IN THE KINGDOM'S NAME

Guardian of Scotland ~ Book Two

by Amy Jarecki

Rapture Books

Copyright © 2016, Amy Jarecki

Jarecki, Amy
In the Kingdom's Name

ISBN: 9781523252794
First Release: February, 2016

Book Cover Design by: Amy Jarecki
Edited by: Scott Moreland

Heartfelt thanks to my beta readers, Anna, Christine and Marti. Your feedback added the finishing touches to this book. I'd also like to thank my editor, Scott Moreland. Without him you'd see all my unflattering *tyops*...I mean *typos*.

Foreword

In the Guardian of Scotland Volume One, *Rise of a Legend*, historical journalist Eva MacKay joins an archaeological dig at the battleground of Loudoun Hill. There, she meets Professor Tennant from Glasgow University who gives her a medallion inscribed in Latin. Translated it reads, "Truth is like a beacon, but few choose to follow".

What she doesn't realize is the medallion has the power to change her life forever.

Falling asleep in a ruined monastery, Eva awakes in the midst of a bloody thirteenth century battle. Just when certain death is eminent, brutal arms surround her and drag her deeper into unknown terror. But her excitement escalates when she discovers she has been hauled to the hideout of William Wallace in Leglen Wood—the very man, the icon, the legend about whom she wrote a series of articles for the *New York Times*.

While she grows accustomed to life in 1297, Eva realizes she has landed the story of a lifetime—if she can find a way home to tell her tale.

What she doesn't count on is her mounting chemistry with the greatest legend Scotland has ever known, or the absolute love swelling in her heart.

But regardless of her growing attachment, Eva gives herself a year, witnesses Wallace in action as he attacks

Lanark, gains allies with Bishop Wishart and the High Steward of Scotland. William takes Scone and Dundee, then forms an alliance with Andrew Murray. Together, they wage the historical Battle of Stirling Bridge. Indeed, Eva witnesses history as it unfolds—uncovers the depth of character of the great man who united a nation.

Rise of a Legend leaves us with Wallace's victory after Stirling Bridge and the deep love that has grown between Eva and William. Join us now as this time-swept couple marches toward the greatest challenge of their lives…*If you dare.*

PART ONE

Cᕼᴀᴘᴛᴇʀ Oɴᴇ

Selkirk, Scotland, late September, 1297

Holding her breath, Eva MacKay shot a glance over her left shoulder then her right. Alone at the rear of the nave, she stood behind a gathering of the most influential nobles in Scotland. Temptation made her fingers twitch. This might be her only chance. Gingerly, she slid her hand into the pouch hanging from her belt and palmed her smartphone. She'd be a total fool not to snap a photo of such a momentous occasion.

But if caught...

With a shudder, Eva looked again to ensure no one watched.

She pushed the "on" button and drew the phone out. With a quick swipe of her finger, familiar icons illuminated. After selecting the camera, she turned off the flash and held it up, snapping two quick pictures. Before Eva dared look at them, she slipped the shiny black rectangle back into her pocket—more like a purse, really, fashioned from the same damask as her thirteenth-century gown.

The sound of a man clearing his throat came from Eva's left. Jolting, her stomach somersaulted with a queasy leap. John Comyn, Lord of Badenoch, stepped from behind an enormous stone pillar. He stood for a moment and squinted at her with suspicion etched across his hard, pinched features. Eva folded her arms and raised her chin in defiance. Then she tiptoed to resume her place beside Lady Christina Murray while watching the snake out of the corner of her eye. In the short time she'd come to know Scotland's nobles, she trusted Comyn the least, with the Earl of March a close second.

As the Lord of Badenoch brushed past her and joined his wife, Eva exhaled and turned her attention to the front of the Kirk of the Forest. Lord John Stewart, the High Steward of Scotland, presided over the ceremony, flanked by Canon Lamberton. "Kneel," Stewart instructed William Wallace and Sir Andrew Murray.

They complied as commanded, wearing full battle armor of hauberks and mail coifs, adorned with surcoats emblazoned with the St. Andrew's Cross. Lord Stewart placed his palms upon their heads. "By the power invested in me granted by the Privy Council of this great nation, I hereby declare Mr. Wallace and Sir Murray joint Guardians of the Kingdom of Scotland. As witnessed by your gallant bravery and cunning defeat of the English at Stirling Bridge, ye shall not only preside over matters of state, ye shall be Commanders of the Army of Scotland and the community of the same Kingdom."

The High Steward paused for a moment and panned his gaze across the gathering of Scotland's highest ranking nobles. "Do ye swear to uphold all laws and decrees of the Kingdom of Scotland?"

"I so swear," Wallace and Murray said in unison.

"Do ye swear in the presence of all in attendance to defend this great nation against Scotland's enemies?"

"I so swear."

"Do ye promise to safeguard the rights of the crown until Scotland once again sees our monarch returned to the throne?"

The two men regarded each other with a solemn nod. "I so promise."

Then Lord Stewart stood back and raised his palms. "Go forth and act to uphold the interests and decrees of Scotland. From this day henceforth, all subjects shall honor ye as the undisputed Guardians of this blessed Kingdom."

Eva pressed her palms together and touched her fingers to her lips while tears blurred her vision. Unwilling to miss a single moment, she blinked in rapid succession. Indeed, this day was the most uplifting in the five months since she'd been hurled into the thirteenth century.

Together, William and Sir Andrew stood, bowed, then turned and strode down the aisle. Though at six-foot, Sir Andrew Murray was inordinately tall for a man of this era, Wallace towered over him by more than a head. Of all the nobles in attendance, William was the only commoner, but by far, the most impressive warrior. Chestnut curls peeked from beneath his coif, framing a handsomely chiseled face made fierce by his cropped auburn beard. Even though he wore thick mail armor, anyone would be impressed with his well-toned, iron-muscled frame. Wrapped in tight chausses, William's powerful legs stretched against his thigh-length hauberk and surcoat with every stride.

When he caught Eva's eye, a slight smile turned up one corner of his mouth, his crystal blue eyes sparkling with the flicker of the aisle candles nested in their tall, iron stands. In truth, William Wallace could make Eva melt merely with a look and today was no different. She drew a hand over her heart to stifle its rapid pounding.

No one knew why the mystic powers behind the ancient medallion chose her, pulling Eva from the twenty-first century ruins of Fail Monastery through some sort of time warp where Wallace rescued her from nearly being murdered by the sharp point of an English sword. Since arriving in the midst of a battle between the English and the Scots, three things had guided her decisions. First: as a historical journalist, she religiously chronicled all of the events she witnessed. The second: she could not change past events. If she attempted anything to materially change the past, her time in William's arms would come to an abrupt end. And finally, Eva refused to lie to William, which always seemed to land her in more sticky situations than she ever would have dreamed possible.

But none of that mattered right now. The only man in the thirteenth century or the twenty-first, for that matter, who could rock her world just strode past and gave her a sexy wink.

"Goodness, Andrew grows paler by the day," said Lady Murray from behind.

Eva's elation immediately ebbed when she turned and regarded her friend's worried mien. Sir Andrew was injured by a crossbow arrow to the shoulder during the Battle of Stirling Bridge and had suffered since. Worse, the bairn in his wife's pregnant belly had begun to show. If only Eva could do something to help him—help the pair of them. She patted Lady Christina's arm. "Today is momentous for him."

"Aye, I am ever so proud."

"As you should be." Eva stepped into the aisle and grasped Christina's hand. "Come, let's join them."

At five-foot eleven, Eva could see over most heads which made it easy for her to pull the petite woman through the throng. Once they squeezed out the thick double doors of the church, she spotted William surrounded by men dressed in more velvet than it would take to stitch together a set of curtains for a theater. She led the gentlewoman off to the side, away from the stream of foot traffic. "Perhaps we should wait here."

The lady smoothed her hands over her silk wimple and nodded. "Verra well."

Lord Comyn stepped to Eva's right and folded his arms. "What's in your purse, lassie?"

"Pardon?" Eva feigned an exasperated expression. "I have no idea to what you are referring."

He smirked. "Och aye, ye do. And whatever it is, I've every suspicion 'tisn't something meant for a house of God."

Eva's chin ticked up. "Are you threatening me, m'lord?"

Scoffing, he gave an exaggerated eye roll. "Heaven forbid someone threaten William Wallace's woman."

Narrowing her eyes, she glared at him for a moment. Even if he'd seen her take the pictures, he wouldn't have a clue what she was up to. And she'd turned the flash off. He had absolutely no grounds on which to make any accusations. With a dismissive nod she turned her attention back to Christina.

"But—" Comyn stepped closer, making the hackles on the back of Eva's neck stand on end. "One day that big fella will fall out of favor and then a pretty lassie such as yourself willna be so smug."

"I beg your pardon, Lord Comyn?" Lady Murray threw her shoulders back. "Ye overinflate your station. Regardless of your noble birth, Miss Eva is the daughter of a knight, and I daresay she ought not be spoken to like a mere commoner."

"Not to worry." Eva flashed a wry grin. "I am very comfortable being identified as among the loyal servants of Scotland. Unlike some high-ranking gentry present whose questionable actions have proved their very hypocrisy, *and* their willingness to change allegiances on a whim only to protect their personal wealth."

"Is all well here?" William's deep voice rumbled as he climbed the steps toward them, a wary glint in his eyes.

"Ye'd best put a leash on your barb-tongued wench." Adjusting his collar, Lord Comyn stretched his neck and strode off.

With a gasp, Lady Christina drew a hand to her chest. "How discourteous."

Wrapping his fingers around the hilt of his dirk, William's gaze shot to Eva.

"He's not worth your ire." She grabbed William's arm with an apologetic cringe. "It's nothing. I baited him, is all. Told him I'd rather mingle with the commoners than a mob of noble hypocrites."

Tense as a lion ready to pounce, William glared at Comyn's retreating form. As the Lord of Badenoch was swallowed by the crowd, Wallace let out a heavy exhale, relaxed his grip and regarded her. "Och, lassie, there's never a want for a bit o' excitement when ye're about." He placed his palm in the small of her back and turned his lips to her ear. "But regardless, if we werena celebrating with half of Scotland's nobles, I'd challenge the sputtering hog to a lesson in chivalry."

Grinning, Eva leaned into him as they proceeded toward the path to Selkirk Castle. "Aye?" she teased. "A man as reed-thin as Lord Comyn would give you no sport whatsoever." Her inflection of Auld Scots phrases became stronger by the day.

Sir Andrew joined them. "Trouble with the Lord of Badenoch?"

"That man is full of self-importance," said Lady Christina, placing her palm atop her husband's offered elbow—the one not in a sling.

Sir Andrew sighed. "Agreed, but so are over half the gentry in our company."

"Well, he's not worth a second thought." With a sideways glance, Eva grinned at William. "Besides, this is a momentous occasion, too important to be filled with misgivings about jealous nobility. Tell me, what has Lord Scott ordered for your celebratory dinner?"

"Anything but swan," said William with a chuckle. "As I recall, 'tis not your favorite."

"Yuck." Eva made a sour face. "It tastes like fishy mutton."

"That it does, though ye use the oddest words, Eva. *Yuck?*" Lady Christina peeked around her husband. "Wherever do ye come up with them?"

William grasped Eva's hand and squeezed. He was the only person in this century who knew the truth about her birthdate being in the year 1988, and even the fearless warrior still had trouble believing it. He needn't worry, because she had no intention of revealing her secrets to anyone else. Momentarily, she strolled along the wooded path with her friends as if she belonged. "I traveled a great deal with my father. In my experience, I'd say sailors use the most colorful language."

William cringed. "Och, dunna tell me ye'll soon be teaching Lady Murray to talk like a pirate."

The lady shook her finger. "Oh no. Miss Eva must spend a month or two with me and I'll set her to rights."

As they moved toward Selkirk Castle, Eva rather liked the idea of spending time with Christina Murray and learning how to be a proper thirteenth-century lady...until her gut squeezed and sank to her toes. *Damn.* Thoughts of the future always had a way of dampening her enthusiasm.

***

If anything, medieval nobility knew how to throw a party. The great hall hummed with music and laugher, dampened slightly by the landscape tapestries hanging from the thirty-foot walls. Heady smells of roasted lamb laced with port wine and fresh bread overwhelmed Eva's senses, which had grown somewhat seasoned to many of the less savory odors of humanity deprived of frequent baths and deodorant. Regardless, the delicious aromas wafting from the kitchens in the cellar below made her hunger ravenous.

The two newly appointed Guardians of Scotland had removed their armor and sat in the highest-ranking positions in the center of the great table on the dais. Eva wasn't always invited to the high table, but this evening she sat beside William as his special guest and stuffed her face with medieval zealousness.

William raised his goblet. "My regards to the host. Everything is delicious."

"That it is." Eva tapped her goblet to William's. "I'll turn into a pumpkin if I keep feasting like this."

"Och, how many times do I have to tell ye to eat when the food's aplenty? It'll be winter soon and Scotland's larders will grow bare afore the green shoots of the harvest again appear."

Eva hid her grin behind her goblet and sipped. How marvelous this man. He not only wanted her to put on a little weight, he expected it.

He leaned closer. "Will ye dance with me this eve?"

"You mean to waltz?" she chuckled.

William grinned, tapping her ribs with his elbow. Good Lord, his smile could make a girl's heart flutter. "I reckon Lady Stewart would collapse with a swooning spell if ye gave her another demonstration of your so-called dance from the Holy Land."

"Honestly?" The sip of wine nearly blew out Eva's nose with her stifled laugh. "I thought they enjoyed our performance at Renfrew Castle."

"Mayhap for a novelty. Perhaps we should retain your newfangled waltz for behind closed doors." He fingered her veil. "'Tis about time ye took part in a circle dance like a proper Scottish lassie."

"All right, then. Fortunately I now have tailored gowns long enough to hide my feet."

He waggled his brows. "A waltzing nymph such as ye should have no problem picking up a few simple *antiquated* dance steps."

"Antiquated?" Across the table, Lady Christina shook her eating knife, albeit delicately. "I'll say there is nothing antiquated about the new court dances." She leaned forward and waggled her eyebrows. "And Lord Scott said he brought in minstrels from Glasgow solely for this occasion."

"Well, then." Eva sat taller. "I hope you will help me stumble along, for I haven't had the opportunity to dance in eons."

The lady clapped her hands. "Oh, this will be fun."

Eva tipped up her goblet and drained the rest of her wine. She'd need a wee buzz to endure the next hour's entertainment.

***

Leading Eva to the dance floor, William's feet skimmed the boards as if he floated slightly above it. Never in his seven and twenty years had he dreamed he'd be Scotland's Guardian. So much had happened in the past year, it all seemed like a blur.

He'd only set out to defend his Kingdom against anarchy—to be one of many who took up their swords. Enraged at Edward Plantagenet's invasion of Scotland, William could no longer remain cloistered behind the walls of Dundee and pray. Both he and John Blair had been trained as Templar knights and, together, they swore an oath to protect the Kingdom and formed a militia.

At first they fought the English interlopers with carefully planned raids, lying in wait for garrisons to pass. With a score of men, they acted like highwaymen and lived in a cave in Leglen Wood. It was then—only five or six months past that he'd rescued Miss Eva from an English swordsman.

Now walking beside him, she made him whole. Who knew how, in the early days, he'd survived without her, but he doubted his success would have come so easily without the lass' love and encouragement.

He chuckled at his achievements. After leading an uprising in Lanark and putting the murderous sheriff under the knife, there had been no stopping the Patriot forces. With the patronage of Lord Stewart, William had led them to capture Scone and Dundee where they joined the rebels to the north led by Andrew Murray.

In short order, they raised a force of six thousand men and stopped the Earl of Surrey at Stirling Bridge with a historic victory over the English. Their success led to a meeting of parliament and the unanimous vote to name Wallace and Murray Guardians of Scotland to safeguard the Kingdom until they freed King John from the Tower of London.

Eva stopped and gave his hand a pat. "Hello? Where are you?"

Blinking, he turned full circle. "Just thinking about all that transpired to lead us to this eve."

She took her place in line and gestured to him. "I have no idea how you cope. Every day brings something unexpected."

"That it does." He bowed.

Following the others, she curtseyed, a cringe turning down the corners of her mouth.

"Dunna worry. Just follow my lead." He skipped forward holding out his arm for her.

"'Tis easy for you to say." She met his gaze as they locked elbows, but she pattered around like a fairy, out of time with the music.

"Ye're doing fine," he said.

She snorted. "And you are a bad liar."

He scooched her back to the ladies line. "I dunna lie."

What Eva lacked in practice, she made up for with enthusiasm, and when the number ended, she laughed and clapped her hands. William did too—not because of the invigorating reel, but because of the infectious nature of Eva's joy. No one could remain around the woman for long without laughing—except mayhap Father Blair. But the goodly friar hadn't much of a sense of humor.

Eva waved to young Boyd, William's squire. "Find a partner and come dance."

At ten and two, the lad shrank behind his tankard, shaking his head. "I prefer to watch ye and Willy. Ye provide more entertainment than a court jester."

Eva curtseyed deeply. "And you are a fraidy cat."

William guffawed. Where she came up with such a twist of phrase, he wouldn't even bother to ask. Instead, he took a goblet of wine from a passing servant, sipped and held it up. "A wee beverage afore the next dance?"

Her green eyes widened mischievously as her tongue slipped to the corner of her mouth. "Yes, indeed." She took the goblet and drank a healthy tot.

Before she downed it all, he stopped her. "Ye might want to ebb your thirst…for I have plans involving the both of us this night, and it will be all the more fun if ye are awake to enjoy it."

Chapter Two

The dancing wasn't nearly as torturous as Eva had imagined, but now that the festivities were over, she thoroughly enjoyed standing alone on the wall-walk with William. The latent effects of the wine made her eyelids heavy. Moonbeams peeked through the puffs of clouds and white streams of light illuminated Haining Loch below.

"'Tis smooth as glass," William said, tightening his arms around her as they faced the still water.

"Mm." Eva relaxed her head against his chest. He was the only man she'd seen in this century tall enough to provide such a comfort to a woman of five-foot-eleven. "We're having an Indian summer."

With a gentle chuckle, he pressed his lips to her temple. "What's that ye say? Indian summer?"

She hummed melting into his lips. "Oops," she said lazily. "I mean the season is staying with us longer than usual this year."

"Aye, and we may as well revel in it. The north wind will be upon us in no time."

She involuntarily shivered. "I hate winter."

He clasped his hands around her midriff. "It can be miserable for certain, but 'tis the way of things. Without it, there would be no spring and no harvest."

William forever saw the practical side of everything. But then again, he'd never lived in the tropics. As long as she

could remember, Eva's winters had been broken up by
vacations in the Caribbean or Hawaii. One year, her family
had rented an islet in Fiji for a couple of weeks—a fact she
definitely would not be sharing with William. She hadn't
shared much about her life prior to landing in the thirteenth
century. As of late, he hadn't asked many questions either.
Her answers seemed to trouble him. Things she had told and
shown William had been difficult for him to accept—like
pictures from her smartphone. Ever since taking a selfie with
him and showing William the results, she'd been very careful
not to pull out her phone when he was watching. Jeez, he'd
even threatened to burn her at the stake for using the devil's
"sorcery". Oh no, she'd never make such a faux pas again.

Besides, she had no idea how much longer she'd spend
with William before the medallion's charms expired. And she
definitely could not stay.

Absolutely not.

To allay her repugnance of the future, Eva preferred to
keep things in the now and refrain from allowing herself to
think about anything except the present. Her own past was
miserable—too awful to remember. William's future? Well, it
was unconscionable.

Seven hundred years separated their birthdays and her
time in his arms was but a passing tryst. Yes, her heart wanted
more, but she could never allow it.

*A year. I can revel in the gift of our mind-blowing passion for a
year.*

She closed her eyes and smoothed her fingers over the
back of William's hand. "So now that you've brought
Edinburgh under Scottish control, what's next?"

"I'd like to drive the English out of our border castles by
fire and sword, but if we cut off their supply of food, that will
happen soon enough and without bloodshed." He nuzzled
into Eva's temple. "We need to resume trade with the rest of

Christendom, then I must devise a way to ensure the English stay off our lands for good."

Eva held her breath. She'd heard William say "and return King John to the throne" so many times, she expected him to say it now. When he didn't, she slowly let the air blow through her lips.

"But then, ye ken what I'm planning next, do ye not?" His voice grew deeper as he rocked his hips into her buttocks.

"Sometimes." A spark of heat ignited low in her belly as she rubbed against him—thank God she still had her IUD and didn't have to worry about pregnancy. "The bigger decisions, anyway."

"All right then, Andrew and I will be joining our forces at Dirleton Castle afore we march south."

She nodded.

"And ah…" He pulled aside her veil and smoothed tickling lips along the curve of Eva's shoulder. "I want ye to remain there with Lady Christina during her confinement."

She inhaled against her urge to gasp, trying to focus on his words rather than melting and agreeing just to enjoy his seductive lips warm against her skin. "You want me to stay with her ladyship to assist her with the bairn, or to keep me from harm when you invade England?"

"Och," he chuckled. "Ye ken my mind better than I."

"Not always."

"I mean it, Eva," he whispered softly in her ear. "By now ye must realize the battlefield is no place for a woman."

She stiffened a bit, leaning aside far enough to regard his face. How much more time did she have with him? Must that question continually needle at the back of her mind?

His eyes grew dark as a midnight storm. "Besides, with my appointment to Guardian, the English will be looking for ways to worm through our defenses and get to me. Ye ken if ye're captured, I'll nay stop until I have ye back."

"I wouldn't want that." There were a great many things coming Eva didn't want, and with the lust and wine swirling in her head, she had no mind to argue. "I told you once I wouldn't try to follow if I knew you would return for me. If you'd prefer me to remain with Lady Christina for a short time, I can agree to that. But do not forget that I am here for *you*. No one else."

She straightened and faced him, her tongue tapping her top lip. "Enough of what's to come. I don't want to talk about war or separation right now." Smoothing her hands from his chest down to his waist, she moved her hips forward, connecting with him intimately. "Kiss me."

William's deep moan rumbled through her as he lowered his head and ensnared her lips. His mouth invited her in, his tongue swirling with a fervent hunger Eva had grown to crave. Instantly intoxicated by his scent curling around her soul, she gave in to her need. Long, languid caresses of his tongue grew more demanding as his hand traveled up her torso and cupped her breast.

With a sigh, she purred, "What does it feel like to be Guardian of Scotland?"

A feral growl rumbled from his throat. "Right now the only thing I want is to guard the woman in my arms."

She nibbled his smooth-shaven neck. "You know how to make this woman melt like butter."

"I'd have it no other way, *mon amour*."

God, she loved it when his Auld Scots laced with French.

Eva increased the pressure of her hips grinding into his thickening erection. Lord help her, she hungered for his touch whenever he was within her grasp. Unlacing her kirtle, he pulled aside the cloth and bared her breast. When his warm lips claimed her nipple and teased it to a hard point, she sucked in a gasp. As he increased the pressure, she threw her head back and swooned into him, goosebumps spreading across every inch of her exposed flesh.

"Perhaps we should retire to our chamber," she managed in a throaty whisper.

He straightened, his hands skimming over her hungry flesh. "Och, there's no one guarding this section of the wall-walk. I've made certain of it."

"You planned to bring me up here and seduce me?" She giggled with delight while his hand grasped her skirts. "I should never underestimate you."

"To do so would be a great folly." He winked with a devilish grin. "A warrior must have a bit o' fun now and again."

The cool air tickled her skin as gradually he slid his warm palm up the inside of her thigh. He fingered the panties she always wore—one of the few items from the twenty-first century she couldn't live without.

His fingers looped around the elastic. "But these have to go." With one swift tug, he slipped them down.

Stepping out of the lace, she parted her legs and he ran his finger over her sensitive skin while she slid her hand down the front of his chausses. "What do you have in mind?" she asked breathlessly.

He kissed her before providing his answer, as his finger worked faster. "Up here."

Still lucid enough to understand the danger of making love on a narrow barmkin wall, she glanced over her shoulder. "But we could fall."

He loosened the tie on his chausses. "I'll nay let ye fall, lass."

Oh, yes. Eva would believe anything William said when he spoke with that deep, lilting burr. Taking in a stuttered breath, she pushed his hands aside and unbound his braies. With a tug, they spilled open and exposed him. It only took one look and Eva's fears smoldered away with her spike of arousal. She swirled her flesh across his.

"Trust me," he growled, lifting her high enough for them to join.

"I do." She wrapped her arms around his shoulders and encircled him with her legs. His cock caressed her slick core as he leaned down and set her in crenel notch. Eva tried to glance over her shoulder.

"Dunna look back." His powerful hands cradled her firmly as he slipped inside.

Inviting danger into their lovemaking made the pinnacle of passion all the more exhilarating. If he let go, she might plummet two hundred feet to her death. She trusted him more than anyone in the world. Gazing into his eyes, she trusted him with her life. The breeze swirled enticingly across their skin as, together, waves of pleasure coursed through them.

Chapter Three

William looked back from atop his warhorse and regarded Eva. Riding beside Lady Christina, the two women chatted quietly. When he caught her eye, the lovely ginger-haired lass' face brightened with her smile. Oh, how the woman could make his heart leap from his chest when she directed a smiling sunbeam his way. Och aye, he would have married the lass if it weren't for the war—War of Independence, Eva called it. His jaw twitched. He might have made an offer of marriage despite the war, but she'd told him more than once she wanted to live for the now.

The now. What else is there?

Though like brushing a horse's coat against the grain, he knew she was right. He could not make a commitment to Miss Eva or to any woman no matter how much he loved her. Now a soldier of Scotland, William once had lofty ambitions to become a Templar priest. But he'd abandoned his training to fight against the outrageous acts of tyranny brought into the Kingdom by Edward the Longshanks. Ever since taking up the sword, Wallace had followed the path of war, leading a band of rebels and fighting for the release of King John from the Tower. William could no sooner take a wife as he could turn his back on his duty.

He'd even tried to leave Eva. At first. Now William could barely tolerate the thought of spending a night without his woman in his arms. But he'd be forced to do that soon, regardless. At least his woman would be safe and thank the good Lord she'd made a bond with Lady Murray. Eva would be far less likely to venture out on her own once he and Sir Andrew took the army south.

Reports of skirmishes on both sides of the border had been trickling in. William needed to take charge, organize these patriotic zealots and stage a full-on invasion of Northern England—and soon. If only Sir Andrew's health would take a turn for the better. They'd joined together as comrades in arms in this rebellion. Unfortunately, the knight had suffered a crossbow arrow to the shoulder at Stirling Bridge and his health had declined since. Worse, Eva regarded Sir Andrew with fear in her green eyes. She'd predicted too many things about the future for her foresight to be mere luck. The lass had the gift of a seer—aye, she'd insisted she was from the future, but regardless, William knew the gift of sight when he encountered it.

A moment of eerie silence mushroomed on the breeze before a flock of birds scattered and flew above the forest ahead. The back of William's neck burned with prickles. Raising his hand, he signaled for a halt. Wallace drew his sword as he made eye contact with Blair and Little.

With his next blink, an arrow whizzed past his ear.

"Attack!" William bellowed, reining his horse toward Eva.

Clutching the reins in her fists, she gasped, her mouth drawing down in a panicked grimace.

Another hiss came. Then a dull whop. Rearing, William's mount whinnied and reared. Clamping his knees to stay on, he reined the warhorse in a tight circle, but the horse's hindquarter gave out and the big stallion spiraled downward. Launching himself from his stirrups, William leapt free. His shoulder smacked into the dirt. A jarring thud reverberated through his teeth.

In the blink of an eye, he forced the pain from his mind as he rolled then rose to his knees. Still gripping his sword in his fist, William's gaze searched the bedlam for his woman.

The roar of battle boomed with the clang of iron in concert with bellows, grunts and shrieks from the wounded. Eva and Lady Christina huddled, hunched on their skittish mounts in the center of the mayhem. They wouldn't be safe for long. Their horses' ears pinned back with heads held high and nostrils flaring.

Gaining his feet, he started to run toward them. Hoofbeats thundered behind. With an upward strike, William spun and met his assailant's sword with a crushing blow. Flung from his mount, the man howled. William advanced and buried his sword in the traitor's chest.

He whirled around. "Andrew! Take the women to safety." His order would not only save the women, it served to remove the wounded knight from danger.

Only able to use one arm, Andrew circled his horse and latched on to Lady Christina's mount's bridle. "Miss Eva, follow me," bellowed Sir Murray, reining his gelding eastward. "Make a path."

Swinging battleaxes and swords, William's men fought to open a gap wide enough for a horse to charge through. Digging in his spurs, Andrew barreled ahead, pulling his wife's mare in his wake.

Following with focused determination, Eva kicked her heels against her gelding's barrel, slapping her reins. "Go, go, go!"

Attacked from the side, William deflected a poleaxe while watching his woman's old gelding lurch into a gallop. Before the horse cleared the skirmish, a brigand dove sideways and caught Eva's gown.

A high-pitched shriek screeched in William's ears as she sailed through the air, arms flinging wide. The bastard dug his grimy fingers into her waist as together they crashed to the ground.

Screaming, Eva thrashed, fighting to break free.

The defiling whoreson trapped her with his leg. Tearing off her veil, he rolled atop her and licked her neck. His sickly laugh rose above the tumult while he yanked up her skirts.

Rage boiled from William's gut and erupted through his chest.

Bursting forward with a thundering roar, he battled through the skirmish. Eva's hem creeped further up her thighs. Swinging her fists, she beat the cur's back and thrashed her head. But the plunderer cackled with bloodlust in his eyes.

Unable to chance striking her with his blade, Wallace grasped the lout by the chin and yanked his head sideways with a sickly crackle of bone and sinew. The slimy varlet's body fell limp and dropped atop her. Eva screeched with staccato yelps while she squirmed under the dead man.

Hefting the corpse aside, William grabbed Eva's wrist and hoisted the only woman he'd ever loved over his shoulder. "I'll spirit ye away from here."

He raced for a riderless horse while the battle surged. A thug stepped into his path. With a kick up the backside, William sent the brigand face down to the dirt and surged forward. No time for decorum, he tossed Eva over the stallion's neck and leapt aboard. Gathering the reins, he dug in his spurs and galloped for the shelter of dense forest.

***

Too frightened to worry about her stomach pounding against the horse's withers, Eva gripped the girth strap and held on for dear life while her knuckles turned white. Her breaths came in gasping bursts. Branches slapped her face and legs as William raced for safety.

Stars darted through her vision before he tugged on the reins and pulled the horse to a stop.

"We're out of danger for now." William dismounted and helped Eva slide to her feet.

Her knees buckled and he gripped his fingers around her waist. "Steady, lass."

She swiped trembling fingers across her face. "Oh God," she shrieked. "They came from n-nowhere. One minute w-we were alone. And the next…"

"I ken." He smoothed his palm over her hip where she'd fallen. "Are ye hurt?"

"I don't think so." Honestly, her entire body felt numb. "Maybe a bit bruised." She shook so violently, her teeth chattered.

"There, there, *mon amour*." William tucked a strand of hair under her veil and pulled her into his arms. "Ye're safe now."

Eva's gaze darted to the path they'd taken. "What if they follow us?"

With a pat to his sword's hilt, William's eyes grew dark. "Then they'll have five pounds of cold iron run through their bellies."

Her stomach squelched. Nothing worse than nearly being raped and murdered to stir the fear in one's blood. "How can you take it? Knowing you could be attacked at any moment? This is no way to live."

He pulled her into his arms and clutched her head to his chest. "Och, ye could be attacked by brigands when lying in your bed. 'Tis no use cowering or hiding from them. The only way is to stand and fight. Show them we will not tolerate their brutality."

"I was so afraid." Gulping, she tried to still her unsteady breath. "I can't fight off a whole band of outlaws. I don't know the first thing about swinging one of those mammoth swords."

He tightened his embrace, like forming a shield of iron around her. Lord, his strength felt so secure, she never wanted him to release her. "Och, Eva. Ye ken I'll protect ye, no matter what."

She buried her face against him and hid in the comfort of two arms hardened by years of training and battle. The reassurance William imparted calmed her thundering heart. But every time she closed her eyes, all she saw was blood and the face of that monster who pulled her from her horse.

"There, there, lass. 'Tis over now." He pressed his lips to her forehead. "I could have killed a hundred brigands when I saw that bastard touch ye."

A shudder rippled through Eva's body. "I feel so safe with your arms around me. I want to stay like this forever."

"Jesu, I hate thinking about leaving ye alone. I must ensure ye are safe behind the fortress walls of Dirleton Castle. There ye'll have an army of men and six foot thick stone walls to protect ye from the vile swine."

He dipped his chin and kissed her cheek, his gaze connecting with hers, binding them together. Warm breath caressed her face as his mouth parted. Those intense blue eyes watched her while he sealed his lips over hers, taking possession of her mouth. There, alone in the forest, their spirits joined—two souls drawn together regardless of impossible odds.

She squeezed her eyes closed and inhaled his spicy masculine scent. "Promise to hold me forever." The words escaped Eva's lips before she had a chance to catch herself. But she didn't care. Not now. Not when her every nerve ending trembled.

"Ye have my sword, m'lady. On that I make my solemn vow." He loosened his grasp and placed his large palm in the small of her back. "Now come. We must haste to Dirleton. I'll cradle ye in my arms through the duration of our journey."

She looked up to his stern countenance and grinned. "As long as I don't have to ride face down draped across your horse's withers."

His eyes sparkled with warmth. "I have to admit there wasna verra much time to set ye to rights." Then a deep chortle rumbled from his chest as a sly grin stretched his lips.

"What?"

He waggled his brows. "I rather enjoyed the view."

Eva thwacked his shoulder. "Oh, please."

With a shrug, he bent down to give her a leg up. "I canna help it if I'm a man."

She bent her knee and allowed him to hoist her into the saddle. "Right, all men running for their lives gape at the woman's butt in their face while they're crashing through the forest."

"Butt?"

"Bum, buttocks, rear end…whatever you want to call it."

A subtle snort trumpeted through his nose. "Will ye never cease to come up with odd twists of phrase?"

"I suppose, but what do you expect? I'm called to the carpet for my odd speech all the time."

He mounted behind her and situated the reins in his hands. "I reckon I like it. Every now and again, ye come at me with a word that almost makes me laugh."

Shifting her hips to find a comfortable position, she asked, "Why almost?" Eva dearly loved to hear him laugh.

"I expect it hasna been easy to draw a laugh from me these past months."

Nor will it. Again Eva shuddered. She hated knowing. Clenching her fists until her fingernails dug into her palms, she steeled her resolve. *Live for the now, you dolt.*

William nuzzled into her temple and slid one arm around her waist, drawing her snuggly against his chest. "Ye ken I'd die defending ye, *mon amour.*"

"And I promise there will never be a need for that." *No, no, no. I mustn't ever again be the reason for William to fight.*

She closed her eyes and with an exhale, forced herself to relax into him. God, to think she'd been yanked from her mount trying to get her old horse to move fast. Horses were so damned unpredictable. "I think I need horseback riding lessons."

"Too right." William's belly shook with his chuckle—not a laugh, but close. "I kent ye were no horsewoman the first time I tossed ye on the back of my mount."

"As I remember it, you accused me of knowing nothing about horses, though I'd never claimed to have ridden one."

"No training at all?" His palm slid up and down her abdomen. "Ye mean even though your da's a knight, ye were never taught how? Not even as a wee lassie?"

She'd told him about trains, but hadn't come across the need to describe a car. "There was never an opportunity. In my time, we have motorcars—four wheels, an engine that burns fuel for energy to propel it forward. You know, a horse gets energy from eating grass, a fire gets energy from burning wood and oxygen."

"Oxygen?"

"Air." She wriggled against him. "If you snuff the air from a flame it will go out, right?"

"Aye."

"Well, around the end of the nineteenth century, they learned how to make an engine that burns gasoline—a fuel like oil—and thrust a vehicle forward—sort of like a horseless wagon."

William, being the inquisitive type had a gazillion questions about how a car operated and after explaining about roads, steering wheels and passenger seats, he finally stopped probing and let her continue.

"So, do you think I should try to ride a pony that isn't an old nag like the gelding?" Eva asked. "Robbie's good with horses. He could give me a few pointers."

William gave her a squeeze. "Dunna ye want me to teach ye?"

"You'd be my preference." Twisting, she regarded his face. "But when would you find time?"

"Dunna ken." His mouth quirked. "Robbie's my squire and I'll have plenty for him to do as well."

Eva huffed. "He's only a lad. Have him stay behind with me for a time. I worry about him being embroiled in the fighting."

"Ye ken I wouldna let him near a battle." William hummed in her ear. "Mayhap ye are right. The borders are no place for a lad of two and ten—and the older he grows, the more he needles me to let him fight."

"I say wait for him to become a man first." Eva raised her eyebrows and grinned. "What is it you say? Let his beard grow in?"

William affected a scowl. "He willna like it."

"Who's the boss of him? Hmm?"

"Och, ye ken he'll do anything I say, but the lad's got to learn to be a man one day."

Eva crossed her arms. "And he cannot learn responsibility providing protection to me whilst you're off invading England?"

"Let me think on it. But ye do need to learn better control of your mount. Had ye been faster, ye would have made it out of the skirmish right behind Sir Andrew."

"Well then, it's settled. I need speed-riding lessons." Today's brush with that vile beast pinning her to the ground and hiking up her skirts still rattled Eva's nerves. She mightn't be able to fight a man like that, but she certainly could learn to outrun him.

"Mark me, there's nothing to replace instruction and practice." With William's slap of the reins, the horse transitioned to a trot. He always made it seem so easy.

"All right, so you'll assign Robbie to the task as soon as we return?" Eva pressed.

William grumbled under his breath. "Ye have a way of bending my ear like no other woman I've ever met."

"I'll take that as agreement." She smiled and allowed herself to relax against him. "How much further to Dirleton?"

"I reckon we'll be there afore nightfall."

"I think it's safer to ride in small groups rather than in an army."

"Oh do ye now?" His chest rumbled with another chuckle. "Next ye'll be telling me how to stage my men on the battlefield."

"I sincerely doubt that."

"Good, then we ought to continue to be agreeable."

"Oh, stop." She tsked her tongue. "Do you know whose men attacked back there?"

"I have an inkling."

"Aaaand?"

"They wore the crest of the Earl of March on their surcoats," William growled.

"Cospatrick," Eva whispered the earl's surname.

"The bastard holds as much land south of the border as he does north. He'll be kissing Edward's arse until pigs sprout wings."

Eva ran her fingers through the horse's coarse mane. "What are you planning to do about him?"

"Mayhap I'll pay the bastard a visit."

Over her shoulder, she regarded the stubborn set to William's jaw. "Just walk up to Dunbar Castle and request an audience?"

"And why not?" he asked, the glint in his eye growing more determined. "Parliament just voted me Guardian. 'Tis my duty to instill peace—at least on this side of the border."

Cɦapτer Foᴜr

A fog rolled in with dusk, making Dirleton Castle but a colossal grey outline on the horizon. With the mist came a brisk wind. And as they rode double, William hovered over Eva to keep her warm. He hated that he'd brought her into this war, but now he couldn't imagine himself ever letting her go. In this world of violence and death, Eva had become the one person who grounded him—served as a constant reminder of his deep moral character.

Still, even with their bodies touching, her teeth chattered. "D-do you think the others have arrived?"

"Most likely. We took quite a circuitous detour." Moving the reins to one hand, he rubbed the outside of her arm. "I'll have ye to warmth in no time, *mon amour.*"

Turning her head, she nuzzled against his shoulder. "I like it when you speak French. How did you learn?"

"All monks must learn languages. Latin first, then French."

"Why did you not whisper your endearment in Latin?"

"Och, lassie, French is the language of love." The true reason was almost embarrassing to admit—even to Eva. "Latin? Well the holy word is written in Latin—'tis just not as romantic."

When the horse's hooves clomped on the wooden bridge, a sentry on the wall-walk waved a pennant above his head. "'Tis Wallace. Open the gates."

As they trotted into the courtyard, Father John Blair, who William dubbed the Archangel of War, hastened to meet them. "Praise the good Lord ye are unharmed. When we arrived and ye werena here, we feared the worst."

William reined the horse to a stop. "Ye think I can be taken down by a mob of bedraggled wastrels?" He snorted for added effect, though no one need mention their attackers were trained soldiers. They came too damned close to capturing Eva.

Spreading his palms to his sides, Blair shrugged and played along with William's show of disregard. "Well, I didna *want* to believe it."

"Have a wee bit of faith, father." William helped Eva slide to her feet before he dismounted. "Come, we must convene. Call Sir Andrew and my lieutenants to the hall. We'll talk whilst we sup."

No sooner had William started toward the keep, when a group of merchants hastened his way. "Lord Guardian, may we have a word?" asked a sizable man dressed in woolen chausses, shirt and a tanned leather doublet showing considerable wear. He removed his merchant's cap and bowed deeply.

Blair stepped between them. "Mr. Wallace can spare no time for idle chat. Be gone—"

William gripped the priest's shoulder firmly and ushered him aside. "Pardon my chaplain's fervor. I was forced to take a detour to the castle and he feared the worst." Wallace extended his hand. "Please, friend. What troubles ye?"

"'Tis grave." The merchant beckoned a group of similarly dressed men who looked no better than tinkers, the lot of them. "We canna sell our goods. All routes of trade outside of Scotland have been closed to us."

Squinting, William regarded the other's haggard miens. "What is the nature of your trade, may I ask?"

"Woolens and woven cloth," said one.

"Grain," said another.

"I trade in livestock—horses." The first merchant pointed. "I import impressive mounts like that destrier ye rode in on in exchange for all manner of goods, sir. But no longer—I canna even make a wager for a nag." He shook his head. "Longshanks has control of the ports. Only English goods are allowed on the ships."

"And he has poisoned our reputation throughout Christendom."

"All of Christendom?" William asked.

"Aye, Norway, Spain, The Holy Roman Empire, even France willna buy our goods."

"Our families are starving," said another.

William thrust his finger northward. "But what of the port at Dundee? We captured the town and the castle. Can ye not sail your ships from her port?"

"Sail, aye, but not trade." The merchant wrung the cap in his hands. "As I said, the English have pushed us out. Our goods are banned and no one seems to have any coin to purchase them in Scotland."

"Please," the thinnest man pleaded. "We've nowhere to turn."

"Of course." William grasped the man's arm and looked him in the eye. "I intended to summon the nobles to parliament within the month, but I see the situation is dire. Mark me, Scotland is a force to be reckoned with. As long as I am Guardian, I will see that all men have means to earn an honest living." He looked to Blair. "Send missives to the barons at once. We will convene in a sennight."

"A sennight?" asked the priest. "That does not give their lordships much time to prepare and many are still traveling home from Selkirk. They willna appreciate a summons so soon."

"When the Kingdom is in such dire need? Are they not suffering from Longshanks' skullduggery as well?" William jammed his fists into his hips. "Haste ye—a sennight."

"Verra well." Blair inclined his head toward the keep. "But I'll have a word with ye afore I put quill to vellum."

Aye, the chaplain was a good man and confidant, but at times William wanted to give him a firm wallop upside the head. He bowed to the merchants. "I shall address this matter forthwith and will send emissaries abroad to reestablish routes of trade. Mark me."

"Thank ye, m'lord," they chorused, bowing deeply.

William hastened toward the keep with Blair on his heels. "Ye must not keep the people from me."

"Aye? Ye thankless mule-brained hog. I was only looking after your welfare. When did ye last eat?" the chaplain demanded like an old hen.

William stopped and jabbed his finger into Blair's shoulder. "My own comfort does not come before that of the sons and daughters of Scotland. Be ever mindful of that."

Blair crossed his arms, his dark eyebrows slanting inward. "Believe me I am."

"So why are ye standing here and not setting your quill to the missives I've prescribed?"

Blair glanced around them with a wary glint. "I didna want to ask in front of the crowd, for ye never ken what spies may be listening. But where do ye intend to hold your session of parliament?"

William pursed his lips. As always, his chaplain made a good point. 'Twas perilous to travel, even with a healthy retinue of armed men. Hell, they'd been ambushed this day, and by a Scottish nobleman's army, no less. The situation was precarious, but one that must be dealt with firmly and soon.

"We need a place of sanctuary. Not public. Where enemies canna dream of taking up their swords."

"Hmm." Blair scratched the shaved patch atop his head. "Perhaps a monastery. Melrose?"

William frowned. "Too big."

"Fail?"

"Possibly." With a squint of his eyes, William pondered. "The Trinitarian monks are too placid. We need a quiet fortress run by men who are bred to enforce order."

"Aye," Blair agreed. "The Templars?"

"Nay. Too many English in their ranks." William would like nothing better than to align Scotland with the Templar Order, but that would take a great deal of time and negotiation—not to mention the risks of playing into Longshanks' hands were too great.

Taking in a sharp inhale, Blair held up his finger. "Scotland's Knights Hospitallers align themselves with France…and they're nearby at Torphichen Preceptory."

"Brilliant." William grinned and clapped Blair's back. "I can think of no better allies than the Order of St. John. Ye are a good man, father."

"Sometimes I bloody wonder if ye appreciate it," Blair said with a rueful grunt.

"Och, are ye now playing the bleeding heart?"

***

When the merchants approached William, Eva moved toward the keep and stood at a respectful distance, though not too far away to overhear the interchange. Then when William led Blair aside, they were out of earshot, but she opted to wait. History was in the making and she didn't want to miss anything. Once they approached, she joined them, ignoring Father Blair's disapproving frown. From the beginning the priest had made it clear he didn't trust her, nor did he believe women had a place in the rebellion. But after her work helping Brother Bartholomew minister to the injured at Stirling Bridge, he'd at least curbed his acrid remarks. Eva even ventured as far as to think she might be wearing him down.

"Ye're here!" Twelve-year-old Robbie Boyd dashed out of the thick double doors with Paden and Adam Wishart in his wake. The lads had grown inseparable in the past month, though Paden still had a chip on his shoulder from William's rather abrupt removal of the boys from their home. When Bishop Wishart led a rebellion in Irvine and then tried to increase his personal wealth by negotiating with the English, William grew so enraged, he looted Wishart's manor and took his sons—nephews as far as anyone else knew. William intended to instill honor in the boys whilst Wishart rotted in Roxburgh Castle's gaol. Honestly, Eva thought William's idea to enlist the lads as squires during their father's incarceration would be a good education for them—as long as Wallace kept them from the battlefield.

Eva opened her arms. Robbie ran a few steps, but stopped and ticked up his chin before he reached her embrace. "I reckon I shouldna be mollycoddled, Miss Eva."

Her bottom lip jutted out, but her frown turned to a grin when eleven-year-old Adam barreled in from the side and gave her a hug. "We're happy to see ye, m'lady."

Closing an arm around Adam, she reached out the other to muss Robbie's hair. "You think you're too grown up to give me a proper welcome?"

He glanced aside and twisted his mouth. A young serving girl hastened away carrying a basket. Eva clamped her lips against her urge to laugh and met Paden's gaze. The older Wishart boy had never been one for affection. "Have Lady Christina and Sir Andrew arrived safely?" she asked.

"They're waiting in the hall," said Adam.

William gestured for them to follow. "Come. We've no time to waste."

As usual, Eva sat at the first table beside the dais with Christina and the lads while William and his men discussed strategy on the dais. Eva didn't mind this arrangement. She was close enough to hear and observe, but far enough away not to interfere—and that kept the medallion hidden beneath her shift cool. Whenever the blasted thing warmed against her skin, it warned her to proceed with utmost care, else she be hurled back to the twenty-first century without so much as a farewell.

She made eye contact with Christina while they both inclined their ears toward the dais.

"I cannot believe we were attacked by our own countrymen." Sir Andrew dipped his spoon into his lamb pottage and stirred without taking a bite. "Any Scots baron in the north would sooner take a dirk to his throat than turn backstabber."

"Aye, the nobles along the borders all hold lands in England." William broke off a chunk of bread and dunked it. "But I'll not tolerate insurrection against us. Any Scottish subject attacking Scotland's army will be arrested and tried for treason. If a man desires to kiss Longshanks' arse, he can do it on his Judgement Day."

"Here, here," boomed the deep voices around the table.

William looked Eva's way and rolled his hand through the air. "Miss Eva, scribe a missive. I aim to send out criers to all corners of the Kingdom to ensure everyone kens the penalty."

Her heart fluttered. "Me?"

"Ye write all day." He waved her on. "Fetch your quill, woman."

Eva retrieved her writing materials before William finished his piece of bread. She'd been practicing writing in Auld Scots, but this was the first time he'd ever openly recognized her as a chronicler. She might even be able to put her Latin to use.

The men shifted down the table and she took a seat beside Wallace. John Blair gave her one of his grumpy looks. With a grin, she shrugged. At least he hadn't made a snide comment.

William dictated the first missive about severely punishing all treasonous acts. Then Andrew made a call for conscripts aged sixteen to sixty.

William gestured toward the two documents. "We'll need a score of copies of each to be sent out on the morrow. Conclude each one with our names, underscored by 'Commanders of the Army of Scotland and the Community of the same Kingdom' then we'll affix our seals."

"Consider it done." Eva pushed back her chair.

"A moment." William held up his hand. "We will scribe missives granting safe passage to Scotland and announcing that by war the Kingdom of Scotland has been recovered from the tyranny of the English."

The medallion warmed against her chest. "You wish for me to write these letters?"

"Ye and Blair." William nodded to his personal chaplain. "There are many to scribe and they must be carried throughout Christendom forthwith."

Blair reached for a piece of vellum. "I daresay, I'll scribe these. They'd best be written in Latin."

Eva cleared her throat. "I can write in Latin."

"Such an education for a woman?" The priest gave her a pointed glare. "Your admission borders on heresy."

Giving him a sober stare of her own, she raped her fist on the table. "Pardon me, but women have every ounce of intelligence as their male counterparts."

Blair snatched the quill from her hand. "'Tis just not done."

She grabbed it back. "You want to scribe the missives yourself? Then have at it, but I'll not listen to another word of your hogwash."

"Bloody hell." Blair shoved his chair away from the board. "I'll fetch my own writing gear. But the next thing we'll know, she'll be wanting to be assigned command of an entire battalion or some fool-born notion of the female persuasion."

Eva dipped the point of her quill into the inkwell. "I assure you, leading a regiment is not my forte." She slapped a piece of vellum in front of her. "But writing *is*, thank you very much."

The priest grumbled something undecipherable under his breath. Eva chose to ignore him. Father John Blair was William's personal chaplain. He mightn't care much that Eva had appeared on the scene but he'd accepted her, grumbling along the way. She'd stopped trying to make him like her. A fondness just wouldn't develop between them. Tolerance was all she could hope for.

For hours, she wrote across the board from Blair with William dictating every word in Latin. It was as if she'd landed in an advanced Latin class at university. The content of the letters was mostly the same, all requesting trade to again flow between the cities and villages of France, The Holy Roman Empire, Norway, Spain and beyond. William and Andrew signed each one and affixed their seals in wax.

Eva's forearm burned from continuous writing and the rims of her fingernails turned black from the ink. By the time they'd scribed the last missive, the candles on the table had burned to nubs. She rubbed the back of her neck. "It must be late."

"I believe I heard the toll of the Matins bell not long ago," said William.

She'd been concentrating so hard, the bell had slipped past her.

Andrew pushed his chair back and swayed a bit. A sheen of sweat glistened on the knight's face. "I reckon I'd best find my bed afore this damn fever gets the better of me."

Eva cast aside her fatigue, hopped to her feet and dabbed his head with her kerchief. "How is your shoulder?"

"Still canna move it, but not to worry, I'll come good in a matter of days." He pushed Eva's hand away.

She cast a worried grimace to William. "Shall I fetch Lady Christina?"

"Nay. Let her sleep." Andrew swayed in place again, the little color he had completely draining away from his face. "I'll not be cossetted by anyone."

Eva stepped back and let him pass, staggering across the great hall to the stairwell.

"I'm off to my pallet as well," said Blair as he collected the scrolls of vellum.

The rest of the men had headed to bed not long after William first started dictating missives.

He stood, took the kerchief from Eva's hand and tossed it on the table. "Come here, lass." A long sigh slipped through her lips as he pulled her into his arms. "It has been quite a day, early rising—attacked on the trail, up until the wee hours setting the Kingdom to rights."

His deep hum soothed her as she relaxed into his arms. "It hasn't been ordinary, I'll say."

"And still ye choose to stay with me, even with the peril that surrounds us."

"I would be nowhere else."

He took her hand and strolled toward the stairs. "I worry about Sir Andrew."

A shiver coursed across her skin. "Me, as well."

The medallion warmed enough to remind her it was there. Sometimes Eva hated the damned warnings the piece of bronze gave. And when it came to Andrew Murray, she was scared out of her wits. She was no doctor—she'd only learned a fraction of medieval healing arts through her time with Brother Bartholomew. She probably couldn't help the knight if she tried, and every time she'd considered it, the damn medallion issued a scorching warning.

She hated being powerless to do anything.

Before William crouched into the stairwell, he stopped. "Can ye help him?"

"I'm not a physician." She shook her head for added emphasis.

"I didna ask that. Do ye ken a remedy?"

The medallion heated like it was burning a hole over her heart. She suspected Andrew suffered not only from a septic infection, but he had lead poisoning as well. She'd seen the arrow after Brother Bartholomew pulled it out of Sir Andrew's shoulder in the tent at Abbey Wood. The tip had been made of lead and was broken—as if a chunk had chipped off inside his shoulder. But she didn't know of a cure, not unless she could hurl Sir Andrew to a twenty-first century hospital.

She shoved the medallion aside. "No, I have no idea how to cure him. Can you summon a physician?"

"Perhaps, but I fear he would want to bleed the poor man. My ma always called the healer—warned against physicians." William scratched his beard as if second guessing his mother's reasoning.

Eva shrugged her shoulders to her ears. "I wish I knew the solution—but if you don't have any other options, maybe Lady Christina should summon a..." she couldn't bring herself to say *physician*. The medallion cooled a bit. Eva's stomach twisted into a knot. *Bleeding never did anyone a bit of good. I have no idea why doctors resorted to it for centuries.*

William groaned and proceeded up the stairs. "There must be something more we can do."

"Is he keeping the wound clean? Changing the bandages several times a day?"

William eyed her over his shoulder. "Have ye asked this of Brother Bartholomew?"

"I told him to only use clean bandages…" Eva pulled the medallion out from beneath her shift and let it rest atop her gown. A few layers of fabric might help—if she didn't end up flung to 2016. "We could try cleansing the wound with boiled saltwater." She cringed, ready for the deafening rush and an abyss of blackness to overcome her, but nothing happened.

"Honestly?" He led her onto the third floor landing. "A cure is as simple as boiled water and salt?"

Eva shook her head. "I didn't say it would cure him—I think he needs antibiotics, but those won't—"

"—be invented for another seven hundred years," he finished. "Good Lord, woman. Why did ye have to attend university to become a chronicler? A physician would have been much more useful to me."

"Or a chemist," she grumbled, biting her bottom lip and brushing the hurtful remark aside. William always spoke his mind, though sometimes he could be a little too insensitive. Eva didn't bother to point out that if she were a doctor, she never would have been chosen to time travel in the first place. The forces behind the medallion picked her because she wanted to take the truth to the world and there was no one better to do that than a journalist with a passion for history.

"Alchemy?" William chortled. "Isna that a tinker's art of chasing magic?"

"I didn't say alchemy. Chemistry is not magic. It's pure science."

He opened the door to her chamber and accompanied her inside. Though for decorum his chamber was through the adjoining door, he rarely slept in his bed. "I'll have to take ye on your word. I shall speak to Brother Bartholomew on the morrow about the boiling salt water."

"Boiled salt water." She held up a finger. "You wouldn't want to scald the poor man."

Chapter Five

Rain spat from the dense clouds. It would make William's hauberk rust for certain, but if he left all the Kingdom's business for fine days, he'd ever accomplish a thing. He chuckled at the irony. Only a few months ago, he'd been content to live in a cave and never paid a mind to the weather unless it was blowing a gale with hip-deep drifts of snow. Now he'd moved into more comfortable quarters. He balked at the rain.

Well, no more. A warrior must endure all manner of discomfort to carry out his duty.

After convincing Sir Andrew to stay abed, William gathered a cavalry of three hundred horse and set out for Dunbar. He didn't expect a fight from the Earl of March on his own lands. The ambush had been clandestine—in the forest with the unlikely chance of credible witnesses.

Regardless, after the Fountainhall raid, Wallace needed to be cautious with his every move. He might be the Guardian of Scotland, but that only increased the size of the target on his back. Before, he'd achieved success with surprise raids. He understood the mind of a raider better than anyone. In no way would he ride into such an ambush again.

With him, he took the missives Eva had written for the chieftains of East Lothian. Once he met with the earl, he intended to visit the southeastern clans to reinforce their fealty to the crown.

He'd also taken Paden Wishart with him this time to stand in as his squire. Though Robbie Boyd had acted as his squire for the past two years, Paden needed to learn to be a man, and hadn't received any training from his father, Bishop Wishart. And the fact that the man was now rotting in Roxburgh's prison did nothing to add to Paden's education. Worse, the lad was soft—preferred his lute to a bow or dirk. He spent too much time strumming and not enough learning the art of war. Unless the lad intended to live his life behind the walls of an abbey, he needed to grow some cods.

Truth be told, William felt more confident leaving Robbie with Eva. The Boyd lad would protect her with his life. Paden? He might try to lull a plunderer with a ballad.

Fortunately, William had found Eva a new mare to keep her out of mischief and he'd decided to humor her by agreeing—Robbie Boyd was just the lad to stay behind and give her a few pointers on handling a more spirited mount. William couldn't imagine what Christendom would be like without horses. His mind still boggled at Eva's description of motorcars. *What about traversing all the bogs? Wheeled carts can only pass where the path is cobbled or dry.*

He had plenty of time to ponder her tales—be them what they may. But doing so helped pass the time while the rain drove harder with each progressing hour. And the wind cutting through William's hauberk told him winter was nigh. Onward he rode, keeping the Firth of Forth on his left until the immense red-stone fortress of Dunbar came into view. Built upon the most strategic peninsula in Scotland, the castle was considered impenetrable and, moreover, William needed its ground advantage for the Kingdom.

William ground his molars. Though they arrived well before dark, Dunbar's gates stood barricaded with archers posted atop her outer bailey.

"What's your plan?" asked Eddy Little, commander of the archers, William's cousin and most trusted spy.

Wallace held up his hand to signal a halt well before the barbican bridge that separated the castle from the mainland. "I'll go in."

"Alone?" John Blair pointed to the archers. "Do ye think they'll allow the great and powerful William Wallace to pass by without skewering him with a few arrows first? Ye canna cross the bridge without riding right beneath their sights"

William sliced his hand downward. "Wheesht. I'll carry the black flag of parley. Even a bastard as two-faced as the Earl of March wouldna kill a man who merely wanted to talk."

Eddy shook his head. "I dunna like it. At least let me and Blair go in with ye."

"Och aye," Blair nodded. "Cospatrick's likely to sit down for a wee yarn, then stab ye in the back as ye're leaving."

"Bloody oath, ye're carrying on like a pair of old crones." Sliding the reins through his gloved fingers, William considered his options. Truth be told, the men had a point. "I'll allow the pair of ye go in with me if ye promise to behave and keep your swords in their scabbards." He turned and faced his man-at-arms. "Graham, mind our horses."

"Did ye think to bring a black flag?" asked Blair.

William pulled a black bit of silk from under his hauberk. "Now ye think me daft as well?"

"I dunna think it, I ken it." Blair tugged his helm low over his forehead. "Planned this all along did ye?"

"I reckon I did." William dismounted and passed his reins to Graham. "I'm putting ye in charge. Be ready for anything—and above all, keep the men out of range of their archers. If ye hear a blast from my ram's horn, make ready for a fight. Only then can ye take out the archers on the wall."

"We'll stand ready for a battle, sir."

"Good lad." William adjusted his sword belt and looked to his two most trusted men. "Come along, then."

Holding the flag above his head, William and the pair of lieutenants marched up to the gate in silence. The breeze off the sea cooled his face as white gannets screeched above. The entire distance William kept his eyes on the men atop the bailey. Not a one made a move.

Blair pounded on the gate.

The viewing screen opened and a ruddy face glared out. "Who goes there?"

"William Wallace, Commander of the Army of Scotland, so appointed by the Parliament of the Kingdom. I carry the flag of parley and would have a word with Lord Cospatrick."

The man's eyes bulged, then shifted with guilt. "Wait here."

The screen screeched as the guard started to close it, but William was faster, slipping his dirk's hilt into the gap before it shut completely. "Long live King John."

After a heated interchange with man's beady-eyed stare, William pulled his dirk away.

Blair rocked back on his heels. "At least we havena been skewered by arrows yet."

William looked up and met the curious stare from a helmed archer regarding them from the battlements. "Cospatrick would be a fool to attack us here. If he were so bold, half the nobles of Scotland would raze his castles, every one."

"After the backstabbing at Fountainhall, that doesna sound like such a bad idea," said Little.

William frowned. "Aye, but if we can win Cospatrick's alliance, we'll be all the more closer to controlling the border—and our ports."

Blair spread his hands to his sides. "And how do ye expect to do that?"

A snort trumpeted through William's nose. "Oh ye of little faith, father."

"God will strike ye down one day for your mockery toward this holy man." John Blair might be an ardent soldier of God, but he didn't always have a vision of what could be.

"Will he now?" William smoothed his palm over the psalter he kept in the purse at his hip. "I think not."

The man door beside the portcullis creaked open and a burly man-at-arms addressed them. "His lordship will see ye now."

"My thanks." William looked to his two lieutenants and waggled his brows. "'Tis time to dance."

The main gate led directly into a tower and an enormous hall with sparse furnishings, clearly barracks for the earl's army. They strode out through the tower and over a sea bridge to the donjon. Once inside, opulence fitting an earl's rank was evidenced from the silk seafaring tapestries to the white marble hearth.

William took it all in with quick shifts of his eyes. *The earl is smart to hide all this wealth behind an army.*

Crossing through the great hall, the guard led them up a stairwell to the second floor landing. He opened the door to the lord's drawing room and gestured for them to enter. A polished walnut table filled the space, appointed with rich hunting tapestries. Yet the Earl of March was nowhere to be seen.

The man-at-arms gestured to the chairs. "Sit. His lordship will attend ye momentarily."

Wallace and his men proceeded as asked, with William taking the seat at the south end of the table. At the north, a lavish and immense wooden chair was clearly reserved for the earl. He watched the man-at-arms pull aside the tapestry and exit into yet another chamber.

"His lordship is taking no chances, I see." Eddy drummed his fingers atop the polished wood.

"Aye. I'd have preferred it if he'd greeted us." William swirled his palm over the pommel of his sword, then stood and pulled the wooden shutter away from the window and looked down to a small courtyard. If this meeting became hostile, they had three options for escape and all except diving into the icy depths meant they had to cross that narrow sea bridge. The window would be the quickest, but a two-story drop to the cobblestones might cause Eddy and Blair injury. No, William had best keep this a congenial gathering as he'd wanted it in the first place.

After resuming his seat and waiting a time, the compline bell tolled. William's stomach rumbled. He considered going in search of the evening meal when the door behind the tapestry opened. Through it marched a dozen men-at-arms all dressed in mail and carrying pikes as if they were protecting the king himself.

Finally, the earl slipped through, wearing a hauberk beneath a red surcoat and a mailed coif atop his head. Topping off the ensemble, a sword and dirk hung from his belt.

William and his men stood and bowed. As he straightened, the corner of his mouth ticked up in a smirk. "M'lord Cospatrick, were ye expecting a fight?"

After assessing the three men with a deprecating glare down the length of his nose, Cospatrick moved to his chair. Two impressive looking men-at-arms took their places behind him and stood with hands grasping their hilts. The earl frowned. "With three hundred cavalry men stationed outside my castle, I should be asking the same thing of ye, *Mr.* Wallace." His emphasis on "Mr." sounded decidedly disrespectful.

"Aye? Well, I suppose I'll make no bones about it then." William looked the earl directly in the eye. "We saw more than one targe bearing the seal of the Earl of March when we were set upon near Fountainhall. I come to ask if the attack was under your orders."

"Och, aye?" The backstabber looked too smug as he sneered and ran his fingers down his surcoat. "And ye think I would own up to such a lawless raid against one with so much newly purchased acclaim?"

William's clenched jaw twitched at the insult, but he refused to take the bait—not with the narrow sea bridge to cross while archers waited above. "I assumed the brigands outlaws, but in the interest of Scotland, 'tis my duty to allay the rumors of your allegiance to Edward."

Cospatrick had the gall to roll his eyes. "And why should I not pay the King of England his due? My holdings in England are nearly as vast as those in Scotland."

"Yet ye make your home here in Dunbar." William intensified his stare. Earl or nay, he would not be spoken to like a fool. "And ye sit on the Privy Council of Scotland. All I ask is that ye own to your lawful king, John Balliol. If ye choose to stay in the Kingdom of Scotland, then ye'll live by her laws of—"

"Are ye threatening me? I am an earl...and ye? Ye are but a poor commoner. The King of the Kyle is all ye are."

Pausing to let the churning bile in his stomach subside, William mulled over his response. The man needed a good hiding, but that would best be accomplished on the battlefield. "I did not come under the flag of parley to withstand your arrogant insults." The chair clattered to the floor as he stood and slapped his palms on the table.

In fluid motion, soldiers leveled their pikes at William's neck.

Blair and Little pushed back their chairs, reaching for their weapons, only to be stopped by guards seizing each burly man's arm.

William glared at the earl and hissed through his teeth, "I am the Commander of the Scottish Army, appointed by the esteemed Parliament of the Kingdom of Scotland and, as such, I have a duty to ensure the safety of all subjects of this land, *commoners* and nobles alike."

The earl emitted a rueful laugh. "Ye are no better than the puppet king."

God's bones, William would welcome the opportunity to meet this bastard on any battlefield. "And your words are treasonous."

"Do ye believe I would ever stoop so low to take heed of a commoner?" Cospatrick leaned back in his chair and threaded his fingers atop his stomach.

William straightened, ignoring the deadly sharp pikes leveled at his neck. "As the Guardian of this Kingdom, I expect ye to honor the edicts of the Privy Council or suffer the consequences—just as any subject, noble or nay."

"Ye are an embarrassment to the nobility of this great land," the earl sneered. "Go home to Ayr, Wallace, and leave the governance of Scotland in the hands of men bred to lead."

"And watch while Longshanks razes our lands? Few of our countrymen have the luxury of being able to cross the border and hide in an English fortress." Heaven help him, William's rage was about to burst from his temples. He clenched his fists to keep from launching himself across the table and strangling that reed-thin neck. "Have ye so easily forgotten the devastation of the battle of Dunbar less than two years past? Your own people—people who bore your arms and tilled your fields were cut down, raped and murdered, all in the name of a foreign king who calls himself suzerain over Scotland. A king whose only interest is to place our sons on the front line of *England's* battles."

"Things are not always as they seem." The earl examined his goddamn fingernails. "King John, the puppet king to whom ye so loyally refer, joined with France. We could have remained at peace with the English, but no, Balliol refused to let things lie."

"King John refused to grovel to Edward with further public humiliation. Ye ken the truth." William leaned forward. "Dunna speak down to me because ye think I'm a lesser man. I've proved my worth on the battlefield and would be happy to meet ye there if ye should doubt my word."

Cospatrick jutted out his chin and sneered. "So ye come into my castle and threaten me, an earl?"

"Nay. I come to tell ye I aim to unite the nobles and demand the release of King John from the Tower of London. And while I'm at it, I aim to see an end to English oppression against all Scotsmen, noble or nay. And I'll let no man stand in my way...even if he is an earl."

Cospatrick clutched his neck before gesturing toward the door. "I suggest ye take your leave, *Mr.* Wallace. I've many things to attend and I do believe we've nothing more of import to discuss."

William stretched to his full height, towering above all men in the room. He made eye contact with each one, silently telling them they'd be the first to die should a one raise their arms against him. "Well then, I'll see ye at the next meeting of Parliament."

The earl narrowed his gaze and thinned his lips.

William beckoned Blair and Little. "Come, men. We've missives to deliver."

Without a word, the guards released their hold as Wallace's men followed. William led them back from whence they came, all the way through the long barracks and out Dunbar's gates.

As soon as the man door slammed closed behind them, Blair spat on the ground. "We should have had Sir Andrew with us. That bastard earl will only pay heed to a member of the gentry."

"Add Sir Andrew's cure to the list of things we need to remedy." William kicked a dried piece of horse dung. "Since when does 'Commander of the Army' mean nothing?"

***

It was dusk when they rode south from Dunbar Castle. William opted to set up camp in the wood near Innerwick. After a meal of bully beef and oatcakes, sleep was fleeting on the damp, mossy earth as rain drizzled from above. Aye, William and his men would need to wrap themselves in wool soon. With what he had planned, there would be many a cold night yet to come.

Restless, Wallace's eyes flew open when he felt a faint tremor of the ground. More than once he'd sensed the approach of horses before hearing their hooves pummeling the earth. Jumping to his feet, he tapped Blair on the shoulder and held his finger to his lips. "Wake the others and keep it quiet."

William strapped on his sword belt and drew his weapon. Creeping to a vantage point, he saw the advancing army but two furlongs away. Cospatrick for certain. Wallace ran to his horse. "Mount up and be ready to fight."

Eddy climbed aboard his steed. "How many?"

"Three, mayhap five hundred."

Blair threw his leg over his horse as well. "The odds are a bit steep."

William grabbed Paden by the shoulders. "Haste ye south and fetch Sir Home—tell him we need reinforcements straight away."

The lad glanced in the direction of the approaching army. "But—"

"Go. Now!"

After watching Paden mount up, William directed his attention to his men and pointed to the ridge. "We'll have the ground advantage if we wait for them to come to us. Make haste, for the Earl of March has decided to play his hand." He circled is hand above his head. "Archers, stand at the ready."

Wallace led his garrison at a fast trot. He caught Eddy's eye and pointed south. "Line up your archers along the ridge. Wait until Cospatrick's forces are upon us afore ye give the command to fire." He beckoned the others to follow while turning his attention to Blair. "We'll hide in the gully yonder and let them pass. Once the archers let loose, the cavalry will hit them from behind."

"May the Lord have mercy on their souls." The priest made the sign of the cross. "At least we'll not have long to wait."

William crossed himself, repeating Blair's motion. "Aye, now pass the word. Quickly."

No sooner had Wallace and his men hid in the gully, the hoofbeats of the earl's army thundered past. Though concealed from sight, he clamped his fingers around his reins and waited, ears piqued for the thud of the first arrow hitting its mark.

Though a seasoned warrior, the rush before battle always made his skin thrum with anticipation. The thunder of his heart beat so loudly in his helm, his every breath rushed like the rumble of the tide. If he'd been an inexperienced lad, he might have feared being caught by the deafening roar of his own lifeblood pulsing through his veins. Placing his hand atop the psalter at his hip, he closed his eyes and concentrated on clearing his mind. Then he offered a quick prayer for his men and for those wayward souls who followed the Earl of March.

A heinous howl screeched through the wind. Then another. Snapping up his head, William dug in his spurs and slapped his reins. "Scotland until Judgement!" he bellowed the Kingdom's war cry.

Thundering the cry behind him, his men boldly repeated the cheer that bound them together as men driven in a united cause.

Ahead, mayhem erupted. Fallen soldiers writhed on the ground, clutching at arrows. The earl's ranks forced out of step, they toiled to circle their horses and face the onslaught.

William drove his mount straight for Cospatrick. By God, he would cut any man down who turned traitor. Narrowing the distance, the direct path to the earl was blocked by a pair of henchmen flanking Wallace from both sides. He roared and swung, meeting each man's sword with gnashing of teeth and a deafening clang of iron. Ears ringing from the booming clash of battle, William fought, hacking off limbs and deflecting blows from battleaxes and pikes while steering his horse with his knees.

Facing nearly twice their numbers, the fighting grew bloodier, but William wasn't about to stop. Cospatrick cowered at the rear of the battlefield, surrounded by his guardsmen.

"I'll carve out your heart and send it to Edward in a bejeweled box," William roared as he fought wave after wave.

His muscles tortured him, burning like limbs being held to the fire as he inched toward the earl. With an upward swing of his great sword, a gap opened—straight to his target. "Scotland until Judgement," he roared, spurring his mount into a gallop.

The stench of fear inflamed William's nostrils before the earl's party turned tail and raced south. Pointing his great sword forward, he dug in his spurs and urged his men to follow. "After them!"

On and on he drove his horse south, making chase toward the border. An uproarious cry came from the east as an army galloped into their ranks, bolstering Wallace's numbers.

The Home pennant flew high, carried by young Paden.

"Good lad," William bellowed, sure his shout was but a whisper on the howling wind.

His horse's snorting breaths became more labored as they continued to make chase. Finally, white froth leeched from his steed's neck as they approached the Whiteadder Water.

"Hold up." Sir Geoffrey Home reined his horse beside William. "We're growing dangerously close to Berwick and the Tweed. Word has it Lord Warenne has five thousand men lying in wait within the castle walls. They'd like nothing better than to sever your head and hang it from the town's gable."

William's gut clenched as he watched Cospatrick gain distance. "Five thousand?"

"Aye, my spies reported as such, reliable men they are as well."

Taking in a deep breath, Wallace lowered his reins. "Ye reckon the Earl of Surrey is ready to stage a revolt?"

"I reckon he's still licking his wounds after ye kicked his arse at Stirling Bridge. But he still wouldna look a gift horse in the mouth." Sir Home beckoned him. "Come, we've much to discuss and I've got a thirst."

William glared across the burn while Cospatrick's red surcoat disappeared into the wood. "First bring me one of the injured men of Dunbar. One who's well enough to carry a missive to the Earl of March." He beckoned Paden. "I need a slip of vellum, quill and a pot of ink."

Not long and William had his missive written and sent the wounded man on his way with a scroll addressed to the Earl of March:

On this date, 25ᵗʰ October, the year of our Lord 1297, the Earl of March, is hereby stripped of his Scottish title. All holdings in Scotland are forfeit to the king. This decree by William Wallace, Guardian of Scotland.

Long live King John.

***

Sitting in the second floor solar of Cocksburnpath Tower, William sipped a tot of whisky. "After the backstabbing by Cospatrick, 'tis good to know we have allies among the eastern border clans."

Sir Geoffrey Home had the look of a warrior. Barrel chested with a bit of grey in his beard, he was the type of man whose loyalty the Kingdom needed. "Most of the clans support ye. We're all sick of having our lands razed by the English. Only barons with holdings on both sides of the border are in question."

William leaned forward and rested his elbows on the table. "True, but that comprises nearly all the most powerful families in Scotland."

"But I dunna ken a man who wouldn't like to see the backsides of the English army retreating across the Tweed." Sir Geoffrey sipped his whisky thoughtfully. "And your victory at Stirling Bridge made ye a legend. Make no bones about it, the people of Scotland are ready to take up their arms and stand behind ye."

"'Tis good to hear. Mayhap if we can continue to drive away naysayers like the Earl of March, even grand families like Bruce and Comyn will stand behind our cause."

"If they can curb their lust for the throne." Home threw back his head with a belly laugh. "Ye mustn't forget in twelve ninety-one Bishop Fraser asked Longshanks to choose between Balliol and Bruce—the two men with the greatest claim to the throne."

William hated that Edward had been consulted, though at the time, the bishop thought he was acting to prevent a civil war. Little did the misguided holy man know, Longshanks would arrive and claim himself rightful suzerain. "'Tis not our place to decide who should have been crowned. Regardless, Edward has wrongfully imprisoned King John in the Tower. I intend to see his crown restored afore I take my last breath."

"Here, here," said Sir Geoffrey, raising his cup.

William eyed a thin sword resting atop the sideboard. "Do ye mind if I have a look at that?"

Sir Geoffrey twisted around and followed Wallace's line of sight. "My mail piercer? Go right ahead."

Pushing back his chair, William strode around the table and picked up the piece. "'Tis light of weight."

"And square at the hilt."

William touched the blade. It wasn't sharp except for the deadly tip. "Did ye say mail piercing?"

"Aye. 'Tis from the Holy Land—bought it off a sea merchant. Its sole purpose is to pierce through a man's hauberk straight through to the heart."

William whipped it through the air with a hiss. "Would ye be willing to part with it?"

Sir Geoffrey crossed his arms thoughtfully. "Nay, but my smithy could fashion ye one if ye're inclined to stay on a bit."

"I could arrange for that." William tested the tip with his finger. God's teeth, it was sharp enough to lance straight through bone. "Besides, I've a parcel of missives to deliver to the surrounding clans."

CHAPTER SIX

"I think I'll call this filly Ryn," Eva said, posting up and down in time with the gait of the horse while she and Robbie trotted through the open lea outside the castle walls.

After a week of taking instructions from an adolescent boy and riding inside the courtyard, Eva finally felt comfortable enough to take Ryn on a real ride. In truth, she'd learned the basics on an old nag out of pure survival—hadn't even let on that the only horse she'd ever ridden by herself was hot pink and part of a carousel at the county fair. Thrown on the back of the gelding, as the daughter of a knight, everyone had naturally assumed she could pick up the reins and launch into a canter. The only thing that had saved her neck was her ability to copy others. Eva probably wouldn't have survived if her gelding had been as spirited as this mare, but fortunately the old fella didn't like to move much. He'd just drop his head and trudge along behind the others. She'd been fine with him until a few days ago when she needed to flee from a mob of attacking outlaws.

A six-year-old mare felt completely different to the old guy. Ryn took off with the slightest tap of Eva's heel and needed a firm rein. Over the past week, handling the mare became easier while Robbie continued to provide instruction, like keeping her heels down and relaxing her seat. She even began recognizing the horse's body language. If Ryn carried her head high, she was more uptight. Pinning back the ears was a definite warning to any human or horse within ten feet.

"Ryn?" Robbie asked after a long pause. "What kind of name is that?"

Eva trotted the mare in a circle. "It's the name of a minstrel I once knew."

"Someone ye met on your travels to the Holy Land?" Robbie asked in an absent tone, as if not too terribly interested.

"Something like that." Eva smiled. Ryn was the name of a new vocalist she'd heard on the radio not long before crashing through time and ending up in the midst of a battle in Fail Monastery. She'd experienced nothing quite as disconcerting as traversing seven hundred years in a matter of seconds. Naming her mare Ryn gave Eva a small sense of connection with her twenty-first century life. A time to which she must return one day. She'd given herself a year. A year to immerse herself in medieval Scotland and learn everything she could about William Wallace. A year to really discover what it was like to love him, adore him, be his woman.

Eva couldn't allow herself to think beyond that. Yet five months of her year had already passed.

Two years?

Shaking her head, she refused to allow herself to consider it.

"Um…" Robbie slowed the pace to a walk. "Er…How would a lad my age go about talking to a lassie?"

Unable to stifle her grin, Eva managed to hold in her laugh. Most likely, it wasn't easy for the twelve-year-old orphan to blurt out such a question. "Well, that depends," Eva tried to keep her voice serious, clinical. "Is the lass old like me or about your age?"

Shrugging, he fiddled with his reins. "Close to my age, I'd reckon."

"Hmm." Eva gave the lad a sideways glance. His brow furrowed as if this topic were very important. "I think it's best to keep things simple at first. Say hello—um—or good morrow. Mention the weather."

Robbie scrunched his nose. "Weather?"

"Yes. Everyone talks about the weather." Arriving at the edge of the forest, Eva reined her horse back toward Dirleton Castle. "You might think of questions you could ask her. If she was a serving girl, perhaps you could—"

"I didna say anything about her being a serving girl." He gaped as if she'd dealt a personal affront.

Waving her hand apologetically, she explained, "I know. I was just using that as an example." Eva cleared her throat and continued as if he hadn't been bothered by the serving girl comment. "If she was, you could ask her about her tasks. What part of the castle does she work in, what are her main responsibilities, does she like it, does she ever have time to herself, do her parents work at the castle…You know, that sort of thing."

He groaned and looked to the sky. "Och, ye make it sound so easy."

"It is, really." She let out a relieved breath. "I've never met a young lady who didn't like talking about herself."

Robbie grazed his bottom lip with his teeth, giving her a quizzical look. "So ye reckon a lad should just go up to a wee lassie, say good morrow and ask her what she's on about?"

"Sort of." Eva bit her lip. She knew enough about living in the Middle Ages to throw out a word of caution, especially since Robbie was an orphan with William overseeing his fostering. The newly appointed Guardian had more on his plate than any army general and Eva wondered if he'd paid much notice to the lad in the past month. "Of course, if she's a highborn lass, you would need a proper introduction. You might ask someone like Lady Christina to introduce you, for example. Then, once you are on speaking terms, it would be all right to ask questions."

The lad's eyebrows shot up as if he liked her idea. "An introduction, aye?"

"That would be proper, but regardless, you should speak to the lass where others can see you, so as not to sully her reputation."

Robbie turned as red as a harvest sunset. "I wouldna want to do that."

"I'm certain you wouldn't. It is always important to be considerate of a young lady's standing. You must understand how devastating it would be for a lass to be compromised in the eyes of society, and it is up to young men like you to protect and honor her virtue." Eva sat a bit straighter in the saddle. Had William been so busy he'd overlooked the need for such important discussions? "You must act chivalrously. Do you know what that means, Robbie?"

The growing boy puffed out his adolescent chest and thumped it with pride. "Och aye, Miss Eva. 'Tis my duty to protect womenfolk and to fight for right."

"Mm hmm. And more." Eva definitely must have a word with William about this conversation. "Do you know many court dances? Dancing is an essential social skill at court and at gatherings."

Robbie's shoulders shrugged to his ears. "How am I supposed to learn about dancing when I'm serving as squire to the Guardian of Scotland?"

Eva shook her riding crop at him. "That makes it even more important—and we mustn't forget that you are the son of a knight, a lad who owns property." *And a man who will become a titled baron in his own right.*

"Aye, but who will teach me?" Robbie gave her a stern frown. "Not ye I'd wager. Ye dunna even ken how to dance. I saw ye at Peebles Castle and reckon ye need lessons more than I do."

Covering her mouth with her hand, she let out a belly laugh. Oh, for the love of God, she'd hoped her skirts had hidden her stumbling feet. "True," she admitted. "Perhaps we both need lessons. Let me give that some thought." Eva slowed her mare and looked to the donjon looming above the bailey walls. Could she ask Lady Christina to help? *But how long...?*

Eva blocked the thought from her mind.

Robbie obviously considered their discussion over, because without another word, he spurred his horse into a fast gallop—a gait Eva doubted she'd ever be able to master. Alas, she did miss driving her red Fiat at seventy miles per hour on the motorway—though less and less as time passed.

Picking up her reins, she sighed and headed toward the gate. The mare hadn't traversed but a few paces when the ram's horn sounded from the wall-walk above. Blinking, Eva nearly jumped out of her skin. Robbie immediately changed course and hollered, waving his hand over his head while grinning like it was Christmas.

Catching sight of the garrison approaching through the trees, Eva's stomach erupted with butterflies. *William!*

She cued her horse for a canter while the little show-off rode in beside William with animated welcoming gestures. And what a sight the big man made, sitting his horse with a commanding presence as if he were born to the guardianship. If she hadn't known him, Eva would have guessed him to be as regal as a king. While he led the garrison along the path to the gates, he looked her way and gave her a firm nod.

She pulled her horse to a stop. There had always been an unspoken code of respectful distance between them when in public—gatherings and celebrations aside. Even when William carried out his duties as leader of the rebellion, and now Guardian of Scotland, she kept her distance and minded her affairs. But at night, William was hers. Fortunately, with the sun low in the western sky, she wouldn't have long to wait.

***

After leaving her horse with the groom, Eva headed to her chamber to dress for the evening meal. Now they were no longer living in a cave, she'd fallen right in to living the comfortable life of a highborn woman. William had even appointed her with a chambermaid, Madeline, who greeted Eva as soon as she stepped inside. "How was the riding, Miss Eva?"

The words "awesome" and "brilliant" came to the tip of her tongue, but Eva knew better. "Quite invigorating." She twirled inside and tossed her circlet on the bed. "Do you ride?"

"Och, whenever there's a need, I suppose." The chambermaid strode to the bed and picked up Eva's discarded headpiece. "I dunna travel overmuch."

Eva combed her fingers through her growing red hair, though it was still too short for a medieval lady. "Were you born here?"

"Aye, and my parents as well." Madeline gestured to the walls. "Everything we need is right here in Haddington."

"Have you ever been to Edinburgh or a city?"

"Oh no." Madeline stepped into the garderobe and retrieved a blue gown.

Eva untied the front lace of her kirtle. "Would you like to go sometime?"

"Never really thought about it." The chambermaid stopped and looked down with a furrow to her brow. "Wouldna it be dangerous?"

"Perhaps not if traveling to Edinburgh when riding with a fortified garrison. And riding a horse, it wouldn't take long. If you left at dawn you'd be there in time to take your nooning." Goodness, Eva had improved at communicating in Auld

Scots. Professor Tennant, the archaeologist who'd given her the medallion, would be impressed.

Madeline drew a hand to her chest. "No longer than that? I never realized we were so close."

"Would you like to see the city?" Eva shrugged out of her kirtle and let it drop to the floor. It always felt as if she could float after removing the heavy woolen day gown and shaking out her shift.

"Oh no, I couldna leave Dirleton." She skittered backward as if terrified of the idea.

"I suppose you'd need an adventuresome spirit." With a sigh, Eva tapped her fingers to her lips. "There's far more to life than what lies in this castle."

"Mayhap to ye. Ye're William Wallace's woman, and ye've traveled all of Christendom. But the mere thought of venturing away from my home scares me to my verra bones. What of outlaws and tinkers and all manner of ill-reputed folk the father preaches about during Sunday mass?"

"Yes, the world can be a dangerous place, though I doubt it is as bad as the priest makes it out to be—especially if you have a proper escort." Eva rolled her eyes to the ceiling. Recently, she'd been giving too much advice. Servants didn't just pick up and take a day trip to a big city. A stroll into the village of Haddington would have been a major deal to Madeline.

"Och, ye dunna need to be filling my head with fanciful dreams of travel. I'm a servant's daughter. No use dreaming where I've no business sticking my nose."

Dumbfounded, Eva stared at the wall for a moment. *My, how different their lives are. A servant who refused to allow herself to dream about traveling twenty miles?*

The door creaked open and William poked his head inside. "Do ye have a moment?"

Madeline darted in front of Eva and held up the gown to cover her as if she were naked and not wearing a shift tied at the neck, draping all the way to her toes. "I'll have Miss Eva presentable in no time."

He craned his neck, peering around the tiny chambermaid. "Verra well. I shall wait in the passageway, then."

"For crying out loud." Eva marched to the garderobe and donned a dressing gown. Was she the only person at Dirleton Castle who didn't see a need to pretend she and William weren't sleeping together? "Please excuse us, Madeline."

Holding out the gown the chambermaid shook her head defiantly. "But—"

"Just leave it. I'm sure I can manage this once."

"Aye, miss." After carefully draping the gown over a chair, Madeline curtseyed then slipped past William and out the door.

Once they were alone, all he had to do was grin.

Swarms of butterflies attacked her stomach as Eva flew into his open arms. "Can you believe it? I stayed behind for an entire fortnight and nothing bad happened. I wasn't kidnapped. There was no attempt on my life."

They both shook with the force of his laugh while he lifted her and spun in a circle. "And ye didna don men's clothing and try to come after me."

Her toes touched the floor. "Right. You did have to bring that up." When he'd found her at Fail Monastery, she'd been dressed in jeans and a month later, when he tried to break up with her and leave her at the same monastery, she'd put on a monk's habit and had gone after him—which didn't work out well for her at all. She coyly twisted a lock of hair around her finger. "But I promised not to try anything rash as long as you vowed to return."

"Mm hmm." His gaze dropped to her lips. "I missed ye." Lordy, he could melt marzipan with that sexy Scottish burr.

With a dip of his chin, he brushed a kiss across her mouth. Hot tingles spread down her back. Eva moved closer and pressed her body flush with his toned, muscular form. If they hadn't been born so many centuries apart, she could have believed they were made for each other, fitting together perfectly as if molded from the same clay. Closing her eyes, she drank him in, allowing her senses to take over. Hot, spicy male kissed and held her in a tender embrace with arms that could crush a man, let alone her fine bones. Yet he cradled her with incredible tenderness.

Pressing friction made her breasts swell and ache with pent up desire she hadn't even been aware she'd suppressed. The forceful demand of his mouth filled her with spiraling pleasure. Rubbing from side to side, her nipples hardened and her need for him grew like an addict's craving. She dug her fingers into his back muscles, needing to savor him. Oh no, no opportunity to hold him in her arms, memorize every curve of his flesh, could be allowed to pass.

Eva's limited time was too precious.

William's body responded in kind, his erection hardened against her mons as his hips swirled in a seductive rhythm.

Taking a breath to clear her swooning head, Eva arched her hips firmly against his as she smoothed her fingers through his wiry red beard. It had grown during the fortnight of his absence. "I missed you every waking moment. I don't like it when you're gone."

He placed a gentle kiss upon her forehead. "But ye ken I've no choice. 'Tis why…"

She nodded her understanding as his voice trailed off. It was why they lived in the moment—why they refused to make promises to each other—the reason she couldn't sleep at night when he lay beside her.

She halted her wandering thoughts and smiled. "Did you see me riding Ryn?"

His expression brightened. "Ye've given the mare a name?"

"Aye, and why not? I like her."

Brushing her hair away from her face, his eyes twinkled tawny from the candlelight—sexier than sin. "I suppose there's no harm in it. I named my first horse."

She trailed her finger from his collar down to the laces of his shirt where a tuft of chest hair teased her. "What happened to him?"

"He grew old." After another kiss, William lifted Eva in his arms and carried her to the bed. "But I dunna want to think on it now."

Oh, how she loved that he could whisk her off her feet like she was a petite young thing. Not only was she tall, Eva had never been a string-bean either. Her curves rivaled Beyoncé.

He set her down with her feet dangling. "I brought ye something."

"A present?" Eva's heart fluttered. Though she never expected anything from William, from time to time he surprised her. She looked between his empty palms, biting her bottom lip. "What is it?"

With a devilish grin, he drew a weapon from his belt. It was long like an arming sword, but needle-thin and squared near the hilt.

She eyed it. "Is that a sword?"

He presented it atop his upturned palms. "Aye, 'tis made for piercing mail."

Not wanting to touch it, Eva rubbed the outside of her arms. "For me?" In truth, she hated all sharp objects, though she'd grown a bit desensitized of late. Hell's bells, everyone around her carried knives hidden up every sleeve and inside every sock.

William sat beside her. "Come, lass. Ye canna turn your back on the realities of the times forever. I promise when I'm away I'll assign ye a guard, but I'd be a damned sight relieved if ye'd accept my gift."

She reached across and brushed her trembling fingers over the icy hilt. "The craftsmanship is marvelous." Smooth as a brass doorknob, the pommel sparkled with the flickering light.

He grinned and held it up. "'Twas made by the smithy at Cocksburnpath Tower." Taking her hand, he closed his fingers around hers until she firmly grasped the hilt. "I'll teach ye to wield it."

She bit her bottom lip and tried not to shudder. "If you think it's necessary. I wouldn't want to carry something like this without some training. You know they say if you carry a weapon it can be used against you."

William rested the sword across the bedside table. "Do they now?"

"Yes."

"Well, whoever *they* are hasna met the likes of me." He waggled his brows with a playful glint dancing in his eyes. Then he brushed his fingers across her cheek. "And I doubt they've met a woman with as determined a spirit as ye, *mon amour*. Ye have more fight in your heart than half the zealots in my ranks."

She leaned into his warm palm and closed her eyes. "I wish that were true, but I'm really as skittish as a finch."

"I think ye have the good sense to flee….but ye ken that is not always possible." The tip of his tongue snuck to the corner of his mouth while he tugged on her robe's sash. He spread open the red wool revealing her shift and cupped her breast as if he were holding a dove. "I've something more urgent to attend, if it pleases my lady."

Such simple words had a way of turning his lady's knees to wobbling jelly. Who could refuse such a chivalrous offer? William Wallace could ignite a raging fire in Eva's belly with merely a half-cast stare and a wee touch. She arched into his palm. "Mm. This lady most certainly would enjoy being pleasured by you, sir."

He let out a feral rumble. "But first I need to see ye bare." He pulled her to her feet and pushed the robe completely from her shoulders, sending it to a heap around her ankles. His lips curled up in a wicked grin as he grasped her shift and drew it over her head, leaving her standing in the only "modern" clothes she refused to part with.

With a chuckle he traced his finger over the mounds of her breasts swelling above her bra. "Do ye ken how much I like your newfangled undergarments?"

"Yes." She inclined her head back and closed her eyes while goosebumps rose across her flesh. "I'm glad you like them."

His hand slid to her back. "They make the prize all the more sweet, but I must admit I prefer it even better once I've removed them." With a flick of his fingers the elastic relaxed and he cast the bra aside like an expert. Next, he slid her panties down. With her legs slightly parted, Eva stood prone to him, every nerve ending alive, anticipating his next move as she kept her eyes closed.

His deep moan resounded through the chamber. "Your scent is more intoxicating than a vat of honeysuckle wine."

A warm hand brushed her pubic hair ever so slightly, tempting her before his fingers skimmed to her waist. Hot moisture covered her nipple as his tongue teased it to a wickedly hard point.

Opening her eyes, Eva placed her palm in the center of William's chest. "You're next." With her wee push, he obliged her and sat on the edge of the bed. Kneeling, she untied his shoes and removed his hose. When she stood, William had already untied the lace of the arming doublet he wore atop his shirt. Eva held up her finger. "Tsk, tsk. You don't want to spoil my fun do you?"

He shrugged out of the doublet with a look of defiance. "It canna hurt to help a bit."

"Come here." She pulled him up by the cord of his chausses. Fingers working quickly, she untied them and his braies, and let them drop to the floor. Then, with a sultry giggle, she slowly tugged the tie on his linen shirt, staring at his eyes while she tortured him, pulling oh so very slowly. "This bit of linen is all that's left between us, William."

He growled through straight white teeth. "And it will be torn to shreds if ye dunna haste to rip it from my torrid flesh."

Laughing, Eva grasped the hem and tugged the shirt as high as she could until William yanked it off the rest of the way. Casting the shirt aside, he gazed upon her with an intense, predatory glint in his eyes. He placed his warm palms on her waist and moaned. Lord, merely the sound of his voice could stir her desire into a frenzy.

As if she were no heavier than a kitten, he tossed her onto the bed. The feather mattress molded around her ever so soothingly, but Eva wasn't about to let him take complete charge. Licking her lips with a purr of her own, she took hold of his hands and pulled him over her. God, he was so hard, with one thrust of his hips she'd have him inside.

But that wouldn't do at all. She wanted to draw it out. Savor him until they both lingered upon the ragged edge of ecstasy.

He pinned her wrists to the bed, hovering just above her, but not touching. "I like your spirit." Dipping his hips, his erection teased her mons. "Ye are the perfect woman for me, Eva. Ye're built like a fine-boned filly, yet ye're not so petite a big stallion the likes of me would crush ye."

She winked. "There is nothing small about me."

"I wouldna say that." He trailed kisses along her throat and moved downward. "Ye're lithe and long and…mm…ever so desirable."

Goosebumps rose across Eva's skin. She arched into him as the swirl of his tongue over her nipples ignited a raging fire deep inside her. Rocking her hips in time with his delectable licks, her need mounted like the onset of a raging tempest.

William's crystal blue eyes regarded her as he slowly moved his mouth down to her navel. Swirling warmth filled her core. "Your skin is like spun silk, m'lady." He uttered these words while urging her legs further open with his shoulders. "But your taste is like ambrosia from the gods— sent to tempt a man and send him to the edge of utter madness."

"Utter pleasure," Eva moaned as his tongue lapped her. Filling her fists with the bedclothes, she closed her eyes and gave in to pure euphoria. A man of many talents, William's tongue was more talented than his sword. Humming into her, he intuitively knew exactly how much friction she needed— she craved—oh, God, how she craved him.

When her thighs began to tremble with the onset of her peak, Eva opened her eyes and forced herself to rise up slightly. She reached down and mussed his hair. "Now you."

William wiped his arm across his mouth and regarded her with eyes that could turn iron molten. "Ye are a vixen."

She managed a hoarse chuckle. "Why is it that we vixens are so desirable to men?"

"'Cause their wiles are irresistible. Just like ye are, m'lady."

Rising to her knees, Eva grasped his shoulders and coaxed him down to the pillows. She traced her finger around his erect nipples, completely aware of the other erect part of his body demanding her attention.

For the love of God, he was magnificent to gaze upon— and so very much more. Though married once, Eva had never connected with anyone remotely similar to William before. Such a powerful presence, commanding, intelligent, brilliance at its best. What he was doing with her, she couldn't fathom. If only she could put him on a pedestal to worship and admire through all eternity.

A more virile man did not exist.

With a lick of her tongue across his nipple, he arched into her. "Merciful father, your every touch sends my heart thrumming into a tumult of desire."

And by her life, he always found the most perfectly charming words. Merely the sound of his voice was an elixir to her confused and shattered soul. She couldn't think about the consequences because loving William Wallace gave her strength, made her life worth living again.

With every inhale, Eva craved him more of him. The spiciness of his scent, the downy auburn curls splayed across his powerful chest. She wanted all of him, the emotional, intellectual, and above all, the physical. She trailed her lips down the center of his chest, swirling her tongue, delighting in his every satisfied sigh.

Lovingly, she prolonged the journey until she nuzzled into his erection. With a low chuckle, she licked his length.

"Almighty stars," he moaned.

Taking his enormous size into her mouth, Eva's own need heightened as she led him to the very edge of climax.

Eva rose up and savored the sight of him, rigid as a poleaxe. His chest heaving, his lids half-cast and his lips slightly parted, William gazed at her with a fervent stare. The corners of his lips turned up and he placed his enormous hands on her hips. "I swear, woman, ye're on a crusade to drive me to the limits of my verra sanity," his low burr rumbled.

Giggling, she straddled him and took him deep inside her core, sliding ever so slowly until he touched her womb. "I'll take that as a compliment," she said, her voice every bit as husky as his.

Gazing into each other's eyes they rode the wave of passion, delighting in every thrust, every swirl of hips, until glorious release claimed their minds and souls and left them panting in each other's arms.

CHApTER SEVEN

"Order," William bellowed, rapping the pommel of his dirk on the board. He needed to take control of this session of parliament before the nobles came to blows. Bless it, the lot of them were more barbaric than commoners for certain. "Ye can settle your petty differences outside this meeting. We've a great many matters to discuss, the first being the return of King John."

Torphichen Preceptory became suddenly quiet, a great feat considering that even the slightest whisper resonated over the vaulted ceilings of the hall. Though many nobles had ignored his summons, half the gentry stared at him as if he were daft—especially John Comyn. William had no doubt the Earl of Badenoch coveted the throne for himself. And Wallace would do what he must to ensure that man remembered his place.

"We've received no response to our demands for his release," said Sir Andrew, his "s" trailing off with a wheezing cough.

"Balliol will never again set foot in Scotland. He abdicated for Christ's sake," said Comyn with a dismissive bat of his hand.

William smoothed his palm over the dirk sheathed at his hip. "Ye're wrong. The king resigned his crown to protect Scotland from entering a war we couldna win—"

"Aye, and see where that got him," said Sir Douglas.

"Ye're the one who lost us Berwick," snapped Comyn.

Douglas shoved back his chair. Standing, he drew his dirk. "I did what I must in order to live to fight the English another day." He pointed the weapon across the table directly at the Earl of Badenoch. "'Tis more than I can say for ye—why are ye here and not kissing Longshanks' arse?"

"Enough," William bellowed and thrust his finger at Douglas. "Sheathe your weapon unless ye want to spend a sennight in the dungeon." He eyed each man. "And that goes for the lot of ye. When parliament is assembled ye'll cast your miserable clan feuds aside."

"Edward will never respond. If ye're intent on bringing the king back from the Tower, ye'll need a miracle." Robert Bruce spoke up for the first time since he'd entered the hall. At three and twenty, the young earl had held his tongue on the few occasions William had seen him—a fact which had made Wallace question the earl's fealty. Another noble with lands on both sides of the border, no one knew where the Bruce Clan's loyalties lay.

William met the Bruce's stare. "Have ye a direct line to the Holy Father, m'lord? 'Cause I'd not be above calling upon him to unleash a miracle or two on our behalf."

"Blasphemy!" Comyn shouted.

"The Lord *is* on our side," said Sir Andrew with a bolder tone than he'd managed of late. "Scotland is ours. By the grace of God, we took back Stirling when no one thought it possible."

Lord Stewart rapped the table twice. "Here, here. But I say we must rid all our castles of English overlords afore we set plans to negotiate for the release of King John."

"Negotiate?" William asked with a snort.

"Lord Stewart is right," Bruce said. "Too many lives would be lost if we attacked. No one can breech the Tower of London—not even the likes of ye, Wallace."

"True. We'd be slitting our own throats," John Comyn said far too eagerly.

William looked to the arches of the barrel-vaulted ceiling while voices rose. Everyone had an opinion, yet not a one of them could agree on a course of action. Seething, heat flared up his neck while the earls and barons posture for their own personal gain. "Enough," he finally thundered loud enough to bring down the preceptory's stone walls. "If ye've nothing further to say on the matter, as Commanders of the Army, Sir Andrew and I have agreed on a course of action." William wasn't about to provide details of their plans to a gathering of men who could turn backstabbers without a lick of remorse. "If King Edward willna respond to our requests, then we shall make known our wishes by other means."

The hall again erupted with taunts and shouts. *Bloody hell. How in God's name can anything be accomplished with these men?* He sliced his hand through the air. "Our next order of business is resuming trade throughout Christendom."

Though not without banter, that topic proceeded a bit smoother with Hay and Ramsay agreeing to be emissaries and carry William's missives across the channel. At least the nobles with holdings solely in Scotland supported the restoration of trade, though it didn't pass William's notice that Lord Bruce again remained quiet.

William was about to call an end to the day's session when Sir Andrew stood, his brow glistening with a sheen of sweat, the poor blighter. "There is one more article of business I would discuss which I havena mentioned to Mr. Wallace."

William's eyebrows shot up. Since they'd joined their forces, there had been no secrets between them.

Andrew faced him and bowed. "I act only in your interest, my friend."

William rolled his hand through the air. "Then I bid ye continue."

"As ye all are aware, William Wallace has risked life and limb for this, our Kingdom of Scotland. He has ignored his calling to become a priest. He has taken up arms and put himself in harm's way so that each and every one of ye can retain your lands and live in peace."

Comyn leaned back and crossed his arms with a blast of air out his nose.

Andrew arched an eyebrow at the earl. "I speak true, m'lord. William Wallace doesna have the luxury of crossing the border and pretending he's not a part of this war. He's a man of the people—loved by the people and I believe 'tis time we knighted him—gave him the title he deserves."

Silence filled the chamber until Lord Bruce raised his cup. "Here, here. We've made Wallace our Guardian. He should be knighted and granted lands."

William blinked. Had he heard Robert Bruce correctly? What did the earl have to gain from such a statement?

Nothing, I'd wager.

Another pause permeated the hall until the High Steward stood. "Agreed. Sir Murray is right. We should have knighted Wallace on the day he was made Guardian. 'Tis an oversight that we must remedy immediately."

Comyn's mouth formed a thin line, though he chose to say nothing.

"I've a deed drawn for four hundred acres and a castle in Ayrshire near Kilmarnock if all are in agreement." Andrew might be suffering from his battle wounds, but on this account, he surely had been most dutiful. "All in favor?"

"Aye!" The word echoed off the walls and swirled around the hall.

"Opposed?"

John Comyn threw his gloves on the board and shook his head.

"'Tis settled." Ignoring the earl, Andrew looked to Lord Stewart. "Will ye do the honors this eve, m'lord?"

"It would be my pleasure. Let all in attendance witness William's knighthood."

"My thanks. Ye honor me and I will endeavor to continue to act in your service." William stood and bowed, his lips quivering a bit. When the day began, he feared every man in the hall stood against him bar Andrew, and now there had not been one "nay" uttered to oppose his knighthood—though he doubted the Earl of Badenoch had hollered an "aye".

Truth be told, the vote of confidence given by the nobles did much to ease William's misgivings about spending the duration of the sennight in their midst. There still were a great many matters to be discussed and they hadn't yet heard petitions from the floor.

After dismissing the day's session, he slipped out the side door to find Eva. True, he did not covet a title and lands—did not expect it. But as a Guardian of Scotland, he'd be a fool to refuse the honor, for a title would carry much weight among the gentry—something that had hindered him on many occasions in the past.

***

Eva's heart leapt when William relayed the news in their rooms at the inn. She'd been fairly certain it would happen soon. Though the history books hadn't recorded the date he was knighted, it was clear that at some point soon after William was made Guardian, he also received a title—something he never would have bestowed upon himself.

Releasing Eva from their embrace, William held her at arm's length. "I did not seek promotion of my own accord."

"Well, thank heavens Sir Andrew did." She grinned. "You may have due admiration from the ranks, but you also need respect from nobility. Now they have no reason not to give it."

He took in a sharp breath. "My appointment to Guardian should have been enough."

"Yes it should have." Eva hesitated. With her next blink the Battle of Falkirk popped in her head. She froze. Why did bad thoughts have to always put a damper on her happiness?

"Is something amiss?" William was too perceptive.

Backing, she shook her head and steadied her nerves with a deep inhale. "It's nothing." Her gaze trailed aside. "I'll fetch Robbie to help you prepare your armor."

When she headed for the door, William grasped her elbow. "What is it?"

Gulping, Eva forced herself to smile. "I'm overcome with happiness for you. This is a night for celebration."

Though his intelligent gaze reflected wariness, he gave her a nod. "That it is, and I intend to enjoy it with my woman beside me." Now he glanced away. "Except…"

With a pinch to her brow, she stepped in. "What?"

"The Order strictly forbids women from entering the preceptory."

Blinking, Eva folded her arms. "Are you kidding?"

With a shrug, William spread his palms. "I wouldna jest about something like that."

He *was* serious. How unfair—William was going to be knighted and she would be banned from witnessing it? "For crying out loud, you are the Guardian of Scotland. Can't you tell them to make an exception?"

"The Order of St. John doesna take direction from me. They pay fealty only to the Pope."

She threw up her hands. "This is ridiculous. You're being honored and I can't even hide under a table and watch the ceremony?"

"Och, I'll walk in, kneel, Lord Stewart will dub me on the shoulders, and it'll be done. Then ye and Lady Murray can join us for the feast."

"Brilliant. I can make an appearance for the food."

He tugged her into his arms. "Come, Eva, dunna be like that. Ye kent no women were allowed in the preceptory afore we left Dirleton."

"I have half a mind to don a monk's robe and pull a hood over my head."

William shook his head. "Nay, ye canna risk it. Ye'd only give the Earl of Badenoch more reason to urge the others to vote for my dismissal. I swear, if Andrew and I werena Guardians, that man would attempt to claim the throne for himself."

She slipped her hands around his waist. "I have to admit I don't trust Lord Comyn any more than you do."

"'Tis difficult to trust the lot of them."

His words rang true—more than he realized. But damn, she wanted to see William knighted.

He fingered one of her curls. "Promise me, ye'll not do anything to give them cause to bury me."

Groaning, Eva gave in. "Of course. I wouldn't want to embarrass you."

"Ye ken I would never be embarrassed with ye by my side." He brushed a rough-padded finger across her cheek. "'Tis just there are men who would snatch any opportunity to see me fail."

Closing her eyes, Eva sighed. This was too important for him. She'd just have to play along with it this time. "Then I'll wait for you at the inn with Lady Christina."

"My thanks." He rubbed his big hands up and down her spine. "Ye are so fine to me, Miss Eva. I wish…"

"Yes?"

"I wish ye would marry me."

God, that stung. Tears filled her eyes. A cry caught in the back of her throat. Why did everything have to be so difficult? Couldn't she just have a six-month affair and leave her goddamned emotions out of it? Why did he have to feel so good pressed against her body? Hell, all William had to do was brush kisses along the curve of her neck and she'd do anything he asked. But marry him? "I can't."

"Ye mean ye willna."

She closed her eyes, forcing herself not to cry. "Please," she pleaded. "You know our days together are fleeting."

"Because ye have to return to your time?" He grasped her shoulders firmly. "What if ye are here to stay?"

She shook her head, the dread she had pushed away so many times hit her full force. "I-I-I know I must return—j-just not when." Her palms started to perspire, her head spun. *Please don't make a scene. Not now. Not when things are at their best.*

He looked at her with eyes narrowing. "Ye want to leave. Is that it?"

Yes. "No. T-that's not it at all," she stammered—she hadn't told him about her one-year plan. Besides, he wouldn't understand it. "I'm already on borrowed time…and…"

"What say ye? Something terrible will happen? Does Lord Comyn murder me? My enemies will betray me?"

Eva blinked, completely dumbfounded. The medallion warmed against her chest, reminding her that if she answered him, she'd be gone in a heartbeat. "I-I'll fetch Robbie and send him to you."

William pursed his lips. "Ye canna tell me, can ye?"

"You *know* I cannot talk about the future." Eva turned and dashed to the door.

"Wait." William followed, placing his hand on her shoulder. "Who among these men are my enemies?"

Over her shoulder, Eva met his pointed stare. She hated secrets. They felt too much like lies. "Honestly, you have very few allies among the nobles. I've been around you long enough to know you are right to limit confidences to your inner circle." Thank God the medallion didn't get any hotter. "Be watchful at every turn. The coming years will challenge you like no others."

"Years?" His voice sounded too hopeful.

She slipped her shoulder from under his grasp and reached for the latch. "Forgive me. I don't dare say another word."

***

Though thoroughly chapped that the knighting was for men only, Eva pinched herself. *At least I'm able to celebrate with him. And I want this to be a night William will remember forever.*

With her adjustment in attitude, Eva applied herself to organizing the evening's events. Fortunately, the menu had already been established and the food preparation was under way—with Eva adding William's favorite plum pudding to the menu. Finding musicians was another matter. Tucked away deep in the woods, Torphichen was more of a hamlet—an escape for the monks with one narrow road and an inn that was too small for such a great gathering of important men. Fortunately, most of them were given accommodations behind the forbidden walls of the preceptory. Only a handful had brought their spouses.

After making inquiries, Eva and Lady Christina were able to hire a lute and drum for music.

But the lady didn't seem at all happy. "What do you mean no one plays the flute? Is this village not filled with knights? Surely there are a host of musicians behind the preceptory walls."

"Aye, but none on this side, m'lady," said the man with the lute.

"I'm sure it will be fine," Eva said. "We only want a bit of music to entertain whilst we sup."

"Pardon me?" Christina moved her hands to her hips. "This is a momentous occasion. There should be dancing and making merry."

"Dancing?" Eva cringed. "Oh no, it will be far too crowded to dance."

"Once the meal is over, we'll have the servants move the tables aside. 'Tis how it's done." Taking Eva by the elbow,

Christina pulled her aside. "Besides, ye've made great progress since we started practicing with young Robert."

Eva had hoped to have a few more lessons with Robbie before trying to impress William, but he did like to dance after all. She bit her bottom lip. "Do you think so?"

"Unquestionably."

"All right. If there is time and William is amenable to it, we shall dance."

Lady Christina clapped her hands. "We most certainly shall."

Eva regarded the lady's belly. "I'll bet the wee one enjoys music and dancing as well."

The woman's face lit up like a beacon—a delightful combination of pride and embarrassment. "Indeed."

The women didn't have long to wait.

True to William's word, the knighting ceremony didn't take long, and soon the noblemen filed into the inn, calling for ale and whisky. First through the door, William strode straight to Eva. She dipped into a deep curtsey. "Sir William. May I be the first to congratulate you?"

He grasped her fingers and pulled her up, brushing feathery lips across the back of her hand. His breath tickled the fine hairs while shivers ran up her arm. The look in his eyes darkened. Lord, how the man could make her feel desired. "I am ever so glad to have ye with me to share this eve."

"Ahem, I do believe there is a feast to be had," said Lord Stewart, brushing past them.

Regardless of whether she wanted to lead William above stairs and enjoy a private celebration of their own, since there was no dais, she gestured toward the head table. "A feast awaits."

"And dancing," Lady Christina said as Sir Andrew escorted the noblewoman to her seat.

William placed his palm in the small of Eva's back and smiled. "It seems her ladyship has a yen to pick up her feet."

"Indeed she does."

"And ye?" he led her to a chair and held it for her. "There'll be no waltzing this eve."

She slid into the seat trying to be as graceful as her ladyship. "I am yours to command, oh knight."

"Aye?" His eyebrows shot up. "So all I needed to do to hear ye say that was gain a knighthood?" Cupping his hands around his mouth, he hollered. "Lord Stewart, ye should have knighted me afore we marched on Scone. 'Twould have made my life a fair bit easier, I'd reckon."

The High Steward raised his tankard. "We've set ye to rights now, Wallace."

"Och aye." Andrew lifted his cup in kind. "I wouldna put it past him to sprit into England and bring King John home."

Nodding to his friend, William took his seat and raised his tankard. "To King John."

"Here, here!" At least everyone was inclined to toast the deposed king when the ale was flowing aplenty.

Eva's insides bubbled as they dined. William was in high spirits, talking about the future of Scotland and sharing some of what he had planned for the army. He mentioned not a word about his unquenchable desire to invade England. Such bravado could very well end up in the wrong hands.

Eva regarded the faces and drummed her fingers against her tankard. "Where is Lord Comyn?"

"Made his apologies and left after this session." William took a long pull on his ale. "I expect, with his absence, parliament may come to close a day sooner."

Laughing, she thwacked his arm. "You are awful."

"I am nothing but honest."

The minstrels hovered in a corner, hopelessly failing to serenade the meal. They played their instruments as if in pantomime. Too many voices drowned them out.

"Oh dear," Eva said, leaning into William. "I'm afraid we needed more musicians."

"Bah." He batted his hand through the air. "They're fine."

After William had two gargantuan servings of plum pudding, he patted his stomach and looked to Andrew. "Sir Murray, I believe your wife has a yen to dance this night."

The knight regarded his wife, wiping his brow with his sleeve. "Then I canna sit idle when I have a duty to attend to my fair lady."

"Clear the floor," he shouted. Standing, William offered his hand to Eva. "Please do me the honor, m'lady."

She loved it when he referred to her as his lady—though her proper title was miss, or missus since she was a widow. Though she hadn't been bothered by it, William had never referred to her as missus. He'd assumed she was a miss when they first met—her mistake, really. Eva hadn't been predisposed to talking much about her past. She'd been with him for about two months before Steve's murder in a New York subway came up—and then they'd never spoken about it again.

Some of the other noblemen escorted their wives into the space hastily cleared by the servants. Eva stood across from William.

"Dunna be nervous," he jested.

She winked. "Easy for you to say."

The boisterous voices died down enough to hear the music. Lady Christina gave Eva a reassuring nod and all launched into a stately line dance that was ever so proper for a bawdy inn in the midst of a dense forest.

Eva followed along, only missing a step or two.

William grasped her hand for the circle and inclined his lips toward her ear. "Ye've had a wee bit of practice."

"Thank you. Robbie and I've been taking lessons from Lady Christina."

"And where have I been whilst ye've been kicking up your heels?"

"Chasing after the Earl of March among other things."

"Well, I'm glad ye've been keeping yourself occupied." She laughed. "And out of trouble?"

"Aye."

With a clatter of chairs, Eva and William stopped. Sir Andrew lay on his back, sprawled across the floorboards.

William rushed to lend him a hand. The proud knight brushed it away. "I'm dunna need mollycoddling."

"He's a wee bit tired," said Lady Christina.

"I'm not bloody tired." Andrew leaned heavily on a chair and pulled himself up, wincing all the while. "'Tis my battle wound that ails me."

"Of course," said William. "Mayhap an early night would benefit us all."

"Och, enjoy yourselves." The knight swayed until his wife slipped under his arm and helped him balance. "The ale must be potent."

"That it is," William said, sober as a judge.

Eva chewed the inside of her cheek. Andrew Murray grew weaker by the day and there wasn't a damned thing she could do about it.

As Christina helped her husband to the stairwell, William frowned. "He needs a cure."

"Aye," Eva whispered, unable to watch the couple any longer. The lady's pregnancy had started to show and the sadness of their plight twisted Eva's stomach into a million knots. If only she could do something. Watching Andrew's health gradually decline was agonizing for everyone.

CHAPTER EIGHT

After his fall at the inn, Andrew had accompanied Lady Christina to Dirleton, leaving William to finish the session of parliament. He and Eva had returned only last eve and this morn, seated upon the dais in Dirleton's great hall, it pleased William to see Andrew exit the stairwell…until he started walking. Wallace chewed a bite of sausage while he watched the man who had grown to become a dear friend stumble and sluggishly approach the dais. Resisting the urge to lend a hand, William washed down his mouthful with a swig of cider.

At the top step, Andrew leaned on the rail, breathing deeply as if he'd just run a footrace. "Good…morrow."

William gestured to the chair closest to the knight. "Good morrow."

Andrew smiled, a sheen of sweat glistening across his sallow face. "How fared the remaining sessions?"

"Well enough. Once the Earl of Badenoch was off home, things proceeded more quickly at least. What's better is we can now proceed with our plans to ride south."

"Good to hear." Andrew's hand shook as he poured himself a tankard of cider. "Regardless, 'tis a shame I missed out on the fun."

"By the looks of your coloring, ye'd best continue to convalesce during the next sortie." William furrowed his brow and looked to ensure no one was near enough to overhear him. "Now tell me true, how is your shoulder? Any better?"

"Worse." Andrew gestured to his arm hanging in a sling. "Canna even move my fingers now."

Wallace knit his brows. "'Tis puzzling for certain. And ye look as if ye're still fevered."

"Have the chills, mostly. Canna eat much either." Andrew shook his head and sipped the cider, then coughed. "What—ahem—news?"

It twisted William's gut to see such a braw warrior knocked down by injury and illness. If only he knew a cure. Hiding his concern, he scooped a spoon of apricot conserve from the pot at the center of the table. "Received a missive from St. Andrews. It has become imperative to appoint a bishop to oversee the completion of the new nave at the cathedral."

Andrew leaned his forearms on the table and bowed his head. "'Tis of grave importance for certain."

"William Lamberton has provided noteworthy service filling in at Glasgow in Bishop Wishart's absence." Wallace spread the conserve on a bit of bread. "And he supports the Patriotic Party."

"Aye, there are not many holy men either side of the border who would oversee our consecration to Guardians." Andrew's tongue moistened his chapped lips. "Agreed. Lamberton would be an excellent choice, and God knows we need an ally in St. Andrews."

"Then I shall offer him a provisional appointment whilst I scribe a missive to the Pope and pray for a swift agreement."

Andrew nodded and again drank.

William held up a trencher of sausages. "Ye should break your fast. A bit of cider willna heal what ails ye."

Andrew rubbed his stomach and grimaced. "I've no appetite. Merely smelling food makes me green."

"Has Lady Christina consulted with a physician?"

"Aye. If anything, they've made me worse. Bled me till I couldna see straight."

William cringed. He'd do anything to avoid a physician's lancet. "There must be something we're overlooking. Ye're young—strong."

Lifting the tankard to his lips, Andrew nodded. "Did ye hear about Lamberton being appointed the Bishop of St. Andrews?"

William stopped mid chew and stared. For the love of God, they'd just decided to send a missive to the Pope to request Lamberton's appointment. Was Murray losing his mind? William pondered his reply for a moment, then opted to play along. "Ah...I believe there is no better suited candidate in all of Scotland."

"Hmm?" Seeming disoriented, Andrew placed his palms on the table. "I'd best attend my mother."

Now William *knew* something was terribly amiss. Andrew's mother had been dead for years. The knight pushed back his chair. Just as he stood, he tumbled to the floor with a clatter of furniture. Dashing around the table, William stopped short. Andrew's eyes clamped shut as if completely unconscious, his body lurched and jerked, then stilled.

William dropped to his knees and grasped Andrew's shoulders, giving him a firm shake. "Guards, Fetch Brother Bartholomew!"

A group of soldiers hastened to the dais.

"I'm afraid the monk has gone to Edinburgh to collect supplies," said Graham.

"When?" William barked, then pointed to the big double doors. "Have a rider go after him."

"He left at first light. I doubt anyone would be able to catch him afore he reaches the city."

"Send a cohort out at once to bring him back." Reaching for Andrew's uninjured arm, William bent down and hefted the big man over his shoulder. "I'll carry Sir Andrew above stairs. Inform Lady Christina she is needed in his chamber straight away."

William huffed under the strain of lugging a good eighteen stone as he climbed the stairwell, bellowing for everything he could think of—bandages, water, fresh linens and more. He pushed through the door, then carefully unfolded Andrew onto the bed.

Lady Christina hastened in behind him. "Oh my Lord in heaven," she gasped. "What happened?"

"God only kens." William's heart filled his throat like a pounding lump. "One minute we were talking, then he said something that made no sense at all, and the next thing I kent, he was sprawled on the floorboards."

She pressed praying hands to her lips. "Heaven help us, and Brother Bartholomew left this morning to consult with the Council of Physicians in Edinburgh to see if there was anything else that could be done."

"God's teeth, I've just ordered the guard to stop him and bring him back." *Damnation, if things couldn't grow worse.*

"But he must go," Lady Christina deplored. "We're down to our last resorts."

Bloody hell. "I'll send word to the guard to wait." William quickly ran his hand over Andrew's burning forehead. "How long has he been fevered like this?"

She wrung her hands. "A fortnight or more. Well before we traveled to Torphichen."

Wiping his hand on a cloth, William shook his head. "I fear he is far worse now than he was a sennight ago." He headed toward the door. "There's but one person I ken who might be able to set him to rights."

Christina pattered after him. "Anything to help him, Sir William. Please."

"Guards," William shouted loudly enough to be heard in the passageway. "Stop the retinue from leaving for

Edinburgh." Grasping the latch, he glanced over his shoulder and regarded Lady Christina. "I'll return anon."

***

Eva's eyes flew open when someone burst into her chamber.

"Get up!" William slammed the door and marched to the bed. "Ye're needed and I'll not listen to a word of excuse this time."

"For Christ's sake, what the hell are you talking about?" Eva jolted up and flung the covers aside. "What do you think you're doing, storming in here like a freight train?"

"I've had enough of your newfangled phrases." William marched across the floor, scowling like a mad bull. "Sir Andrew collapsed in the hall."

Springing from the bed, Eva covered her mouth with her hand. "Oh my God. Is Brother Bartholomew with him?"

William threw his hands to his sides and huffed. "The bloody monk left for Edinburgh at first light."

With her head whirling from the news, Eva dashed to the garderobe. "Oh for heaven's sake, that's horrible." She grabbed her kirtle and slipped it over her head. "Have you sent for a physician?"

William strode in behind her. "Ye have been here at the castle all along. Did ye not ken the physician bled him to within an inch of his life?"

She yanked the laces on her kirtle. Jeez, William resembled an angry bear. He acted like Andrew's illness was her fault. "Lady Christina oversaw his care—same with Brother Bartholomew. I only lent a hand when asked."

"Damn it, woman!" William grasped her shoulders and shook. "Ye claim ye are from the future. I've seen your newfangled treasure. I ken ye know more than ye let on. Ye canna say with advancements like telephones and trains there has been no development of the healing arts in seven hundred years."

Her teeth rattling, Eva twisted from William's iron grip and rubbed her shoulders. "First of all, I will not tolerate your bullying." Her entire body trembled. How dare he storm into her chamber and treat her like a liar. "I don't care if you're a hundred times stronger than me, I will not be treated like a doormat—I-I mean thresh on the floor."

"Jesu." He dropped his hands to his sides. "Ye push me to the brink."

"Me?" She stamped her foot. "It's you who are acting like a *hothead*."

He looked to the ceiling and groaned. "For all that is holy, I need ye to heal him, damnation!"

Eva stared at him in disbelief. He expected her to heal Sir Andrew? How on earth could she do that?

I can't. First of all, I'm completely unqualified, and secondly...I just bloody can't.

But she needed to make him understand. "You're right. There have been huge advancements." She'd explained a gazillion times. "It's just I'm not a doctor. I'm a *journalist* for Chrissake. I don't know what to do to make him better."

"Och." He shook a defiant finger. "Ye always say ye canna heal him, yet ye ken what's ailing the poor blighter. I see it in your eyes every time we speak of Andrew—and I ken ye're holding back from me."

"I have a suspicion. I cannot say I know for sure what is wrong." Eva folded her arms and hugged them tight to her trembling body. "I think aside from an infection, he has lead poisoning."

"What? He's been poisoned?"

"It's not quite what you think." She held up her palms. "At Abbey Wood after the Battle of Stirling Bridge, I found the arrow Brother Bartholomew removed from Sir Andrew's shoulder. It was made of lead and had a broken tip. I'm afraid a bit of it might still be lodged inside the wound."

Knitting his brows, William leaned into her. "Ye mean ye've known this all along, and ye've kept it to yourself?"

"No!" Eva stepped backward as the medallion heated against her skin. "Brother Bartholomew said there was nothing more he could do. I'm not even sure the piece is still in his shoulder."

"Christ, woman. Do ye think ye are God Almighty? This is *Andrew Murray* of whom we are speaking. The man who took the north from the English—the only man in the resistance who can bridge the gap between commoner and noble. Did ye not consider that?"

Eva's face grew hot and she clenched her fists against the urge to slap him. Jeez, she loved William, but at the moment, she'd taken just about enough of his medieval hot temper. "Of course I've thought about it. Every time I see his face I——"

"Ye shirk away," he accused. "I've seen it."

"I do not." She stamped her bare foot so hard, shooting pain spiked up her leg. "I wish I could take him back to my time so he could be cared for in a proper hospital and receive antibiotics—I *told* you about antibiotics."

"Aaaaye, but still I've not seen ye lift a finger to help him." William pointed to the door. "Finish tying your bodice and haste ye to Andrew's bed. I'll not hear another word about what ye ken and what ye canna do. Ye'll help him so help me God."

Eva pulled her laces taut, then shoved her feet into her boots. It was no use reminding him that she had no ability to change the outcome of Andrew's illness. That fact had been shredding her insides to pieces since the knight was injured at Stirling Bridge. And dammit, she hadn't hidden anything. She'd told Brother Bartholomew to use boiled salt water, clean bandages, and to ensure there was nothing of the arrow remaining in Andrew's shoulder. Hell, she wasn't a goddamned doctor. She hardly knew how to apply a Band Aid back home. The little monk had taught her everything she knew about medieval healing and herbalism and now William assumed she was some sort of miracle worker.

She grabbed her healer's basket—the one she'd put together under the tutelage of Brother Bartholomew. With a huff, she barged past William and out the door.

Of course the man plodded after her, his anger radiating through the passageway as if a fire blazed around him.

Eva stopped before entering Sir Andrew's chamber. "I have no idea what I'm doing."

"Ye may not, but my wager is on your knowledge. Ye dunna give yourself credit for the things ye ken. Bartholomew never cleansed the bandages afore ye set him straight."

Eva met William's stare. "Then I'll need your help, dammit. You're not going to mosey out to the courtyard and spend the day sparring with your men."

He gave her a narrow-eyed nod. "I'll hold vigil beside his bed for a fortnight if that's what's needed for his recovery."

When they entered, Lady Christina stood and faced them. Wringing her hands, worry and fear pinched her ladyship's features. Eva glanced back to William, wishing she could run, but he wore that expression on his face—the same determined stare he assumed before he rode into battle.

Planting her fists on her hips bolstered her utter ineptitude. "I need boiling water. The sharpest knife available, pure alcohol—uh—whisky, and piles of clean cloths."

"What can I do to assist?" Lady Christina asked.

Eva couldn't even look the woman in the eye. Worse, she couldn't think of any task to occupy her. *Andrew's fate is in history's hands.* "We need a miracle." And she couldn't endure Christina hovering over her along with William. "Perhaps if you go to the chapel, drop down on your knees and pray like you've never prayed before."

"Yes, of course," she said with a tremor in her voice. Wiping the tears from her eyes, Lady Christina whisked past and out the door.

"I'll set to collecting all ye need," William said as he followed the lady out.

Eva nodded. Taking in a stuttering breath, she moved to Andrew's bedside. His face ghostly white, he looked cadaverous with sunken cheeks. "Sir Andrew?" When he didn't move, she folded the linen sheet down to his waist. "I'm going to try to help you. See if I can remove the piece of lead left by the arrow," she said as if he could hear.

Finding a pair of shears on the bedside table, she cut the bandage from his shoulder. With a gasp, she clapped her hand over her mouth and stared at the wound in horror. It was worse than she'd imagined. The entire shoulder was distorted with swelling, and she didn't need to touch it to tell it was fevered. The swollen skin gleamed angry red. Worse, it stank like the castle middens fermenting in the hot sun. Puss oozed from the jagged hole where the arrow had entered over a month ago.

Eva swallowed against her revulsion, rubbing her fingers together. Cringing, she stepped toward him and scrunched her nose as she reached out to press her fingers around the grotesque wound. *If only I had a pair of latex gloves.*

But she didn't.

She had no choice but to touch the repugnant, infected skin with her bare hands. Sickly bile burned her esophagus as she started at the outer edge of the swollen red ring, swirling her fingers as she felt for a sign of the lead tip she suspected might still be embedded in muscle.

Working her fingers completely around the hot, burning flesh, she came up with nothing. She stared at the puss weeping from the open wound and couldn't bring herself to stick her finger in it. After taking in a deep breath, she picked up the damp cloth Lady Christina had been using to wipe his forehead. It wasn't sterile, but Eva doubted that mattered at this stage.

Before she brushed the ooze, the door opened and William strode inside carrying an iron kettle filled with water. "I'll just put this on the grill."

Robbie followed with an armload of rags.

She beckoned the boy. "Put them at the foot of the bed, then you'd best go."

"Aye, Miss Eva." The lad's face scrunched as if sickened by the stench. "Do ye need anything else, Willy?"

William kneeled beside the hearth and set the pot on the iron grill above the fire. "Nay, be off with ye."

Eva tossed the wet rag aside. "Is the water hot?"

"Warm," he said over his shoulder. "Couldna carry it up here if it was scalding."

"Did you bring the whisky and the knife?"

"Aye." William stood and pulled a very small knife from inside his sleeve.

Eva peered closer. It looked like a scalpel. "Where did you find that?"

"'Tis a bloodletting lancet."

With her pincer fingers she took the thing and examined it. "It's sharp?"

"Like a razor." He pulled a second knife from his belt—a good sized dagger. "But if that one's too small, I've another."

Eva shirked from the sharp point. "Let's try the lancet first."

William replaced the knife in his belt, reached to his back and pulled out a flagon. "Here's your spirit."

Eva took the whisky and poured a bit into a cup, and then rested the lancet inside.

"I was wondering why ye wanted a wee tot," William hummed.

"It isn't for me." She gestured to the cup. "I needed it to act as a sterilizing agent."

"Ye see." He shook his pointer finger under her nose. "I never heard the term sterilizing afore I met ye."

Taking a clean cloth, she doused it with whisky and pulled it taut around her fingers. She held her breath and pushed against the eye of the wound. Yellow puss surged forth as she applied more pressure and swirled her fingers in a circular pattern. Eva clamped her lips taut to keep from retching.

"What are ye doing?"

Aside from trying not to puke all over Sir Andrew? "Seeing if I can locate the piece of lead," she said soberly. "He's awfully swollen." Feeling nothing, she pressed harder. Then she found it—something hard at least. With a quick inhale, she used one finger to rub deep. Embedded in the tissue she'd found a hard lump no bigger than the tip of her pinky finger. "Give me a pen."

"Pardon?"

Pens don't exist you dolt. While holding her finger on the spot, Eva shook her free palm. "A bit of charcoal—anything with which I can make a mark."

William grabbed a stick of charcoal from the hearth and brought it over. "Did ye locate the arrow tip?"

"I think so." She made an "X". Thank goodness, she'd probed first because the tip was about a half inch below the open wound. She picked up the flagon. "This will prevent infection." She looked at the puss. "I mean further infection."

William grumbled under his breath. "Ye pour that directly on and it'll hurt like Hades' fire."

He's not wrong there. "Fortunately, Sir Andrew's unconscious." She drizzled about a thimble full of whisky directly on the wound and watched it coagulate with the ooze. Then she added a bit more.

With an ear-splitting bellow, Andrew's eyes flew open. Flinging his hands up, he gaped at her as if she'd run William's knife across his throat.

Eva clutched the flagon to her chest and skittered backward. "It-it-it's okay."

Andrew's arms dropped and his eyes slowly rolled back until his lids closed. Together they watched for a moment until the knight's chest rose and fell in a steady rhythm.

Letting out a stuttered exhale, Eva's shoulders dropped. "I didn't think he'd wake." When she blinked, an image of Professor Walter Tennant with his thick glasses and wiry, grey-streaked hair flashed through her mind, but only for a fleeting second.

William pointed to the flagon. "Ye'd wake the dead pouring whisky on an open wound that size."

"Well, I don't have any other options." She shrugged, blocking the professor from her mind as she picked up another cloth from the foot of the bed. "I'll need you to sop up the blood and keep it dry so I can see inside."

He took the cloth. "Verra well."

Her fingers trembled as Eva pulled the lancet from the cup and held it up. "No matter what happens, I love you." She did—probably not the best time to declare it. God, she wanted to throw her arms around William's neck and tell him never to grow angry with her again. Plead with him not to make her do something they would both regret, but from the hard line of his jaw, she knew, whatever the cost, she must prove the extent of her love.

William pursed his lips and nodded. His action spoke volumes—aye, he loved her, but desperately needed a miracle to save his dying friend. Stepping to the very edge of the bed she bent down and placed the razor-sharp edge against Andrew's flesh. The medallion flashed hot like a branding iron scorching her skin.

The lancet dropped from Eva's hand and clattered to the floor. An agonizing rush of air filled her ears as blackness consumed her mind.

***

William bent down to retrieve the lancet. A brisk breeze swept past his face and a shudder slithered up his spine. Shaking off his trepidation, he straightened and held out the tiny knife.

Gooseflesh crawled across his skin.

Gasping, he blinked in disbelief.

Eva had vanished—in the matter of a heartbeat.

There'd been no footsteps.

The door hadn't sounded.

His gut clamped and twisted.

God in heaven, what have I done?

Cɦ Ꭺ ꝑ ꞇ ꬲꝛ Ninꬲ

"Holy *fucking* shit!" Eva rubbed her hands over her face and pressed against her temples. Blinking rapidly, her mind caught up with her body as she sucked in consecutive shallow breaths.

An intense, grating voice spoke loudly with affected importance. Eva turned toward the sound. *A television?*

She spun the other way. "Walter?"

The professor sat on the couch, gaping as if he were as stunned as she. Through an open door, papers rustled and a chair scraped across the floor.

"Eva?" asked Chrissy, one of Walter Tennant's students. She stepped into the living room and leaned against the door jamb. "Where the hell did you come from?"

Walter flicked his wrist at the undergrad. "Please give us a moment. I need a word with Miss MacKay."

Chrissy coughed out a grunt and backed into what looked like an office and closed the door. Thank God. All Eva needed was a nosy student finding out about the medallion and time travel.

Walter motioned with his head. "She's doing some research for me."

Eva shrugged. It wasn't any of her business why a fifty-something man would shack up with twenty-year-old student. Thank God they weren't naked when she arrived. Eva bit her lip, realizing she'd never set foot in the room before. "Where the hell am I?"

"My flat in Glasgow."

"What about the dig? Where's my stuff? What happened to the tent…and where's my car?" Her head shook as she glared at Tennant. "Fuck! This can't end. Not. Now."

The professor shook his palms. "Slow down. One thing at a time."

With a huff, Eva clamped her fists to her hips and tapped her foot.

Looking over the top of his inordinately thick lenses, Walter cleared his throat. "First of all, it's November. The dig ended two months ago. Your things are safe. Your car is in the garage below and your suitcase and attaché are in my spare room."

She turned in a circle. "How did I end up here?"

"I've no idea."

She reflected back to the moment she was about to make the incision in Andrew's shoulder. "I pictured your face. That must be it. The same thing happened the last time I was hurled back to the…" She looked toward the office and lowered her voice to a whisper. "Twenty-first century."

"I never expected you to be gone for this long. What in God's name has been happening?"

"Too much. I need to go back. All my scrolls are still there. This is the absolute worst time to leave William."

He inclined his head and held up a finger. "Now come lass, you cannot spew a string of ambiguities and expect me to sit back and let it pass. What. Have. You. Been up to?"

With an exasperated sigh, she looked to the ceiling. "The last thing I remember, I was trying to remove a lead arrow tip from Andrew Murray's shoulder."

"Murray? Well, undoubtedly that's what sent you back. The history books are very clear as to the timing of his death."

"Don't you think I know? But William was adamant I try to do something to save him. He even accused me of withholding information about a cure."

The professor crossed his arms. "Didn't you? I mean, you knew you could do nothing to change the past. I would think you would have avoided helping Sir Andrew at all costs."

Eva groaned. "And William suspected me of doing just that. I tried to help as much as I could. I told Brother Bartholomew to keep the wound clean, though I suspected Sir Andrew was suffering from lead poisoning."

"Fascinating." Walter beamed as if the world hadn't just collapsed. "We all know he died from wounds incurred at the Battle of Stirling Bridge, but how did you arrive at lead poisoning?"

"He was shot in the shoulder with a crossbow arrow and a bit of the tip broke off."

"And you were about to remove it because Wallace didn't want to lose his friend?"

"Sir Andrew was more than that." Eva threw out her hands. "He was William's ticket into the gentry. You wouldn't believe all the backstabbing that goes on between the nobles."

"Wouldn't I?" Walter chuckled. "That's exactly why Scotland ended up in such a mess in the first place. The nobles would have preferred to fight each other for the throne than fight for King John."

Eva combed her fingers through her hair. "I have to go back to Fail. If I drive there, can you pick up my car?"

The professor had the gall to slip his stockinged feet onto the footstool. "Do you honestly believe the forces behind the medallion will allow you to travel again?"

"I did nothing wrong." She stamped her foot. "By the looks of Sir Andrew this morning, he wouldn't have lived even if I did successfully remove the lead."

"But how do you know for certain?" Goddammit, did the man have to look so smug, comfortably sitting in his lounger?

She narrowed her gaze and balled her fists. Lord she wanted to throttle him. "I don't."

"Wasn't Sir Andrew a young, virile man? Someone who might recover from the brink of death?"

Eva threw up her hands. "I suppose there was a remote possibility that he would have survived, but that doesn't allay the fact that I must try to return."

Walter sat back and clasped his hands behind his head. "Well, not before you have a word with your mother."

"Pardon me?" She glared at him. "I am twenty-seven years old, and I'll not be listening to a college professor tell me I ought to call my mother."

"If you want your keys, you will. The woman has been growing quite irritated. I'm afraid she and your father are on the brink of notifying the Royal Marines. Lord knows I've been putting them off, but with every phone call your mother becomes less understanding."

"Ugh." Eva rubbed the needling knot in her neck. "Bloody hell." She dug in her pocket for her mobile phone and pushed the "on" button.

Nothing.

"This is dead. Can I use yours?"

Walter unclasped his phone from his belt. "Go in the spare room—down the hall, last door on the right."

Eva did as asked and found her gear neatly stowed in a corner. Before dialing, she pulled her charger out of her briefcase and plugged in her smartphone to start it charging. She watched it illuminate while she dialed her mother on Walter's phone, almost shocked she remembered the number after being in a time warp for six months.

The phone didn't even ring once when her mother picked up. "Hello?"

"Mum?"

"Eva? Oh my God! Do you have any idea how worried I've been? I've left messages for you day and night. Your father and I have been beside ourselves thinking the worst of Professor Tennant…"

Eva glanced at her mobile while Mother continued her rant. *Only a thousand fifty-three voice messages?* Otherwise, the thing was still going through the gyrations of updating unread texts and e-mails.

She tuned back into Mum's rant. "…how could you have gone for so long without calling? I taught you to respect your parents. I should—"

After taking in a deep breath, Eva interrupted, "Sorry. I'm fine, in good health, wonderful, actually. How are you and Dad?"

"Pardon? You sound as if you've been away for a weekend holiday, and—"

"I know it's been a long time, but I literally have not been near a phone or a post office or a computer for that matter."

"For heaven's sakes, have you been on the *moon?* I have a mind to hop on a plane and fly to Scotland right now. Regardless that your father will be entertaining the Russian ambassador, *you* need me more." Eva's parents lived in Washington DC.

"No. Mother, please do *not* fly here. I am perfectly fine and I doubt I'll be around when you arrive."

"You mean to say you will be off again? What? Are you working for MI6? Oh my God, save us. Have you…have you become a *spy?*" Mother's voice ratcheted up with her every word. "Do you know how dangerous that is?"

It would have been easy for Eva to say yes, but she abhorred lying, even when Mum played the hysterical card. "No. It's a journalism job. I'm researching a story undercover…it may take a year…maybe longer."

"Undercover? I knew it all along. You *are* putting yourself in danger. I shoul—"

"No! You aren't listening to me. I am perfectly safe." Eva believed that to her toes. She'd convinced herself she would be hurled back to her time if any medieval zealot ever tried to kill her. That's what happened when Professor Tennant fell through the *time warp*...though he'd never been able to accomplish time traveling again. But Eva had. "The only problem is I am unable to make contact with you or anyone else while I'm there."

"This is ludicrous. No contact at all? What you're doing *must* be dangerous. If nothing else, give me the name of the outfit you are working for and I'll have your father investigate. You know your father has contacts in high places in London—"

"Jeez, Mum. How can I make you understand?" Eva clenched her fist. "There is *no* threat and there is *nothing* for Dad to concern himself with." Eva's father, Sir David MacKay was the UK Ambassador to the United States and if he leaked a scandal, it would make the headlines of every newspaper between Washington DC and Edinburgh— not to mention the bloodbath by television.

Mother huffed on the other end of the phone. "I don't like this."

"I'm sorry you're worried. But I'm happy and doing something that makes me feel alive for the first time since Steve's death. Finally I've been able to move on with my life. Please, just give me a little time. Don't you want me to be happy?" Gritting her teeth, Eva held her breath for a long pause.

"Oh, sweetheart." Mum's tone completely changed. At last. "I've only been thinking of you—of your safety. Of course I want nothing more than to see you happy."

Eva grabbed the carrot and fast. "Good. Then it's settled. When I return, I'll fly to the embassy and we'll have a wonderful reunion."

By the time she clicked off, Eva had her Mum's hysterics under control. *Maybe I should write a few ambiguous letters for Professor Tennant to send from time to time so that doesn't happen again*. But she had no time to lose. Opening the door she headed for the loo.

The water ran before Chrissy stepped out the door.

Great.

"So, what's going on?" the cute, brown-haired girl asked, planting a sassy hand on her hip.

Eva looked toward the living room with a shrug. "What does Tennant say?"

"Same thing I just heard you tell your mum."

"You were listening in?" Now Eva knew she needed to watch her back whenever Chrissy was around.

"How else would I find out? Prof Tennant doesn't tell me anything. One day you were working with us on the dig. Then you unearthed William Wallace's seal and disappeared—and the professor seemed to think nothing was wrong. It's just weird."

Eva pushed past the lass and grabbed the doorknob. "I can only tell you what I told Mum. I'll spill the beans after I'm done and not before."

"Come on. At least tell me why you're dressed like that?" Chrissy pinched Eva's sleeve and rubbed the wool between her fingers. "It looks so authentic."

"It's part of my disguise. Now if you'll excuse me." Eva shut the door and turned the lock. As soon as she finished taking care of her bodily needs, she'd head straight for the ruins of Fail Monastery.

Chapter Ten

William sat in the dark chamber—dark like the black scourge spreading through his heart. Two days ago he'd retreated into solitude and hadn't emerged since. Without a candle or lamp, and the furs pulled across the window, the only hint to the time of day was the regular tolling of the chapel bells. All the while he sat in there as his heart sank deeper into the abyss of self-loathing.

Only he was to blame.

He'd lost not only a patriot, but a true friend.

And he'd lost Eva, the one woman he'd ever loved.

After Eva's disappearance, William had removed the bit of lead from Andrew's shoulder himself. But his efforts were for naught. He even doubted such a small piece from the arrow tip would cause so much illness to an otherwise healthy man in his prime. Regardless, Sir Andrew Murray died that eve and there hadn't been a damned thing William could do to prevent it.

Aye, Murray's death was a devastating loss for the Patriotic Party, but that wasn't why William sat motionless in his unlit chamber. Once he'd searched every corner of Dirleton Castle, he'd realized his deepest fears had been realized. She was gone for good.

Faster than he could blink, she'd vanished. He'd only averted his eyes long enough to collect the lancet from the floor. But just as she'd warned him time and time again, by his insistence, Eva had tried to do something that was meant to alter events already written in the stars by God Almighty.

William touched his cheek where a wee puff of air had skimmed past—his last hint that she'd existed—the only hint that something grave had happened. There were no footsteps, no creaks, or banging of doors. Eva had made no movement whatsoever.

She'd vanished.

Mayhap it was Satan's magic that brought her.

But William's heart told him differently. It ached like someone had reached through his rib cage and crushed his heart between the jaws of a vise.

"Whatever happens, I love you." He recounted Eva's last words. *I was too embroiled in my own bloody anger to acknowledge her. I just glared at the woman like a damned, ox-brained bastard.*

A rap sounded at the door.

William did nothing but blink.

The door creaked open and the blinding light from a torch shone inside. "Willy, are ye in here?" It was John Blair's voice.

"Leave me be."

The priest stepped inside and closed the door. "I have for near two days." He strode to the hearth and used the torch to light the peat and the candles, then snuffed it.

All the while William stared at the floor.

With a grunt, Blair sat in the chair opposite at the small, round table. "All men die. And ye ken as well as I, every time a man picks up his sword, he places his life in peril. Sir Andrew will be remembered for his service to Scotland."

A fire flared in his gut. "Aye. There's no need to lecture me."

"Ye've been holed up in here for days whilst the Kingdom in your care crumbles about our ears." Blair pulled a flagon from his belt. "Have a tot. It'll set ye to rights."

William licked his chapped lips and raised his chin. He didn't want a blasted thing, especially a sermon from a damned priest.

Blair poured and pushed the cup across the table. "Now put this into your gullet."

William stared at the cup for a moment. *Did I hear Blair right? Is something amiss? Why couldn't the monk have just left me be?* He groaned. *Damnation, I have a responsibility to the Kingdom of Scotland to wrench myself away from this miserable melancholy. But Lord in heaven, I dunna want to.*

With a sharp nod, he pursed his lips, grasped the cup, and sipped.

Blair rocked back in his chair. "I'll wager that's better already."

The whisky burned a fire down William's throat and sloshed in his stomach like it was still ablaze. William watched the remaining amber liquid swirl.

"What happened to the woman?" Blair asked.

Clenching his fist, William looked up. "Why should ye have a care? Ye never favored Eva overmuch."

"'Twasna a matter of whether or not I liked the lass. 'Tis just I ken when something's amiss and nothing ever seemed right with that one." The priest shook his head. "She spun a thick blanket of wool across your eyes for certain."

The whisky twisting around his stomach shot through to the tips of his fingers. "I ought to plant my knuckles in your flapping jaw for that." William held up his fist. "She only tried to help. Though she was unfamiliar with our ways, she was always willing to learn and do what she could—far more than most of the men in our garrison."

"But ye just said it—she was unfamiliar with our ways. I always thought there was something sinister about her— something *unholy*."

"Och, ye daft friar, that wasn't it at all. Ye didna appreciate her for her efforts."

"Oh?" Blair's eyes grew wide. "Then confess to me, your personal chaplain. Show me the error of my ways. What are these secrets locked in your heart that are eating ye from the inside out?"

William turned the cup between his fingers before tipping it up and sculling the rest. "Ye'd never believe it."

"Och aye? I'm a man of faith. I believe that Jesus walked on water and Moses parted the Red Sea. Come, lad, have out with it."

Hell, William would probably never see Eva again. What would it hurt to share the truth with his closest friend? "I trust ye more than my own kin."

"I reckon that's why I'm sitting here and not your brothers Malcolm or John."

Reaching for the flagon, William poured himself another tot. A larger portion this time. "She came from the future." He snorted. "Sent here to write my story."

Blair gaped. "Now I've heard some tall tales in my life, but that one's got to be taller than the highest peak in Scotland."

William pounded his fist on the table. "I said ye wouldna believe me. Worse, she told me over and over that she couldna do anything to affect the outcome of events already foretold, but I forced her into Andrew's chamber—forced her to attempt something to help him. I only averted my eyes for a moment, and the next thing I kent, she'd vanished. Just like she'd warned would happen."

"Vanished?" The priest's jaw dropped like a simpleton.

William batted his hand through the air. "Believe what ye like. I ken what happened and I'm sick to death that I forced her to do something that would rip us apart."

Blair narrowed his eyes. "Ye're serious?"

"I should have kept my mouth shut."

Clutching the wooden cross at his chest in his fist, Blair shook his head. "But 'tis not like ye to believe such sorcery—

that which can only be from Satan himself. 'Tis a good thing she's gone. The woman was a temptress, I kent it in my verra bones."

"Ye're wrong about her. Have been all along." Clenching every muscle in his body, William glared back at Blair, personal chaplain or nay, the man was dead wrong.

"I suppose that doesna matter now."

"Aye?" William slammed his fist on the table. "I'll not stand for ye sullying her name. Eva MacKay was a good woman. She had a kinder heart than ye or me, and I'll not tolerate an evil word against her."

Blair jolted upright. "Bloody Christmas, I think ye need a slice of roast mutton with your spirit."

"Nay, ye'll not skirt around it. I'll have your word right here and now, ye will not speak out against her."

"Och, ye ken I wouldna, and it vexes me ye feel ye have to ask."

"Then we'll not speak of her again." William took another sip of whisky and blinked to clear his watering eyes. He'd been wallowing in his misery long enough. No commander ever held his ground by hiding in the dark. "What was it ye said about the Kingdom falling to pieces?"

"Reports have come in about plundering all along the border. Word spread of your chasing the Earl of March out of Scotland and everyone is raring for a piece of it."

William sat a little straighter. "'Tis good to hear." And there he'd expected news of another English invasion.

"Aye, but they're looting churches and monasteries."

William frowned and drew his fingers down his unkempt beard. "I say we join them. The only way we can ensure the English stay out of Scotland is to invade and attack the very heart of the lion that attempted to oppress us." He stood and swayed a bit. "Assemble my lieutenants at once."

Blair hopped to his feet and snatched the flagon. "I'll have Robbie bring up some food as well, else ye'll be in your cups afore ye reach the solar."

Chapter Eleven

Cranked up to the fastest setting, the wipers beat a relentless rhythm, sweeping away water from the windscreen, but still could not keep pace with the driving rain. Eva gripped the steering wheel in her fists and leaned as far forward as possible. She strained to focus on the stretch of road in front of her as she punched the brakes for the turn at the unmarked road at Fail.

She hadn't been behind the wheel for months. Everything seemed alien. The car fishtailed until it came to a stop sideways on the B730. Thank God no other vehicles were in sight.

"Shit," she cursed, frustrated with the weather and everything else that had delayed her.

Having attended high school and college in the United States, she'd only driven with the steering wheel on the right side of the car for a couple of weeks before ending up in 1297. Driving in such bad weather, her instincts took over and she'd already ended up on the wrong side of the road twice.

Downshifting in to first, the gears ground as she let out the clutch and proceeded onto the unmarked road until she reached the ruin on the Fail Water. Shrouded in the colors of autumn and darkened by pelting rain, the remains of the old monastery looked completely different than they had the last time Eva parked outside the abandoned rubble.

When she clicked the handle, the wind caught the door and yanked it from her grasp.

She snatched her hand to her chest and peered through the windscreen up at the dark grey sky. "You're really mad, aren't you?" A gust of wind yanked back the door further as the car shuddered.

With a shiver, Eva reached inside her shift and pulled out the medallion. Running her thumb over the Latin inscription, she translated, *truth is like a beacon.* Turning it over, she digested the second part of the axiom, *but few choose to follow.*

I have always built my life upon the foundation of truth.

From the look of the dark clouds hanging low above, it could be days before it stopped raining. And in no way could she allow herself to be flung into the thirteenth century with an umbrella or a rain slicker. If anyone besides William saw her, she'd be in deep shit.

A little rain never hurt anyone.

After she hid the keys under the passenger seat as she and Walter had discussed, she took in a deep breath and made a mad dash for the center of what once would have been the nave of the ruins. Grabbing the outsides of her arms, Eva hugged herself against the instant cold and wet from the driving rain.

As she'd done on the two other occasions when she'd time traveled, Eva stared up at the rose window embellishing the only complete wall left standing. "It's me again." Her teeth chattered as rain pelted her face and dribbled down her chin. But she forced her arms down and stood completely straight. "I know I let William push me too far, but how on earth would I have saved Sir Andrew? He was so sick. I've never seen anyone suffer so badly from a wound. But I still stand by my point. I couldn't have saved him. For goodness sakes, I have absolutely no medical training whatsoever."

Nothing happened—no lightning overhead like the last time, just the downpour continuing to soak through her kirtle and shift.

"Please, the truth is my beacon and I will always follow it." She held up the medallion. "Just as it is inscribed right here. You wanted me to have this—encouraged Walter to put me on the dig team last summer. I know it wasn't fate."

She stared at the rose window and watched heavy droplets of water streak from the ledge twenty feet down to the ground. "This cannot be over."

Rain streamed into her eyes, but she wasn't about to give up. "Why did you send me there in the first place, if you intended for me to be hurled back without my writings? What was the purpose of my visit? You knew I would fall in love with him. You knew I wouldn't be able to take losing him—at least not yet. Dammit, I planned on a year. Couldn't you give me that? One lousy year of happiness with him?"

She walked in a circle, rubbing the outsides of her arms. "I tried so hard not to change anything—to be helpful—to prove that I could survive. Do you know how difficult that's been for me? I'm from a wealthy family that takes luxurious vacations on private islands in Fiji. But did I complain about bathing in a river? About sleeping in a cave when William's rebels were just getting started? No! I accepted everything thrown my way without complaint."

All the memories from the past six months hit her in the gut like the force from an iron hammer. "Jesus Christ, I've even overcome my fear of knives…well, almost. Sharp objects will probably always make me squeamish, but I haven't freaked out in months. I've hung in there. I stood by and watched the horrific Battle of Stirling Bridge and was on hand to assist Brother Bartholomew. I helped Paden and Adam, and especially Robbie—stood in as their surrogate mother. And I'm only twenty-seven fucking years old!"

Eva slammed her fist into her palm. "Come on. I'm pleading. I'm begging. I cannot walk away from William right now. I'm not ready. I need him. He needs me. We need each other."

She stamped her foot so hard, pain seared all the way up to her thigh. "I'm a widow for Chrissake. The first love of my life ended up stabbed to death in a New York subway, and now you cut short the fleeting bit of happiness I had with William? How can you do this to me? I'm. Not. Ready. Goddammit!"

Shivering, her gown soaked through, Eva stood in the center of the ruin and glared at the rose window while unrelenting rain pummeled her body. Her throat thickened while the rain commingled with her tears.

"I'm not leaving."

Distant thunder rumbled, and Eva finally gave in and rubbed the outside of her arms and bounced her legs to keep warm. "Please, send me back."

Her teeth chattered and she stole a glance at the Fiat. She could turn on the engine and run the heater, but that would be like giving up. "Please," she whispered. Closing her eyes, she pictured the monastery with walls and a solid roof as it had been when she'd arrived in the midst of a battle in 1297. She saw William's face—the intensity of his crystal blue eyes when he stared at her from across the fire.

Eva rocked to assuage the cold. "Please."

She dropped to her knees and curled into a ball. "I have no other place to go. William is my home. I can't just leave it like this. Please, please, please, send me back."

***

By the time the headlights of a car bombarded her with blinding light, Eva had grown numb to the icy cold of the pelting rain, though her teeth refused to stop chattering. The car door slammed. Eva squinted and shaded her eyes against the brightness. The outline of a man moved toward her, carrying an umbrella in one hand and a torch in another.

"Eva?" It was Walter's voice. "Come, I'll drive you back to Glasgow." As he walked forward, the torch blinded him—the battery-operated kind. Then his car drove off.

Eva stared at the black galoshes that stopped beside her. "I-I'm n-not going." So wracked by excessive tremors, she could hardly force the words out.

"You can do what you like, but you'll most likely have pneumonia by morning."

"I h-have to find a way back." Water streamed into her mouth.

"I'm afraid that portal has been closed, just as it was for me—and I only spent a matter of minutes in the past." He held the umbrella over her, though it didn't make much difference. "Come, let's see you dried off. Do you have a place to stay?"

"N-no. Hotel, I guess."

He gave her arm a gentle tug. "It's time to give it up, lass."

She yanked away. "Never. Not g-giving up."

"Well, at least come with me for tonight. Chrissy has gone to see her parents and I'm here to take your car as you asked. You may intend to die of exposure out here in the driving rain, but I assure you, I'm planning on having a long life."

Eva didn't budge.

"Look, I reckon you've been out here at least five hours. The magic would have worked by now. It's not only dark, it's cold, and I'm not about to leave you in the midst of this downpour."

With a shudder, she looked up at the wheel-shaped window. "I might concede defeat for today, but I'm not about to give up."

Walter offered his hand. "There's a good lass."

He led her to the car and helped her climb into the passenger side. "Do you have anything dry to change into?"

She crouched forward, gripping her arms tight to her body. "I might have a blanket in the back."

The gravel crunched under his feet as he went around and opened the hatch. "You're in luck." He tossed up the plaid she'd left there when she'd first joined the dig team.

That seems like an eon ago. Eva pulled the wool around her shoulders and used the edge to wring out her hair while she still shivered.

Walter revved the engine and cranked up the heat. "It'll be toasty warm in here in a minute."

Her lips quivering out of control, all she could do was nod.

"Tell you what." He put the car in gear and headed north. "I'll let you stay in my spare room until you can find a place of your own."

She gave him a sideways glance. She had no intention of staying anywhere for long.

"How does that sound?"

But still, he'd gone out of his way to pick her up. "T-that's very kind. Thank you." The warmth from the heater brought back the feeling in her toes.

"Do you have any money? I might be able to find you a position at the university until you can find a job."

"Are you serious?" He knew she was loaded. Nonetheless, she shook her head. "I have the money from the insurance settlement." She snorted with a smirk. "Unless someone cleaned out my bank accounts while I was gone."

Walter chuckled. "Well that's good, then. You can start in on writing the articles about your time there—I've no doubt they'll sell."

She nodded and stared out the window.

"Have you any ideas for a title?" he asked as if he seriously believed she'd be staying more than a day.

She blinked and studied a stream of water as it trailed sideways on its way down the glass. "No." A tear leaked from her eye and slowly dribbled down her face—just like the rainwater she watched.

He clicked on the blinker and proceeded through a roundabout. "You know, this is probably for the best. If you'd stayed much longer…well, it would have been that much more difficult."

Eva's gut clamped into a knot. "Look, I gave myself a year. That means I've got six more months." She pulled the blanket tighter around her shoulders. "I'd give anything to spend that time with him." *And maybe a wee bit more.*

"And then what?"

She whipped her head around. "What are you doing? Are you trying to talk me out of going back? Because if you are, you can stop it right now. I do appreciate that you came after me, but I never felt for anyone the way I feel for William, and God dammit, I'll take every moment I can with him. I don't think about the future."

"No?"

"No. I do not. All that exists for us is the now."

Walter pursed his lips and drove on while the wipers hammered a morose rhythm.

Chapter Twelve

With eight thousand soldiers behind him, William led the march to Berwick. Sacked by the English nineteen months ago, they were finally ready to reclaim the border town for Scotland. It hadn't taken long and he'd gone from living in a cave and leading a score and ten men to being in command of the combined forces of Scotland.

In their company, marched the powerful border clans of Home, Graham, Hay and Ramsay—trained armies carrying pikes, sword, battleaxes and longbows.

Marching eight thousand foot soldiers across the rolling hills of the Marches made the going slow. But it gave William time to think—and stew. God's bones, he needed a good fight to release the seething angst boiling just beneath the surface of his skin.

Ever since Eva had disappeared, a black hole had taken up residence in his chest The chasm's only positive purpose served to feed his relentless drive to rid Scotland of the English all the more.

As dusk set upon them, Sir Geoffrey Home pointed to a copse of trees near the shoreline. "We can make camp yonder. We're a mere two miles' march to Berwick."

"Do ye reckon there's enough cover to keep us hidden?" William asked.

The knight inclined his helmed head. "Aye, beyond those trees, there's a gully well out of sight of any passersby."

William peered through the wood. He never would have guessed there was a ravine beyond. He circled his hand over his head and pointed to the forest. "We shall bed down in the gully. Blair—station the watch around the perimeter. Eddy—send your spies ahead. I'll not be leading the men into a trap on the morrow."

Though the weather had turned bloody cold, William's orders were for no fires and no smoke to alert the enemy to their location. He did allow the men to pitch tents to keep from freezing their cods and for a bit of shelter from the drizzle.

Huddling beneath the white canvas, William and the barons discussed their plans.

He picked up a stick and drew an outline of the town, with the castle and the river behind it all. "Our greatest advantage is the Tweed. If we corner them between the bailey walls and the river, we'll win for certain."

"They ken we're coming, no doubt. They've spies everywhere." said Sir Home.

"Most likely, but the question is, what are they planning to do about it?" William drew an "X" where their army would stage their attack. "Ye said the Earl of Surrey had called for conscripts. How many have answered the call?"

"Not as many as there will be," said Sir Ramsay.

"Then now's the time to strike for certain." Wallace jabbed his stick in the center of the "X". "Right here. Home—wait until my ram's horn sounds, then flank us with the cavalry. That'll stop any English bastards from fleeing."

The sound of clipped voices approached outside the tent. "He's not leading a raid on Berwick without me."

Wallace recognized the deep burr and his gut clenched. In the past, he'd had one too many run-ins with Sir William Douglas. The man was unpredictable and vainglorious to boot, but he commanded a contingent of well-trained cavalry men. William ducked outside and stretched to his full height. "Ye come for a fight, did ye?"

Sir Home joined them, crossing his arms over his barrel chest. "Ye had your chance to fight the English over a year past, and ye lost Berwick Castle. Then ye lost at Irvine. I reckon ye've done enough damage."

Reaching for his hilt, Douglas lunged within a hand's breadth of Sir Home's face. "I ought to skewer ye for that." At least the baron had the good sense not to draw his sword.

"With what?" Home closed the distance until their noses practically touched. "Your ma's eating knife?"

Bellowing, Sir Douglas threw his arms around Geoffrey's trunk and the two men crashed to the ground, fists flying.

"Cocksburnpath Tower s mine," Douglas bellowed, slamming an undercut to Home's jaw.

Geoffrey responded, jutting the heel of his hand into the side his opponent's chin and twisting his head back. "Get off me ye milk-livered swine. The tower's mine. Always has been."

Douglas twisted back, then dove atop Home with a fist to the nose before the older man could right himself. Blood streamed from Sir Home's nose.

William rolled his eyes and shook his head at Sir Ramsay. "Does anyone have a bucket of water?"

Shouts resounded from the gathering crowd—a bit of pushing and shoving, too.

Ramsay smirked. "Are ye aiming to stop the flea-bitten dogs or let them have it out?"

"I'd boot both their arses out if we didna need their armies." William stepped into the brawl, grabbed Sir Douglas by the scruff of the neck and hefted him across the clearing onto his backside. "Boar's ballocks, can the pair of ye not wait until the morrow to take out your aggression? And not against each other. Ye're a disgrace to your men."

Sir Home shook his finger. "He'd sooner cut my throat in the wee hours of the night."

William eyed Douglas. "If ye want to be a part of this, I expect ye to obey my orders." He panned his gaze across the dirty faces of the bedraggled onlookers. "That goes for the lot of ye. There'll be no infighting amid the ranks, else ye'll be out on your own with nary a sword at your back."

Sir Douglas lumbered to his feet. "Och, ye're still sore about burning the barns in Ayr, are ye now?"

Slowly, William strode toward the wayward knight. "Among other things. No man wants to be backstabbed by a colleague."

"Ah." Sir Douglas shifted his eyes side to side, then smacked his lips. "Do ye have that tall redheaded lassie hidden away in your tent? As I recall, I didna have an opportunity to show her how the gentry does it."

Before he blinked, William had the bastard in a neck hold with his dirk leveled at Douglas' throat.

Around them, the Douglas men drew their swords, met immediately with battleax and pike from the Wallace army.

William pressed his lips against the insolent hog's temple. "Dunna ever say an ill word against my woman. And ye'll nay forget she's as highborn as ye are."

The bastard tried to struggle, but his smaller frame was no match for Wallace. "I was jesting ye enormous, goat-brained brute."

"I'll not stand for Scotsmen fighting Scotsmen." William pushed the sharp blade into Douglas' flesh, drawing a stream of blood. "Tell your men to sheathe their weapons, else I'll end this right here and now."

Sucking in his spittle, Sir Douglas raised his chin a wee bit. "Stand down."

William didn't release his grip until every last weapon had been sheathed. Then he shoved Sir Douglas into the crowd while his gaze darted to Sir Home. "I'll not tolerate your petty feuds. Backstabbing is part of what led us into this mess, and ye'll stand together and fight like true Scotsmen, else I'll send ye home to your mas right now."

Sir Douglas swiped his hand across the blood trickling down his throat. "I come to kill the English bastards and no one will stop me, not even ye, Goliath."

Smirking, William took the jab as a compliment. "If ye dunna follow orders, I will stop ye, and I can." He again looked to Sir Home. "What say ye? Can ye fight beside Sir Douglas and his men?"

Sir Home used his fingers to dab a gash just below his lower lip. "Scotland until Judgement. On that I give my solemn pledge."

William's gaze shot to Sir Douglas. The man brushed off his mail and gave him a nod. "Agreed. Until Judgement." He scowled at Sir Home. "But when the war is over, we'll have a reckoning."

Stepping between the two, Wallace planted his fists on his hips. "I'll hold ye to your word, and ye'll fight alongside each other and all soldiers present on the morrow."

A soft whistle came from the top of the gully. It was too dark to see who approached, but William recognized the sound. Eddy Little had returned from his reconnaissance. The rustle of rocks and leaves tumbled down the slope as he neared.

Eddy bounded into view. Leaning forward he rested his hands on his knees and drew in deep breaths. "They're waiting for us—soldiers are camped in a perimeter around Berwick Castle."

"We have them right where we want them," Douglas said.

William narrowed his eyes. "How many?"

"Three thousand at the least." Eddy chuckled. "And they're flying Cospatrick's pennant."

***

William sat up panting, his heart hammering. "Eva?" he called out, wiping the sweat from his brow.

His hand trembled as he ran his palm over the place beside him where she usually slept, only to be met with chilly earth. But the dream had been so real. As clear as the birds outside the tent, he'd heard her crying, felt her trying to reach out him.

He scrubbed his hands over his face and groaned. Eva was out there somewhere, desperately trying to come back to him. *If only I could do something to help her. God in heaven, I miss that redheaded vixen.*

The tent flap opened and Robbie poked his dirt-smudged face inside. "Are ye ready for a battle, Willy?"

William tossed aside his plaid. "Och aye. I need something to stop this miserable ache in my chest."

"Pining for Miss Eva, are ye?"

The sound of her name made William shiver. "Silence your gob. She's left us and there's naught we can do about it."

"Where did she off to?"

William gave the lad a stern look.

"I ken ye said not to talk about it, but I miss her, too. She was the closest thing to a mother I ever had." The lad's eyes turned watery and he wiped his nose with the back of his hand. "Bless it, Willy, if ye tell me where she is, I'll fetch her. She loves ye, even if ye did something to make her madder than a hive of stinging bees, I ken she'll come back."

The boy's face turned bright red and William pulled him down beside him on his pallet. "It isna that easy. Miss Eva had to go. She didna want to, but she had no choice."

"But where?" Robbie persisted.

"Far. Over the sea."

"The Holy Land?"

William's tongue went dry. "Near enough." It was no use trying to tell the lad what had really happened. Robbie was old enough to know vanishing into thin air was only achieved through the powers of dark sorcery. William wanted no one to think ill of Eva or to deem her a master of the black arts. What if she did come back? No, it was best if everyone thought her off on a long voyage from which she may never return.

Robbie shoved the heels of his hands against his temples. "Why would she leave without saying goodbye?"

William ground his knuckles into the lad's mop of sandy hair. "I wish I knew, but we canna muddle our minds with woeful thoughts about a lass. We've a battle to fight and we must harden our hearts to face our foe."

"Will ye let me ride with the cavalry?"

"Ye ken ye canna. When your beard grows in and your bones grow strong enough to wield a great sword like mine, I'll be proud to have ye fight beside me."

Robbie's shoulders dropped. "But that will take forever."

"Ye'll reach your majority afore ye ken." William shoved the lad to his feet. "Help me don my armor and then tend the oxen with Brother Bartholomew. There'll be wounded for certain and ye'll be of more use helping them than becoming one of the poor souls bleeding on the battlefield."

CHAPTER THIRTEEN

Eva's eyes flew open when she heard him call her name. Heart flying to her throat, she jumped to her feet and turned on the bedside light. Blinking rapidly, her gaze darted across Walter's small guest room. "William?"

Holding her breath, she listened.

Nothing.

She dropped to her knees and looked under the bed.

Finding only dust, she coughed. With a harrumph, she tugged up her pajama pants, strode to the window and opened the roll-up blind. Raindrops pattered against the pane which overlooked a deserted close. Heavy clouds loomed above and the inky black sky threw shadows in every crevice. With the heavens giving no hint of the time, she retrieved her cell phone from the bedside table: 4:44 a.m., the exact time she used to wake when suffering nightmares about Steven's murder.

Eva's entire body shuddered. Though her head told her Walter made sense…it was over, she wasn't ready to walk away. While with William, she'd gathered a ton of information, and even without the pages upon pages of vellum she'd scribed, she could still write one helluva series of articles. But this wasn't how it was supposed to end. In a blink, she'd just disappeared. There was no closure, no lingering hugs, no sharing of tears, no goodbye kiss.

It can't be over.

She tugged the medallion from beneath her sweatshirt and smoothed her thumb over the Latin inscription. "Now I'm hearing his voice? Why in God's name are you messing with me? By now, you should know I pose no threat to the past. I've honored the single rule." She whipped the medallion over her head and threw it on the bed. "But it seems as though you have a lot more secretive unwritten covenants than that."

With a groan she slammed her fist into the mattress. She'd spent the past three days frantically staring at the computer screen, researching time travel. She'd hardly slept. Worse, for all her efforts, she'd come up with nothing and with her every inhale, it became harder and harder to breathe. William Wallace was her soulmate. She couldn't make sense of it—she hadn't even tried, but in a few short months, Eva had grown closer to William than she ever had to Steven.

Heaven help her, the memory of her first husband was fading.

Climbing onto the miserable bed, she propped herself against the headboard and opened her laptop. She'd read Physics article after article and they all rambled about the same theories quoting traveling faster than light, worm holes, bending space. Eva hated Physics and after three days of research, she'd arrived at one conclusion. Nothing existed online about the medallion or how it worked or if there was a little man somewhere up on the moon who watched her every move and decided what century she would be in today.

While her computer booted, she reached for the medallion and studied it in the bedside light. Nope, no trace of a recording device of any sort. After another groan, she put the miserable thing back over her head. God forbid, it change its mind and decide to send her back to William.

The bronze flickered in the mirror before it dropped to her chest.

C.S. Lewis' *The Lion, the Witch and the Wardrobe* came to mind.

Setting her laptop aside, she crawled off the bed and stood in front of the wardrobe. Made of walnut, it looked like an antique with double doors and an oval ornamental relief at the top. Though she hadn't unpacked her suitcase, she had opened the door the first day to hang up her thirteenth-century gown. Nothing seemed untoward then.

Her palm perspired when she reached out and grasped the brass pendulum handle. The door stuck at first, but with a tug, she opened it about six inches. Peering inside, she couldn't see a thing. The hinges creaked when she pulled the doors wide. Her gown and shift were the only garments hanging inside. On the left was a banker's box. The type she used to store past documents like tax returns. Jeez, she definitely didn't want to meddle into Walter's taxes.

A manila folder stuck out beneath the box. She started to close the doors, when the tab of that folder caught her eye. The words "time travel" were written in block letters.

Sucking in a gasp, Eva bit her thumbnail and looked at the door. No noises had come from Walter's room, nor had he clomped down the hallway. What harm would there be in taking a peek at his notes?

She bent down and slowly pulled the file from under the box, trying not to make any noise. With a tug, the folder slipped free. She closed the wardrobe and resumed her seat against the headboard. Leafing through the file, she found pages of handwritten notes.

The professor's handwriting was pretty sloppy, but if she could decipher Auld Scots without spelling convention, this ought to be a breeze. It started out yammering about the same theoretical, unproven, untried scientific stuff she'd found on the internet. Still, Eva read every word, praying she'd find a nugget—the slightest hint to lead her in a new direction.

It wasn't until she reached page twenty that she stopped and re-read the title he'd written on that page. "Psychic Traveling."

Only an hour-and-a-half ago, she'd awakened when she'd heard William call her name. Was his voice a form of psychic time travel? It had seemed so real. At this stage, she'd grasp threads. Indeed, she'd grasp anything to move forward.

It's not over. I heard him. I know I did.

For another ten pages, she read about out of body experiences and self-hypnotism where people sent their minds to foreign places. But the professor's scratchings were so damned vague.

The floor creaked in the room across the hall, followed by footsteps.

Walter was up.

Eva pored over the next several pages while listening for him to walk down the hallway to the kitchen.

The man must have spent an hour in the bathroom, because by the time his loafers clomped down the wooden floorboards, she'd finished reading.

Eva neatly placed the papers back into the folder and carried them out to the kitchen. Walter stood with his back to her, ladling a teaspoon of instant coffee into a mug. "Good morning." He didn't turn around.

"Hi."

He held up the jar of *Nescafé*. "You want a cup?"

"No thanks. I kicked my caffeine habit a few months ago. May as well not take it up now—the withdrawals aren't worth it." Though Eva might enjoy a tall, decaf, nonfat latte if there were an espresso machine nearby. She placed the folder on the counter and leaned against it.

"Suit yourself." The electric kettle rumbled to a boil and clicked off. After adding water and stirring, he faced her. "How's the flat hunting going?"

"It's going." Having done absolutely nothing to look for a place to live, her gaze trailed aside. "I'll be out of your hair by the end of the week. How's that?"

He shrugged. "Well, it's time you picked up the pieces and returned to your life in this century. What about applying for a job at the Herald or the Daily Times? You may not need the money, but a job is a start—you'd meet people, you ken—start to assimilate."

She shook her head. "Probably a good idea." But she didn't believe it for a minute. Her fingers wandered over and grasped the folder. "What can you tell me about psychic time travel?"

Color spread up his cheeks. "Found my notes, did you?"

"They were in the wardrobe."

He opened the cupboard and pulled out a box of Weetabix. "You want some?"

"Thanks."

"I've tried it some." After retrieving two bowls, he added two biscuits in each. "Would you mind handing me the milk?"

Eva opened the fridge. "Did you have any success?"

"A bit." He poured and handed her back the bottle. "Come, let's sit."

The table in the bay window was stacked with newspapers, leaving barely enough room for each of them to eat.

Eva took a bite. "So tell me more. Have you traveled with your mind?"

"Only after you disappeared."

"Me? Why?"

"Having been the one who gave you the medallion, I felt responsible." He shook his spoon at her. "Cripes, your da is the U.K. Ambassador to the U.S. and it only took a few days until your mother was sending me panicky e-mails. I had to do something to ensure you were all right."

It was Eva's turn to blush and heat ran from the tips of her toes to the top of her head. *God I hope he didn't see everything.* "Y-you were spying on me?"

"Not exactly. The few times I tried it, I just got a sense that you were okay—kind of a feeling that you were unharmed, and…"

"And?"

"You *wanted* to be there."

"Did you ever hear my voice?"

He chuckled. "No. Just sensed your emotions, I guess."

"How did you know it was me you were connecting with?"

He pointed his spoon at her. "As a scientist, these words shouldn't even escape my lips, but I just knew. I wish I could explain it."

"When you were meditating, did you hold an object of mine or something?"

"That would have been a good idea. But no, I just focused on remembering your face and all that red hair." He held his mug to his lips. "You need to let go, Eva."

Her swallow caught in the back of her throat. "I can't."

He pushed back his chair. "In that case, I have to insist that you be out of my spare room by the end of the week as you suggested. I don't mind helping you, but I'll not sit idle while you wallow in misery. And don't you think I don't know that all you've done since you've been here is try to figure a way back? You went to Fail and literally *failed.*"

She stared at her bowl while tears blurred her vision.

"One day you'll thank me for pushing you back into the life you were born to lead." He strode out of the kitchen. "I'm off to work like a real twenty-first century Scotsman." The door slammed behind him.

Wiping her eyes, she stared at the folder. *Dammit, I can look for a flat any time. Besides, I'm from Edinburgh, not Glasgow.* Then she opened it and memorized the steps to psychic time travel...comfortable chair, focus on the one thing you want to change, rid your mind of fear, stress and anxiety...

She wandered into the living room and sat in Walter's recliner. Flipping up the foot rest, she leaned her head back. *I am capable of contacting William. I can let him know I am trying to return to him.*

The difficult part was to rid her mind of anxiety. For the past three days she'd been wound tighter than a hunter's snare. But she closed her eyes and focused on taking deep inhales and letting them out slowly, all the while repeating, *I am capable of contacting William.* Focusing her gaze on a vase sitting on the mantel, Eva relaxed her toes, then her feet. All the while, she took calming breaths as the stress fled from her calves, knees and stomach. Her pent up anxiety melted from her shoulders and out the tips of her fingers. And finally, her face didn't feel drawn so tight anymore. She stared at the vase awhile longer as her eyelids grew heavy.

By the time Eva could no longer keep her eyes open, the sensation of floating and weightlessness swirled around her. She pictured herself alone in the midst of a grassy lea. A gentle breeze caressed her face and made her long skirts dance and flutter around her legs.

Still floating, she walked up the rolling hill. William must be there. She felt his presence as if his aura surrounded her like a shroud. "William?" Eva wasn't sure if she'd spoken his name aloud or not, but she repeated it until she reached the crest of the hill.

What she found stopped her short. In the distance raged a fierce battle. A drum beat a steady rhythm while men grunted and howled on the wind. Beyond the blue sea stretched to the east, and to the south, motte and bailey surrounded a four-towered castle. Eva's gaze quickly honed on the fight. Horses whinnied and metal scraped.

William fought in the middle of it, swinging his great sword. No, she couldn't see him, but his presence swirled around her. Her muscles twitched with every swing of his blade as he attended each wave of attack.

Her heart clamped tighter than a fist…William's heart. God, he missed her as much as she missed him—he needed her. Without her, anger and hatred drove him into a rage.

Taking in a sharp gasp, Eva tried to run toward the mayhem, but with each step, they grew further away. Terrified that she might lose the vision, she stopped.

"William," she cried. "Fight well, my love. I am trying to return to y—"

With a jolt, Eva's eyes flew open. Every nerve ending trembled as she stared at the vase. God, of course she wasn't the only person wallowing in self-pity. From the agony she'd experienced in William's heart, he was dying on the inside, filled with remorse, pain and sorrow so great it would send a sane man into lunacy. Eva clutched her hands over her heart.

Lord, the man had seen more death and oppression than she could possibly imagine. Yes, she'd been there for six months, seen her share of misery and suffering, but she hadn't lived it every day of her life.

Patting her cheeks to regain her senses, Eva hopped to her feet and began pacing. Both times she'd time traveled, she'd done so from the Fail Monastery ruins. But the first time she awoke in the monastery and the second she awoke exactly where she'd left—in the Lanark torture chamber, staring at the sheriff's back. Was there a portal at the Fail ruins or did the place not matter? What was she missing?

Dirleton?

One thing was an absolute certainty. William needed her as much—perhaps more than she needed him. Eva raced back to her bedroom and threw open the wardrobe.

I have an idea.

CHAPTER FOURTEEN

Wallace wrenched his blade from the attacker's belly and spun in place, ready for the next assault. His muscles burned, torturing him from endless exertion, but he dared not blink, lest he lose life or limb.

"*William!*" Eva's voice rang in his head. "*Fight well, my love. I am trying to return to y*—"

"Eva," he roared, spinning again, praying she wasn't in the midst of the battle, but frantic to find her all the same. He could spare only a glimpse across battlefield.

Thank God she was not in harm's way.

A battleax whooshed through the air, straight for his temple. As if a bolt of lightning flashed inside his arms, Wallace regained his strength and swung his sword with brutal force, deflecting the attack, the ax's wooden shaft splintered in two. Maintaining his hold on the broken stick, the brigand hefted it over his head and swung it downward with both hands. Wallace caught the pole with his palm, then used its momentum to flip the swine onto his back and finished him.

On and on the battle raged with William in the lead, sometimes fighting three at once. With attackers targeting him from every side, on any other day he'd be dead. But he'd heard Eva call his name. She existed out there somewhere. As he fought, all he could think of was her—her love, her strength, her support and understanding of Scotland's cause.

He needed her like he needed the air he breathed. Her memory would infuse him with courage until he once again held her in his arms.

A break in the wall of the attackers came all at once. Ahead, a loud roar rang out as the English fled over the bridge and across the Tweed. William turned to Sir Ramsay. "Seize the town." Waving his great sword above his head and running for his horse, he beckoned the others. "Scotland until Judgment!"

Roaring the battle cry, the men sped behind him.

The pennants of the Earl of March and the Earl of Surrey flapped in the wind as William and his men made pursuit. South and west the brigands rode, fleeing like a herd of timid sheep.

William's heart raced with the prospect of catching two of the nobles who were eating from Longshanks' palm. Blair and Little thundered beside him, leaning over their horses' necks, demanding more speed.

But the English mounts galloped just as fast. Ahead, the sandstone walls of Norham Castle came into sight. Before William and his men could close the distance, the bloody English bastards clomped over the barbican.

Wallace dug in his spurs, determined to blast through the bailey gate before they dropped the portcullis.

As his horse's hooves hit the wooden slats of the bridge, the black iron teeth of the gate boomed, shuddering through the ground. William reined his horse to a halt. "Ballocks!"

Blair stopped beside him. "What now?"

William looked to the top of the ramparts. Archers were running along the wall-walk, moving into place. "Fall back," he bellowed, reining his horse around. "We mightn't have the siege engines to attack a fortress, but we can wreak havoc everywhere else. No man who takes up arms against us is safe. We shall invade the lands of our oppressor!"

"To Rothbury Forest and beyond," he shouted over and over as he rode though his ranks and led them on the journey south. The forest was his greatest ally. He'd rid Northern England of all fighting men—anyone who posed a threat would flee or meet their end.

***

The foot soldiers soon followed and, within a day, William had established his military base high on a crag in the thick wood of Rothbury. When finally he had the plans for the invasion laid out with his lieutenants, he headed to his tent. Fatigue hung on William's limbs like a heap of sodden blankets.

The last time he'd had a decent night's sleep? He closed his eyes. *Ah yes, it was the last night I slept with Eva in my arms.*

With a sigh, he lumbered to his pallet and sat, resting his head in his palms. The battle at Berwick flashed before him. This was the first time he'd had a chance to think on Eva's voice—the one he'd heard in the midst of hell. Yet the words had come from an angel, had uplifted him, renewed his strength.

He rubbed his eyes. *She said she was trying to return to me. But where is she now?*

She hadn't told him much about her world. He'd even discouraged it for the most part. A few times she'd tried to explain things—he remembered telephones, motorcars that burned fuel to run without horses, and trains that would take a man from Edinburgh on the lauds bell and have him in Glasgow well before prime an hour later.

And oh, how Eva loved her baths. She'd said heated water ran straight into the bath with no need to boil pots and dump them into a wooden tub as his mother had done for him. Eva could recline in a bath for ages—had even told him about whirlpool jets that massaged sore limbs.

William dropped his hands and cringed. Though her father was a knight, he had no need to carry a sword or weapon of any sort. He'd once heard her say that people were free to worship the religion they chose and that all children went to school to learn mathematics and to read and write. She could read and write like no one he'd ever seen. In truth, he was beginning to realize her education surpassed even his own.

She'd gone to university in the United States of America—a place yet to be discovered.

With so many comforts, why would she want to return to a war-torn land?

But I ken I heard her. Clearly she said she was coming back.

William's heart clenched tight. He never should have insisted she try to help Sir Andrew. No wonder she avoided the knight. *She kent—God damn me to hell—she kent saving him would mean the end of her time here. And I wouldna bloody listen and she did my bidding. Such a bitter tonic to swallow. Now I've lost them both.*

William pulled his psalter from the purse he wore on his hip—the very leather pouch Eva had given him in Renfrew when they visited Lord Stewart. God bless her. He held his most precious possession between his hands and bowed his head. "Dear God in heaven, I beseech thee with all my soul. I do not understand how she came to me, but now that ye have brought Eva MacKay into my heart, please dunna keep her away. She grounds me, completes me as a man. To do your will, and restore Scotland to the great Kingdom it once was, I ask for this one thing. Though no small matter it may be, I beg of ye…"

William prayed until so overcome by fatigue, he could no longer sit upright. Reclining on the pallet with his psalter tucked under his arm, he drifted off to sleep with Eva's words repeating in his head: *Fight well, my love. I am trying to return…*

Chapter Fifteen

An eerie sense of déjà vu made goosebumps rise across Eva's skin. She stood on a footbridge in the exact spot where a grand and menacing barbican once had crossed the ditch at Dirleton Castle. She'd ridden Ryn across that very motte only days ago. So vivid her memory, Eva could still hear the clop of horse hooves on timber.

Though ruined, the castle appeared in relatively good condition. Astonishingly, the tower she'd stayed in with William still stood, though it looked dilapidated in comparison to the sturdy fortress in her mind's eye. In better condition stood a tower house to the west of the main gate, built in the sixteenth century—called the Ruthven Lodging. When she'd stayed at Dirleton, the space had been taken by a wooden structure comprising the great hall.

She leafed through the guide book she'd purchased at the gift store. They did a nice job explaining the thirteenth, fourteenth and sixteenth century additions, though they missed all the wooden outbuildings. No surprise—any remains of earlier construction would have been hidden by the remodels. The only mention of the Wars of Independence was the damage done, which would have happened after the Battle of Falkirk.

The fine hairs prickled the back of her neck. She didn't want to think about Falkirk. Not ever.

"Excuse me, are you giving tours?" asked a middle-age woman with an American accent. Though Eva had spent ten years in the United States, the accent now sounded grating, broad and completely foreign to her ears. But the woman and her companion grinned with friendly expectation.

Eva dropped her gaze to her gown and realized she indeed must look like a tour guide—or a complete loon. She stared at the couple a moment, at a loss for words. "Uh...sorry, no. I—I'm a medieval history zealot, you might say."

"Too bad," said the man with a quirky look. "These old castles are fascinating."

"Well, have a good day." The woman offered a faint wave and followed her husband across the footbridge.

Eva waited for them to pass, then took a deep breath and slowly proceeded across the bridge. Her hands began to tremble as she strode beneath the grand arch and guardhouse. At least it had once been grand. The uppermost part where the best archers were stationed had been ruined. Right above her head was the kill hole used as a last resort to drop boulders or boiling oil onto intruders.

Once inside the courtyard, her stomach sank to her toes. The mighty fortress was but a shell of its former glory. Crumbling and broken walls surrounded her.

I guess seven hundred war-torn years isn't kind to even the grandest of fortresses.

Eva cast her gaze up to the remaining battlements and turned in place. She hardly recognized anything. Pressing the heels of her hands to her temples, she tried to picture it—the great hall, the gardens, the donjon. She wandered into the oldest remaining tower, now a roofless shell. Closing her eyes, she focused on deep breathing. The last time she'd been there, she'd stayed in a chamber on the third floor. Ah yes, she could picture it now. She opened her eyes and looked at the very spot were her chamber had been. Though the tower floorboards had all rotted ages past, the masonry still remained. The hearth surrounding her fireplace looked much the same, and further along, the window embrasure still cut into the stone. Eva pictured the heavy furs that covered the pane-less windows to stave off the cold, and the red satin cushions she sat upon to take advantage of the sunlight when writing.

She'd been a guest at Dirleton for only a few weeks, but it seemed more like home than any of the other castles she and William had visited during his rise to greatness. The wind blew a gale off the Firth of Forth, but she didn't care. She spent the day climbing over the ruins and reading the placards with historical tidbits. Odd, not a one mentioned that William had been there—or that Andrew Murray had died there.

If they only knew, they'd make a mint.

At least she reckoned Sir Andrew must have passed away not long after she'd traveled back to the present. He certainly was too sick to move elsewhere.

Fortunately the weather didn't invite a horde of tourists, and after the American couple left, Eva had the place to herself. Slipping back into the old tower, she moved to where she could see her chamber and sat in the middle of the gravel that covered the missing floor.

She stared up at the empty hearth. It looked odd suspended in the middle of the stone wall, about thirty feet up. She'd warmed herself beside that hearth, watched Madeline light or stir the coals to life every morning. Yes, the carved granite mantel suspended above connected her to William. They'd sat in front of that very hearth, held hands and kissed. They'd talked about politics and the weather. He'd given her the mail-piercing sword in that very place. Unfortunately, her sword hadn't made the journey with her— lost like her scrolls.

If only she'd been able to hold onto the important things—things that connected her to Wallace.

Eva stared up until her eyelids grew heavy and her neck sore. With a deep inhale, she closed her eyes and pictured William grinning. He'd looked almost innocent when he'd presented her with the sword—excited to give her such a treasure. And she'd been a stupid lout and shirked from it at first.

Eva then pictured him leading the garrison when they returned from their sortie to Dunbar. No greater warrior could there be. He sat his horse like a king. Though humble. William would never be so presumptuous as to covet the throne, but he would protect it with his last dying breath.

William Wallace was nothing like the man she'd studied when attending NYU. Oh no, he was so much more.

Love swelled in her heart and she reached out her hands. *Where are you, William?*

Her mind jettisoned to a walled-in city in flames. Shouting, men with torches galloped horses through cobbled streets, igniting thatched roofs as they pillaged. Women shrieked and ran from burning homes with bairns in arms.

"Spare the innocent," William's voice rose above the pandemonium.

Eva's mind's eye honed in on the source of his familiar bellow. His features drawn, he drove his horse hard, shouting orders as his men sacked the town.

Durham?

He circled his hand over his head. "Let this be a warning to all English who march against Scotland. We will not be beaten. We shall tolerate the tyranny of King Edward no longer."

He rode on, slapping his reins against his steed's neck. "Return King John to Scotland!"

The men echoed William's demands with fervent cheers as he led them northward from the burning city.

"William," Eva whispered.

Riding at breakneck speed, he looked all around him, even to the sky. "Where are ye?"

"Dirleton—but in my time, not yours."

"Come to me in Rothbury—"

"Miss?"

Eva jolted when someone touched her shoulder. Her heart practically beat out of her chest as her eyes flew open. "Jesus Christ, you shouldn't walk up behind someone and scare them like that."

"With all due respect, I've been trying to gain your attention for a while now." The man from the gift shop pointed his thumb toward the main gate. "We're closing."

Eva's heart raced. "Now? Can't you wait a while longer?"

"Actually, it's well past time I locked up." He gave her a concerned look. "You weren't trying to hide or anything, were you?" He assessed her gown. "Are you homeless?"

Yes, I'm bloody well without a home at the moment. She wanted to tell the man to leave her alone. She'd actually exchanged words with William. Surely she was closer to time traveling again. She just had to figure it out—like she was missing a key element to this whole thing.

"Are you ill?" the man asked.

Blinking, she regarded him. "I'm fine. I saw a bed and breakfast up the road. I'll stay there for the night."

"Do you need a lift?"

She'd left the Fiat in Walter's parking garage beneath his flat and had taken a train and a bus. Damn, she'd been absolutely positive Dirleton would hold the answer to send her back to William. She felt it in her bones. All she needed was more bloody time.

"Miss?" Damn he was persistent.

"Yes, thank you. I took the bus here." Eva stood, slinging her bag over her shoulder. At least she'd had the wherewithal to pack some things for overnight just in case.

PART TWO

CDAPTER SIXTEEN

Modern day. Eight years later.

Eva sat at the back of Torwood Castle's renovated great hall. The rows of chairs filled with people all faced the newly constructed dais. Everything was perfect—just like it would have appeared in the late medieval era—William's time. Rubbing her outer arms, even she was impressed at the work the restoration crew had accomplished since she'd hiked back through the wood to find the crumbling ruin eight years ago. She couldn't believe the time had passed so quickly.

After failing to time travel at Dirleton Castle, she'd gone everywhere she and William had been together, all the while experiencing snippets of psychic traveling as she grasped fleeting bits of conversation with him. Their last communication had been right after the disastrous Battle of Falkirk—a devastating loss for Scotland and for William.

If only she could have been there while he suffered. He'd blamed himself for Scotland's failure, though betrayed by a band of noblemen.

Taking refuge at Torwood Castle, William had expressed his grave remorse and horror at watching so many of his countrymen butchered on the battlefield. The Scots had been decimated by Longshanks' Welsh archers sporting new-fashioned bows with a longer range than those of the Scots.

William's remorse had been palpable—even across time. The depths of his depression—desperate and dire. Had Eva not known his future, she would have been terrified that he'd do something...something *unthinkable*.

But the strength of his character prevailed, just as it always had.

The aftermath of Falkirk led her to Torwood Castle—the modern-day ruin anyway. The record showed he'd fled there, and that's where Eva raced to attempt to travel back to the thirteenth century, this time frantic, painfully aware of how desperately he needed her. As they both huddled behind the walls of Torwood in the wee hours of 23rd July—albeit in two different centuries, William had cried out for her, begged her to return and take the pain away.

But the powers behind the medallion had shut down for good.

That was the last time she'd had any contact. Not even the sensation of a puff of air on the back of her neck had heightened her senses since the frigid night she'd spent prostrate on the craggy, dust-covered floor of these ruins.

To her disgust, Torwood had been in abominable condition—she'd wandered through crumbling passageways covered with graffiti. Moreover, the historic site, overgrown with vine and moss, sat tucked away deep in the wood where it could not be admired by the public.

Not long after her visit, Eva contacted the Clan Forrester Society—caretakers of the castle—put up twelve million pounds of her own money and took on the project of seeing to Torwood's restoration.

Her writing and this project were the only two things that had kept her sane in the past eight years—kept her so busy she scarcely had time to think. In fact, life had passed her by. All her college friends were settled and had children. Eva doubted kids would ever factor into her life. After all, she was thirty-five and didn't even have a boyfriend. Jeez—*boyfriend* sounded so adolescent. Perhaps Torwood Castle became a sorry substitute for a lover?

Initially, Professor Tennant and his band of archaeologists had excavated the site, revealing all the old foundations and digging up relics for the museum. Eva then hired an archaeological architect to draw the blueprints. Modern stonemasons and carpenters were brought in and now the castle was complete—a monument to be revered through the ages. A four-story donjon connected by long passageways adjoined three other towers forming a square, guarded by a fortified gate, including a guardhouse and portcullis. Inside, Eva had seen to every detail of medieval decoration from the tapestries, to the furnishings, to the display of silver behind the high table on the dais. Even Eva marveled at the magnificence of the work done by the Scottish restoration team.

And today marked the end of the project.

She swallowed. Hard.

Endings are so bittersweet.

Laird Forrester, standing at the podium on the dais, gestured toward her. "I'd like to present the key to the castle to the woman who has made this all possible. Please join me in welcoming Miss Eva MacKay, bestselling author and renowned Pulitzer winner."

The intro was her cue. Taking in a deep breath, she smiled as the crowd applauded and faces turned her way. The past eight years may have been lonely and frustrating, but she'd suppressed her depression with hard work. After she stood, with purpose she strode to the front of the great hall with its enormous exposed rafter beams, and climbed up the dais steps. Lord, it almost felt like she'd gone back in time—but that would never again happen. Eva had finally accepted it. Besides, she wore stockings, stilettoes and a navy pinstriped skirt-suit.

After shaking Laird Forrester's hand, he placed the enormous key around her neck.

Clearing her throat, she stepped up to the podium and waited for the applause to abate. "As I gaze out over the faces of all present, I see so many who helped bring this project to fruition, and I thank each and every one of you. Due to your efforts, Torwood Castle is now a welcoming relic where anyone can step back in time…"

Eva had her speech memorized backward and forward, and delivered it flawlessly. If she left no other legacy in her lifetime, this was the grandest. Sure, she'd written an in-depth history about Wallace that had been a blockbuster—won her a Pulitzer—and, better yet, the film would be out next summer. Her success had enabled her to increase her personal wealth, to be a benefactor of substance, and that's what she would be remembered for.

Later at the cocktail party, nearly everyone had gone by the time Walter Tennant approached her with his arms wide. "You've done a splendid job, my dear."

Eva welcomed his embrace, but smirked. "I didn't do much aside from consult and write checks."

"I do not believe that for a minute. No one could have made this place look so authentic. The detail in every chamber could only have been conjured by someone who had actually spent time…" He glanced over his shoulder, then lowered his voice. "You ken as well as I, little of the authenticity in the renovations would have been accomplished without your *unique* perspective." He grasped her shoulders and held her at arm's length. "Do you remember what you said to me when I asked you what you wanted to do with your life—right before I gave you the medallion?"

A rueful chuckle rumbled from her throat. "Oh yes, I'll never forget." She'd said she wanted to find a story so intriguing, the whole world would say *wow*.

He grinned—his face even craggier after eight years. "I think you found your wow, my dear."

Eva forced a smile. "I guess I did." She should be ecstatic about her achievements—elated—ready for the next great adventure. But finishing the project at Torwood was akin to losing an old friend. It was almost as if she'd found a connection to William in the old castle. Renovating a thirteenth century relic at least made her feel like she'd kept one foot in William's time.

"So what's next?" Walter asked.

With a startled blink, she chewed her bottom lip. "Ah..." Returning to war-torn medieval Scotland was no longer a remote possibility.

The professor grinned. "I'm leading a dig this summer. Going to excavate Tappoch Broch. Would love to have you on the team."

"I'd like that." Indeed, Eva would need a new diversion. Seeing they were the last two remaining, she started toward the door.

"Can I pencil you in?" he asked, following.

"I don't see why not." She held the big oaken door with blackened iron nails. It might be new, but it looked as medieval as the doors had at Dirleton Castle when she'd been there with William.

He stepped over the threshold. "Can I escort you to your car?"

Eva held up her enormous key. "I think I'll stay for a bit—do a final walk through before the place is opened to the public tomorrow."

"Very well." The professor gave her a nod. "I'll e-mail you the paperwork for the dig."

"I'd like that. Thank you."

After closing the door, she locked it and placed the key inside her purse, right beside her first aid kit. Ever since she'd returned from the thirteenth century she'd kept a "healers" kit in her purse—containing plenty of antibiotic ointment and a ten-day supply of penicillin. Thank God the family doctor humored her and wrote a script. She still couldn't lie and feign an illness. Besides, she had to replace the medicine every couple of years.

Pulling out her penlight, she climbed the stairwell to the east wing. That part of the castle had been renovated for Clan Forrester and wouldn't be open to visitors, though they'd given Eva full access to every chamber. Her one caveat had been complete access for life. The foundation had been so overwhelmingly pleased to receive the funds for the restorations they'd been planning for years, her request had been granted without hesitation—they'd even given her an upper chamber of her own to do with what she would—she'd even spent a few nights alone locked within…secretly hoping to find William again. Alas, it wasn't to be. And now? Well, now it was too late.

Opening the door and turning on the light, Eva stepped inside. A long sigh slipped through her lips. She'd almost asked them not to run electricity to the replica candelabra, but then decided it was time to stop pretending. Yes, perhaps the chamber was appointed with a four-poster bed with red silk curtains. The grillwork on the hearth, the round table and two matching wooden chairs were carved with lion's feet—similar to those she'd seen at Lord Stewart's castle in Renfrew. Regardless if nearly everything in the chamber breathed life into the medieval era, it was lit with the miracle of electricity.

***

After returning from five years traveling throughout Christendom trying to rally support for Scotland's cause, William had come home to a Kingdom beaten and without hope. He'd never seen people so afraid to take up arms. His failure to free Scotland from tyranny hung around his neck like with the weight of an anvil.

Freezing beneath the bridge, William rubbed his right shoulder. The damned appendage had pained him since the king of France had forced him to fight the lion. Aye, he'd killed the ravenous beast in the end, but not before the back of his shoulder was shredded by claws sharper than iron nails. Worse, that had been five years ago. He doubted the wound would ever heal properly.

God's teeth, I've fought in more battles than I can count, and a lion ends up being my downfall?

William groaned. Mayhap his trip to the continent had been a mistake.

So many things had fallen apart since Falkirk.

The horse beneath him snorted and sidestepped. William smoothed his hand along the gelding's mane. "Wheesht."

"Where are the bastards?" Blair grumbled in a whisper.

Upon his return to Scotland, William may have been forced back to raiding, but the few informers who remained were loyal. Regardless, fewer than ever could be counted on for certain. "They'll be here. Mark me."

"If they dunna come soon, the rumbling of my stomach will give away our hiding place," said Robbie. If the young man would ever stop growing, his stomach might last more than an hour without food.

Bloody oath, looking at Boyd's broad shoulders made William feel old. At five and thirty, he should be settled with a half-dozen bairns at his feet. And when did the cold start making everything hurt worse? Lord in heaven, eight years of battle had taken its toll.

The worst of it?

He hadn't achieved a damned thing.

There were more Englishmen in Scotland now than when he'd left for the mainland after his tragic loss at Falkirk.

"Horses," Eddy Little whispered.

A sharp stirring thrummed through William's blood. He wrapped his fingers around his hilt and slowly drew the great sword from its scabbard. Making eye contact with each of his score of men, they all indicated their readiness with a nod.

He held up his hand, ready to give the signal.

The wooden planks on the bridge above thundered as the retinue began to cross.

Beneath his helm, his heart roared in his ears. This was another chance to stop English spies bearing missives and supplies from England.

Three and two score of footmen crossed with twelve horse. The odds had been worse. When the softer steps of the foot soldiers paraded onto the bridge, William dropped his hand and dug in his spurs. "Scotland until Judgement," he growled under his breath as his mount lurched toward the unsuspecting horsemen. Racing against time to cut off the foot from the horse, William's men rallied behind him.

Galloping out of the ravine, the first thing he saw was Comyn's pennant. The earl had become the greatest turncoat in the history of the Kingdom. At the first sign of danger, the unsuspecting foe began drawing their swords and reining their horses.

William drove the gelding toward the head of the retinue. God's teeth, Lord Comyn was in the lead. How tragic things had become. In the early days, the Lord of Badenoch had fought a few battles alongside William, but like many of the nobles, he'd turned at Falkirk—put his personal wealth ahead of honor and his duty to his countrymen.

Bought for lands and riches.

Gnashing his teeth, William rode straight for the backstabbing leader.

"Protect Badenoch," bellowed a man at his flank.

In the blink of an eye, four horsemen blocked William's path. He didn't pull up. Strengthening his seat with a downward press of his heels, he eyed the first, swinging his sword back for a deadly blow. William glared into the wide eyes of his opponent.

Ye're the first to die.

The pain in his shoulder shot thorough his arm like he'd been bludgeoned with a pickaxe. The lion's claws sinking though his flesh plagued his mind with every bone-jarring strike. But William would never allow an injury to stop him. Only death would still the rage of battle that poured out from his heart to the tips of his fingers.

Iron scraped and clanged as blood splattered and men fell.

Behind the bridge, the foot were running with John Blair leading the pursuit.

Attacked from the side, William had no time to spare. Gritting his teeth against the pain, he forced his arm to keep swinging, defending every blow.

When his opponent fell, he set his sights on the prize. He'd have Comyn's traitorous head. "Sssss," William hissed, leaning forward in his saddle and demanding a gallop. "Ye venomed swine-eared rat!" He raised his sword, ready to meet his foe head-to-head. "I'll send ye to hell for selling your loyalty for a bit o' land."

Comyn's eyes grew wide with terror as William swung, aiming for the bastard's neck sinews.

Struck from the side, a hammer collided with his helm. Stars blinded him. The great sword flung from his hand. Squeezing his knees, he fought to stay mounted while his body hurled sideways.

William's sight cleared in time to see the ground approach. Tucking his shoulder, he hit with a jarring thud. A thousand knives needled his torturous scars.

His pulse thrummed.

No time to think.

Drawing his dirk from his belt, he tried to spring to his feet. His stomach squelched. Everything went black as he dropped to the mud.

***

"Give me a wee bit o' help would ye, now?" a voice strained.

William gulped back his bile, his eyes flashing open. God's teeth, Robbie was trying to heft him onto his horse.

"I'll be right," Willy slurred. "Go a-f-ter Comyn."

"They're long gone." Robbie grumbled as he shoved against Wallace's backside.

"Let me help," said Little's voice. "We need to spirit him away afore they double back with an army."

Wind coughed through William's throat as he landed across his saddle on his gut. Consciousness slipped in and out, his vision blurred. Was this the end? Finally?

"Eva," he bellowed at the top of his lungs.

All strength fled as his head dropped and bobbed against the horse's barrel.

CHAPTER SEVENTEEN

Bitterly cold as if she'd plunged into a snowdrift, Eva sat up and shook her head. Lord, it was darker than midnight. Her teeth chattered. Where the hell was she?

Putting her hand down, her palm filled with wet slush.

How in God's name did she end up in the Highlands?

Scrubbing her hands over her face, her eyes adjusted a bit. Icy prickles shot across her skin.

Good Lord, she wasn't in the mountains.

A tightness gripped her chest so powerful she couldn't breathe. Though overgrown, she'd recognize the cave entrance anywhere.

But how did she end up in Leglen Wood in the snow? Yes, it had been cold at the reception, but snow hadn't been in the forecast.

Her next problem? The surrounding forest was so dense, there was no way to wander out of there until daylight.

Pushing herself to a stand, her feet wobbled. Jeez, she still wore stilettoes, stockings and suit. She rubbed her outer arms. *Where's my coat?*

Shaking her head, the last thing she remembered was lying across her bed at Torwood.

A flicker came from the cave.

She gasped.

Who's in there? Shit.

She wouldn't last the night out in this cold. But before she just marched inside and met up with a band of hoodlums or drug addicts, she reached into her purse and pulled out her smartphone.

It only took one blink for the realization to sink in. Her throat closed. With the sudden perspiration oozing from her palm, the phone slipped.

Oh God, no.

Clutching the phone to her chest she paced while her teeth chattered.

Twelfth February, 1305?

I can't do this.

The medallion chilled like ice against her skin.

"Take me back, dammit."

Bouncing her knees to stave off the cold, she squeezed her eyes shut.

Please. I can't. Please, please, please, please.

If it got any colder, she'd turn into an ice sculpture.

What if he wasn't there?

What if she'd been sent back to fall in love with someone else?

No. Fucking. Way.

With a gulp, she pushed the torch icon on her phone and hobbled inside, trying not to twist an ankle on the craggy ground. The last time she'd been in this very spot, she was wearing hiking boots and a down vest—much more practical attire for the woods.

She hadn't seen another flicker. Maybe her eyes had played a trick on her? With luck, the place would be empty…and then she'd need to build a fire. Did she have a book of matches in her purse? She certainly didn't have a flint.

A hiss echoed through the passageway.

Ice coursed through her veins. Eva hadn't heard the sound of a sword sliding from its scabbard in eight years.

"Hello the cave," she called in a panicked voice. "I'm in need of shelter." Lord, the Auld Scots came back, too.

"There's no room to be had. Be gone with ye," a young man's voice resounded—one she didn't recognize.

She turned off the torch and slipped the phone back into her bag, replacing it with a vial of pepper spray—not a fantastic defense against a sword, but it might buy her some time. *To run where?*

Should she chance it?

"I'm looking for William Wallace," she said.

A wry chuckle followed. "Ye and everyone else. He's nay in these parts—now be gone with ye."

She ventured to guess the reason for her sudden appearance. He had to be in there. If her hunch was right, asking for shelter would be met with a firm rebuttal. "I am Eva MacKay come to see William. I have no weapons." *Not even a miserable coat or a practical pair of shoes either.*

Silence filled the cavernous walls.

She held her breath, trying to stay her chattering teeth.

"Come into the light," said a deeper voice.

Blair?

Her pulse sped.

Skimming the balls of her feet over the craggy surface, she rounded the bend and stood at the entrance to the big cavern, bracing her hand against the wall.

"Lord have mercy," a young man said, staring at her legs.

"Robbie?" she asked. Goodness, the sandy-haired lad had grown nearly as big as William.

John Blair held up his sword with a sneer. "Satan, get thee from me."

Backing, she glanced down at her legs and cringed. Bloody hell, over a dozen hungry eyes gaped at her. "Does anyone have something I can use to cover up? It seems I've arrived a bit over dressed."

Blair snatched a blanket and tossed it to her. "A bit under dressed is more apt."

She tugged the musty wool around her shoulders. Ah yes, the acute odors of the—now—fourteenth century. Warming ever so slightly, she regarded the men's swords, still leveled at her midriff. Funny, they didn't make her jittery at all. Perhaps she'd mellowed after eight years. "If you'll be so kind as to sheathe your weapons, I could use a pair of shoes as well."

"Bloody hell, woman." The overzealous priest shoved his enormous sword into the scabbard hanging from his belt. "Where did ye come from, and why in God's name did ye stay away for so long?"

"I…" She chanced a glance around the cave. *Where is William?* "I tried to come back for years." *And now that I'd finally accepted my fate, I've suddenly appeared. Why the hell didn't I give the medallion back to Walter when I saw him at the reception?*

John Blair hadn't grown any more welcoming during her absence. If anything, his face was gaunter, more foreboding.

But Robbie on the other hand—he'd turned into a man. Tall, ruggedly attractive, shiny blue eyes, shoulders as broad as a horse's rear end. "Och aye, Miss Eva. Willy pined for ye something awful."

She rubbed her outer arms. "As I did for him."

"Then what happened?" demanded Blair.

She shifted her foot to the side, regarding the latest Louis Vuitton style—sinfully high heel, pointed toe—a slip of black leather. Everything she wore oozed twenty-first century. "You'd never believe me. William didn't at first."

Blair nudged Robbie's arm. "Go tend the fire. I want to have a word with her *ladyship*."

Eva folded her arms as the priest neared. "Where is William?"

"That is none of your concern."

Her gaze shot to the alcove where he slept—had slept with her at one time. Furs covered the entrance like they had

nearly a decade ago. "I believe he's the reason why I'm here."
Surely he must be somewhere near.

"Ye think so?" He backed her down the passageway.

"Well, I certainly didn't travel through a time warp to seek
forgiveness for my sins. There are plenty of priests who can
offer me absolution in the twenty-first century."

"Blasphemy!"

"No. It is the truth." She glanced down at his sheathed
sword, then met his gaze. "Why do you think I've suddenly
appeared wearing clothing not of this time?"

"Wearing the devil's garb. Ye are disgraceful."

She crossed her arms tight over her gabardine jacket,
huddling under the blanket. "My clothing is of the best
manufacture in my time."

Lunging forward, Blair pinned her against the stony wall,
his forearm across her throat. "Willy said ye were from the
future." His eyes narrowed. "How do I ken ye'll not put a hex
on him?"

Gulping, her knees started to quiver. *If I show weakness I'll
lose his respect.* "Did I ever do anything to harm him before?"

"Och, he pined for ye something awful—never forgot
your bonny face. Damnation, I ought to burn ye."

She refused to shift her gaze away from his penetrating
stare. "Father Blair," she said, stressing her modern
Edinburgh accent. "I have no idea why I am here, but
something in my heart tells me William Wallace needs me." In
a bold move, she pushed against his shoulder. "Is he in the
alcove?"

The monk's eyes shifted.

Shoving her way out of the priest's trap, she started off,
but he grabbed her wrist and squeezed. "Ye hurt him again,
and I'll hunt ye down and carve out your heart myself."

She yanked her hand away. "I see you haven't lost any of
your charm." She flung her finger toward the center of the
cavern. "Now, I will forgive your boorishness if you find me a

more suitable pair of shoes before I break my ankle on these stilts."

The man grumbled something imperceptible under his breath, but then continued to follow her. "Can ye heal him?"

Eva stopped. "He's ill?"

"Wounded in battle."

"Jeez. Why didn't you say something when I first arrived?" Clutching her purse, she kicked off her shoes and sped for the alcove.

***

Pulling the furs aside, Eva's hand flew to her tingling chest. Turning upside down, her stomach fluttered with a gazillion butterflies. Her knees buckled, made worse by the swooning of her head. She'd been in shock before—swore she didn't want to come back. Not now. Now when things would… Shaking her head, her entire body trembled as she regarded the sleeping form stretched out atop a pile of furs.

Lord, he'd aged. Deep lines etched the corners of his eyes and made furrows from his nose to where they disappeared beneath an unruly auburn moustache and beard. Still mahogany brown, his hair had not a wisp of grey. Regardless, his face was drawn, a bit gaunt and pale.

Eva glanced over her shoulder. "How long has he been unconscious?"

"A day," said Blair.

She crawled inside. "Bring me some ice from outside—and clean rags." After sliding her bag from her shoulder, she set it on the ground. "Where is Brother Bartholomew?"

"Gone," said Blair, his voice trailing off.

"What happened to him?" Eva loved the little monk.

"Died of consumption on the return trip from Rome."

Eva gasped, her heart clutched into a knot. *God, no.* "I-I'm sorry. He was…um…I liked him." She had to keep it together. How many others had perished during her absence?

Seeing William unconscious—being back in Leglen Wood was like stepping into a nightmare. For so many years she'd ached for him, cried herself to sleep, angry that their time together had been cut short. But now. Did she want to be here?

Hell, no, no, no, no, no.

She knew what was coming.

Death.

The most hideous, painful, humiliating, barbaric death ever imagined—the brainchild of an insane king, Edward Plantagenet. Her flittering stomach squelched and threatened to heave.

Blair didn't budge. "Why, may I ask, do ye need ice? Is it not cold enough already?"

Eva had nothing to hide from the priest—not anymore. The medallion needed to send her home. Besides, Blair already thought her a heretic or worse. "You said he's been unconscious for a day?"

"Aye."

"Well, he most likely has a concussion. Ice is to help decrease the swelling of his brain—if he hasn't suffered brain damage already." In addition to keeping a first aid kit in her purse, she'd taken first responder classes with St. John's Ambulance—in the days when she was sure she'd end up traveling back to William. She might be a bit rusty, but the knowledge she'd gained was a damned sight more than she'd had the last time she'd visited medieval Scotland.

Blair slapped his hand through the air. "Ye dunna make a lick of sense."

"To you, perhaps not, but if you want him to wake, I'd suggest you stop lingering and fetch me the ice."

"Ye havena quelled that barbed tongue of yours, I see," Blair grumbled, dropping the curtain. "Pushy wench," carried through the shroud.

And you haven't mellowed your grumpy, opinionated attitude.

Alone, she scooted toward William's head and tested his temperature with the back of her hand. "At least you're not fevered. But you're awfully pale." The friction from touching him made goosebumps rise across her skin. Her fingers trembled. "I'll tell you here and now, I cannot possibly stay."

William didn't move, though a puff of air whistled through his lips.

Eva's gaze slid down his body. Wearing a dirty linen shirt encrusted with blood, a plaid covered him to his waist. "Do you have any other injuries?" Wet blood seeped through his sleeve at his left shoulder. Untying his laces, she peeked beneath. "Jesus Christ you've been pummeled. What? Did they just shove you in here and leave you to live or die?"

Her pulse racing, she reached into her purse and pulled out the first aid kit. The jagged wound looked as craggy as the Grand Canyon. *Hit with a mace?* Lord only knew. Medieval soldiers carried all manner of weapons meant to maim.

She snatched a pair of shears and cut the shirt right down the middle. Pulling it away, the fabric stuck to his wound. Carefully she cut around it. "Robbie! Bring me some boiled water," she hollered. Hopefully the lad remembered how important it was to keep things clean.

"Still harping on about hot water?" After some rustling, he popped his head through the shroud, holding a tankard of ale in his fist. "It'll take a wee while to set a pot to boiling."

"All right. I'll put that ale to use in the interim." She waved him inside. "Did you know his shoulder was this bad?"

"I havena seen him since we slid Willy in the alcove." Wariness filled his sideways stare as the lad handed her the pewter tankard then scratched his bearded chin. Lord, Robbie had grown up. "Och, he looks foul."

"Wait until I pull the cloth away." Eva drizzled the ale atop the linen, praying the alcohol in it wouldn't provide too much of a shock to William's already weakened body.

Robbie grimaced. "Do ye have to do it now?"

"If not, the wound will fester."

After letting the ale seep in and moisten the cloth, Eva slowly tugged it away.

"Ssss," Robbie hissed. "He still looks as if he lost the battle with the lion if ye ask me."

Panning her gaze from the gnarled wound down the puckered scars across his chest, her gut turned over. "My God." She glanced at the lad. "Lion?"

"Aye, King Philip wouldna give Willy a letter of passage until he fought the lion—with his bare hands. Killed the bastard, too."

A cringe stretched the corners of her mouth while she examined William's mangled flesh. "But not until the big cat got in a few nasty swipes of his own, I see."

Robbie nodded, his gaze falling to her open first aid kit.

She snapped the plastic container closed. "Thanks for the ale. I'll take it from here."

He glanced up—his expression guarded as his teeth grazed his bottom lip. "Ye'll help him will ye not?"

"I'll do everything I can."

Then his gaze swept to her legs. "Bloody hell. Is that your skin?"

She tugged the blanket over her stockings. "Do you think you can find me some suitable clothes?"

He knit his eyebrows as if considering.

"Please, everyone will be calling for me to be burned if they see me like this."

His mouth twisted. "I'll see what I can find—not too many tailors in the wood."

"Thank you."

He again looked to the kit. "What…?"

"Please, Robbie. Don't ask."

The lad shook his head. "'Tis probably best."

No sooner had Robbie left when Father Blair showed up with a handful of chipped ice and a few rags—dirty ones at that.

With no time to haul them to the burn for a good scrub, she wrapped the ice in the cleanest and held it out. "This isn't going to last. Can you fill a bowl with ice?"

"Bloody hell, woman. I'm not your squire to order about."

She looked up with a pointed glare. "I'm sorry if I've offended you, father. Can *someone* fetch more ice? William could die…" But she knew he wouldn't. *Right? Is this why I'm here? What if I refuse to help him?* The medallion warmed against her chest for the first time in eight years.

Except, this time it didn't give her the same panicky effect. This time her throat thickened as she considered her options. Then the worthless lump cooled as fast as it had warmed.

Heal him and get the hell out of here.

God, yes.

The priest let out a noisy sigh and dropped the furs. "I'll fetch more ice, but this is the last time. 'Tis colder than a year of Januaries out there."

"Thank you," she called after him.

Beside her, William moaned.

A gasp caught in her throat. Would he wake soon? How should she act when he did?

Holding the ice between her palms, she studied him. Lord, he might be weathered and worn, but even unconscious, he made her blood stir. The mere sight of him brought on every emotion she'd ever experienced from joy to terror.

For years Eva had pined for this man—hid from the world with her medieval castle project. Everything she had done was an attempt to be closer to him—closer to *them.* Through the ages their souls were irrevocably connected by love—a love more powerful than the medallion or Father Time himself.

But would William still feel the same?

All she wanted to do was throw her body atop her lover and bawl—tell him how much she'd tried to come back—yet tell him she couldn't possibly stay. Regardless of the feelings she had for him, their love no longer mattered. Staying with William now would kill her—take her insides and rip them into tiny shreds.

No possible way. Not this time.

Nurse him back to health and get the hell out of here.

"William?" she whispered, applying the ice to his head. "Can you hear me?"

CHAPTER EIGHTEEN

William shivered. Something hard and cold pressed against his throbbing head. Water trickled. A warm cloth swirled over his chest and under his arms. Lord, his shoulder punished him like someone had bludgeoned it with a pickaxe—mayhap someone had.

Heaven help him, the myriad of sensations addled a poor warrior's mind. A miserable pounding in the head—a shoulder that felt like it had been run through with an iron spike…combined with the most soothing bath…

Mm. Bless it, the gentle hands caressing him must be those of a woman. He inhaled. An unusual scent—strong but oddly clean.

A woman?

For eight bloody years one woman had consumed his thoughts. A woman lost to him.

His heart jolted.

Jesu, the scent. I'll never forget.

He tried to open his eyes. "Eva?" The question sounded like a hoarse whisper. And why did her name have to always be on the tip of his tongue? Merciful madness, he was daft. He'd thought about the lass every waking moment since that dreadful day when he'd lost her *and* Andrew. God save his idle cock, he hadn't looked at another woman in eight years. Hell, he should have taken his vows rather than accept the guardianship. He was more suited to life as a monk. Mayhap he'd be tending a garden at Melrose rather than hiding in miserable caves.

The swirling stopped with a feminine gasp. "William? Are you awake?"

In a rush, his heart well-nigh leapt out of his chest. His eyes flew open—Miserable hell, he couldn't focus. "Eva? Is it ye?" Blinking rapidly, he tried to sit up.

"Shhhh. Easy," she cooed with a soft, lulling voice. "I'm here. I've been sent to help you."

Giving in to her gentle palm pressing against his chest, William lay back and slid his tongue over dry lips. "I never thought—"

"I know." She smoothed lithe fingers over his forehead. "I'd given up hope—and then poof. Without warning, I awoke outside the cave in a snow drift."

Chancing another peek, his vision grew clearer. Oh, and such a vision—one worth enduring a decade of hell. "God's teeth, ye are more beautiful than ever."

Leaning over him, long red tresses skimmed his chest. She smiled. William's heart stuttered—could it really be her? "Eight years older," she said. Aye, 'twas Eva's voice for certain.

"Och, I've aged as well." He reached up with a trembling finger, aching to touch her to see if she was real. "But ye—ye havena aged a day."

A flicker from the fat-burning lamp danced in her green eyes. "I'll say you're still the most handsome man I've ever seen—even if your body is scarred beyond all imagination."

He looked down and frowned. "I suppose the lion in France did the most damage."

"Robbie told me."

She pointed to his throbbing shoulder. "I think you must have been hit with a mace. Whatever it was turned your flesh into mincemeat."

He looked—a pure white bandage covered the wound—it didn't hurt too badly either. "I must be coming good."

"Healing. Though I won't say you're out of the woods yet." She adjusted the cold compress atop his head. "You have a severe concussion."

"Och, there ye go, using your odd speech," he teased. But he loved it, could listen to her twists of phrase for the rest of his days.

She pursed her lips looking like she was trying not to grin. "Are you thirsty?"

"More parched than salt in the sunshine." Heaven help him, he wanted to pull her atop his body and smother the lass with kisses—but it had been so long. Though smiling, she seemed coolly distant. And what had she been doing the past eight years?

His gut twisted.

Had she married?

Eva reached for a tankard and spoon. "I have some watered wine. It'll give you strength."

He watched her ladle a wee bit. She *had* changed. Aside from growing her tresses down to her waist, she was more poised—mayhap less excitable. He blinked in succession. Without a doubt the years had increased the woman's beauty.

Growing more beautiful with age is something only achieved by a sorceress for certain. But Eva is no witch. She proved that to me a hundred times over.

The brew slid over his arid tongue and down his gullet. Lord, sipping made him even thirstier. "More."

"Go easy."

He gave a nod, wishing he could grab the tankard and guzzle it. But instead, he coughed like an invalid. "Bloody hell."

She offered him another spoonful. "You had quite a blow to the head. Father Blair said it's a good thing you were wearing your helm."

Licking his lips, William closed his eyes. Ah yes, the raid at Johnstonebridge—and that bloody, backstabbing Earl of Badenoch.

"Do you remember what happened?" she asked.

William looked at Eva's face. God's teeth, she was fresh as a newborn lamb in spring—so full of life—yet something wizened her face—a tad thinner, perhaps? "Och, I dunna want to talk about that now." He brushed a finger over the back of the hand holding the tankard. "What is it about ye? I see no lines etched around your mouth or at your eyes. Like I said—'tis as if time has stood still for ye."

"Oh, I've definitely aged. It's just…" Her gaze drifted sideways as she set the tankard and spoon down. "I'm not running for my life at every turn."

He grasped her hand. How in God's name did the woman manage to keep her fingers softer than rose petals? "Aye. Ye come from a time of peace?"

"Yes."

"Then why did ye come back after all this time?"

Her feminine Adam's apple bobbed. "I wish I could say I willed it to be so." Then she let out a nervous chuckle. "But it just happened. Much like the first time—I had no idea that I would even drift off to sleep, let alone awake in—" Her mouth drew down in a grimace.

"Did ye see a ghost?"

She shook her head and blinked rapidly.

"Are ye unwell?" he asked.

"No."

"But something is troubling ye." He knew it.

She pursed her lips and stared at him as if she, indeed, had seen a ghost.

He grasped her wrist. "What is it?"

"I cannot say."

His gut squeezed. Ah yes, the secrets. But forcing her to reveal them is what had ripped her from his arms so long ago. "By the look on your face, 'tis grave."

She nodded and wiped a hand across her lips. "There's so much we have to talk about, but you need to rest. It will take you a fortnight or more to regain your strength."

He moved his shoulder. Och—that hurt like nails driving it into the cross. "How long have I been abed?"

"Two days."

That wasn't good. "I'd best be mounted by the morrow."

"You cannot be serious," she coughed out.

"Longshanks has a hefty price on my head. The bastard willna rest until he sees it on a spike atop the tower."

Lord, Eva turned green. "But aren't you safe here? The men don't seem overly nervous."

"I'm safe nowhere. Spies lurk in every corner of the Kingdom. I've scarcely had a wink of sleep in three years—the bastards."

"Is there no one to whom you can turn?"

A smirk snorted through his nose as he slipped his finger under the medallion around her neck and flicked it. "Not unless ye can spirit me to your time."

"If only—I'd do it in a heartbeat." She bit her bottom lip and looked up. "What about the Steward?"

"Bought—just like all the nobles—sold out for a bit o' land."

"All of them?"

"Aye. Every last one—even those who rode with me when we invaded England. And the common men are all afeard; hiding in their cottages, praying their families will be spared from further cruelty by that *murderous* English king."

"He's still razing Scottish towns?"

"'Tis worse than before—'tis a reign of terror."

"What about the Earl of Carrick?" she said with all the solemnity of Job.

Now that made William's head throb all the more. "Och, no one ever kens what side the Bruce is on. His mind changes like a swinging pendulum."

Eva dunked a cloth in a basin and wrung it out. "I believe he's an ally."

"Well then now I ken ye've been gone eight bloody years. The only ally Bruce has is himself. He owns enough land on both sides of the border to command an army of reckoning."

She ran the cloth down his arm. "If you had to choose between Bruce and Comyn, which one would you pick?"

Eva made the question sound innocent, but it gave him pause—and he hadn't a mind to answer such a pointless query. He snatched her wrist and held it firm. "Ye ken I met King John in France?"

She nodded. "I thought you may have—I knew he was exiled there after Edward released him from the Tower."

"Aye." William swallowed. "Ye ken he refused my plea to return?"

"I am only aware that after his abdication, John Balliol never again set foot in Scotland."

William stared at the stony ceiling of the alcove and let out a long sigh. "'Twould have been good to ken afore I spent an entire year imprisoned in King Philip's dungeon."

She pulled her hand from his grasp. "It pains me to see the years have not been kind to you, William."

Suddenly bereft of fight, he closed his eyes. The years had been anything but kind—and not only to him. All of the Kingdom had succumbed to oppression. "Is there nothing ye can do to ease the pounding in my head?"

Reaching into her shiny satchel, she pulled out a white vile. "That, I *can* help with."

***

Though John Blair acted his usual gruff self, eyeing her with distrust, fortunately he did unroll a hide that had protected all the clothing she'd collected during her last stay.

She even found her mail-piercing sword in the middle of the bundle along with two pairs of shoes and a fur-lined cloak. Thank God. If only the powers behind the medallion would see fit to provide her with proper attire before dumping her in the midst of winter, seven hundred years into the past.

Regardless, once again, Eva was clad in a shift and kirtle, and hiding out with a band of rebels in a cave.

Robbie walked past carrying two buckets. "I'm off to fetch some water."

"Would you mind if I come along?" Eva asked. "I need a bit of fresh air."

One side of his mouth ticked up. "Are ye daft? 'Tis cold as ice out there."

"I know. It's just I've been cooped up in this cave for three days and I'm going stir crazy."

"Huh?"

"I'm going mad," she corrected.

He shrugged. "Och, if ye want to come along, I'll nay argue."

Eva pulled her cloak tight about her shoulders and hurried after him. Since her arrival, no one had been overly welcoming—pretty much looked at her warily. She couldn't blame them. How often does a scandalously dressed woman arrive in the middle of a forest in the midst of winter? The high heels and stockings had to be the icing on the cake. In the fourteenth century? It was a miracle no one had a heart attack.

Jeez, she was lucky John Blair didn't tie her to a stake and set fire to rushes beneath her feet.

Fortunately, William had slept most of the time since her arrival. True, he wanted to ride, but he'd been in no shape to do so. Even Blair agreed—said they had plenty of sentries posted and Leglen Wood was still the safest hideaway in all of Scotland. As long as they lay low—no comings or goings beyond the confines of the forest—people in the surrounding villages would be none the wiser.

Eva followed the young man out the cave and along the narrow path. Of all William's men, Robbie had changed the most. Of course that wouldn't have been difficult to guess. As a lad, he'd just accepted her, quirks and all. But now, he looked at her with wariness that almost surpassed Blair's distrust. Well, Eva needed more than one ally—especially since William was in no shape to defend himself, let alone her. Once they were well away from the camp, she ventured to strike up a conversation. "I can't believe how much you've grown. What are you? Six-two? Six-three?"

He stopped and faced her, his eyes filled with ire. "Bloody hell, ye talk like nothing I've ever heard afore."

"Do you not remember?" she affected her Auld Scots as best she could. "My speech has always been different."

"Aye, but I thought ye cared for us—cared for me—cared for William at least." He spun and trudged onward.

"Did I hurt you when I left?" Eva kept pace.

"Nay." By the clipped edge to his voice, she didn't believe him for a minute.

"Did William tell you I had no choice?"

Robbie stopped and threw the buckets into the bushes, snow shaking from their naked limbs. "Ye vanished without a word. Ye didna even see fit to say goodbye."

"I—"

He sliced his hand through the air. "And then ye show up in our secret camp—the only place Willy can go where he has a wee chance to rest. Ye appear out of nowhere. Bless it, there were no tracks. I ken 'cause come the morn, I searched for them myself."

Eva glanced down and bit her bottom lip.

"What in the devil's name were ye wearing when ye arrived? Ye looked like a harlot—though none I've ever seen." He sauntered forward, narrowing his eyes. "And what were all those things in the box ye pulled from your satchel? Dunna lie to me."

Jeez, he sounded too much like William. He'd not only grown up, he'd grown hard, just like any medieval warrior would. And Eva had no illusions. She must choose her words carefully, regardless if this was the lad she'd known years ago, he was a man now—a man who might sooner run a dagger across her throat than await her answer. "Don't worry about that. I cannot lie to you."

He wrapped his fingers around the hilt of his dirk. "Ye'd best not."

"I couldn't lie to William either, and then he still didn't believe me for months."

White lines formed around Robbie's lips as he nodded.

Taking in a deep inhale, she pulled the medallion from under her shift. "I come from the future. My clothing, my medicine—everything I had when I arrived came from the twenty-first century."

"I thought ye said ye wouldna lie." After throwing up his hands, he grabbed the buckets. "Ye're a witch. Blair always thought ye were a witch and now I ken it."

"I am not." She stamped her foot. "Bloody hell, I didn't ask to be sent here—not after eight years of putting the pieces of my life back together."

He continued to the river. "Then why are ye here? To build up Willy's hopes and then smite them again?"

She looked away—what about *her* hopes? What about all the time she'd pined for *him*? "I have no idea—except..." Why in God's name would the medallion send her there now? Would William have survived his wounds without the antibiotics she'd forced down his throat? Overwhelmed with a flood of possibilities, she shrugged.

"Except what?" he demanded. "I want to ken what ye were about to say."

She folded her arms, clutching them tight to her body. So much for swaying the lad to her side. "Perhaps he needed me?" *I most assuredly didn't need him—or this.*

Bending down, he scooped the first bucket, filling it with water. "Well, I think it would be best if ye returned from whence ye came. Blair and I both do. Willy has enough woes without having his heart carved out by a barbed-tongued lass."

So that's why Robbie was so hostile? He'd been talking to Blair. Well, this time he was right. The sooner Eva returned home the better. "I wish it were that easy." Maybe she could deliberately do something to change the past. That should see her hurled home without so much as a blink.

He filled the next bucket. "Can I help ye?"

"I don't know." She shivered, suddenly noticing the cold. "Perhaps after William recovers?"

He gave her a heated glare, then started back, water sloshing out of the buckets.

"Robbie," she called. Her idea just might work.

He stopped but didn't turn. "Aye?"

"I must urge you to seek out the Earl of Carrick."

"The Bruce?" He looked back and glared at her. "Now I ken your mind is addled."

"One day he will become your greatest hope." Damn. The medallion didn't do a thing—just sat there like a cold lump of bronze.

When she looked up, Robbie had disappeared into the brush.

Damn. Damn, damn, damn.

CHAPTER NINETEEN

William sat across the fire from Eva and watched her turn the oatcakes on the iron griddle. He didn't like that the men had left without him. Bloody Blair had to go off and prove his point—make him feel like a worthless old relic. They'd argued, then the priest knocked William on his arse. With that, the men had left him behind whilst they headed for a raid.

He hated weakness. All his life he'd fought for the weak, the oppressed. He'd be damned if he would become one of them.

But, Jesu, his legs wobbled.

She glanced up. "Whatever happened to Paden and Adam Wishart?"

"Went back to serve their da after his release from Roxburgh gaol."

"Ah." She got a faraway look in her eye. "How is the bishop?"

"Forced to pledge fealty to Longshanks." William pursed his lips and glanced aside. "He's dead to me."

"But he—"

Bile roiled in William's gut. "What? Is a traitor?"

Eva shook her head and pressed the spatula atop the cake, making it flatter. "Never mind." She said it like she disagreed.

Bloody oath, the woman hasna been in the midst of this hell in years. Wishart is a lost cause, just like the others.

"I'll start training on the morrow," he said more to himself than to her. God's bones, it was awkward to see her again. She made him feel like an inexperienced pup—and he was nothing the like—he was bloody five and thirty and felt like sixty.

Why hasna she aged?

Aye, he couldn't deny his fingers itched to touch her, to pull her into his arms and feel those breasts mold into his chest. But it had been too long. Too many battles and too many years—centuries separated them. And Lord knew his heart couldn't withstand losing her again. It was best if he didn't allow himself leave to succumb to her allure this time. Hell, he almost wished she hadn't returned. But then he'd made a speedy recovery. The last time he'd endured such a grave injury, he'd been abed for a month—fevered with the sweat—delirious. Aye, he'd been close to death for certain.

William leaned back against the furs, resting on his good elbow. Why death continued to elude him, he had no idea. If Eva had not come, would he have survived? *I suppose I'll never ken.*

She used the wooden spatula to remove the oatcake and placed it on a trencher beside a lump of cold mutton. Then she passed it to him. "I hope the men bring supplies when they return."

"Aye." He took the trencher and regarded her face. Could he still trust her? Had she turned like so many others? Days ago she'd talked about Robert Bruce. Why? What did she know? True, she had the gift of a seer.

William drummed his fingers. The man was nearly as large as he—a stout warrior for certain. But Willy didn't trust him, couldn't trust any nobles.

Bruce? The earl has a claim to the throne—mayhap weaker than Comyn's, but nonetheless, a solid royal birthright.

She picked at her food as if nervous. "Why are you looking at me like that?"

Shifting his gaze to his food, William tore at the meat with his teeth and shoved the bite to the side of his mouth. "I'm trying to figure why ye're spewing babble about the Earl of Carrick."

She nudged the meat with her eating knife and shrugged. "Perhaps I'm wrong."

"Ye made me think." He washed his bite down with a bit of ale. "If King John willna return, the two men with the greatest claim to the throne are Bruce and Comyn." He shuddered at the thought. Comyn had become a staunch supporter of Edward. And Bruce? Well, the bastard was an enigma.

"Didn't Bruce lead a raid on Edward at Rosslyn?" she asked with an intelligent arch to her perfectly formed ginger eyebrows. She knew something—was leading him toward some sort of insight. Everyone else would just blurt out what needed to be said—but Eva? She had a way of building her argument and then ramming it home once her sharp tongue had backed him into a corner.

But William could hold his own. Even with her. "Two years past. Since, Longshanks has teamed with the Earl of Ulster to quash the remaining rebels." He held up his oatcake. "Ye ken Richard de Burgh is Bruce's father-in-law?"

A delicate red eyebrow arched. "I know families have been torn apart by feuds for centuries."

"Bruce was seen riding for Longshanks," William drove his point. "I canna trust him."

Her mouth twisted as if trying to piece together fragments of a puzzle. "Why do you think he took up the English side? Was Ulster there? Was that before or after he led the rising in Rosslyn?"

"Och, ye twist things about. Bruce is a traitor. Why would ye think he's any different from the rest of the gentry? They're all a mob of backstabbers—not a one proved his loyalty to King John or to Scotland. They signed the Ragman Roll, then sold out to Longshanks at Falkirk, and they'll do it again. Mark me."

She moved her fists to her hips and eyed him. "If you're so sure the war is over—that England has won and there is no hope for Scotland's nobles, why are you hiding in a cave? Why do you not sail for the Holy Land and go on a pilgrimage?"

He snorted. Now he remembered how maddening Eva could be—especially when she affected the self-righteous, fisted-hip pose. "Ye make it sound easy," he grumbled. "I'll never give up the cause. My countrymen are still suffering the yoke of tyranny. English armies are still leading raids into our villages, frightening everyone into submission—they're still raping women and hanging men. And I'll tell ye now. I. Will. *Never*. Submit."

A tic twitched in her jaw as she shifted her gaze away. He sensed she didn't care for his answer—would have been happier if they'd planned to board a galley for Jerusalem on the morrow.

"So, what are your plans?" she asked.

He'd hoped to gain the support of the clergy, but even Bishop Lamberton, who William had appointed to the Bishopric of St. Andrews had turned his back. "I'm still devising a plan." Now a tic twitched in his jaw. Bloody hell, Eva had been gone for too long. She didn't understand a damned thing—she had no idea what it was like to watch a thousand men be butchered while carefully laid plans were foiled by backstabbing earls and barons.

She crossed her arms—Lord, she wasn't about to let it lie. "Was Bruce at the battle of Falkirk?"

"Wheesht, woman. He may not have been there, but I swear on my da's grave he's a snake."

"Do you think he may have stayed away on purpose?"

William stabbed his meat. "I'm certain of it."

"My guess is he stayed away because he couldn't usurp Ulster, Longshanks…and Comyn all at the same time—he'd face anarchy." Eva shook her head. "Lord Bruce and the Earl of Badenoch are no allies."

Losing his appetite, William threw his eating knife atop his trencher. "Ye see? They've all colluded to make themselves richer—at the expense of the common man."

"It is all so very tragic." Her shoulders fell with her sigh. "But I ask you to think about Robert Bruce. What are his motives? What would happen if you showed him fealty?"

Jesu, will she not give up on this mindless quest? "Have ye turned backstabber as well?" He gave her a pointed glare. "We'd best find something else to talk about afore your babble makes me lose my temper."

A hellacious battle warred inside Eva's head. What did she care if the medallion hurled her home? That's what she wanted, God dammit. But she couldn't allude to too much—couldn't tell William he only had six more months until…until the unthinkable. The mere thought made her want to retch. She still cared for him—couldn't put the poor man through that kind of hell. But there was something else she *could* tell him that might be as strong. Sure, he'd told her to back off. Eight years ago she would have—the medallion would have burnt a hole through her heart by now, too.

Who knew why it now sat cold atop her chest while she blabbed about Robert the Bruce.

She took a sip of ale and then looked at him. His color had returned—the spark in his eye—the handsome grin…er, scowl. Lord how she'd missed him. No man back home could hold a candle to William Wallace and she'd dated plenty. Well, a few. After walking away from her third dinner date, she decided widowhood wasn't so bad. Work became her lover, her one driving passion.

Before she told him, she wanted to drink him in. There was no chance to rekindle the romance—no way on earth she'd allow herself to give her heart—be so stupid. She still couldn't believe she was there alone with him. All the nights she'd gone to sleep begging the forces behind the medallion to send her back once more—give her the rest of that year she'd planned.

God, I was an idiot.

He knit his brows as she stared at him. "Do I have a pustule on my face?"

"No." She continued to stare. He may be a bit more time-weathered, but that only served to increase his allure. And his eyes. Lord, his eyes were the same crystal blues that could pierce through her soul.

Tilting his chin up, he folded his arms. "Then why are ye looking at me like that?"

"I want to remember."

His gaze softened. "I've never forgotten."

"Nor have I."

His eyes grew dark.

"We can't." She tapped her top lip with her tongue.

"I ken." His mouth twitched. "Thank ye for setting me to rights with that newfangled tincture of yours."

"Any time." *Right—dumb response.* She would have tended him every time he'd been injured if the damned medallion would have allowed it. And now he was well on the road to recovery, she really should be going. "What would you say if—" She covered the medallion with her palm. Odd, it still hadn't warmed in the slightest.

"Aye?" William asked.

"What if I told you Robert Bruce would one day be crowned King of Scotland?" There. She'd said it—put the truth out there for him to ponder. And what the heck was she doing still sitting there? She yanked off the medallion and shook it.

"Burned ye, did it?"

"No." She watched it twirl. "What I just said should have hurled me back home, dammit."

His grin fell. "Ye mean to say 'tis true?"

"Did I ever lie to you?"

"Well..."

"I mean after I realized who you were." Goodness, the man could hold on to a grudge forever. She'd fibbed about her identity when they'd first met, but at the time she'd thought he was a murdering nutcase.

His teeth scraped over his bottom lip as he slowly shook his head. "Nay, lass." He reached for the ewer of ale and poured himself another tankard. "Bruce?" he growled. "The maggot."

Eva slipped the medallion back over her head. Evidently, the lump of bronze had other plans for her this trip. "Yes."

"How?" William leaned forward. "He defeats Edward?"

"In time he defeats his son, Edward the Second."

"God on the cross, I never would have guessed." Picking up his tankard, he smoothed his fingers back and forth around the base, his brow pinched as if deep in thought. "Scotland will again be at peace?"

"Eventually." Eva didn't want to talk about it anymore. Obviously mentioning Robert the Bruce was a dead end. Besides, William might ask questions she couldn't bring herself to answer regardless of the medallion's warning, or its ridiculous notion of going into hibernation just at the moment when it should be transporting her home.

How long will I be stuck here this time?

Chapter Twenty

After breaking his fast, William lumbered outside. Donning his hauberk caused so much pain in his shoulder, he'd cast the heavy mail aside. Aye, he would need another day or so of healing and then he'd be right to wear his full kit.

Bloody Christmas, he hated to be injured. Pain? If he could avoid it, he would, but this life brought agony that mounted with every passing day. If he gave in to it, he may as well slit his own throat.

Sword in hand, he tried to hold the damned thing straight. Stars crossed his vision as the sensation of stabbing knives paralyzed his shoulder. The heavy weapon dropped to the ground. *Christ, I'm abed a few days and I cannot hold on to my sword?*

Worse, neither shoulder worked now.

For the love of God, aging sapped a man.

Gritting his teeth, he closed his eyes and forced his mind to focus on one thing. Every twinge of pain had been caused by one power-hungry tyrant and William would never forget it. Either in this lifetime or in death he would face Edward Longshanks face-to-face, man-to-man, and that thought always infused him with strength. For nine years, the quest to liberate the Kingdom of Scotland had driven his every action. Hatred took his pain and honed it—drove it toward an unquenchable purpose. Come Judgement Day, they would both stand naked before their maker.

He raised his sword with a steady hand and lunged. His blessed arm shook. Sharp jabs tortured him. Tremors wracked through the wounded limb. Steadying his weapon with both hands, he fought against his urge to quit.

With a bellow, he raised the sword above his head, turned to the side and swung it down, then level with the ground. Recoiling, the sword flew from his grasp. His mouth contorted at the sensation of razors slicing open his sinews, so agonizing, his gut seized.

Dropping to his knees, William's spine curled and he balled his fists. "God in heaven, help me or take me to my judgement this day."

"No warrior suffers an injury like yours and immediately resumes fighting." Eva stepped from the shadows of the cave. "You know that as well as I. Andrew Murray never did recover from the arrow wound to his shoulder."

William straightened and regarded her. "If I canna fight, I am worthless to the cause."

"Hardly." She had the gall to snort. The last thing he needed was Eva's sharp tongue. "You have one of the greatest military minds in history. Surely your value falls not in your physical strength, but in your ability to lead."

He hadn't expected her to be complimentary—coax his arse back to bed, mayhap, but tell him he had a great military mind? If only he could believe it. His shoulders slumped. "Aye? My army has been reduced to a score of men."

"But the commoners still remember you. Your name is still on their lips. Perhaps it is no longer shouted, but they *want* to follow you."

William lumbered to his feet. "The only problem? Every time I show my face, I'm relentlessly chased by Edward's brigands." He raked his fingers through his hair. "Everyone who follows me puts their verra lives in peril."

"Do you fear being caught?"

"Nay."

She stepped toward him. "Then what is it you fear?"

A flame flared from his gut up through his throat. "I fear nothing, damn ye."

"I don't believe that for a minute." She bent down and retrieved his sword.

"Ye seem to ken everything since ye've returned. If ye are so sure of yourself, then tell me: What is it I fear?"

"Failure," she said without hesitation, handing him the hilt. "And your own weaknesses."

He snatched it from her, the shooting jabs causing an unwelcome grimace. "Failure is not an option."

"What about failure for the common good?"

"Now what are ye on about? Jesu, Eva, a man needs a cypher map to unravel your prattle."

Rubbing her outer arms, she glanced back to the cave. "Forgive me. I spoke out of turn." She dipped into a quick curtsey. "I interrupted your misery. Carry on."

He watched while the hem of her cloak swung with her turn. Ballocks, she could raise his ire like no one else. Aye, the nobles had tested him, but they were men. He could reconcile any differences with a good sparring match. But Eva? She toyed with his mind—his thoughts. She twisted everything he believed to be true, chewed it up and spat it on the ground. Lord, she should have been knighted—should have been the damned Guardian.

Interrupted my misery? Cheeky wench, I'll not allow such a barbed-tongued remark to pass.

Sheathing his sword, he marched after her. "I'll have ye ken I've failed plenty, and every time, I've faced it like a man."

Her foot slipped on the damp, uneven surface. "Yes, you have."

"Then why the blazes did ye say I fear failure?"

She stopped and whipped around—those spiteful fists jamming into her hips. "Because you have closed your heart—you no longer have allies. How do you expect to win with a score of men? Huh? I tried to give you a tidbit of information, but you are so bull-headed, you'll just bumble on without paying me a bit of mind."

He chopped his hand through the air. "Did I say I wouldna listen? So ye want me to seek out the Bruce even though I dunna trust the man? Is that it?"

"Who *do* you trust, William? Anyone outside of your inner circle?"

She hastened toward him.

"Careful!" He pointed at a rock.

Before she could stop, her toe caught.

William opened his arms.

Squealing, all five foot eleven inches of her fell into his body. Breasts molded to his chest as if she'd been made to fit his form and his alone. His arms closed around her as Eva's breath skimmed his cheek. A fragrance sweeter than a field of wildflowers consumed his mind. God's bones, he'd missed her. Missed holding her in his arms every night—listening to the sound of her voice—sitting beside her in front of the hearth while a storm brewed outside.

But those days of glory were but a passing dream.

And now he felt like a wet-eared lad. They'd been so distant, so awkward, since she'd returned.

Nonetheless, he chanced dipping his head to inhale the heavenly scent of her hair. Only Eva smelled sweeter than a vat of simmering honeyed mead.

"God, I've missed ye," he heard himself say. Fear of failure? Mayhap when it came to *her*. He'd endure a mangled shoulder any day if he never had to suffer losing Eva again.

Her inhale spluttered as she looked up into his eyes, moving her hand to his whiskered cheek. "I—"

Dipping his head, he kissed her. Aye, finally kissed her, like he'd been aching to do for three days.

And God bless it, she kissed him back.

Lord, his mind filled with everything Eva. The soft length of her body flush against his, the scents, the wisps of hair tickling his face, the warmth of her skin. The little sucks of her tongue, plying his just the way he liked it.

Aye, he'd missed her. Needed her every night, needed to be inside her and let her take him to a place of release where every man became a king. Plunging into her mouth, he never wanted to let go. He could lean against the cave walls and kiss her for the rest of eternity, rub his hardness into her body, listen to her sweet sighs of desire.

God had given him a gift when he opened his eyes to see her smile and the lovely glimmer of fathomless green pools. Her gaze reminded him of the rolling hills of his beloved Scotland. With Eva, he was home. With her in his arms, he could achieve anything—fear nothing. If only...

Taking a shaking breath, she pulled away, her eyes shifting. "I can't."

"What?" No, no, William wasn't ready to release her.

When she again met his gaze, he read fear in her eyes. Something wasn't right.

She bit the side of her lip. "I—"

"Is there another man?" Gulping, he forced himself to hold her at arm's length. He'd been so wrapped up in his own problems he hadn't asked her how she'd fared all this time. Hell, she could have married—could have had bairns. His gut squeezed.

But she shook her head. "I've never re-married."

Aye, she'd been wed before they'd first met—she'd been a widow.

She slipped a hand over her mouth and inclined her head toward the cave. "I'd best see to the evening meal."

William nodded dumbly. She *was* afraid. And it didn't take him but a moment to realize why.

***

Eva trembled as she made her way back to the fire pit. God, she'd kissed him. Oh, man, how she'd kissed him. And it had felt so damned good—too good. Heaven help her, she was in trouble. She must never fall into that man again. Yes, he could make her knees turn to wobbly jelly with his blue-eyed stare. His musky scent confused her. She was too weak to resist him when their bodies touched—when he wrapped his powerful arms around her, inclined his lips toward hers with a faint hint of spice on his breath.

No, no, no.

This—*they*—were not going to happen again.

Thank God she'd put on the brakes.

Her lips still tingled from being pressed against his seductive mouth. In a blink, all the memories, the passion, came flooding back. What kind of masochist was she? Why hadn't she dated? Married? Had children? Jeez, she was thirty-five already.

Heaven help her, his rock-hard body made her want him—want to hike up her skirts and let him take her right there against the cave's wall. What kind of whore was she? She'd had her IUD removed five years ago. She hadn't slept with a man since William—hadn't wanted to—hadn't met anyone who stirred her blood like he'd just done with one kiss.

But boy, could he kiss. Delectable swirls of his tongue instantly harmonized with hers as if eight years had never passed. His big hands sliding down her back. The blast of heat from the length of his body pressing against hers. The hard column of flesh teasing her—*God*—just a tiny bit north of where she needed him.

No!

Stepping beside the fire, she clutched her fists beneath her chin and closed her eyes. *Please take me away from here! God, what do you want from me? You know how difficult it is for me to resist him.*

She wandered over to the pallet she'd fashioned to sleep upon since William occupied the alcove. She needed a bath and her computer and a good steak dinner with a baked potato slathered in butter, and broccoli and a salad and a piece of double chocolate cake for dessert. Three days of leathery venison and bland oatcakes was enough to make any modern girl long for home—or lose her mind kissing a condemned seven hundred-year-old Scotsman.

She plopped down on the musty furs. Everything was musty, just as it had been before William had started taking back Scotland's castles. The food had been bland then as well, yet she didn't seem to mind as much. Last time she'd been too excited about the opportunity for a story and mind-blowing adventure.

So, the medallion was in no hurry to send her home? There must be a reason. Perhaps this new quest would yield another book. She hit her head with the heel of her hand. Cripes, Eva had so many speaking engagements to attend before the film debut in late August. Then a gasp caught in her throat. She couldn't miss the red carpet—not for the world.

Reaching into her purse, she pulled out her phone—her calendar was synched with her laptop. Damn, the battery was dead. But then? She grabbed the leather satchel that had been with her things. Whew—her solar charger was still there. She'd upgraded her phone, but…she gave the connector a shove. Cooler yet, the micro fittings hadn't changed. She might be able to snap a photo or two.

She chuckled.

Maybe I'll get caught and the medallion will take me out of here.

"What have ye got there?" William asked from behind.

With a spike of her heartbeat, she shoved the phone into her satchel, then smirked and pulled it out again. "I found my solar charger."

"I beg your pardon?"

"Remember my telephone?"

"Och, the shiny black box." He folded his arms, not coming too close. "Dunna tell me ye still have it."

She held up the phone. "A newer model. Takes even better pictures."

"That's all we need." He sat on the rock across from her. "Just keep it hidden when the lads are about."

"Okay." She frowned. If only the thing were charged now, she'd snap a photo of him. Walter would love it—so would her publisher—though no one aside from Walter really believed she'd traveled through time.

William took the armor piercing sword from amongst her things. "I never did teach ye how to use this."

She smiled—the memory of his face when he'd given it to her was priceless. "It's a whole lot lighter than your two-handed sword."

"Aye, but with a great sword a man doesna have to move too close to his opponent to lop off his head."

She grimaced. "How charming."

His shoulder ticked up. "'Tis the way of war." He twirled her pointy blade in his hand, then set it down. "I'll give ye a lesson on the morrow. It'll keep me from going mad whilst the lads are off on their raid."

Chapter Twenty-One

"Again," William growled as if he were speaking to one of his men.

Eva groaned and lunged, thrusting her little sword forward.

For the umpteenth time, he twisted her wrist and disarmed her.

She stamped her foot and clutched her arm against her waist. "Ouch. That hurts, goddammit."

"Ye must block your mind to the pain. When ye're in the midst of battle, there's no time to think—or feel. Ye must rely on your training."

"Well, I'm not intending to fight anyone."

"If ye remain around me long enough, ye'll need more than a sharp tongue, mark me." He beckoned her with his fingers. "Now come again—aim for the loins, or the throat, the eyes—any place not protected by mail."

Eve crouched and eyed him. She'd had about enough sparring for a lifetime. If he'd showed a modicum of patience at first, she might not feel like stabbing him in the eyeball right now, but he'd done nothing but act like an asshole since they started. She had to be insane for even thinking about lunging in with her sword again. He'd just grab her wrist and twist until the damned thing dropped.

Unless?

She bit her bottom lip.

His fingers twitched as he stood opposite, poised for her next attack.

When she'd played basketball for NYU, the way to the basket was by faking out your opponent. Eyes, foot position, momentum, a turn of the head—body language spoke volumes about the ball-handler's next move.

She stilled her gaze and focused on his feet, imagining a basket behind William's head. With her next breath, Eva faked right, spun backward on her left foot. Raising the blade, her head snapped around and set her sights on his exposed neck. Cold iron hissed through the air.

Time slowed.

Then her heart flew to her throat.

Impact became imminent.

Where was William's block?

Just as the blade met with flesh, he jerked aside. A steely grip clamped around her wrist and twisted—but the pain didn't come. William grunted and grabbed his shoulder.

"Ballocks," he spat.

Eva looked at her hand—Lord, he hadn't disarmed her. "Are you all right?"

"I'm fine." He stood straight with a grimace. "Come again," he barked.

She lowered her arms to her sides. "Your injury hasn't healed enough for this."

He shook his head with vigor. "The only way to recover is to work through the pain."

"Oh no. You might have a tear—and the only way that will heal is rest. You must do nothing that makes it hurt."

"Och, then I may as well be dead, 'cause I canna move without suffering torment from old wounds."

"That's awful."

"'Tis the way of it." He beckoned her with his fingers. "Come, now."

Ignoring him, she slashed her sword diagonally through the air. "So, was I better that time?"

"Ye're learning."

"But all you've had me do is come at you." Her feet danced like a boxer. "What about technique?"

"Ye need to learn how to hold on to your weapon afore I can teach ye more."

She grinned. "Then I *was* better."

"Come again," he growled.

Eva performed the same maneuver again with much the same results. William grabbed his shoulder and winced.

No matter how much he wanted to be healed, he clearly wasn't ready to spar with anyone. Even a novice like her. Eva moved toward the cave. "I've had enough sparring for one day. I'll heat some water for hot compresses."

The big man crossed his arms. "I dunna need your mollycoddling."

"Did I say the compresses were for you?" Turning up her nose, she headed off to find a bucket. William mightn't think he needed her help, but he'd receive it all the same.

***

How she convinced him to remove his shirt, he'd never know. He didn't want to be pitied by anyone. If she'd shown a modicum of interest in him as a man, he'd feel a damned bit happier about his state of undress, but since he'd kissed her, she'd scarcely looked him in the eye.

Hot compresses? Ballocks to that.

She used a pair of tongs to pull a cloth from the simmering water. Then she wrung it out. "Tell me about the pain in your right shoulder—from fighting the lion, was it?"

"Aye." William reached back and rubbed the spot that always needled at him. "The bastard's claws cut me deep. It has never been the same since—weaker. I've had to rely more on my left."

She traced her finger along the deepest scar, pressing fairly. "Does this hurt?"

He winced. "Has your touch grown rougher over the years?"

"Sorry," she said, cringing.

"Can ye fix it?"

"Afraid not." She eased his pain with feather-light swirls of her finger. "I should have studied medicine during my absence."

"Ye mean ye havena?"

"Not as much as I should have." She placed the warm cloth over the sore spot and rubbed—much more gently this time. "So the lion incident happened four years ago?"

"Five." He glanced at her face. "I suppose the scars of battle canna even elude me."

"You're five and thirty—and have been a warrior most of your life." Her hand stilled. "What do you expect?"

Closing his eyes, William rolled his shoulder and reveled in her kneading fingers. "Everyone grows old. Most soldiers dunna make it to thirty. I suppose I'm fortunate."

She picked up the tongs and fished another cloth out of the pot.

"So what of your time?" he asked. "What does a man do when he's past his prime?"

She didn't look up whilst she wrung out the cloth. "Do you consider yourself past your prime, William?"

"At five and thirty? Och, aye—and I've two mangled shoulders to prove as much."

She draped the cloth over his left.

William hissed. The sutures she'd made were itchy and still angry sore. "Ye didna answer my question," he said through clenched teeth.

She busied herself with the tongs again. "To be honest, a man at five and thirty is still in his prime—as is a woman."

What was this future world where people aged so slowly? Were they protected in cocoons of silk? "What say ye? Are there no warriors?"

"There are soldiers who join the army—and they learn combat, but most of the fighting is done…" She glanced aside.

"Pardon?"

"You wouldn't believe me."

He snorted. "The fighting is done by banshees and fairies?"

She threw back her head with a belly laugh. "Now that would be a good name for a video game."

"Jesu, I ken ye've lost your mind." Since she'd returned, she was using even more twists of phase that made not a lick of sense.

"I'm sorry." She slipped a hand over her giggles and shook her head as if trying to stop her laughing hysterics. "I'll try to sum it up—most of the fighting happens in the Holy Land, just as it has for thousands of years, and sometimes men fight face-to-face, but usually not…um…Have you heard of black powder?"

"Aye—heard tale of it when I was in the Holy Roman Empire. 'Tis said it is from the Orient—'tis like fire and brimstone."

"Yes, I couldn't have been more accurate if I had tried to describe it for you. But in the twenty-first century—and well before, men have learned how to make devastating bombs with such concoctions—bombs that can wipe out an entire city like Edinburgh."

"Or London?" he asked.

"Yes—and wars are fought more with bombs. In fact, sword fighting is only a sport."

He studied her face—it twitched not a bit. "Ye're serious?"

"Why would I not be?"

He stared at the fire for a time mulling over all she had said. "In your time, when has a man passed his prime?"

"I don't know—perhaps sixty, I'd say."

"That old? Then how long do people live on average?"

"I should know that off the top of my head, but it's not unusual for a person to live into their eighties, even their nineties. Jeez, people usually don't retire until they're sixty-five."

"Five and sixty?"

"Excuse me, five and sixty." She tapped a rock with her toe. "I'm afraid my Auld Scots has gone a tad rusty over the years."

William watched the firelight dance across her red tresses. He liked that she'd grown her hair long during her absence. The locks hung in thick waves all the way down to her waist. He flicked a curl with his finger. "I'm glad ye didna cut your hair."

She clasped her hand around the tresses at her nape and drew the length to her opposite shoulder. "I should replace your compresses."

She'd been with him for days and had only grown more and more distant. He grabbed her wrist. "What's ailing ye, Eva?"

She looked his way with a hitch to her breath. He recognized the fear in those green eyes. But something inside William's gut told him not to push her. "Ye're not used to living around so much death—never have been."

She shook her head.

"'Tis good to ken people of your time live long lives." He gripped his fingers a tad tighter. It was as if she were building an invisible wall between them. Was their precious time together fleeting? Most likely—just as it had been before. What could he say to tell her it would be all right? What could he say to convince her to leap over that wall and love him for the now? That's what they'd always agreed. "Perhaps all the sacrifices made by men in my time help the lives of their descendants?"

This time she nodded. "Every era brings more advancement."

"I am pleased to ken it."

They sat in silence while the fire crackled, sending swirls of wood smoke through the air. So many times he'd wanted to hold Eva in his arms—her memory saw him through the depths of melancholy whilst he berated himself for the deaths of his men at Falkirk—it seemed so long ago he'd heard her soothing words on the wind and knew she loved him as deeply as he loved her. That same love gave him strength to endure a year in the bowels of King Philip's dungeon after the French king refused William's request to send troops to defend Scotland.

Even though her voice had stopped coming to him.

And now that she sat beside him, it seemed they were still separated by different worlds. "What happed to live for the now?" he finally asked. "Ye ken things in my world are brutal and the devil follows me like a shadow."

"I—" She turned green like she might heave up bile.

"Dunna try to tell me it willna happen. In your time, perhaps a warrior can live a long life, but I ken my days are numbered."

She looked up abruptly. "How do you know?"

Something squeezed in his gut—his hunch just might be right. "What good am I if I canna wield my sword—fight for the weak and oppressed?"

"As I recall, you wanted to become priest—why not seek a life behind the walls of an abbey?"

"Do ye think Longshanks will sit idle whilst I take my vows?" William tossed another stick of wood on the fire. "Nay. I carved my path years ago."

With a heavy sigh, she reached for a long stick and poked the flames—he'd never known the lass to be so short of words. That something troubled her was an absolute certainty.

William intended to find out—and make it right. Surely she didn't come all the way from the future to pay him no mind. "What happened to ye—all that time away?"

"Not much." Her shoulder ticked up. "After I realized the medallion would no longer work for me, I wrote a book, won a few awards, and then set to restoring the Torwood Castle ruins."

"Torwood is a ruin?" He'd never forget having taken refuge there—it was the last time he'd felt Eva—spoken to her in his dreams—the most devastating eve of his life. "Writing a book and building a castle. And ye won awards? Those are not simple feats."

"No. I kept myself busy...so..."

"So?"

"So I wouldn't think of you," her voice ebbed to a whisper.

He lightly brushed her shoulder. "Ye didna stop thinking of me?" The hair on his arms stood on end.

She shook her head.

He leaned near enough to inhale the intoxicating fragrance that could only be Eva. "And now, why are ye fighting to suppress your feelings for me?"

She drew away slightly, but he heard her wee gasp. "Did I say I was fighting?"

His little finger brushed the tip of hers. "Ye didna need to say it, lass."

She looked at him with fear in her eyes. He'd seen that look before—every time she regarded Andrew Murray before he died. He knew it.

"I can't," she said.

William traced his finger along the curve of her slender neck, studying the blue vein thrumming with life beneath her skin. "Ye mean ye willna."

CHAPTER TWENTY-TWO

Too bottled up with her warring emotions, Eva was almost glad to see John Blair's face—until he opened his mouth. "The English are hot on our trail. I hope ye're fighting fit, Willy, 'cause we must make haste."

William sprang to his feet. "How much time do we have?"

"Not long—an hour at best."

Eva grabbed her "medieval-looking" satchel and stuffed in her first aid kit and purse. Her modern clothing wouldn't fit. She clutched her stilettoes against her chest.

William peered over her shoulder. "Ye should toss those stilts on the fire."

She'd paid five hundred pounds for that pair of shoes. God knew it wasn't easy to find classy size elevens.

Robbie rolled up his gear in his pile of skins. *Of course.* Quickly, she did the same, saving her shoes and medieval clothes in the roll.

It took no time for the men to pack up their belongings and tie them to their saddles. The only problem? Eva didn't have a horse.

William patted his saddle. "I ken it will annoy ye to ride double with me, but it doesna appear ye have another option." He reached for her gear and used a leather thong to secure it atop his.

Riding double? How much more torture can I take? She stepped up to his big warhorse. "You'll give me a leg up?"

He bent down and cupped his hands. "Ye remember how to ride?"

She put her foot in his makeshift cradle and hoisted herself into the saddle. "If it's anything like a bike, I should be fine."

"A what?"

"Never mind."

Eva hoped she'd be fine—hoped she could block her annoying pangs of desire until William sidled behind her and took up the reins. His brawny arms surrounded her in a protective cocoon. The allure of raw, spicy male swam over her—the only male who'd claimed her heart since Steven's death. Yes, she'd been young and in love with her first husband, but that love amounted to little in comparison to the love she harbored for William.

No matter how hard she tried to push him away, his soul called to her. His crystal blue-eyed stare, his alluring deep burr, his ruggedness. Licking her lips, she glanced down at the forearms in repose on her thighs, the big hands holding the reins. Peppered with dark hair, pink scars slashed in random directions and rose in contrast to lightly tanned skin.

Eva's lips parted as her mouth grew dry. She knew exactly how gentle or brutal those hands could be. Indeed, she'd never experienced a gentler touch in the bedchamber—a more capable or caring lover.

She slowly traced her finger along a scar between his thumb and pointer finger. "How did you get this?"

"Och, ye expect me to remember every time I have a wee cut?" the deep rumble of his voice vibrated against her back.

She tapped the pink flesh. "This one's deeper than the others—I suspect it caused you a great deal of pain."

His hips shifted behind her. "It did." His voice sounded gruff. *He did remember.*

"Oh," she whispered.

"Falkirk."

Goosebumps sprang up across her skin.

He needn't say more. The Battle of Falkirk was the worst loss in Scotland's entire history as far as Eva was concerned. And William was the man deemed responsible, though several nobles had accepted bribes to change sides in an attempt to ruin him.

"Ye may as well sit back, lass," he whispered in her ear. "We'll be riding all day."

Eva glanced over her shoulder and regarded his face. Lord, she shouldn't have done that. The man was riding for his life and he could still smile like he hadn't a care in the world? Could grin and mask all the pain coursing beneath his skin? How did he do it day in and day out, without a Fiji vacation?

"If ye keep looking at me like that, I'll have no recourse but to take a quick detour into a quiet glen."

"With Comyn's men on your heels?"

One dark eyebrow arched. "Well, it would have been a bit more convenient if ye'd have joined me in the alcove." Then he raked his sexy gaze down her body. "Ye ken ye were meant to be with me. Ye may as well stop fighting that which is in your heart."

She crossed her arms and sat ramrod straight. Jeez, he could be maddening. Worse? He was right. How much longer could she resist when every time their gazes met, her stomach somersaulted a dozen times? What of the now? Before, she'd convinced herself that all that mattered was the now—until she'd endured eight years of loss. And now she had no illusions. She would lose—if she didn't die first.

Then her stomach squelched. *Will the medallion ever send me home?*

It had to.

She needed to stop worrying.

With an exhale, she relaxed against his chest. God, how a man could be so incredibly warm in this chilly weather, Eva would never know. Dammit, she was a woman for Christ's sakes. She lived like a nun for eight years. Mourned the loss of this man for all of them. And now…

She couldn't think about it.

She glanced over to Robbie. The lad had a determined scowl on his face. Gone was the carefree boy who had often made her laugh—who had taught her how to ride a horse—who she'd comforted in her arms when he mourned the loss of his friend. Riding with him would no longer be an option.

***

She caught a glimpse of a big monolith in the distance. "Are we heading toward Loudoun Hill?"

"Aye."

Eva had been there before in medieval times and modern. Presently, the terrain was so different—far more forested. Traveling through Scotland was rough with few roads cutting through thick scrub, and the pass that ran past Loudoun Hill was not only treacherous, she herself had witnessed William stage an ambush there.

"What if the English are lying in wait?" she asked.

"I've sent Eddy ahead to scout." He ran the reins through his fingers. "And I'm praying the bastards behind us dunna ken I trapped Heselrig there."

"I remember."

"Ye were a feisty wench."

"Were?"

"Well, I reckon ye've mellowed a bit," his deep burr rolled across his tongue, hypnotizing her. "I ken I have."

Heat spread across her face while her fingers smoothed up and down his arm. Had she wanted to do that or had her fingers grown a mind of their own? Worse? She could swear he sighed with a long exhale.

She could ride with him forever on the one side. On the other, she hoped they'd find her a horse soon.

It was late afternoon by the time they rode to the crest of the hill. The best vantage point for miles, Eva turned her face away, pretending she hadn't looked. Being in the fourteenth century hadn't been too scary until she saw movement in the distance—an entire retinue moving toward them like a dragon with iron fangs.

She leaned forward in the saddle. "Can't we just make a run for it?"

"To where?" William asked with an edge of sarcasm in his vice. "Sooner or later we'll have to make a stand and the hill gives us the best ground advantage in the shire."

"But you're in no condition to fight."

He snorted with a sarcastic smirk. "Och, believe me, when the enemy attempts to run a man through, he can no longer feel pain. The only thing that matters is staying alive. The pain comes later."

She squinted, looking at the riders in the distance. "How long until they arrive?"

"Afore dark for certain." He dismounted, then turned and reached for her. "I want ye to hide up here."

Lord, her legs nearly crumpled when her feet touched ground. Taking a few bow-legged steps, it was all she could do not to rub her inner thighs and make a spectacle in front of the men.

William sniggered behind her. "Ye're not used to riding, are ye?"

"Not anymore." She pushed her palm into the small of her back and stretched. "I prefer driving. It would have taken an hour." *With paved roads and a car.*

"Wheesht." William grasped her arm and led her out of earshot of the others. "'Tis well enough ye talk about your time when we're alone, but I dunna care to hear it around the men—'twill only bring trouble, and not for me."

She glanced back to John Blair who wielded a whetstone, honing the razor-sharp blade of his great sword. Yes, it was careless of her to be so brash. Father Blair was the type who might just enjoy putting a rope around her neck—ever so Christian of him.

Rubbing the outside of her arms, she nodded her agreement. "You want me to stay up here?"

"Aye."

"While you set an ambush down below?"

"Well, ye havena exactly mastered the art of swordplay."

She smoothed her palm over the pommel of the little sword in her belt, doubting she'd ever be a master at wielding a weapon with a blade. But more than anything, she worried about William. She'd seen his weakness back at the cave. "And you're about as fit to fight as I am. Why can't you stay up here with me?"

"And let my men fight my battles?" He grasped her shoulders with his two enormous hands and focused on her eyes. Lord, she'd agree to anything when he looked at her with that kind of intensity. "Dunna ask me again."

"Then promise me ye'll be careful."

"I'll gladly do that." A hand move to her nape, a finger tickling the side of her neck. "Ye ken why?" he asked with a devilish grin.

"No." Her tongue grew dry.

His gaze dipped to her mouth. "'Cause ye still love me, lass." With one step in, his chest lightly brushed the tips of her breasts as he lowered his lips to hers. She caught a drift of his scent, part leather, part iron, part musk and entirely intoxicating male. With a rush of heat between her legs, Eva could no sooner resist him than to say no to warm double-chocolate-fudge-melting lava cake. The deep rumble of his sigh made tingles spread through the tips of her fingers as he deepened the pressure with soft, demanding lips.

Closing her eyes, Eva moved her hands around his waist and sank her fingertips into thick bands of muscle. She leaned into him, giving in to her pent up desire to experience the ecstasy of his length pressed solidly against her, fully aware they could take it no further. One delicious, naughty kiss she could allow herself while the men gathered just beyond the tree.

But no more.

Yes, she did love him. She always had and always would. Forever she would treasure this man in her heart and keep him locked away deep inside. That's where her feelings belonged—sealed inside an impenetrable barrier in her heart.

CHAPTER TWENTY-THREE

Left alone at the top of Loudoun Hill, Eva wasn't about to sit idle. Rain drizzled while she hurried to collect boulders and line them at the cliff's edge. Lord, her stomach squelched. It didn't look so high from below, but now she tottered at the precipice. One wrong slip and she'd plummet to her death.

The drive to help steeled her nerves. There was nothing worse than feeling helpless while the enemy advanced. Who would be injured this time? She cringed. Who would die?

She stopped for a moment and rubbed the medallion beneath her kirtle. "Why haven't you sent me back?" Damn, what else could she try to invoke the powers that be? Why was her presence needed? William had obviously recovered enough. Her stash of penicillin was half gone.

Every time he touched her, he chipped away a bit more of her resolve. Seeing him, touching him, inhaling his provocative scent—every sensory detail drove her to the ragged edge.

The dull thunder of horse hoofs carried on the wind.

Eva's heartbeat spiked as she peered up to see the English heading straight toward William and his men, crouched in the ravine below, weapons at the ready. Across the glen, Robbie and a handful of archers sat their horses, bows loaded, waiting to fire.

Everything grew quiet.

A chilly breeze flicked her hair. Eva crouched down so not to be seen.

Her heart beat faster.

The enemy rode past William and his men, none the wiser.

Nearly to the hill, she placed her palms atop a boulder.

Her breath rushed in her ears as she waited.

William would sound the attack with a blast of his ram's horn.

Wouldn't he?

But the enemy soldiers were so close—she could do some damage for sure.

She leaned out further to glimpse the invading troops, all wearing orange surcoats atop their hauberks.

The rock in her hands slid forward on the slick mud and slipped from her grasp.

The first hit ricocheted off the cliff like a blast from a cannon. By the second boom, men bellowed and arrows hissed through the air.

When the rock crashed into the helm of an enemy soldier, William and his men were already upon them, swords clanging, embroiled in a bloody fight.

Five English were down, clutching arrows.

Robbie and his men thundered ahead, blocking the pass.

Eva clutched another rock, searching for her chance to let it fall.

An English soldier broke away.

Closing her eyes, she hurled the rock.

It thudded behind the man's retreating horse.

Thank God. What am I doing? But Eva knew the answer. She couldn't see William or any of his men hurt.

She picked up another boulder and cursed. "Damn them to hell."

She stood at the ready, waiting for an opening, and vowed not to hit a patriot.

"Too right. Wallace has resorted to using women to fight his battles?" The sound of a hostile male voice slithered up her spine like a snake.

Trapped at the edge of the cliff she turned and faced the mounted man—the same blackguard she thought had fled.

She let the boulder drop. *Now would be a good time to time travel home.*

The cur dismounted.

Fuck.

Sidestepping, Eva purchased enough room to keep from falling to her death.

He reached for his sword.

She drew hers, hands shaking like palsied limbs.

As he sauntered forward, she assessed his armor. A sleeveless coat of mail, helm, neck bare—loins covered only by a linen surcoat and woolen chausses. "Ye think ye can take on the likes of me with that wee blade?"

She gaped at his pock-ridden face.

Basketball.

She faked right.

He lunged.

She spun left.

The little sword hissed.

Snapping her head around, Eva eyed his neck sinews.

With a clang reverberating from her wrist clear up her neck, the tyrant deflected the blow.

Heart flying to her throat, Eva backed, teetering on the edge of the precipice. Out of the corner of her eye, the deadly crags glistened with moisture as if daring her to misstep. Her sword slipped in her sweating palm.

"I'll carve out your liver and eat it raw," he growled, lunging with a thrust.

Shrieking, she dove aside. The blade caught her sleeve, slicing it open.

Her hip hit hard.

"Get me out of here!" she screamed.

The man lunged. "I'll send ye to Hades!"

Angling her sword up, Eva cringed.

This is the end.

Midair, the bastard's face changed from one of aggression to stunned. His jaw dropped. His eyes bulged. The weapon dropped from his grasp.

He tumbled from the cliff, howling until his body thudded on the sharp rocks below.

Gasping, Eva looked up.

"I thought I told ye to hide." William shoved his sword into his scabbard and offered his hand.

"I—I wanted to help."

"Bloody near gave us away." When he tugged her up, he jerked forward with a grunt.

Eva's gaze snapped to his flank. "You're injured."

He pulled his hand away from his side. Red blood glistened on his fingers. "Just a flesh wound."

"Oh Lord, please don't tell me I'm the cause of that."

"Nay," he muttered. "Come, we must haste."

Eva stole a glance down the hill. "Did we win?"

"For the now." He bent down to give her a leg up. "But it willna be long afore another mob is hunting us down."

She ignored his hands, putting her foot in the stirrup and hoisting herself up. "I need to dress your wound. Take me someplace safe."

Mounting with a strained groan, he picked up the reins. "I'll come good in a day or two."

"I've heard that before and I'm not buying it." She glanced back. "I mean it—someplace safe."

They headed west toward the setting sun.

Eva expected to hear horses following, but when she turned they were alone. "Where are the others?"

"Split up—'tis the only way to ensure we're not followed."

***

William hated it when he was wrong, but he kent he shouldn't have been fighting, even before Eva had told him not to. Good God, his limbs hung like sacks of fatty mutton. His stomach growled. Hell, he even shivered against the cold. So they'd stopped another mob of bloodthirsty soldiers? They'd only be replaced by more.

He should drop Eva at the nearest village and tell her to go. She had no business staying with him. No wonder she'd been keeping her distance. It seemed like the whole world was hunting him and every time he took up the sword, more followed. "Blair said Longshanks has offered a thousand Ayrshire acres and a purse of gold to anyone who turns me in, dead or alive."

"Lord," Eva whispered. "Why not sail for the Orkneys? They're still under Norse rule. I doubt Longshanks would find you there."

"Och aye, that sounds like a coward's dream. I've never run from my enemies and I'm not abou- to start." His words began to slur.

"I didn't mean it that way." Eva straightened her back against his urge to slump. "We could rebuild your army up there. Like Andrew did in Ross Shire before you conquered Stirling."

The path ahead suddenly spinning, William blinked to clear his vision. He wanted to hold on to that thought—give it some real consideration. Mayhap a year away and he could recruit enough men from Ross to join him? He shook his foggy head. *I'm going daft.*

Eva tapped his ribs with her elbow. "Lady Christina could help spread the word—send Highlanders to join us." Then she turned and gave him an endearing grin. "It would give you time to heal."

"Too right, give all my men a reprieve…If only…" He swayed in the saddle. "Be li…ol' times."

"William?"

He hunched forward trying not to lean on her.

"Are you all right?"

Chapter Twenty~Four

Dammit, why did things always have to go from bad to worse? The rain drove sideways, spitting in her face while Eva clutched William's arms around her waist with one hand and took charge of the reins with the other. Even wearing a fur-lined mantle, she was miserably cold, soaked through and totally lost.

Get a freaking grip.

She knew this area—had not only been a part of an archaeological dig at Loudoun Hill, she had ridden through Ayrshire with William, albeit eight years ago. The burn that ran past the hill flowed into the River Irvine, which meant Kilmarnock was due west.

Though the villagers had welcomed William with open arms last time, she had no idea who would welcome them and who would turn them in. She couldn't risk taking him to a town—or even a farm.

Lord help.

Bowing her head against the deluge, she led the horse to the burn and urged him onward. With few roads and overgrown scrub, the going was rough.

Hooves sloshed through the burn and mud, the muck making every step an effort. Branches slapped her face and the westward wind drove the rain into her eyes, making the visibility impossible. On each side of the gully, mud oozed down the embankment making the horse stumble. The water in the burn rushed faster, roaring louder than the icy wind. Without gloves, Eva couldn't feel her fingers—couldn't move them either.

When they passed beneath the cover of an enormous sycamore, Eva pulled the warhorse to a stop. At least the tree provided some shelter and the rain only slapped them with sloppy droplets. But the wind cut through to the bone. Neither one of them would survive the night without shelter.

Riding in the gully, they were out of sight, but that made it impossible to see—to find her bearings. She had to take a chance. Ahead, a game trail led from the water with a decent coverage of trees above.

Squinting, grey stones peeked through green vines and moss.

A wall?

Gently tapping her heels, she urged the horse to move toward the structure. With William's torso leaning on her with dead weight, Eva didn't dare dismount—but she couldn't support him much longer. Nearing, a perpendicular wall came into view—and a partial roof, completely overgrown by foliage. Goodness, it was an abandoned shieling—and the roof hadn't caved in on the far end.

Perhaps Eva's luck hadn't completely run its course.

The horse crept forward, taking a bite of green foliage while tugging his head to the side. Eva gave him tap. "Hey, big fella, you can eat your fill once we're under cover."

They picked their way to the entrance of the ruin.

"Hello?" she called peering into the darkness.

Sudden rustling came from within.

Eva clamped her fist around the reins, her eyes nearly popping out of her head.

The horse stutter-stepped as five deer barreled toward them.

Eva shrieked.

The horse reared.

Dropping the reins, she clutched William's arms tighter around her stomach.

Mistake.

Together they careened backward, landing with a thud.

Eva blinked, rain filling her eyes. William's chest rose beneath her. His damned horse skittered about six feet to a patch of grass. "I hope it was worth it, you mongrel beast."

Sliding off the poor unconscious man, Eva looked longingly at the shelter. A few more paces and she would have easily been able to slide William off the horse under cover.

The man was a behemoth. Hefting up his shoulders, Eva tugged. Jeez, William didn't even budge.

She stood, planted her fists on her hips, and regarded the horse. "Are you happy...you miserable, lazy lump of lard?" A total non-horse person, Eva opted to clear away the debris and rolled William until he was under cover. Dirt and mud smudged across his face and plastered his entire body.

She couldn't worry about that now. They still could die of exposure. Working urgently, she ran to the horse and used a length of rope to hobble his two front legs—thank God she remembered how. After untying the rolls from the back of the saddle, she raced back under cover.

Lord, the wind and rain cut to the bone. Droplets streamed from her hair and down her face as she regarded the giant gelding. Damn. She had to venture out one more time to pull the saddle, bridle and blanket off the beast.

Once certain the horse was set, she found a bit of old timber and straw at the back of the lean-to, then fished the flint out of the leather purse William carried on his belt—the same one she'd given him in Renfrew.

I can do this.

She'd seen William, Robbie and a host of others start fires countless times. She found enough dried tow—plant fibers that would burn. She made two balls and placed one in the center of her makeshift fire pit, then made a nest out of the other and set it aside. Stacking dry twigs around the tow on the ground, until she had a three-quarter teepee like circle, she drew her eating knife from her sleeve and scraped the flint into the nest until a white dusting of powder covered the bottom.

So far so good.

Turning the flint over in her hand, she struck the serrated end into the powder until it sparked.

Holding her breath, she waited while a tiny flame licked up.

Yea!

Carefully, she pushed the nest under the a-frame she'd built and prayed while smoke billowed around her.

Come on.

Bending her head down, she gave the base a wee blow.

The fire crackled.

Grasping more twigs, she carefully piled them around the growing flame.

I am not helpless. Girls Scouts, here I come.

Well, maybe Eva was too old to be a Scout, but this wee boon of accomplishment certainly helped to bolster her confidence, especially after a disastrous day.

But there was still much to do. Their clothing was soaked clean through. She untied the oiled leather around William's bedroll. At least the plaid inside was dry. She draped it over him.

Removing her cloak and kirtle, she hung them over the only remaining rafter. Working in her shift, she found a handful of bully beef and oatcakes in William's kit. It wouldn't last long but if she rationed it, the food might see her through till he regained consciousness.

The fire was a help, but without a door, and a gaping hole in half the roof, the cold still had Eva's teeth chattering and her nose running. She glanced down. William's teeth chattered too. Those wet clothes had to go before he caught pneumonia.

Tugging off his hauberk took every shred of strength she could muster. William wasn't only the size of an ox, his mail had to weigh eighty pounds. Grunting, she pulled and pulled until she had it halfway over his head. Bending over, she sucked in a few deep breaths. Then she crouched, gritted her teeth and finally yanked the heavy thing all the way off. Her fingers trembled as she removed his shoes, hose, chausses, quilted jerkin and shirt.

"Ssss." She examined the gash at his side. The bleeding had ebbed, but from the broken skin and purple bruise spreading across his entire flank, he'd received a good whack—probably would have killed him if he hadn't been wearing his mail. Eva regarded her dirty hands and looked outside. If anything, the rain pelted harder as night turned the forest darker than soot. She wasn't about to pick her way to the burn to wash.

Instead, she gave them a good rub with a dollop of alcohol soap from her bag. Once clean, she pulled the tube of antibiotic ointment from her first aid kit. Using the tube to spread it over the wound, she applied a gauze bandage and stuck it in place with two Band Aids.

She worked quickly to hang his clothing beside hers and then stoked the fire. The last thing she draped over the rafter was her wet shift. Wearing only her panties and bra, she slipped under the blanket and lay beside William, draping an arm and leg across him.

Briskly rubbing his arms, she chuckled. "Don't get the wrong idea here, big fella."

But honestly, she could think of no other way to stave off hypothermia. As she warmed his body, his also helped her shivers to subside.

Not a suite at the Balmoral Hotel in Edinburgh, but her work would see them through the night. Nothing to make a girl tired like a brush with death and hours on the back of a horse fleeing for her life while her savior flopped unconsciously behind her.

About to drop, Eva needed to sleep.

But how could that happen when she was lying on top of the man she wanted with her very soul with only her panties and his braies separating them?

He'll be okay.

She rested her head on his chest.

And I think he warmed to the idea of going to Orkney.

Her fingers slipped up and caressed the nape of his neck, sliding into thick tresses—so incredibly soft.

Is it possible to break the only rule and change the future?

She brushed his cheek with her lips.

I damn well aim to try.

***

Something weighed on William's chest, something soft with a stirring fragrance. He moved his head, his nose lightly brushing silken tresses.

Eva.

With an arch of his brow, he opened one eye. "Mm." He smoothed his fingertips over a bare shoulder. Then he peeked under the blanket. Holy Moses, she was all but naked, wearing nothing but her newfangled undergarments. Come to think of it, he was stripped down to his braies.

Did we?

Nay. I wouldna slept through that, even if I was half dead.

Inhaling, he peered around them. Where were they? Wherever it was, their clothes hung from the rafter and beyond that, daylight shone through a gap. Beside them, warm coals glowed. The last thing he remembered, they were riding west.

How did Eva manage to get me off my horse—moreover, remove my hauberk and clothes?

He grinned. *That would have been a sight not to miss.*

But he finally had the woman of his dreams sleeping in his arms. He rubbed his hands down her back.

"Mm," she purred, moving against him.

Good God, his cock instantly sprang to life—shot up like a mast catching the wind. Bless it, her allure had driven him mad for the past sennight. Did she have any idea how utterly ravishing she appeared to a battle-weary warrior? Every night for the past eight years, he'd thought about how heavenly it would be to lose himself in her arms, melting into her feminine core. If only for a moment, sail with her to heaven and take his mind away from the world that had become his hell.

With a low sigh, she rocked her hips ever so slightly.

William's heart nearly stopped. God save him, her every little move practically brought him undone. Hell, if he'd been standing, he'd be on his knees by now. He slid his hands down and cupped her buttocks—Jesu, his fingers sank into unbelievably supple flesh. "Eva," he whispered as quietly as he could.

Those delectable hips swirled in an even more provocative arc. "Mm."

He slipped his finger under the leg opening of those wee braies she called panties. Pillow soft skin met his rough pads. William's breathing became shallow as he smoothed along the curve of her bottom until he met her core—hot, wet, molten. God's teeth, she was ready for him. If he pulled the slip of fabric away, he could be inside her in the blink of an eye.

He slipped his free hand between their bodies and released the cord tying his braies.

Again she moaned and rocked her hips while he worked his finger, tantalizing the wee button he knew would drive her to the precipice of oblivion.

With an easy lift of his hips, his bare cock slipped between her legs. Heaven help him, he was too close to resist her.

Closing his eyes he kissed her forehead. "Eva?"

"Mm."

"I want ye."

A pair of sleepy green eyes turned up to him—not dull green, but vivid, like spring leaves.

William parted his lips as her mouth covered his. Lord save him, Eva's entire body turned wicked, writhing, groping. Her mouth sucking, dictating a frenzied pace as she lifted her hips and let him tug off those damnable panties.

Ah yes, she slid her moist center up and down his cock until it caught at her entrance. All the while her mouth explored his with the fervor of a skilled seductress—the wanton woman who'd oft brought him pleasure in the bedchamber had finally returned.

With a wee chuckle that rolled through his chest, she took him inside. Gasping, William dug his fingers into her hips and slowed the pace. "I'll spill if we go too fast."

She said nothing, but watched his eyes as she worked him with languid strokes, her lips red and swollen from kissing.

"I love ye, *mon amour.*"

A gasp caught in the back of her throat as she grinned and sped the rocking of her hips.

He didn't need to ask. She was close to her peak—as close as he.

Thank the stars, 'cause he'd not last but a few more strokes.

Her breathing came faster.

A cry caught in his throat.

As she arched up, William took her breast into his mouth as his seed burst forth in concert with her shuddering flesh.

Taking in deep gasps, Eva held herself above him. "Did I hurt you?" she asked breathlessly.

William couldn't help but laugh, and by God, it felt good to do so. "Och, lassie, ye couldna hurt me if ye tried."

"Oh?" She cringed. "You might be a bit stiff when you try to sit up. Aside from the gash on your side, your horse spooked when a herd of deer darted out of here last night."

"Truth? The big fella spooked?"

"Yes." She nodded. Good Lord, she was too damned beautiful. "And while you fell on your back I crashed on top of you—could hardly believe you survived an Eva 'dive bomb'."

He laughed out loud. Mother Mary, it felt good. "Och, ye make me smile on the inside." How could he ache with his woman in his arms? *Finally*. Still, William moved his shoulders. Aye, he was sore, but he'd been hurting for years. What were a few more aches and pains to add to it?

Her face grew suddenly serious as she cupped his cheek in her palm. "Oh how I love you, William." The angel had spoken.

He closed his eyes and let her words seep into his soul.

CHAPTER TWENTY-FIVE

It was amazing how rekindling their love affair had a way of shedding all of Eva's anxiety. Eight years ago she'd been able to compartmentalize her fears and focus on the now. Thank God she'd rediscovered how to do that. If she'd known all she had to do was love him the way she'd done before, the way she'd longed to do ever since returning, she might have given in—gone with it rather than letting her mind run the gamut.

This had to be the most glorious week of her life. Spent alone with William, the dirt and cold hardly bothered her. And a week away from his men with nothing on his mind except snaring a rabbit here and there eased his troubles like nothing else. His tension calmed further when she massaged his shoulders and more so when they made glorious love.

If only they could hide there forever.

But Eva didn't compartmentalize her thoughts so much to be a fool.

William came in from saddling the horse. "'Tis time to ride to Fail."

"The monastery?" she asked.

"Aye. I'll leave a message with the abbot for my men—tell them were to find us."

Us—she liked that he included her. "And where will that be?"

"I've decided to have a word with Lord Bruce—as ye suggested."

"So, after Fail we're heading to Galloway?"

"Torwood."

Her spine straightened. "Why Torwood?" Oh, how exciting. She'd be able to see the castle as it was when the first tower was built.

"Sir Alasdair is an ally for one—it will be neutral ground for our meeting. Not to mention, he commands a fleet of galleys."

She rolled her hand through the air. "Aaand you're then planning on sailing somewhere after you talk to the Earl of Carrick?"

"Not certain yet." His shoulders hunched. "Your Orkney idea has merit."

Oh yes, yes, yes, if only it could be true. And Eva's heart filled with too much excitement for it not to be. "It is colder up there."

"Aye. 'Twill turn a man into a warrior. Besides, we're heading into spring."

She cringed. Time could stop marching ahead right now as far as she was concerned.

But march ahead they must.

The trip to Fail took far longer than she expected because they couldn't ride on the main roads—which were more like tracks with two ruts carved by wagon wheels. The byways were not much more than game trails, winding their way through, up, and around Ayrshire's rolling hills, which were a great deal more forested in medieval times than modern.

At the monastery, William made quick work dispatching his missive for Robert Bruce and leaving word for his men. The abbot had said John Blair stopped by two days past and left word he'd return soon.

They then headed north to Torwood. The going was slow at best, but Eva didn't mind. Riding double with William, the warmth of his body protecting her back felt heavenly. She hardly noticed the ache in her thighs from hours in an unaccustomed saddle.

After a cold night camping in a cave, it was a foggy morning when they approached the big castle. Good Lord, she expected it to be different but not this much so. Yes, the ruins she'd helped to restore had dated back to the fifteenth century, but the original fortification had been constructed in the twelfth. Made of stone, the donjon rose above the barmkin wall. She'd misjudged the height of the curtain wall—it had to be closer to fifty feet than thirty. The foreground of the fortress buzzed with activity. The clang of the blacksmith's shack rang above lowing cattle, crowing roosters and a bevy of merchants selling their wares under flapping canvas tents.

William slipped his hood low over his forehead and crouched above Eva, enveloping her in his arms. "Hunch down so we dunna look so large."

Neither one of them was small—or even average. She tried to play along, but trying to shrink could make them even more conspicuous to anyone who might really be looking.

"I thought Forrester was an ally?" she asked. Regarding his dark stare beneath the wool made her flinch. The man could appear as menacing as the devil when he wanted.

A guard stopped them at the gate. William pulled the medal of the Guardian from beneath his surcoat. The guard glanced up with a stunned expression. "Ye've business with Lord Forrester Sir Wal—?"

"Indeed," William cut him off. "And speak of this to no one."

The guard looked both ways, then leaned in. "Will there be another rising? 'Cause if there is, I'll take up my sword beside ye, sir."

"'Tis what I like to hear. I could use ten thousand men like ye, soldier."

"Scotland until Judgement," the guard growled under his breath.

"Can ye spirit us inside?" asked William.

"Och aye." The man latched on to their horse's bridle. "Come."

He led them beneath the iron spikes of the portcullis and after tying William's mount, they hastened into the great hall.

"I'll tell his lordship ye have arrived."

William bowed. "My thanks."

Turning to Eva, he gestured to a bench, but she walked into the middle of the hall, taking in every inch. The exposed beams supporting the ceiling were very similar to those that had been restored. But so much was different. Fine tapestries lined the walls depicting pastoral scenes of men and women tilling the fields with horses and oxen. She passed her fingers over the top of a table, roughhewn, made of solid, thick wood.

All the tables and benches were well worn—used by the soldiers and common folk who supported his lordship, no doubt.

"Is it much like the castle ye worked to restore?" William asked from behind.

"Similar," she whispered in awe.

Eva looked to the dais—where she'd received an award only a few weeks ago. She'd got the placement right but this dais was so much more authentic. Who knew how many renovations had taken place in seven hundred years? High-backed chairs surrounded the oblong table, covered with a burgundy damask woven with gold thread. Along the far end, a sideboard displayed ornate silver goblets and plates—a testament to his lordship's wealth.

The guard returned with a woman dressed in servant's garb—a blue gown and white linen apron. She stared at William with wide eyes as the soldier gestured toward the stairwell. "Sir Forrester is waiting in his solar. Tara will show the lady—um…"

"Eva."

The guard cleared his throat. "Lady Eva to her chamber."

Eva's knees could have given out. After sleeping in a cave or a decaying shieling since her arrival, a chamber sounded like pure luxury.

William grasped her shoulder. "I shall see ye anon."

She curtseyed, then looked to Tara. "Thank you so much."

The lass regarded her, arching her eyebrows. "Where do ye hail from? I dunna recall hearing a burr such as yours afore."

Eva almost laughed. Goodness, she'd need to be more careful now they were surrounded by strangers. "My father took me on a pilgrimage to the Holy Land."

"Oh my heavens." The chambermaid patted her chest, then led Eva to the stairwell. "Is that where ye met Sir William?"

Eva loved that he'd been knighted. It made absolutely no difference when they were alone together, but when around others, the title commanded the respect he deserved. "No." She gave the lass a wink. "'Twas even more romantic than that."

"Ahhh," Tara sighed. "Ye dunna say? Would ye mind telling a simple lass your tale?"

"Tell you what. If you'll arrange a bath for me, I'll relay every last detail." Auld Scots rolled off Eva's tongue while she followed Tara up the winding stairs, chuckling all the way. She'd never forget how William rescued her from a battle with the English at Fail Monastery.

They exited on the fifth landing. A sense of recognition prickled the back of Eva's neck as they walked through the narrow passageway. When Tara opened the door and gestured inside, Eva snapped a hand over her mouth.

It was *her* chamber—the bed with a red canopy—the round table with two chairs—the hearth—the narrow window. The likeness was eerily similar—too familiar. Would she time travel soon?

Oddly, she didn't want to go right now.

"Is something amiss, m'lady?"

"Ah, no, nothing at all," Eva said, stepping inside.

"Is there anything I can fetch for ye?"

"Just the bath." Eva looked down at her dirt encrusted kirtle. "You wouldn't suppose there'd be a spare dressing gown about?"

The lass curtseyed. "I'm certain her ladyship will have something to suit. 'Tisn't often we have visitors as important as ye and Sir William, m'lady."

Eva dipped her head respectfully and held her breath until the door closed behind the chambermaid. As quickly as she could, Eva fished in her satchel and pulled out her smartphone.

I must snap some photos of this!

***

Eva sat in a plush dressing gown belted around her waist while Tara gently brushed her wet hair. She'd sighed about a gazillion times since dousing herself in the wooden tub of warm water infused with lilac oil. Enjoying the luxury, she'd soaked until the water turned cold. Medieval baths might be few and far between, but a girl sure did appreciate one when she had it, especially in a beautiful bedchamber that felt so much like home.

"I wish I had thick ginger tresses like yours," said Tara.

"Mm?" Eva eyed the lass. Pretty, she couldn't be older than seventeen. "Aye? But ye have lovely eyes—the color of the sky."

A rap came at the door.

Tara set the brush on the table. "A moment."

Watching, Eva smoothed her hands over the soft wool of her robe. Oh yes, if she had been born in the Middle Ages, she would have had to be an aristocrat. Being pampered was far more enjoyable than starving and freezing in a broken down, old shed, or in a cave for that matter. She didn't abhor hard work, but when given an option…

"I need an audience with Miss Eva," William's voice echoed from the passageway.

Tara glanced back and cringed. "Apologies, but my lady is not dressed to receive callers."

Eva stood and tightened the belt on her dressing gown. "I'm covered. 'Tis all right."

Wearing a pair of clean leather breeks and a linen shirt, William bowed to the chambermaid who was dwarfed by his immense height. "If ye'll please leave us, miss."

The lass turned scarlet as she dipped into a curtsey. "Verra well, sir."

Once the door closed, he cross the floor and wrapped Eva in his brawny arms. She took in a deep inhale—mm—spicy male and rose oil soap. Quite a provocative combination. "You had a bath."

"Aye." He twirled a lock of her damp hair around his finger. "As did ye."

"It felt wonderful." She reached up and stroked her fingers over his neatly cropped beard, cut close enough to accent the bold line of his jaw. "How did your meeting with Lord Forrester go?"

"Verra well. He's agreed to host the meeting with Lord Bruce."

"Fantastic news."

William kissed her forehead, then took her hand and led her toward the hearth. "Is your chamber to your liking?"

Eva again chuckled and spread her arms wide. "I must say, this is much preferable to the decrepit shieling we camped in."

He faced the fire and wrung his hands—not to warm them, but as if he was nervous. "Or a cave," he muttered.

"That, too."

"Would ye prefer to live in a castle…ah…or with me?"

She chuckled. So that was what was bothering him? "Of course, I'd rather be where you are, William. The only reason I've returned is to be with you." *That, I can say for certain.*

He splayed his fingers and rubbed his palms, staring into the fire. Perhaps there was more to his worries?

"Is something troubling you?"

"Ah…" He glanced at her with a pinch to his brow, then fished in the purse at his waist. Goodness, his hands were shaking. "I ken when ye were here last, ye wanted to live for the now."

"True." She tried to peer inside, but the pouch was too dark. "We agreed. I'm here on borrowed time and…" Lord, thinking of anything beyond tomorrow gave her the willies.

He removed his hand, then crossed his arms. Was he holding something in his fist? "What if I want more?" He looked at her with that determined stare—the one Eva had never been able to resist.

Clutching the dressing gown closed at her chest, she scooted back, shaking her head. She guessed what he was doing. *How can I stop him?* "N-n-n-no."

His eyes grew darker than coal as he sauntered toward her. "Ye've said that afore."

"Yes. I-I'm from another time. Who knows when I'll be spirited to the future?" She backed into the bed's footboard. "We could be separated again at any moment."

"Is that what ye want, lass? To go home to be alone with nothing but your memories?"

"No." She shook her head. "I mean yes."

"I think not." William grasped her hand and dipped down to one knee. She tried to tug her fingers away, but he gripped her just tight enough that she couldn't pull away.

Oh God, no. No. No. No. No.

"Bonny Eva, I have loved ye since the first day I chanced to espy ye cowering under that altar." He brought the back of her hand to his lips and bowed his head, his breath ever so warm and soft as he kissed her. "I have never loved a woman the way my heart pines for ye. My soul was but an empty shell when ye left me—I ken it was my fault the black magic took ye away, but without your tenderness I was nothing but a fighting engine, existing like a hairy beast."

"But—"

He squeezed her hand again. "I dunna ever want ye to leave me again, though I ken it could happen. I, too, want to live for the now, but every time we come to a great man's home, it pains me to have to tell them ye are not my wife."

She nodded, clenching her teeth. Tears burned the back of her eyes. Lord, he was right.

"Eva, ye are my wife in every sense of the word, except we have not pledged our love before God. Please. I ken our time together is fleeting. I ken ye could be taken from me on the morrow. I ken my own days are numbered, for I can no longer fight with the strength of Goliath. And though I ken all this, I still want ye to be mine in the eyes of God. No matter how long we have together, even if only a day, I want to make things holy and pure between us."

A lump the size of her fist formed in Eva's throat. She could scarcely see his handsome face through the blur of her tears. God, why did she have to come back? How could she deny him? She loved him with a passion that burned so deep it scorched her soul. Would she spend an eternity with William? Yes. In a heartbeat she'd marry him—if this man kneeling before her was not...

He opened his palm and revealed a silver ring woven in a Celtic knot. "I had this made for ye at Dirleton ever so long ago, and I would be honored if ye would agree to be my wife." His hand shook and his eyes pleaded. "Please, I want ye to be my lady."

He slid the ring over her finger—a perfect fit.

Eva stared at it with tears streaming down her cheeks. So intricate, such detailed work. *How did he know my size? And he's been carrying this all these years?*

"Yes," her voice said as if it had grown a mind of its own.

Wrapping his arms around her, he pulled her into his body and rested his head against her abdomen. "Praise be to God. I dunna ken if I would have been able to live if ye had denied me."

Chapter Twenty-Six

William considered it a blessing when John Blair and the men arrived the next day. He wanted to wed Eva as soon as possible before the lass had a change of heart—or did something that would return her to the future.

He might be completely daft to marry, but something deep inside his soul told him the black magic behind that damned medallion would be crushed by holy matrimony. He'd spent many a day in quiet repose thinking about this, searching for answers in the lines of his psalter, and marriage was the only answer. *What God hath joined together let no man put asunder.* Yes. Marrying the lass was the only way he knew to keep her. He should have insisted they wed ages ago.

He stood beside John Blair and Sir Forrester on the dais tapping his toes inside his boots. Hell, if the men had any inkling of the extent of his jitters, they'd never let him live it down.

"Have ye a mind to settle nearby?" asked Forrester. He was a crusty sort with rheumy eyes and a bulbous nose, but he had a forthright and honorable mien.

William stared at him blankly. He couldn't settle anywhere—not until he booted Edward out of Scotland. Lord, had he been selfish to ask for Eva's hand? Would she want to settle? Blast, he should have asked her.

"Perhaps up north," William mumbled.

"Good choice. Ye might have a chance of living the family life up in the isles—somewhere out of reach of English galleys."

Family life? If only William could allow himself to dream of such luxuries. He was marrying Eva to keep her by his side. Of course if bairns came, he'd be overjoyed—and terrified. What if she did birth a bairn? What was that she'd told him? She wasn't barren but had a way of preventing pregnancy. Like a simpleton, he'd accepted her explanation without pursuing it further.

A bairn? Good Lord, no one could ever know about it. The child would never be safe.

By the time Eva descended the stairs and exited the stairwell, William had worried himself into a simpering pile of worthless bones. A man who faced death and stabbed it in the guts near every day, stood staring at his bride while pure terror pulsed through his veins. He could call the whole thing off right there and now. Probably should.

"Holy Jesus save us all," said Blair.

William blinked. Good God, if his knees were a pile of worthless bones before, they just turned to complete mush. Aye, he'd expected her to clean up well—to look like a queen. But this—this *woman* looked more like a goddess. Jesu, she embodied a vision. Never in his life had he seen a woman look bonnier.

Blair elbowed William and turned his lips toward his ear. "If ye didna believe her a sorceress afore, I reckon ye ought to now."

He'd given the tailor a few pieces of silver and told the man to have her ready by vespers. But holy merciful Mary and all the saints, she looked so beautiful. Dressed in gold from her veil to a gown lovelier than anything he'd seen at the French court, a glowing aura surrounded her. A snug fitting bodice, the low, square neckline framed her breasts like gifts for the unwrapping.

A radiant, golden goddess.

Better, her vivid green eyes regraded him as if they were the only two people in the hall. His heart leapt when she smiled. No woman could ever take control of his heart with a mere smile. No woman but his Eva. *His.* Och aye, she would finally be William's wife to have and to hold, and God willing, till death draws them apart.

With a swish of her skirts, Eva climbed the steps and joined him on the dais. He took her hand, so petite in his beefy mitts. At five foot eleven, Eva might be tall, but she lacked nothing in femininity from the wispy curls of red framing her face, to her slender neck, to the lithe fingers resting in his palm.

"Ye look ravishing," he managed through his arid voice box.

"As do you." Her gaze trailed down his doublet and chausses as the tip of her tongue snuck out and tapped her upper lip.

"Ahem," Blair cleared his throat. "Are ye ready?" William loved the priest like a brother, but he lacked a genteel nature—always the gruff warrior-monk.

Nonetheless, he nodded. "Proceed."

Holding both of Eva's hands in his, he watched her eyes as Blair launched into a litany of Latin prayers. The green flickered with gold from the candelabra above as she boldly met his stare. Their gazes bonded, as if an invisible current connected their souls, as if they would never be parted and live as one throughout eternity. Two souls brought together from different ages. What were the chances of their meeting? Nil, for certain.

Whatever brought them together carried power beyond William's reasoning. Something so supreme and mighty could not be ignored. Their love exceeded all bounds. *Faith, hope, love...and the greatest of these is love.* In the depths of his heart,

William knew the passage he'd read over and over in his psalter to be true.

Suddenly the hall became silent. Eva inclined her head toward Blair.

Right. The vows.

His mouth suddenly dry, William licked his lips. "I take ye as my wife."

"I receive you," Eva said, her voice sure.

"I give my body to ye, Eva, in loyal matrimony."

"And I receive it."

William glanced at Blair, who, ever the somber warrior, couldn't manage a wee grin. The priest gestured to Eva.

She took in a deep inhale. William tensed. She'd agreed to recite the vows from his time, though she'd chewed her nails a bit when they'd discussed it.

"I take you as my husband," she said.

Sunshine radiated through his chest. "And I receive ye."

"I give my body to you, William, in loyal matrimony."

"And I receive it."

Together they recited the rest, "I will keep you in health and sickness and in any condition it please our Lord that you should have, nor for worse or for better will I change toward you until the end."

But there would be no end. William knew it to the depths of his soul.

***

Floating, Eva still couldn't believe she'd gone through with it. She'd actually married William Wallace, the man of her dreams.

But this was no dream.

And she'd never been happier in her life.

Or more afraid.

What if she ended up pregnant? A lump of ice spread throughout her chest and made the back of her neck tingle. She already could be. *But what if? Would it be so bad?*

Blinking in rapid succession, Eva pushed her thoughts to the back of her mind. She refused to allow herself to think of the long term.

Tonight she would cast her fears aside and enjoy the celebration. She'd finally pledged her love to William and sealed it with an everlasting bond—and the medallion had remained cool against her skin. Living for the now took on new meaning. The present was all that existed. There could be no past, no future.

Only by adhering to this creed would she cling to her sanity.

"What say ye, Eva?" William asked beside her.

Unable to fake her way out of obliviousness, she looked up with a blank stare. "Pardon?"

Everyone at the table laughed.

"Perhaps she isna as talented as ye say, William," said Sir Forrester.

"Och, she sings prettier than a meadow lark," said Blair. Her singing was about the only thing the priest approved of.

His lordship made a sweeping gesture toward the musicians accompanying the feast with flute, drum and harp. "Well then, haste ye to the gallery and sing us a wee ballad."

Eva clung to William's arm. "But this is my wedding day. Is the bride to provide the entertainment? Is she not supposed to be regaled, instead?"

"She does have a quick wit about her, Wallace. Are ye certain ye can handle such a woman in the bedchamber?" said Forrester, guzzling yet another tankard of ale, his medieval humor making the hairs on the back of Eva's neck prickle a bit.

"Come." William gave her a nudge. "Sing us the one about being raised up."

"You remember that?" she asked.

"Aye. 'Twas the first time I couldna take my eyes off ye."

"How can a lass refuse when her spouse pays such a compliment?" said Forrester.

Eva sighed.

William patted her hand. "There's a goodly wife."

Climbing the winding steps to the gallery, Eva recited the modern Irish folk tune *You Raise Me Up* in her head. She hadn't done much singing in the past eight years. Hopefully she still had a voice.

"Good evening gentlemen," she said, stepping onto the gallery platform. "Ah, I'm going to sing a wee tune for my husband. You're welcome to chime in…"

Before she started, Eva gazed out over the great hall filled with tables lined end-to-end. One face stood out in the crowd. Robbie Boyd met her gaze, his mien expressionless. The young man was one of the few in the hall who'd heard her sing before. At one time he'd been a good friend, a young lad Eva had nurtured.

But now he held her at arm's length—didn't trust her just like John Blair. Well, now she and William had married, perhaps the time had come to rekindle their friendship. If only she knew what to do to make him trust her again.

Closing her eyes she took a deep breath and cleared her mind of all worries before she began. "*When I am down and, oh my soul's so weary…*" How could she have doubted herself? The old pipes didn't let her down. All banter in the hall ceased. William watched her throughout the duration of the ballad— the look on his face reverent, yet predatory. She sang for him because she knew how much he loved this song. She sang for him because he'd asked her to do so. She would not deny him.

If nothing else, she vowed to make the coming months the happiest of his life.

Chapter Twenty-Seven

A fortnight later, William sat alone in Sir Forrester's chamber with the Earl of Carrick, Robert Bruce. The man was broad-shouldered and comely with a hawkish gaze. William didn't know Bruce well, but aside from Eva's confidence, he didn't trust the earl. Ever since Falkirk, he'd learned to hold the nobility at arm's length altogether. Probably a foolish notion. Scotland would never again stand on her feet if a lofty nobleman did not step forward.

At least the man across the table looked the part.

But does he have the heart of a lion?

Lord Bruce placed his arms on the table and leaned forward with a commanding glint in his eye. "I received your message—now ye'd best make haste to tell me why I am here. Torwood is too bloody close to Stirling for my tastes."

William liked Bruce's unrest—it spoke volumes that the earl harbored no deep-seated love for Longshanks. The English had more spies between Edinburgh and Stirling than anywhere in Scotland. "What better place to hide than under their noses?"

"Aye, ye may need to hide, but not me."

"Hmm." William clenched and unclenched his fists. "Playing with two decks are ye?"

"That, sir, is none of your concern." The earl pushed back his chair. "I assume ye didna send for me for a discussion about avoiding the English."

"Nay." William stroked his fingers along his cropped beard. "Why did ye not fight at Falkirk?"

Lord Bruce tugged on his jerkin, frowning like the question gave his stomach unease. "Why should I be inclined to reveal my hand to the likes of ye? Ye're no longer Guardian."

"Aye, but I still have the ear of the commoners." William shifted in his seat. "I lost a great deal at Falkirk and Scotland lost more. If nothing else, I am due an answer."

Pursing his lips, the earl nodded. "I suppose ye are right, damn it all. 'Twas my father's request—and my future father-in-law's as well. I was in negotiations with the Earl of Ulster when he received the order to march with Edward."

"So ye opted to remain impartial?"

"I couldna exactly throw away negotiations to win Lady de Burgh's hand and take up arms against her father. 'Twas far too advantageous an alliance."

Putting lands and titles afore duty to king? "Did ye ken the outcome of the battle?"

Frowning, Lord Bruce studied his fingernails. "I kent your position was precarious."

"Because certain nobles would turn backstabbers?"

The earl looked him in the eye and nodded.

"So ye sat idle while Scottish blood soaked the battlefield?" William's fists clenched into balls.

"I didna come here to be interrogated by the likes of ye, sir. I acted and continued to act in the best interests of the Kingdom."

"Is that so?" William sat back and crossed his arms. "Yet ye own lands on both sides of the border."

"I was born in Scotland." The man sat square and smacked his pointer finger into the table. "My alliances on the other side of the border only serve to strengthen our defenses along the boundary of Galloway. If I did not employ loyal men across the border, my lands would undergo endless raids."

William couldn't argue Lord Bruce's point. The earl had suffered more than most trying to protect his lands against the senseless border reivers. Yet, Wallace needed more. "What is your quarrel with the Earl of Badenoch?"

Bruce threw back his head and laughed. "Aside from John Comyn being a sniveling arse?"

William didn't smile. "Aye."

"There is no noble in all of Scotland more loyal to Edward than Badenoch. As Guardian, he's no more effective than the puppet king. I couldna tolerate Comyn's milk-livered deference when I served beside him. God's blood, I've sworn on my first wife's grave I will never pay heed to that tyrant again."

"Strong words." William moved to the sideboard and pulled the stopper from a flagon of whisky. "I must say your actions make it difficult to determine which side ye're on."

The earl flung his arms to his sides, the span nearly the breadth of the oblong table. "Do ye not think that is by design? Damnation, man, England has us by the cods. My position is perilous. There are times when it is best to lay low so a man can live to fight another day."

William poured two drams. "That's what worries me."

"Pardon?"

After placing one in front of Lord Bruce, William returned to his chair. "Do ye agree Scotland is in worse condition now than when I ruled as Guardian?"

"Aye, especially now that Comyn is eating out of Edward's palm." The earl sipped.

"But still there are unanswered raids against our countrymen. Our people are huddled in their homes at night afeard the bastard will next turn on them. Do ye plan to sit

idle whilst Longshanks further sinks in his talons until he has
bled us dry—until all of our sons have died fighting his battles
on foreign soil?"

"I—"

William slammed his fist on the table. "Or have ye a plan
to do something about it?"

Bruce leaned forward, both hands splayed wide as he eyed
Wallace. "Ye are the cause of much of the bloodshed."

William shoved back his chair and stood, his fingers
itching to draw his dirk. "Explain yourself and ye'd best do it
quick afore we come to blows."

The earl smirked, folding his arms. "Think on it. Every
sennight the price for your head rises a wee bit higher. With
every plunder of Scottish villages, the soldiers are demanding,
'where is Wallace?'. Do ye believe with your petty raids ye are
doing the commoners a service—running the English out of
Scotland?"

William threw up his hands. "Bloody hell, someone must
take a stand and I seem to be the only man bold enough to do
so."

"Aye?" Bruce stood and sauntered around the table, hand
resting atop his sword's pommel. "Ye canna stay anywhere
without being hunted. To be perfectly clear, my presence here
is a threat to *my* life."

William narrowed his eyes and examined the earl. "Then
why'd ye come?"

"Because I respect ye." Bruce lowered his hand to his
side. "And because I am as sick as ye are, watching
Longshanks' tyranny unfold time and time again."

Tension shed from his shoulders as William resumed his
seat. "I need someone—a nobleman who is strong enough to
commit to end Longshank's madness—a man who willna turn
his back on Scotland no matter what."

"England's army is too strong." Following William's lead,
his lordship shook his head and sat. "As ye said, Comyn has

allowed Edward to sink his claws deep. There is no corner of Scotland without its spies or well-trained English soldiers within a day's march."

William took a long sip of his whisky and slowly lowered the cup to the board. "We stopped them afore."

The earl leaned back and scrubbed his fingers through his beard. "We must build our numbers."

"Aye, but first we need commitment from a man like ye. A man with the pedigree to become *king*. A man brave enough to push the Comyn line aside and take the crown— not for himself, but to save his people."

Robert Bruce, Earl of Carrick, stared at Wallace for a long while before he blinked. Then he opened his mouth and took in a sharp gasp.

William's heart squeezed. He knew his words struck deep. "Can ye unite the nobles—bring together their armies?"

"It will take time." Lord Robert drummed his fingers against his lips. "Ye may have been efficient at dispatching the matters of state, but ye didna make alliances when ye were in Stirling."

"I ken, and the more I've thought on it, the more I realize I should have smoothed a few feathers, especially after we invaded England." Shaking his head, William looked to the ceiling. "If I had stopped and rallied them behind me—played the political game—perhaps we might have won at Falkirk."

"It sounds like ye've put a great deal of thought into it."

"Aye. I had an entire year to ponder the error of my ways whilst I rotted in King Philip's dungeon."

"I dunna ken." Thoughtfully, Lord Bruce stroked his fingers, smoothing his whiskers. "I fear ye burned too many bridges."

"'Tis all the more reason to have ye behind us—keep my role quiet." Tension again clamped William's shoulders. He'd brought Robert Bruce here for a reason and now was the time to reveal his hand. "I aim to travel to the far north. Build a secret army."

"Ye mean to disappear?"

"Aye, give Longshanks time to forget his hate."

Bruce reached for the flagon and poured himself another dram, his expression pinched as if thinking. "That man is insane with loathing for ye. It burns so strong, he'll take it to the grave for certain."

"If the reports of sightings ebb, do ye think the English raids will stop?"

"There's no way of knowing until we try. I reckon the problem is now that the war in France is over, Edward needs somewhere to focus his bloodlust. Unfortunate the man has chosen ye to pursue with relentless insanity. At least France had a fighting chance. 'Tis an entire country."

"So is Scotland." William chuckled—but the reality of Edward's lust for vengeance struck a chord in his gut. "What would Longshanks do if he took my head? Would one man's life save a nation?"

The earl shrugged with a hiss. "Dunna ken. He needs Scottish coin and men."

"Aye, but as ye said, with every raid, the soldiers are demanding information seeking *my* whereabouts."

Bruce narrowed his eyes. "If we used ye as bait…perhaps 'twould quell his bloodlust long enough for us to move against him." Drumming his fingers, he continued, "But your plan to assemble an army to the north has merit."

"Only if ye can send me men—with the English none the wiser."

"'Twill be a challenge keeping your whereabouts a secret."

"Aye."

William topped up Bruce's cup and poured more for himself while they formulated their plans to secretly send men to Orkney. Only the best warriors would go—hand-picked by the earl. And all the while, Bruce would send out spies to watch Longshanks' officers. God willing, this would be a giant leap toward taking back the Kingdom.

A loud boom shook the walls in the solar. Muffled shouts hailed from above.

The door swung open. Sir Forrester barreled in with sword in hand. "Haste ye to the postern gate. We are under attack!"

William's hand flew to his sword. "To the battlements!"

"No!" Lord Bruce clapped his meaty palms on the board. "If ye have learned nothing from our discussion, do ye not understand there is a time to fight and a time to flee? Let us build our forces so we can fight another day. Fight to win!"

William gritted his teeth and jammed his weapon deep into its scabbard. "I will hold ye to your promises."

***

Eva sprang to her feet with a jolt of alarm. Though she'd heard the boom from the portcullis before, it hadn't closed with so much force the whole castle shook. Clipped shouts came from above and rose from the courtyard below.

Whipping around, she spotted her satchel with its contents spread across her bed. Taking in a sharp gasp, she raced for it and started shoving her things inside.

The chamber door burst open. "We must haste!" William snatched their cloaks from the hooks and ran to her as he swung his mantle around his shoulders. "'Tis the English. Quickly now."

After slinging the satchel over her shoulder, Eva tied her mantle closed. "Where is the earl?"

"Gone." Clasping his fingers around her arm, he pulled her toward the door. "We've not a moment to waste."

Eva stumbled over her skirts and fell into him. Damn. If only she had a pair of practical shoes. Her slippers were but thin strips of pigskin with hardened leather soles. A good pair of running shoes would come in handy about now.

As she straightened, William bent his knees and grasped her waist. Before she could skitter away, her enormous husband hefted her over his shoulder.

She kicked her legs. "Put me down. I can run!" His shoulder digging into her gut, she smacked him on the back.

William didn't even slow down. "I can run faster," his deep voice growled.

Eva had no choice but to hold on to his belt as she flopped, draped across his shoulder like a sack of oats. William crouched as he entered the stairwell, winding down the servants steps. Her head thudded into the wall.

"Ow." Just as she clapped a hand to her temple, her bum hit even harder. "Easy!" she yelled.

"Nearly there."

Dashing outside into the mud, William threw her over a horse's withers as if she were a bedroll. "Are the men ready?"

"Aye," Blair said. "We must haste."

Eva slung an arm around the horse's neck and kicked her leg, only to be met by something hard.

William mounted in the saddle behind her. "Hang on, lass. 'Twill be a bumpy ride."

Bumpy wasn't the half of it. With a firm jab of William's spurs, the horse lurched into a thundering gallop. Eva's body bounced like a flopping fish out of water. Worse, her gut hit hard with the stallion's every stride, making each breath whoosh from her lungs.

"Latch on to my leg," he barked with such intensity, Eva dare not question him. Good God, why did she always end up upside down across William's mount with her ass in the air?

Hoofbeats boomed toward them from the flank.

With a hiss, William drew his sword.

Gasping, Eva tried to reach for her mail piercer with her free hand, but the relentless pounding gave her no chance. The horse beneath them lurched and spun. William's enormous hand latched on to her bum while a bloodcurdling bellow ripped from his throat. "I'll cut out your liver, ye mongrel dog!"

Iron screeched with a clash of swords.

Gritting her teeth, Eva held on, ducking her head as low as possible, praying for their lives. The horse jerked as it responded to William's cues—a tap of his spur, a squeeze of his knee, the rocking of his seat. His expert horsemanship seemed effortless as he battled his opponent with broad, striking glances of his weapon.

Eva had never been so close to a swordfight. Her every heartbeat thundered in her ears. Time slowed.

She turned her head. William bared his teeth. His great sword cut through the air with a whoosh. A dull thud hit bone. The attacker's eyes bulged beneath his helm. His mouth gaped. Momentum ripped him from his mount.

William didn't hesitate. He slammed his heels against his horse's barrel, hissing through his teeth.

Eva clutched William's leg, squeezing tight in a desperate attempt to stay the pounding against her abdomen. Stars darted through her vision as she opened her eyes to glimpse the path ahead. Shrieking, a clump of broom slapped her cheek.

"Ow!"

With her next breath, William's arm gripped around her waist and wrenched her up, settling her across his lap. Her head spun so fast, she toppled backward.

"Hold there, lassie," he said, nudging her upright with his shoulder. Lord, the warhorse didn't miss a step.

She glanced around his shoulder. "Are they after us?" she shouted over the rush of running horses and the wind howling in her ears.

William inclined his mouth toward her. "Ye can wager your life on it."

"Can we outrun them?"

"Isna that what we're doing?"

"Yes, but how do we know when we've lost them? Won't the horses tire?"

"Theirs will tire sooner. They had to ride to Torwood afore they attacked." William slapped the reins, demanding more speed.

"How long will you drive this pace?"

"Until we hit the Forth."

"We're sailing?"

"Aye."

Eva crouched as they rode under the branches of an enormous sycamore, then dashed into the open lea. On and on the horses raced, snorting through their enormous nostrils. Ahead, a shimmer of blue flickered off the waves of the Firth of Forth. Behind, the enemy made chase, galloping into the sunlight.

"There they are!" Eva shouted.

"How many?"

She counted then searched beyond for more. "Only six."

"Good. If they dunna turn back, they'll meet their maker this day."

Curling into the warmth of William's chest, Eva sought the comfort of his brawny arms. With eight in their escort, their English pursuers didn't stand a chance. She prayed they'd gain their senses and turn back. She hated fighting—hated blades even more. If she never saw another battle it would be too soon for her.

"Weigh anchor!" Blair shouted from the lead.

A sea galley bobbed in the water, its sail unfurled—looking like an ancient ship Eva had seen in a museum, eighteen oars and all. Was such a vessel seaworthy?

Queasiness twisted her gut at the mere thought of climbing up the narrow gangway.

CHAPTER TWENTY-EIGHT

"Orkney," William said, answering Eva's question as to their destination. Jesu, he would have fought a hundred men with one hand tied behind his back to see her face turn from seasick green and light up like a sunburst.

"You took my advice?"

He shrugged. After all, he couldn't let the woman think it was all her idea. Her head might swell so large it mightn't fit through the neck of her gowns. "It seemed a logical move. At least one worth trying. If reports of my whereabouts stop, there's hope Longshanks will put an end to his mindless pillaging."

A crease formed between her ginger eyebrows. "Who else knows where we're headed?"

"The Bruce. Lord Forrester." William flicked a lock of hair away from her cheek with his finger but the wind snapped it back with a vengeance. "Hell, the master of the ship didna ken where we were off to until Blair told him. Dunna worry, lass. The Orkneys are a part of Norway." He thumped the missive tucked under his jerkin. "And I still have the letter from King Philip requesting safe passage—a kindness not extended to the English."

"Aye." Father Blair waddled toward them in concert with the rocking galley, then leaned against the hull between the pair. "Besides, 'tis too cold for Longshanks' men to attempt to invade Norway."

Eva pulled her cloak tighter around her shoulders. Indeed, white puffs of air escaped her nostrils. "I do believe you are right."

Blair scoffed. "That'd be the first time." He thwacked her shoulder. "Would ye mind saying that again just to appease an old friar's ears?"

She gave him a solid punch in return. "You heard me, you turkey."

He pulled back with a snort. "What is this? Turkey?"

"It's a stout, gobbling bird they eat—uh." Her eyes shifted to William.

He glanced at the others. The boat was too small for her to start spewing gibberish about the future. "Enough."

Looking out to sea, she nodded. "How long will the passage take?"

"Depends on the wind and the sea." He looked at the sail, filled with air. "Mayhap a day—especially if the breeze continues to favor us."

A castle surrounded by stone bailey walls came into view, jutting into the Forth on a slip of a promontory. Eva gasped and drew her fingers to her lips. "Is that Blackness?"

"Aye." It looked as menacing from the sea as it did from the shore.

"There's only one tower." She pointed. "I hardly recognized it but for the location."

William looked over his shoulder. The others were tending oars or coiling ropes—having lost interest now that Blair had returned to the stern to take up the rudder with the master. William led her to the bow and kept his voice low. "What is the Forth like in your time?"

She grinned and scraped her teeth over her bottom lip. "It is so different. Towns and houses line the shore and ahead, two bridges cross the Forth at Queensferry."

"Two? Span the entire body of water?"

"Yes, and they nearly have a third completed." She spread her hands in front of her face then opened them wide, as if painting a scene. "The railway runs across Forth Bridge with its three expansive red arches giving it support." She chuckled. "I can see it now in my mind's eye."

He wrapped his arms around her middle and pulled her back against his chest. "I wish I could see it just once."

"Oh, that would be something. You'd hardly recognize it." She pointed. "There's no dim cloud of smoke hanging over Edinburgh like it's doing today—and there's so much more to the skyline—old and new."

"Is the castle still presiding atop the hill?"

"Yes." She offered a sheepish grin. "It's a tourist attraction."

"A what?"

"Oh dear, that must be another one of my modern words. People pay to go there and look at old relics—old construction—to find out how things used to be."

"Ye mean to tell me people have time for such malarkey?" He gave her a playful squeeze.

She wiggled against him with a squeak. "It is not malarkey. It's important to study the past—interesting, too."

"More important than tilling a field or tending the sick?"

"Of course not, but everyone needs a vacation—ah—a bit of rest from time to time."

I conjure up a mob of lazy laggards. "It sounds like people from the future have too little to do if they pay good coin to climb around old relics."

"You're insufferable."

"And ye've more tales than a long-toothed bard."

"I'm not lying."

"I didna say ye were." He tickled her between the ribs with his pointer finger. "'Tis just I'm the only sop in all of Christendom who's daft enough to believe ye, truth or nay."

***

Their arrival in the Orkneys brought about more rough living and crude accommodations. But Eva held no illusions that she'd been brought back to the fourteenth century to live a life of a privileged noblewoman. She'd returned because of the deep love she harbored for William, and he for her. Eight years had done nothing to quell it. After they'd been separated, she'd only managed to mask her feelings, push them to the deep recesses of her mind so her heart didn't hurt so badly.

Yes, she loved William with a fervent passion unsurpassed by anything she'd ever experienced or ever again would know. Their souls were entwined and woven together by a vine of impenetrable iron.

And that terrified her.

When they'd first arrived, Eva often experienced flashes of dread, covering her skin with a sheen of sweat. It took a few blinks and a bit of fist clenching to chase the fear back to the recesses of her mind. Fortunately, she kept herself busy tending to the needs of William's small band of rebels. Simply existing in this era brought heavy labor. Nothing was easy— no taps to turn for instant, pure water, no light switches, no thermostat for heat, no grocery stores to buy food or refrigerators in which to store it.

Death and darkness lurked in every crevice. They'd even been met by an army of teeth-gnashing Norsemen when their galley ran aground on the Orkney beach.

Thankfully, William's letter of passage from King Philip had been impressive enough to avoid a battle. And after making enquiries, they'd re-boarded the sea galley and sailed a wee bit south to the tiny isle of Eynhallow where smooth-tongued, multi-lingual William Wallace employed his Latin to convince a group of Monastic monks into giving them sanctuary.

In the past month, a handful of mercenaries had joined them from the mainland—sent by the Earl of Carrick. But it wasn't enough and William had already grown restless.

By the time May rolled around, Eva had resumed her writing. While William and his men trained the new recruits who were trickling in, she also helped the monks tend the garden and went for long walks along the craggy shore of the islet. Accustomed to the city, it surprised her that she hadn't grown a bit antsy as the months passed. The remoteness of Eynhallow gave her a sense of calm—a sense of being detached from the rest of the world.

She'd finally figured it out—and perhaps that's why a calm sereneness filled her with contentment. She no longer had to push future dreads from her mind. Convinced the medallion had sent her back to change the horrific course of events, she fully intended to keep William on Eynhallow through summer at the very least.

Summer came late in the Orkneys and the weather still drizzled. The abbot had given the couple a chamber with a narrow window overlooking the sea and Eva had moved the table where she could look out when writing. In the mornings she took up the quill and recorded every detail about her time there.

She'd just dipped the tip in the inkwell when the door to the chamber opened.

"Och, Willy, I dunna need to be mollycoddled," Robbie said as William ushered the young knight inside.

William thrust his finger in Eva's direction. "Ye'll have her look at ye and that's the end of it."

Groaning, the young man plopped into the chair opposite Eva. Blood soaked his sleeve.

She rested the quill in the holder as she hissed. "What happened?"

"The lad got a wee bit too close to my blade," said William, then he pointed to young Boyd. "Take off your shirt so she can have a peek."

Robbie knit his brows with an annoyed huff. "Bloody hell." But he whipped the garment over his head. Indeed, he'd grown muscles as thick as a Brahman bull. But the laceration on his arm bled profusely.

Eva cringed and placed her fingers above the wound. "Oh dear, that's quite a cut."

"'Tis nothing," said Robbie.

William bent down and gave the wound a once-over. "I reckon it needs to be stitched."

"I agree." The laceration had to be at least four inches long. Eva retrieved her basket from the bedside table. "We need to staunch the bleeding first." She pulled out one of the cloths she'd sterilized with boiling water, rolled it and pressed against the wound.

Robbie winced. "It'll come good in a day or two. 'Tis merely a scratch."

William clapped him on the good shoulder. "Let Lady Eva tend ye, then I'll see ye in the courtyard for another round."

The lad grinned. "Ye're on."

Eva dabbed at the wound, regarding Robbie's well-muscled bicep. "You've grown strong over the years."

"Aye? Who wouldna? I've been watching Willy's back since I was a lad of eleven. If I'd been a milksop, I couldna survived."

"I admire you for standing by him through both the good and trying times. Not many have done so." She fished in her basket for the tub of antiseptic ointment and squeezed a small dab onto her finger. She'd been using less, trying to make it last.

He smirked. "Ye had the good sense to leave him when times were at their best."

Holding her finger still, she regarded the lad and frowned. "It wasn't my choice to leave."

"Then why did ye? And dunna lie. I was just a lad. Ye were the only mother I kent—ever, and ye just up and disappeared without so much as a goodbye."

The lad's words cut deep. He still resented her for her disappearance. She carefully applied the ointment, trying to think of something to say to make him understand she hadn't abandoned him—at least not on purpose. "I wanted to stay. I wanted to say goodbye to you, to William. But I couldn't."

"Ye mean ye wouldna."

"No." Standing back, she pulled out the medallion. "Can you read Latin?"

"Willy taught me a bit."

She handed it to him. "What does this say?"

"Truth is like a beacon."

"Mm hmm." Then she turned it over. "And on the other side?"

"But few choose to follow."

"The magic—or whatever it is—behind this medallion chose me of all people to travel through seven hundred years to write William's story. Do you know the only rule?"

He shook his head warily.

He seemed so reluctant to believe her, but Eva figured she might as well finish. "I cannot do anything to alter the past. I suspected Andrew Murray was suffering from lead poisoning caused by the arrow tip lodged in his shoulder—but I'm not a physician. I'm a chronicler, regardless, when William insisted that I try to help Sir Andrew, I was hurled back to my time before I made the first incision."

His nose twitched. "It sent ye away 'cause ye were trying to help? But ye're always trying to help."

"Yes, but this time, evidently helping Sir Andrew would have altered history." She threaded a bone needle.

He regarded his arm. "And ye're not changing history by helping me now?"

"If I weren't here, I imagine a monk would sew you up—regardless, I doubt you'd die from this cut, though without my ointment it might take a bit longer to heal."

When she bent forward, he pointed to the medallion. "Why are ye wearing the blasted thing if it could spirit ye away? It would ruin Willy to lose ye again. Do ye ken what he went through after ye left?"

Eva made the first suture. "I can imagine—though I doubt his pain was worse than my own broken heart. At least I returned to a time of peace."

"Aye, Willy hasna had a moment of respite since he took up the sword for King John."

"I worry about him."

"As do I—especially now ye're here."

She looked the lad in the eye. "You do not trust me, do you?"

He shrugged. "With that medallion around your neck, I fear ye may snap your fingers and be gone."

She tied off another suture. "It isn't that easy. I have absolutely no control over it whatsoever."

He jolted when she pushed in the needle for another stitch. "If ye are from the future, tell me what happens? I've been at war my entire life. I dunna have a home. I havena seen my own lands in years and now we're hiding on this Godforsaken isle. When will it all end?"

She sucked in a sharp inhale before stepping back and regarding his face. "You know, I refuse to lie, but there are things better left unsaid?"

"Aye?" He batted his hand across his face. "Ye speak with a forked tongue if ye ask me."

"Things will grow worse before they improve," she said, wrapping her fingers around the medallion.

"Are ye planning to leave again—afore the bad comes? Abandon Willy when he needs ye most?"

Her hands trembled. A sudden queasiness attacked her stomach. She couldn't leave William. The only thing she could do was influence him to change his course of action. Could she do it subtly enough not to invoke the ire of the medallion? Removing it from around her neck, she placed the bronze disc on the table. "He is my husband now. I will stand beside him no matter what." Her words made the anxiety melt from her shoulders. She rubbed another swipe of ointment across the wound. "Listen to me. *Your* future is what you should focus on now. You will become a renowned knight—one who bears a legacy through the ages. It is time you pledged your fealty to Robert Bruce."

"Is that right?" Robbie said with an edge of sarcasm.

Picking up his shirt from his lap, she stuffed it into his chest. "Think! King John abdicated the throne, and now he's retired to France. He's *never* coming back. Who is strong enough to be king? Who among the gentry has the grit to take on England and throw the bastards out of Scotland?"

The pupils of Robbie's eyes shrank into tight beads. "Bruce?" he whispered. "Is that why he met with Willy at Torwood?"

"I think you know the answer, Robert Dominus Boyd. Who do *you* think is man enough to take up the king's mantle and finish the work William has spent his life trying to achieve?"

CHAPTER TWENTY-NINE

More than anything, during his stay at Eynhallow, William enjoyed his afternoon walks with Eva. Today she let her tresses fall loose. He loved how the breeze picked up her curls and made them dance.

Opening her arms, she twirled along the path as if they had not a care in the world. "I love it here."

"What do ye like best?" William caught a lock of her hair in his palm and held it to his nose.

Giving a wry look, she giggled and fell in step beside him. "The remoteness, the quiet, the fresh smell of the sea." A seal sounded on the shore ahead. "Look—where else have you watched seals sunbathing on the shore?"

"Ye like the seals, then?"

"I love the seals and the seabirds." She pointed. "And look there, the daisies are in bloom since yesterday." Taking his hand, she skipped for the flowers. "We must make a daisy chain."

"I like seeing ye carefree like this." William's rigidity eased with her exuberance. He helped by picking a fistful of the flowers and held them up. "Is this enough?"

"Yes." Laughing, she led him to the stony shore and sat with her legs crossed. She spread the daisies in her lap. "Have you made a chain before?"

"With flowers?" he asked. "Nay. Repairing my mail is about all I've done with chains."

She broke the stem near the top, then made a hole with her fingernail. "See, you slide the next stem in like this, then pull until the base of the flower hits."

William picked up a daisy and followed her instructions. "Like this?"

"Yep. Easy, huh?"

He chuckled. When they were away from others, she relaxed into her normal speech. Now he'd grown accustomed to it, he loved to hear her talk when she wasn't trying so hard to be *her ladyship*. "What do we do with these once we've used up all the flowers?"

She held up her strand of three flowers. "Make a necklace."

Stilling his hands, he gave her a flabbergasted smirk. "Ye expect me to trudge back to the monastery with a ring of daisies around my neck?"

"Why not?" Eva pushed another daisy through her chain, looking unfussed.

"I'd never be able to show my face to my men."

"Oh? I think if anyone were bold enough to tease you, they might end up regretting it, and in short order."

"Och, ye're right there." He pulled a stem a bit too hard and broke off the bloom.

Eva reached for it. "Oops." Her movement graceful as a swan, she plucked it from his thigh and tucked it behind her ear as if she were born to be adorned by daisies.

William brushed her windblown tresses from her forehead. "It suits ye to have flowers in your hair." Watching her bonny face, his heart squeezed. Jesu, he would never cease to adore her beauty. "Och, ye are so fine, wife."

The green of her eyes gleamed when her gaze met his. She reached up and cupped his cheek. "You know I love you with all my heart—always have."

"Aye." A lump filled his throat while his fingers worked the flowers.

She rubbed her outer arms and looked toward the horizon. "Are you happy here?"

He shrugged. "I'd be a fair bit more content if Lord Bruce would send more men." He completed his ring of daisies and slipped it over her head. "And news from the mainland has been sparse."

"I rather enjoy having you to myself in the afternoons. There's nothing more romantic than a quiet stroll along the secluded shore." She held up her palms and grinned sheepishly. "No daily running for our lives."

"'Tis romance ye want?" he teased, prodding her with the tip of his finger. He could be happy spending the rest of his days walking the shore holding Eva's hand. He couldn't deny her point either. Living without fear was what every man desired. William sighed. If only he could walk away from the cause, but he'd never forgive himself. He owed his life to Scotland and his kin. Images of his murdered countrymen haunted him nightly. Every time he closed his eyes, he saw his slain father lying face down in the mud, his sinews cut behind his knees. This respite in Orkney could not possibly last. Did he want to stay and pretend he and Eva were all that mattered in the world? *More than anything.*

But his desires were selfish musings of a mortal man.

She draped her chain around William's neck. Then her eyes grew dark with a waggle of her brows. God's teeth, the woman could make him hard as a bedpost with one wanton look. "I wish we could remain here forever—let the world's problems pass us by."

"Problems have a way of catching up with a man." He slid an arm over her shoulder and squeezed. "We canna hide from our destiny." Mayhap they could steal an hour or two of respite. Inhaling, he closed his eyes and succumbed to her intoxicating allure.

"I don't know." Frowning, she drew away from his arm, then moved behind him and sunk her fingers into his shoulders. Good God, she could also pacify an angry mule with her hands. "You've been regaining your strength with rest and my massages. Perhaps a year on Eynhallow wouldn't be too much to ask."

"And ye have more fanciful dreams than I." But William doubted his strength would ever be equal to his prime. He'd suffered too many injuries—and no matter how hard he tried, he didn't improve.

Eva swirled her thumbs between his shoulder blades. "If the war was over, what would you do?"

He rolled his shoulder as the tension in his muscles responded to her magic. "That's easy. I'd take ye to my lands in Ayrshire. We'd have bairns and till the paddocks. I'd build ye a fine cottage with an enormous hearth."

She leaned close enough for her warm breath to caress William's ear. "I'd like that very much."

Gooseflesh rose across his arms. *Jesu, so would I.*

Since the first time they'd made love, they hadn't talked about taking *precautions*. It seemed of no consequence before, but now he wondered. "Are ye able to have them?" he asked in a whisper.

"Have what?"

He clutched her arm and pulled her onto his lap. "Bairns."

Green eyes opened wide. Her mouth formed a perfect "O". "Ah…I think so."

"What is it that prevents ye from conceiving? We've been together often enough, I would think…"

A rosy blush spread across her cheeks—och aye, he adored how easily she could redden. "Um…I used to have an IUD in my uterus—ah—my womb. It's a device that prevents pregnancy. But five or so years ago, I had it removed."

"Why?"

She rubbed her palm over her belly. "It's not healthy to leave them in forever."

William's tongue tied, but there should be no secrets between them. "Did ye plan to have children?" he managed hoarsely.

"No." She fiddled with his daisy necklace. "After you I…"

"What?" He tilted up her face with the crook of his finger.

Gazing upon him with half cast lids, her pink tongue slipped to the corner of her mouth. "I didn't want anyone else."

His heart not only thundered in his chest, it swelled and made him want to roar. God, how he loved her. "Och, Eva, I love ye with all my heart." He drew his arms around her and squeezed. Soft breasts molded into his chest, pebbled by two of the most alluring tips he'd ever felt in his life. "I only wish we'd have met in your time rather than mine."

"Wouldn't that have been a boon? You could have found your own seal." Leaning forward, she nibbled his neck as she rocked her hips against his growing erection.

His chuckled came out deep, filled with desire. "Ye mean that lump of rust ye showed me in your shiny black box?"

"The very same. It's on display at the National Museum of Scotland."

He blew out a guffaw. "Unbelievable." He captured her mouth with his lips, kissing her with long, languid swirls of his tongue. He tugged the neckline of her bodice down until he exposed her nipple. "I dunna want to think of things to come right now." Cupping her luscious breast, he teased her until she arched her back and moaned with ecstasy, grinding her hips against him. He adored how his woman could show her ardor, how she could growl and moan with unabashed passion and take him to heights he'd never dreamed possible.

With a wee giggle, she lifted her skirts and straddled him. "Make love to me here while the cool breeze tickles our skin."

William glanced back toward the monastery. Sitting against the embankment, they were well hidden. He chuckled and loosened his chausses and braies.

Lithe fingers surrounded him—knew exactly what he liked as Eva stroked.

Shuddering, William's eyes rolled back as she took charge and she lowered herself over him. Cupping his hands around her buttocks, together they began a slow rhythm while the breeze tantalized their flesh and the surf sang a rolling song of love.

Together their bodies rocked as one while the gnawing problems of the Kingdom faded into oblivion. Her lips parted as her breathing sped. A spike of desire shot through the tip of his cock, but Eva controlled the pace, gradually increasing while she clung to him for dear life.

A cry caught in the back of her throat—a wee sound that sent him over the edge of no return. With three deep thrusts, together they peaked with a rush of shudders that wracked his body and soul.

A warm glow spread through his insides as Eva nuzzled into his neck and plied him with fluttering kisses.

But all too soon, she looked beyond his shoulder and frowned. Then she shifted her hips aside. "I think you're needed."

Retying his braies and chausses, he glanced back as well.

"William," Robbie called, approaching at a run. "A galley of recruits has arrived—say they have a missive from the Earl of Carrick."

He gave Eva a peck on the cheek. "Ye see? We canna hide from our accountabilities."

"Well, go on, then." She gave him a playful shove. "I'll stay here for a while longer and keep the seals company."

The tightness in her chest returned while Eva watched William's retreating form as he walked beside the younger man. Her husband had a slight hitch to his step and he carried his lion-mangled shoulder a bit higher than the other. Doubtless he needed this time of respite. If only he wouldn't be so anxious to return to the battlefield. Irrespective, she'd keep working on him—wearing him down. His numbers weren't growing as fast as he liked, and that fact might make him stay put through the end of summer—as long as men continued to show up.

What does the missive from the earl contain? She'd find out tonight. Hopefully it would be like the others, introducing the conscripts who'd sailed from Ayr—or wherever.

A seal barked from the shore. Eva diverted her attention to the pod. An infant nuzzled his mother, looking for milk, no doubt.

She slipped a hand to her flat belly and rubbed. Pregnancy? Honestly, with her gift of blocking things from her mind, she hadn't thought about the possibility of conceiving. Her period was a little late, but that wasn't usual.

Heat spread throughout her chest. What if she did end up pregnant? No one needed to tell her about the mortality rate of having a baby in medieval Scotland.

Shuddering, she rubbed her stomach again. *I need to start taking precautions.*

But what if she did conceive? What a blessing to have William's child—and at thirty-five, her maternal clock was ticking.

No. Not now. After August, yes. Not until.

***

Once he received dismal news from the Earl of Carrick who was unable to recruit anywhere near the numbers they needed, it was William's idea for Eva to sail for Moray Firth and Ormonde Castle with John Blair.

"Ye've been wound tighter than a snare since we set sail," Father Blair said stepping up to the side of the hull beside Eva.

She regarded his gaunt visage—even the friar looked worried. "I need your help."

He let out a rueful chuckle. "What can *I* possibly do to help ye, m'lady?"

"We must ensure William stays on Eynhallow through the end of August at least."

"That long?" He placed his hands on the rail. "I'd hoped the troops would be ready to march by then."

"They won't," Eva said a little too quickly. "Um…I mean, I doubt you'll have the numbers."

Blair regarded her with pursed lips. "Why do I sense there is something ye're not telling me?"

She grabbed his woolen sleeve in her hand and squeezed. "Because it is far too awful to discuss. Can you not go along with me on this one thing? William needs to stay on that bloody island though August, and it's up to us to keep him there. Do you understand?"

The priest grumbled under his breath.

"Please." Eva tried the emotional tact—perhaps the friar had a heart. "If you love William, you'll do as I ask."

Blair looked to the shore with a huff. "Verra well. I'll go along with ye this once." He pointed. "But first 'tis up to ye to solicit the lady's assistance. If ye fail, William willna listen to either of us."

A chill of dread spread across her shoulders as the galley approached the grey fortress looming over the north shore. Pushing her palms against her face, she feared what they might encounter. The castle had been attacked by the English in 1303 for the sole purpose of capturing Andrew Murray's five-year-old son, named for his father. Lady Christina remained there, living under house arrest. Whatever that meant, Eva was sure to find out soon.

Nonetheless, her visit must be a success. Eva would do anything to ensure William stayed in Orkney at least until autumn and if Lady Christina could help rally soldiers and send them to Eynhallow, history just might be changed.

Last time it was easier not to think of things to come—years would pass and she'd had no intention of staying on. But this time things were so different, so much more dire.

Stop thinking about it!

Eva set her sights on the heavily-armed soldiers marching onto the shore.

"State your business afore ye drop that anchor," bellowed an officious looking man-at-arms.

Eva opened her mouth to speak, but Blair pushed in front of her. "Lady Eva MacKay from Edinburgh accompanied by her chaplain, Father John." He bowed. "My lady wishes to visit the Lady Christina to offer prayers for the safe return of her young son."

Eva clasped her hands and demurely smiled. It was proper for Blair to make the introductions. The soldier gave her a once-over, then turned and looked to the top of the outer bailey walls. Through a crenel notch, Eva spotted a woman in the shadows, wearing a black veil. She gave a subtle nod and then disappeared.

Recognition needled at Eva's nape. Surely the woman was Christina Murray.

"Very well," the man-at-arms said to Blair. "Follow me."

Covered with moss and vine, the castle looked as if it needed a bit of maintenance. Eva shouldn't be surprised. These were difficult times, made more perilous by the English occupation.

They proceeded under the iron-toothed portcullis and into a courtyard. Footsteps pattered toward them until Lady Christina stepped into the light, breathing deeply, wearing a black gown and veil. Her cheeks flushed, there was a strained sadness in her smile as she held out her hands. "Eva, how wonderful to see ye after all these years."

Clasping the offered palms, Eva grinned. "Oh my, it is ever so good to see you. We have much to discuss."

The lady's gaze trailed to Blair. "I've see you've brought Father—"

"John." Eva gave a wink. They couldn't chance repeating his last name, lest a spy catch wind of it.

"Ah yes." Christina greeted the priest with a curtsey. "And how have ye been, father?"

"Well, thank ye. My lady is ever so anxious to gain an audience with ye. I do hope our presence brings no intrusion."

"Of course not." Turning, she led them into the hall. "I am not allowed beyond these castle walls and callers have grown fewer in the past two years."

Eva pursed her lips against her urge to reassure the widow about her son. Instead, she looked to the stairwell. "Is there a chamber above stairs where we ladies might take refreshment in solitude?"

"Indeed." Lady Christina glanced upward. "We can retire to the ladies' solar."

After directing the priest to the chapel, the two women shut themselves inside a small chamber filled with a large table and overstuffed chairs, made warm by a brazier of burning peat in the hearth.

Christina poured goblets of watered wine before she sat. Her eyes and cheeks sunken like a cadaver, unfortunately the years hadn't been kind. "William never did tell me what happened that day."

Eva swirled the ruby liquid in her goblet. She didn't have to ask for clarification. The lady referred to Eva's sudden disappearance as Andrew Murray lay dying. She'd hoped to avoid such a question. "I was called away."

"Oh?" Christina brushed her hands over her gown, high color spreading across her face. "To where? Was there something more important than my husband's life?"

"No." There wasn't and Eva couldn't bring herself to lie. "I had no control over my destiny."

"Ye say that as if ye are the archangel of God," the lady said with a snort.

"I definitely am no angel of any sort…but sometimes I must do things I'd rather not."

Christina batted her hand through the air. "Who doesna in these trying times?"

"'Tis something that haunts me even now." Eva pressed her palm against her forehead. "I tried to help and my efforts completely failed."

"Everyone's efforts failed." Christina looked up with an unconvincing smile. "Even the almighty Wallace couldna save him."

With a wee sigh, Eva sipped her wine. "You did birth a healthy son."

"Aye, named him for his father." She placed her elbows on the table and covered her face in her palms, her shoulders shaking. "And now King Edward has taken him from me."

The strain in Christina's voice pulled at Eva's heart. Why did there have to be so much suffering? She reached out and smoothed her fingers along the lady's forearm while a tear streamed from her eye. "You will have your son returned."

"How should ye ken? It has been two years. He's just a wee lad with no father. He needs his ma." Removing a kerchief from her sleeve, she blotted her face.

"That he does, but he will not forget you—his time in captivity will only serve to strengthen his love of Scotland— and for you."

"How…?" Christina dropped her hands to the table and regarded Eva through swollen, red eyes. But then she leaned forward, her visage hopeful. "That's right. Ye are a seer."

Dragging her gaze aside, Eva nodded. That's what William had told everyone ever so long ago, but she'd use it to her advantage now. "Do you recall I told you the bairn inside you would be a lad?"

"Aye. I haven't forgotten to this day."

"Then you can believe me when I say your son will be returned to you on twenty-fourth June, the year of our Lord thirteen-fourteen." The medallion warmed against Eva's skin—but she could not worry about the damned thing now. She knew the date well because young Andrew Murray's release from the Tower of London would be part of the negotiation Robert the Bruce would undertake after his success at Bannockburn.

Lady Christina drew a hand over her mouth, her eyes wide with horror. "So long? Why, at six and ten he'll nearly be a man by then. He willna even recognize me."

"A boy always recognizes his mother." Eva leaned in, painfully aware she would probably be better off if the medallion took her away right now. "He will remember and cherish you."

"If only…"

"Your son will rise to greatness, come into more lands and title."

Her ladyship's eyes narrowed. "Ye're certain of this?"

"More sure of his future than I am of what will happen on the morrow."

"Oh, thanks be to God." Lady Christina took hold of the cross covering her heart. "They are treating him well? He willna suffer whilst in Edward's clutches in London?"

"He will be looked after and receive an education." Eva hoped—all she knew was that the boy would be one of the prisoners exchanged at Bannockburn.

"Goodness, I cannot tell ye how much such news lightens my heart. Though…" A tear escaped her eye. "'Tis so very long to wait to see him again."

"I can only imagine your suffering."

"And ye? Have ye children?"

"I'm afraid not, though William and I did exchange vows at long last."

"'Tis good to hear." Christina dabbed her eyes with a kerchief. "And how is Sir William? Well I hope?"

"Reasonably so. He is plagued by injuries—not nearly as agile as he once was."

"Unfortunately, war has a way of making young men old far before their time."

"Very true." The medallion cooled. *Darn it*. But Eva had a new goal in mind and she'd need all the help she could find. "William is on the Isle of Eynhallow up north in the Orkneys and I'm frightened to my very bones."

The woman narrowed her gaze, her teeth grazing her bottom lip. "Ye ken something, do ye not?"

The damn medallion heated up again. "Aye. I've had a vision that frightens me to the tips of my toes."

"About William?"

Gulping, Eva nodded. "I must find a way to make him remain in the Orkneys through the end of summer. But he needs men. He's trying to build an army whilst in hiding."

"Och, even William Wallace has resorted to hiding."

"No. It's not what you think. If no sightings are reported for a few months, he's hoping King Edward will end his raids. But William is anxious to return to the Lowlands and renew the fight." Her throat constricted as thoughts of the near future burst to the forefront of her mind. "I must ensure he stays in Eynhallow."

"And he doesna think he can build an army in exile?"

"Exactly. If word of his whereabouts leaks out, it's over." Her voice trembled. God she was on the edge of a breakdown. "Can you help? Can you send loyal Scottish soldiers north?"

Christina shook her head. "I am but a prisoner in my own home. The sheriff has spies watching my every movement."

Eva couldn't give up. No, this mission must be successful—for her and for William. She gulped down her urge to cry. "Do you know of a loyal soldier—someone who can move through the Highlands without suspicion?"

Standing, the lady crossed her arms and paced. "All of Scotland is afraid. It could take years to rebuild the forces which William and Andrew pulled together in mere sennights before Stirling. My heavens, a man can have his throat cut for the slightest trifle."

Eva stood and grasped her friend's hands. "How can we continue to live like this?"

"I, too, am under scrutiny." Christina took in an enormous breath. "If I agree to help ye, and the sheriff discovers me, they'll put my son under the knife for certain."

"Please." Eva clenched her hands tighter. "Of course you must exercise all care, but anything you can do to send loyal Scottish troops to William will be an immense help."

Christina pulled away and faced the fire.

"Will you help us?" Eva asked, pressing praying fingers to her lips.

"Aye. I ken of a Highlander who'll bear your message— but he willna have any clue it came from me. I've far too much at stake."

"Thank you."

The lady held up a finger. "My runner will bear word as if directly from William. I've no idea if anyone will come forward. Even in the Highlands, people are being forced into submission. If the clans do nothing, they can live in relative peace—if they take up arms, they will face the ire of Longshanks for certain."

Chapter Thirty

By the time the first of August arrived, Eva couldn't sleep, eat, or function. She'd tried to act as if nothing was afoot, as if the end would never come. But August arrived with the speed of a brakeless freight train and she now must do everything in her power to ensure William remained on the isle.

For the past few months, men had been trickling to Eynhallow under the pretense of becoming monks—some coming from the Highlands as a result of Lady Christina's efforts. William trained religiously during the days and succumbed to Eva's massages and warm baths at night. Though he worked tirelessly, his past injuries plagued him. In her time, a rugby player would often retire at the age of thirty-five. William had been battle scarred and wounded year after year—and not just muscle tears and sprains, which were bad enough. He'd suffered cuts to his every appendage, not to mention his abdomen, back and shoulders. Every inch of the man's flesh was crisscrossed with puckered scars. Eva could only imagine the damage he'd sustained beneath the skin.

But today was Sunday, a day of rest even observed by Wallace. Eva found him facing the sea, the wind in his hair as he sat reading his psalter. She stood still for a moment and watched, her breast swelling as if the waves crashing into the shore roiled inside her.

God bless it, the man defined magnificence. In quiet repose, alone with his maker, he looked gentle, content, at peace. If not for his deep-rooted passion to emancipate his people, he might have been suited for a life in the clergy. But then again, William was the type to find a cause—drawn to the persecuted—driven to unfetter their shackles no matter the cost.

How such a man could be so desirable in every way, she could not fathom. His bold profile punctuated by a straight nose, angled mouth, the coppery fullness of his beard—she adored everything about him. Could observe him for hours.

Licking her lips, she pulled her smartphone from her pocket and snapped a couple of pictures. Ever so peaceful, this was the man who'd claimed her heart, the man she would never forget no matter what. No other could possibly fill his shoes.

He turned the page. Eva smiled inwardly. The leather binding of his psalter was nearly worn, brown leather showing through the black where his hand gripped it. Several leaves had long since separated from the binding, but though William had the means, he refused to purchase a new one. No, this book had been his constant companion since the days when he'd studied to be a Templar knight. He kept it whole and secure with a leather thong. A more ardent soldier of God did not exist. Truly, William's passion came from his faith and his love for the oppressed.

If only men like him existed in my time.

Marking the page with his finger, he looked out to sea as if contemplating something profound in the text.

Just a few more days. She must ensure he stayed on the isle. In a week she could sleep. Even if the medallion sent her home, it would be worth it as long as she succeeded.

I'm convinced this is why I've been sent back. Not to heal William, but to save him.

He glanced her way and grinned—the charismatic smile with the white teeth that never ceased to make her knees crumble. "How long have ye been standing there?" he asked, his deep voice carrying on the wind.

"Not long." Eva strolled to his side and sat. "Would you like some company?"

He opened his arm and enfolded her in his plaid beside him. "'Tis always a pleasure to have ye by my side, wife."

She leaned her head on his shoulder. "It warms me inside to hear you call me wife."

"And all that time ye feared marrying me." Inhaling through his nostrils, he kissed her cheek. "Is it so awful?"

She curled into his warmth. God, she loved this man. "I never thought it would be."

"But ye ken something. I feel it in my bones—something ye canna speak of."

A knot the size of a fist clamped in her neck. Jesus Christ, she couldn't speak of it…couldn't even think about it. She looked down.

"Ye see?" he pressed, lifting her chin with his pointer finger. "I ken your heart, Lady Eva, and whatever it is has ye rattled."

She closed her eyes. "It is too awful to speak of." Though tucked away in her satchel, she couldn't stifle the medallion's warmth as if it were flush against her skin. Heaven help her, she *had* to stay—had to save him.

William's arm squeezed around her shoulder and drew her close. "I've seen enough death and brutality for a hundred lifetimes. Do ye not think I canna stomach any vileness no matter how wretched?"

"But what of a heinous crime against you?" Cold chills seeped across her skin. "What of unconscionable suffering—a hideous death?"

He brushed his lips across her temple with a tender kiss. "Och, lass. I've been tortured within an inch of my life. Cut open by the claws of a lion. Ye think I fear death?"

"Doesn't everyone? I mean the end is so final."

"Is it?" He held up his beloved psalter. "This life is but a passage to the next."

She gazed at him in awe. "You are so secure in your belief."

"If I wasna, I'd have gone completely mad by now. Mark me, wife, there is a greater glory waiting for those who take up the sword and fight for justice. Blair spoke true when he said 'rebellion to tyrants is obedience to God.'"

"Well then I expect you to be an exalted commander in heaven's army." Jeez, she almost bit her tongue off when those words escaped her mouth. She didn't want to talk about death—didn't want to even acknowledge it.

He crossed his ankles as if this conversation were idle chat. "I would be happy to be a servant who washes the feet of the great men who have gone before me."

For the love of God, they were both only thirty-five. They could grow old together on this tiny island. William could build a cottage. There were plenty of fish and rabbits. They needed nothing else. She hugged his arm. "Promise me something."

"What is that, *mon amour*?"

"You will not leave the island in the next month at least." She wanted to say never, but that would have been met with a sharp rebuttal.

He narrowed his gaze. "Why a month?"

Because I aim to rewrite history. "Can you just promise me this once?"

He shrugged. "A promise for my Scottish rose?"

"Please."

"I'd promise ye the moon if I owned piece of it." Pulling her into his lap, he softly brushed his lips over hers, his crystal blue eyes reflecting the waves. "Ye mean more to me than anyone in all of Christendom. But I canna make promises I mightn't be able to keep."

He covered her mouth before she could speak, his kiss melting into her like succulent chocolate. Showing him the depth of her love with fervent sweeps of her tongue, Eva's heart swelled until she could burst.

As a tear slipped from the corner of her eye, she clutched him to her for dear life. This man was her savior. His breath alone commanded her heart to beat. She must not give up. She moved her fingers to his psalter and made a silent vow.

I swear I will watch over my husband and keep him safe from harm.

Chapter Thirty-One

When William looked up, it was no surprise to see a galley approaching, flying the pennant of the Earl of Carrick. He'd known something was afoot for sennights. His wife mightn't be able to predict small events, but Eva couldn't hide it when she knew something big would happen. Only he'd never seen her so distraught before.

The color drained from her face as she straightened in his lap, digging her feet into the stones on the beach. "Lord Bruce," she whispered as if suddenly chilled.

"Aye." He stood, pulling Eva to her feet with him. "Go to the kitchens and ensure a feast is prepared for our guests."

"But."

"Do it, I say." He pointed back toward the cloistered walls. "Doubtless, the earl and his company will have a sore hunger."

Pursing her lips, she gave a sharp nod. "I shall see you in the dining hall anon." Her voice took on a commanding tone William didn't care for, though he chose not to argue. He just pointed, urging her to obey.

He didn't know why, but he wanted to meet the Bruce alone. In the past sennights, Eva had been too outspoken and uppity. Whatever news the earl brought, William needed to hear it with a clear head, without Eva's opinionated comments making him doubt his convictions. Aye, he loved her more than any person in all of Christendom, but no matter how much he wanted to, he could not place her or any mortal ahead of his duty. The image of his father lying lifeless in the mud, his sinews sliced as if he were worth no more than a slab of meat on the butcher's block burned into William's memory. On that day long ago, he'd committed himself to the patriot's cause and would live by its creed.

Dressed for battle, the earl alighted from the galley unassisted. Most men of his affluence would have their men-at-arms carry them through the knee-deep surf, but not Robert Bruce. The man bore his nobility with an air of command, of strength. Something William hadn't found in the others.

Wallace bowed deeply. "M'lord, it pleases me to see ye havena forgotten us."

The hearty warrior took Wallace's hand with a firm grip. "Och, Sir William, the memory of our last meeting weighs on my conscience with every passing day."

"'Tis music to a weary soldier's ears."

"Weary? Ye've been in repose for the past four months." Lord Bruce gestured forward, leading him away from his retinue. "Tell me, how goes our army?"

"We need more men for certain."

"What are your numbers?"

"Five hundred." William's shoulder ticked up. "They're trickling in and, with them, bringing tales of oppression and fear."

Lord Bruce strode thoughtfully, his hands clasped behind his back. "I'd hoped for greater numbers by now. Ye're right. We need ten times that to put an end to the senseless raids."

William stopped. "Ye mean to say after all this time, things have not yet settled—even on the borders?"

"'Tis grave and the borders are suffering the worst of it." A dark shadow passed over the good man's face. "More villages are being put to fire and sword than before, all the while the marauders are calling your name. The murders and hangings have grown out of hand. 'Tis as if Longshanks' madness increases with every passing hour."

William's fingernails bit into his palms as he clenched his fists. "I thought my disappearance would serve to settle the bastard's ire."

"As did I."

"Is there someone else inciting the English garrisons playacting in my stead?"

The earl chuckled. "No one would be brave enough to take on your mantle."

"Ballocks." Scratching his beard, William looked toward the courtyard. It was eerily quiet, even for a Sunday. "We need an act so powerful, 'twill provide a spark to ignite a fire in the Kingdom's breast."

"I agree. If only we had the numbers we could strike now. God kens we need a miracle." The earl heaved a heavy sigh and looked to the heavens. "After all this time, the people still love ye. Still long for the day when Wallace—their savior—will ride on the heavens and bring them liberty."

Such a verbose assertion made William scoff. "No mortal man is capable of such heroism."

"Nay?" Lord Bruce bowed. "Not even William Wallace, sir?"

Looking the earl directly in the eye, William's gut clamped with the power of his conviction. "Mayhap a young king with cods of iron could rise up in my stead."

The Bruce's hawk-like stare narrowed. "What are ye saying?"

"Your time has come, m'lord. It is up to ye to take up the gauntlet and rise above the mire."

"Take a stand against all of England?" He spread his arms wide and raised his chin. "Now? When we have been beaten and burned through eight years of tyranny? How will I find an army of forty-thousand brave Scots who can stand against the greatest fighting machine in all of Christendom?'"

"Ye will, 'cause I will start a riot so grandiose nary a tiller of the land will be able to step away from his sword." William stepped in and held his pointer finger under the earl's nose. "And ye must let nothing and no one stand in your way."

The Bruce folded his arms. "What is this grandiose plan of which ye speak?"

"I'll tell ye once we are on our way." William inclined his head toward the galley. "We've a good wind, m'lord. We'd best take advantage of it."

***

"His lordship's galley has set sail," a crier bellowed from the tower.

The bowl of apples dropped from Eva's hands, crashing to the floor, shattering into hundreds of pottery shards. With a shrieking gasp her hands flew to her mouth. "William!"

The monks in the kitchen stopped and looked her way.

"Where is William?" she demanded.

One shrugged his shoulders.

Eva didn't wait for his response. Running to the courtyard, she grabbed the front of Father Blair's black vestments. "Have you seen William?"

"I thought he was with Lord Bruce."

"Aye, and the ship's sailed." Shoving the priest away, Eva raced out the gate. Tears burned her eyes. In the distance, the sea galley's sail billowed with wind, heading away at full tilt.

"William!" she screamed, scanning the shore for his robust form—his dark hair blowing in the wind, his physique in repose, reading his psalter as he'd been doing only an hour before.

"No! You cannot leave me here. What in God's name are you thinking?" Her mind spinning, Eva ran into the surf. "What did the earl say to make you board that ship?"

Icy water soaked her gown and slowed her progress, but onward she went. "Come back! I am your wife. Come back to me—" The undertow whipped around her legs and drew her downward with the ebb of the tide.

As water filled her mouth, a large hand clamped onto her shoulder. A burst of hope shot through her heart until Blair's grey-eyed scowl met her gaze. He dragged her toward the shore as she tried to wrench from his grasp.

"We must stop him," she shouted, sputtering saltwater out of her mouth.

"Why in the blazes did ye not stay with him?" He pushed her onto the stony beach.

"Me? I told you he sent me to the kitchens." She clutched her arms tight to stave off the shivers and her chattering teeth. "Why did you not follow him?"

"Bloody hell, ye said they needed a meal."

"Jesus Christ." Eva's stomach convulsed, her breathing grew shallow. "He cannot be on that ship."

Blair grabbed her by the shoulders and shook. "Dammit, woman. Ye've spoken in cryptic gibberish long enough. Tell me what has ye so riled."

With a burst of ire, she twisted out of his grasp. "I know you do not believe that I am from the future, and honestly, I no longer care what you think. But trust me when I say William will be captured by the English on August third, the year of our Lord thirteen hundred and five."

Dropping his hands, Blair looked to the sea galley, now only a speck on the horizon. "Good God, that is only two days hence."

"Exactly." Her teeth chattering, she tugged on his arm. "We must leave immediately. He will be betrayed by Sir John Menteith, taken to Dumbarton Castle for one night before they haul him to London for a mockery of a trial."

The friar didn't budge. "Ye kent all this and yet didna tell me?"

"If I had, the words would not have escaped my mouth before I would have been swept away for good." Eva ran her palm over the spot where the medallion should be. Her damned skin was as icy cold as the droplets of water sprinkling from her hair. What if she *had* tried to tell him? Would William still be there?

"There is only one rule." Walter Tennant's voice rang in her head. Those were the words he used when he gave her the medallion.

Her sudden disappearance when she'd tried to help Andrew Murray was an experience she could ill afford to repeat. She must tread with utmost care—must not divulge too much or she'd run the risk of losing William. Eva curled over, her fists tight against her forehead. Why couldn't she stop him from going? Why couldn't she convince him to stay?

Would he have done so if she'd revealed the whole truth? She knew the answer, though she wasn't about to accept it.

She started toward the monastery to collect her things—including the damned medallion. "Gather a crew. We must sail after them straight away."

CHAPTER THIRTY-TWO

After their galley set sail, the wind changed and with it came a violent tempest. Refusing to turn back, Eva and William's most loyal men suffered the ire of the Atlantic as they tacked through thirty-foot waves toward Glasgow.

Two days it took them to negotiate the angry swells, all the while Eva prayed they'd catch up to Lord Bruce's galley. The storm cleared as their boat headed up the River Clyde.

As soon as they alighted onto the pier, they were intercepted by the Earl of Carrick. "Sir Wallace told me ye would follow."

"You're bloody right I would." Eva reached into her satchel and pulled out a handful of shillings. "We need horses. We must haste to Robroyston a once."

Bruce frowned. "Ye are too late."

"Then to Dumbarton!"

The earl knit his brows with a menacing glare. "How do ye ken this?"

"She's a seer," said John Blair, stepping beside her.

"And William's wife." Robbie Boyd hopped on her other side, gripping the hilt of his sword. "Lady Eva will gain an audience with her husband anon."

"Ye'd best watch your backs." Lord Bruce eyed each one. "Ye men all have prices on your heads. If ye're seen within a mile of Dumbarton ye'll not live to tell tale of it, mark me."

"What about me?" Eva asked. "Is there a price on my head?"

"I didna ken Wallace had married," said Bruce.

"Only his most trusted men were a party to the ceremony," said Blair.

Eva took Robbie by the elbow and pulled him forward. "You must stay with Lord Bruce. He will need your sword and your fealty."

The young man yanked his arm from her grasp. "No. Not while Willy is in peril."

Eva looked to the man who would seize the Scottish crown in less than a year. Placing her palm in Robbie's back, she led the lad toward him. "Sir Robert Dominus Boyd is named for his father. A knight hanged by Edward the Longshanks. During his youth he acted as squire to William Wallace who taught this young man to be a knight and to keep him, a lad of noble birth, from King Edward's grasp." She dipped into a deep curtsey. "There would be no greater sword at your side than Sir Boyd. He knows how to fight like Wallace—he is bred to guard a king."

The Bruce's eyes widened as he assessed the young warrior. "William wed a wise woman."

Robbie took a step back. "But—"

"Go," commanded Blair. "'Tis your destiny, lad."

The promising knight threw out his hands. "I canna leave William behind."

Taking Robbie's hands in her palms, Eva squeezed. "Remember what I told you? Your time has come. You must follow the path of your future."

The lad's face flushed red. "I—"

Lord Bruce gripped Robbie's shoulder. "Come, Sir Boyd. We've a new rising to plan."

Shifting his gaze to the future king, Robbie's Adam's apple bobbed. But he nodded.

Eva wasted no more time. Beckoning the priest, she inclined her head toward the stables. "Go find us some horses."

Crossing the street, Eva glanced over her shoulder. Robbie made wide gestures of disbelief until the future king placed his hand on the lad's shoulder and spoke. Something happened then—the Bruce's words must have been profound because the young knight took one step back and bowed deeply.

***

By the time she arrived at Dumbarton Castle it was dark. Father Blair and Eddy Little hid in the shadows of the trees while Eva climbed the stairs and pounded on the gate.

The screen opened and a helmed head popped through. "Go away. The gates are sealed closed until the morrow."

"Please. I must see the prisoner William Wallace."

The guard cackled with a rueful laugh. "That sorry bastard is headed for a public execution, he is."

"Please just let me speak to him."

"Too right, Sir Menteith will receive lands and riches for ensnaring that slippery eel," the guard spewed in a brogue sounding thick like cockney English. "But ye're too late, wench. They set out hours ago. Menteith didn't want to chance on risking a raid by Wallace's men—not when we have the traitor in our grasp."

If only she could reach through the panel and wrap her fingers around the guard's neck. "Sir William is not a traitor. He is a patriot. And you, sir, are trespassing on Scottish lands."

He shoved his ugly face further out the window. "Ye're one them are ye not? Off with ye afore I haul your arse into the dungeon and lock ye away for the rest of your days."

Backing away, Eva gaped. The panel slammed closed. She took in consecutive gasps while clutching her heart. *Not there? The history books got it wrong, goddammit.*

***

Eva thought they'd never reach London. When they crested the last hill, the smoke hanging above the medieval city gave the impression of hell—it had a sulphur stench, too. Only Satan himself would enjoy wandering the streets of such a cesspool. But she would tread through hell and sell her soul to see William. She could not allow him to go through this madness—not while she remained in this century.

Pointed spires jutted toward the sky, surrounded by the slate roofs of wooden townhouses. The twin gothic towers of Westminster Abbey stood as prominent as the Tower of London nestled by the Thames. The river itself had a green tinge, and as they neared, the stench became unbearable. Eva held her cloak across her nose, but it did little to allay the burning of her eyes. The streets grew narrower, sloppy with mud and excrement. Hogs wandered freely, gnawing on the rotting flesh cast aside from the butchers' blocks.

Eva had experienced the filth of medieval cities before, but nothing compared to London. She thanked God a horse carried her toward the tower. She'd loose her meager breakfast of oatcakes if forced to sink her feet in the mire. But even sickness from revulsion would not sway her determination.

Dressed in a nun's habit, Eva slipped to the gatehouse of the Tower. John Blair and Eddy Little remained behind at an inn while they awaited her return. Again she hailed the guard, but this time she knew William was locked away in one of the dank chambers. She would not leave until she saw him.

A panel slid aside. "Who goes there?"

"It is Eve, a holy woman who wishes to pray over the prisoner William Wallace." She purposely called herself by the first woman to allay doubt of her being a nun.

The soldier gawked, looking her from head to toe. "Are ye daft? That beggar is a vile beast. Such a man could do ye harm."

"I am a bride of Christ. The Lord's mercy is watching over me. Surely you would not deny the vilest of men an opportunity to atone for their sins."

"But he has seen a priest."

"Ah yes, but a man will confess more to a woman." She held up Blair's bible. "Please, I have selected a scripture to ease his troubled soul."

The door creaked with the sliding sound of the crossbar. "I'll allow it, but only for a moment."

As it opened, Eva made the sign of the cross. "God will look favorably upon you come the Day of Judgement."

Following the stocky guard through a maze of dank passageways and wheel stairwells, more than one rat scurried through the shadows. Eva recoiled at the filth. When he stopped at a thick wooden door, reinforced with blackened iron nails, she peered through the crossbars in the tiny window.

William sat on a cot, his head bent over his psalter. Eva swooned as she clutched a hand over her heart. When the door opened, she curtseyed to the guard. "Leave us."

"But—"

"I will be unharmed. The prisoner needs solitude."

With a nod, he shut the door behind her and bolted it.

William didn't look up. He merely held a finger to his lips while footsteps clapped and faded down the passageway.

Then his eyes met hers. The same eyes that could see to her soul and carve out her every secret. But she'd never seen such an expression on William's face before. Yes, there was bold determination, strength, intelligence, but this was the first time she'd ever read defeat.

He set his psalter aside. "I wish ye hadn't come."

She moved further inside. "Did you think for one moment that I would not?"

"Nay. I kent 'twas a matter of time."

Choking back a gasp, Eva rushed to him, falling to her knees and clutching his hands between hers. "You cannot go through with this."

"I have made up my mind." His eyes pleaded. "One man's life for an entire Kingdom. The people will rise at the outrage. I ken they will in my heart. It is what Lord Bruce needs to rekindle the Scottish spirit."

She suddenly wished she'd never uttered the Earl of Carrick's name. "Do you know what they will do to you?"

His head dropped forward. "I have an inkling. After so many years of chasing me, Longshanks willna make my death easy."

"It will be the most atrocious, painful death imaginable." She took off the medallion and wrapped it around both their wrists. "Go back to the twenty-first century with me. Please. I will show you everything. I-I-I never told you that men can fly."

He snorted and shook his head. "Och, Eva..."

"They can. In airplanes. Planes can ferry a great number of people like a ship at sea." She closed her eyes tight and concentrated, squeezing William's fingers. "Take us back. Take us to a gentler time. I want to show William my world. Please!"

He wrenched his hands out from under the leather thong. "Nay, lass. It is done. I stand firm on my conviction. This old warrior's bones are weary."

"Old? Why, you might very well have fifty more years to live—over half your life."

"And then what? Die an old man in my bed? That is not a death that will inspire a nation to arms."

A tear streaked down her cheek. Her mouth quivered. "Please, William. I cannot lose you. You will be tried on the morrow. Once the sentence is passed they will drag you behind a horse and—"

"Hush." He held his fingers to her lips. "I ken what they will do and I will meet my end."

Shaking her head, she couldn't breathe. "No—"

"Wheesht, now." He pulled her into his arms and silenced her mouth with a deep kiss. Raw passion surged from him, for the fear he could not express with his words electrified her with the intensity from the pressure of his lips and the desperate swirling of his tongue.

Inhaling deeply, he leaned his forehead against hers. "Our souls are one, m'lady. We will meet again in heaven and ye will be my bride through eternity."

How can he say this? Be so calm when my every nerve ending is on fire? "I cannot let you go."

"Ye have no choice. I want ye to return to your time. Go now, for there is nothing left for ye here."

He placed her on her feet and hollered for the guard.

***

All three disguised in peasant's garb, Eva attended William's trial with Eddy and John.

Dark paneled benches in two tiers and filled with English noblemen lined the Westminster courtroom walls. Onlookers were allowed to stand in the public gallery beyond the justice's table. People crammed into the space, shoulder to shoulder, the air heavy with the sickly pall of unwashed humanity.

Eva's entire body shook as they led William into the courtroom in chains and forced him to stand inside a cage tipped with sharp iron spikes. She reached out toward him, her throat thick and dry. Boos and rumbles of dissention rolled between the chamber walls.

The justice hammered his gavel, demanding silence. "William Wallace of Scotland, ye have been accused of sedition, homicides, plunderings, fire-raisings and a litany of other felonies and crimes."

William stared at the black-robed man, his face devoid of emotion.

"Ye are not allowed to speak during these proceedings as ordered by His Grace, King Edward of England."

"That'd be right—not allow a man a defense," grumbled Blair under his breath.

"All hear the case and evidence against the felon who stands before ye. The charges are lengthy. The evidence irrefutable." Lord Justice stood, unrolled a scroll and cleared his throat. "The King of England in hostile manner conquered the land of Scotland over John Balliol. The prelates, the earls, the barons and other Scottish enemies of England were in forfeiture along with the same John, and by the conquest of him submitted and subjugated all the Scots to right of ownership and Edward's royal power as their king. After which, Edward of England received in public the homages and pledges of the prelates."

Eva frowned. *The Ragman Roll was signed by Scotland's nobles under duress.*

"The King made his peace to be proclaimed through the whole of the land of Scotland. He appointed and set up Guardians of that land, including sheriffs, provosts, bailiffs and other ministers to maintain his peace and issue justice to all according to the laws and customs of England. The aforesaid William Wallace, forgetful of his fealty and allegiance—"

"I did not pledge fealty to the English king," William's deep voice resonated across the chamber.

Boos and shouts of vile discord came from the gallery.

"No!" Eva shouted at the top of her lungs, only to have Blair slap a hand over her mouth.

The justice hammered his gavel on the board. "Silence. The prisoner is *not* permitted to speak."

William stared at the man, his eyes dark, his lips in a hard, thin line. Though he was not allowed to speak in his defense, Eva doubted he would. *Someone must stand up for him.*

"Forgetful of his fealty and allegiance, Wallace unlawfully raised up all he could by felony and premeditated sedition against our lord and King. Having united and joined to himself an immense number of felons, he invaded and attacked the guardians and ministers of the same King. He insulted, wounded and killed William de Heselrig, Sheriff of Lanark, without reason or provocation."

After panning a scowling gaze around the courtroom, the Lord Justice continued reading the scroll. "Thenceforth he invaded the towns, the cities and the castles of that land and sent his orders through the whole of Scotland as if they were the letters of the superior of that land. He held and appointed parliaments after the guardians and ministers appointed by the aforesaid lord, the King of the land of Scotland, had been evicted by William himself. He decreed to all prelates, earls and barons they were to press for the destruction of the Kingdom of England. William Wallace then proceeded to invade the Kingdom of England, laying to fire and sword the counties of Northumberland, Cumberland and Westmorland. All whom he found who were in fealty to the King of England, he feloniously put to death in various ways. He seditiously slaughtered religious men and monks dedicated to God. He burned and laid waste to churches constructed for the honor of God. And it is clear that after such outrageous and horrible deeds, the aforesaid lord, the King, together with his great army, invaded the land of Scotland and defeated the aforesaid William who bore his standard against King Edward in mortal warfare."

Lord Justice made a verbose gesture, swinging his arm over his head. "William Wallace seditiously and feloniously, whole-heartedly and undauntedly preserving his above noted *wickedness*, disdained to submit himself to the King's peace. He was publicly outlawed as a traitor, robber and felon according to the laws and customs of England."

The man paused, deepening his scowl. "On these charges the accused stands guilty without recourse and will hereby be sentenced."

Again, the crowd's angry voice rose with dissention, feet stomping the floorboards.

"Silence," bellowed the bailiff, pounding his staff on the floorboards.

"For the inarguable sedition which William committed against our lord and King and trying to bring about His Grace's death, the attempted destruction and weakening of the crown of its royal authority by bringing his standard against his liege lord in war to the death, William Wallace will be tied to a horse and dragged from the palace of Westminster as far as the Tower of London, and from the Tower as far as Aldegate, and thus through the middle of the city as far as Elmes, and for the robberies, murders and felonies which he carried out in the Kingdom of England and Scotland, he shall be hanged there and afterwards drawn. Furthermore, for the measureless wickedness which he did to God and the most Holy Church by burning churches, vassals and shires, the heart, liver, lung and all the internal parts of the same William by which such evil thoughts proceeded should be dispatched to the fire and burned. And because he had been outlawed and not restored to the King's peace, he will be beheaded. And also because he had committed both murders and felonies to not only the King but to the entire people of England and Scotland, the body of said William Wallace will be cut up and divided into four quarters. The head shall be affixed upon London Bridge in the sight of those crossing both by land and water. One quarter should be hung on the gibbet at Newcastle Upon Tyne, another quarter at Berwick, a third quarter at Stirling and a fourth quarter at Perth as a cause of fear and chastisement in all who pass by.[1]"

When Lord Justice stopped and gazed out over the crowd, not a soul uttered a word.

Breaking away from Blair, Eva pushed through the gallery—her eyes streaming with tears, her head spinning so fast the chamber spun. "No! William is a patriot," she screamed at the top of her lungs. "Scotland is oppressed by Edward's sadistic tyranny! *You* are the murderers—"

As the words escaped her mouth, the medallion burned a hole in her chest, earsplitting screeches deafened her ears. Her entire body ripped apart in a spiral of agonizing darkness.

---

[1] Adapted from J. Russell's translation of *Documents Illustrative of Sir William Wallace*, his Life and Times, ed. Joseph Stevenson, Maitland Club, 1841.

CHAPTER THIRTY-THREE

William ~ The Calm of the Condemned

When Eva's voice rose over the roar of the crowd, I glanced her way for the first time. Though I'd asked her to leave, I kent she'd come. If I have any regrets from my decision, it is saying adieu to my sweet Eva and seeing her bereft with grief. But Scotland needs me more—needs my end.

Heaven help me, I loved that woman more than any earthly being.

As the bailiffs tugged my arms, her tall figure was soon swallowed by Blair and Little while guardsmen pushed their way toward her. But I knew she was gone. I felt it. A wee puff of air skimmed my face, and I kent she'd vanished—returned to her time. Why the magic allowed her to remain for so long, I could not fathom.

Mercifully, the medallion's powers swept her away, just as they had done the day Andrew died. With that silent wisp of air, my wife went to a better life—one in which I pray she will live fully, peacefully.

Lord Clifford held my psalter high as the bailiffs marshalled me out of the courtroom and into the street. I didn't fight. There was no sense in doing so. My actions this day were for my beloved Scotland. I gladly gave of myself for the Kingdom. Praise God a new king will rise. I will not see her restored to greatness, but I go to my death knowing my sacrifice will be a catalyst for change.

Eva was right about Lord Bruce. I, too, felt his greatness in my bones more than once.

The angry jeers from the crowd met me like a wall of soaring arrows. My heart thundered in my chest, betraying me. I did not allow fear to creep into my consciousness often, but her evilness seized me in her hands and a cold sweat covered my skin.

I harbored no illusions. I would endure horrendous pain—pain I had inflicted on others during this war. I'd watched men die at the point of my sword. Their faces stunned at first, followed by listlessness.

I would meet those men by this day's end.

There would be no turning back. I'd made my decision. I caught sight of my psalter in Lord Clifford's hands as the bailiffs bound me upside down to the hurdle, then lashed a hog's skin around my arms and body to ensure I survived the four-mile journey to my death.

Death.

My Judgement Day had come at last.

Closing my eyes, I forced myself to overcome my fear, to reach for joy. I would stand before God this day and atone for my sins. The proceedings at heaven's gates would not be a trial like Longshanks' crookedness I'd just endured. It would be a discussion of my errs. A chance to face them with honesty and to kneel before my maker. Aye, God will judge me harshly, but not unfairly.

Rotten food slapped my face when, at a slow walk, the horse dragged me through the mire. Taunts from the crowd followed me. People opened their shutters and threw the contents of their chamber pots upon me—rocks pummeled my body and the horseman ensured I hit every bump in the road. Humanity at its worst, I felt no contempt for these misled vassals of King Edward. I had fought their sons. I had invaded their country, and in their eyes, I was guilty of every charge read by the justice—except sedition. In their eyes, I deserved every ounce of indignity, brutality and revenge imposed by their dragon-hearted sovereign.

How could a man commit treason against a country to which he'd pledged no fealty? Edward came to Scotland, humiliating our king and murdering men, women and children. The King of England was as guilty as I. *Guiltier.* My actions were all carried out as an act of war to protect and liberate the oppressed. Longshanks' motives were to gain more lands, more riches for himself, and he turned butcher to do it.

At least I can go to my death knowing liberty isn't lost. My respect for Robert Bruce grew as I sailed south to Glasgow with him. During that journey he unveiled his vision for the Kingdom—one not unlike my own. He is my choice to accede to the throne and Eva's unerring predictions of the future cemented my conviction that I am doing the right thing.

Would I like to grow old and die in my bed with Lady Eva in my arms? Had I not been born in a time of turmoil, I would give my eyeteeth to do so.

The horse rounded the bend and my body slammed into the corner of a stone building. A man kicked my side. A pot smashed into my face. Aside from a grunt, I forced myself not to bellow with the throbbing pain of my broken nose. My eyes watered. I clenched my teeth as well as my fists. I'd suffered as much on the battlefield. Except this time, the taunts hurt worse than the blows.

If only I could hold a sword in my hand during these my last hours. To die with a weapon in my hand—that is the wish of every warrior.

When the horse finally stopped, they cut me from the hurdle, my body bruised and bleeding. At Smithfield, a vast concourse of onlookers jeered as the hangman tied a rope around my neck and by the point of a sword forced me to climb a ladder.

I stood there teetering on the fourth rung whilst he paraded around the gallows, holding a headman's axe above his coif. "The traitor William Wallace has been drawn through the streets of London. I see by the state of his face you good people have shown him what we think of traitors and felons."

"He's not fit to eat with the swine," screeched an old hag while I teetered on an unstable rung.

A shove came from behind. My feet slipped from beneath me. I instantly gagged. Swinging, kicking, my eyes bulged from my face as I wheezed and coughed. Stars darted through my vision as I tried to gasp, but my airways were choked.

Taunts of "justly deserved", "he's more hardened in cruelty than Herod", and "make him suffer" piqued my ears. Yet still, the good Lord Clifford held my psalter high.

My body shuddered as I lost all control.

I shall fear no evil.

Blissful words of faith gave me solace as the rope strangled the life from my throat.

Just as my mind went blank, my body crashed to the wooden gallows. Aye, it would have been too easy to expire in the hangman's noose.

"This is far from over," said the headsman, waving an axe in front of my face.

Sputtering against my crushed voice box, they forced me to my feet and again lashed my neck and ankles to a hurdle to keep me upright. No one need warn me what was next. I'd run many a man through on the battlefield. My throat dry and ruined from the hanging, my mouth didn't seem to work. A stream of drool bled from my lips, the pain from my broken nose throbbed clear to the back of my head.

I didn't give the bastard the satisfaction of watching my eyes as he took a dagger and cut off my clothes. All I could see was my psalter.

Lord Jesus, I am coming to you soon.

Chilled by the wind, my naked skin quivered with gooseflesh. Still I stared at the black book that had brought me solace throughout my life.

The jesters danced around me, pointing to my genitals, pretending to cut me.

If only I had use of my hands, I'd bat them senseless. These sadistic vassals of an insane king wanted to draw out my death, to mock me and to be entertained by my humiliation.

They might break the flesh, but they could never shame the man. I go to my maker without regret.

Emitting a cackling laugh, the executioner stepped up to me, his head covered with a black hood—the coward. He held a dagger to my eyes, sharp as any blade I'd seen. "You will watch whilst I carve out your bowels and burn them to atone for your evil deeds."

My stomach squeezed with the chills running up my spine.

Clifford held the psalter higher.

Thy rod and thy staff they comfort me.

My gut seized with the first thrust of the blade. Bile spewed from my trembling mouth. My eyes crossed. My hands and legs shook uncontrollably. Blinking to focus on my psalter, sickly tasting water dribbled from my lips. My breath came in short gasps. Agony consumed my mind. This was nothing like being cut on the battlefield with the lust for a fight rushing through my veins.

As the murderer carved out my innards, the pain grew duller. Darkness encroached as my vision faded. My head dropped sideways but I could still see my psalter.

The crowd heckled as the stench of my own entrails sizzled on the fire.

My life's blood oozed hot down my quivering thighs.

With a long release of air, my vision failed before I heard another taunt and the pain mercifully ebbed into oblivion.

CHAPTER THIRTY-FOUR

Crouched in a fetal position, Eva wailed, her throat burning from endless hysterical screams. Curling into something soft, she rocked back and forth while staccato breaths cramped her sides. After all that time, the force behind the medallion ignored her until the critical moment when she could have done something to stop the course of history.

It wasn't fair. She hadn't asked to be sent back to William. The whole time she'd dreaded what would happen, begged to be sent home, but no. Whatever sordid mystical powers sent her to William wanted her to suffer.

Aye, she'd been given her six months. God damn them.

The single rule could not be changed.

Jesus, she'd never be the same again. The pain shredded her heart into a million pieces. How could she go on? Yes, after Steven's death she'd wept, wandered the halls of her New York flat aimlessly, but that grief was nothing compared to the sickly horror of this loss—and William's brutal end.

Eva bawled until no more tears would come. Realizing she'd landed on her bed at Torwood Castle, she pulled the comforter over her shoulders and hid in the darkness.

Why did she give her heart when she knew the ending?

Why didn't she push him away from the beginning?

The damned medallion didn't send her home because it knew she could do nothing to affect the past.

Hiding alone in a modern century, she felt like a stranger. She didn't want to put the pieces of her life together. Not again.

Eva must have fallen asleep because she awoke to a ray of light streaming in the window, a lark singing beyond.

Feeling like she'd been pushed through a set of iron rollers, she took in a deep breath and sat up. Stretching her arms did nothing to allay the pounding of her head.

Taking her weight on her feet, she started for the ensuite. She'd been wearing the same gown for weeks—something that would be disgusting in her time. Was disgusting when she thought about how badly she would smell to modern folks.

Turning the dial on the water heater, she stood under the stream of soothing warmth and closed her eyes while her tears began anew. Out of necessity, she went through the motions of washing her hair and scrubbing the dirt and sweat from every inch of her body. Scrubbing the brutality of the fourteenth century from her every pore. Washing away the whole sordid, sickening mess.

If only she could have brought William back. Hot showers could have soothed the tears in his muscles, the scars riddling his flesh. But she would never know the joy of being in her lover's arms again.

After toweling off, dressing in a pair of jeans and an old sweatshirt, she dried her hair and stared in the mirror while trying to bring some life to her miserable face with a tad of makeup. Then she picked up her gown and gave it a good shake.

A slip of vellum cascaded to the floor. With a quivering hand, she stooped to pick it up and took it to the padded chair in front of the hearth.

Her throat closed while trembling fingers opened the letter.

My dearest Eva,

As I take up my quill, I am in Robroyston awaiting my betrayal. Ye are most likely already aware that I have agreed to play into Longshanks' hands to bring about a new era for Scotland. Ye were right about Lord Bruce. He is a steadfast warrior. A man of decision. A leader who the people will follow.

My time here is done. My role played out on the battlefield long ago, and I must take steps necessary to help the Kingdom gain its freedom from a monster. Ye understand the cause of a rebel. Ye understand my heart, perhaps even better than I.

I, however, harbor no illusions that this "betrayal" and my death will be difficult for ye, my dearest wife. Ye are the most loving and giving person I ken. Please remember ye are the only woman I have ever loved. Our bond transcends the ages. Our bond will again join us when we both stand together in heaven.

Lead a full life, my love. Ye once said people in your time enjoy long and healthy lives. Pour your passion into your castle, for ye are a woman who can do anything once your mind is set.

Eva, mon amour, ye will always be the keeper of my heart.

Your loving husband,

William

The walls closed around her. How could she pick up and go on with life? Pretend all this hadn't happened? Eyes blurred by tears, mucus streamed from her nose and over her lips as she clutched the missive to her bosom.

Staggering into the passageway, Eva raced down the stairwell. When the steps opened to the great hall, she broke into a run.

The enormous door opened.

Through her tears, a ray of light illuminated the tall form stepping inside.

"Hello," said an imposing voice in a deep lilting burr. "Is the castle closed to visitors?"

In a blink, Eva had no idea what day it was. She dabbed the tears beneath her eyes and forced herself to gain control. "I-I'm afraid we're only open on weekends at the moment."

Her vision cleared. Her heart raced and goosebumps spread across her skin. "It's *you*."

"Pardon?"

"William?" The man surely looked like William—aside from the shorter hair, the shaved face and dress officer's uniform, complete with three lines of impressive medals, sporran and kilt.

"Do I know you?" His eyebrows pinched together just like William's, then he stepped closer.

"Not sure." Her breath caught in her throat. What in God's name was happening? "Y-y-you look surprisingly similar to someone who was very dear to me." Should she run? What kind of sick game was the medallion playing now? Lord, just looking at this man crushed her heart.

He reached out his hand, but stopped midair and pulled it behind him. "I'm sorry to have bothered you. I wanted to organize a tour for my regiment."

"I can help with that," she heard herself say. *God, Eva. What the hell are you doing?* "Have you been to Torwood before?" Jeez, if she'd only keep her mouth shut.

"No." He turned full circle, looking up. "Though it seems oddly familiar."

She gestured inside with a shaking palm. "Shall I give you the five-cent-piece tour?"

"That would be lovely—ah—if I'm not imposing, of course."

"Not at all." She held out a trembling palm. "I'm Eva MacKay."

"Bill Wallace." Warm fingers encircled her hand and gave a firm but gentle shake.

Completely dazed, she stared mouth agape.

He held up a copy of her book. "I just realized, you're the author. My, this story is fascinating—so much detail."

It *was* William—his mannerisms, his presence, the scent that lingered on her palm as she moved her hand to her chin. "Thank you. I learned from the best, and Torwood is my ah...project."

"Your legacy?" he asked.

"No, these halls will always herald William's epitaph—the greatest hero Scotland has ever known." Regaining her composure, she gestured to his uniform. "You are a military man, I see?"

"Aye." His cheeks flushed. "A colonel, Special Ops, stationed in Stirling on a top-secret mission about which I cannot discuss."

Crossing her arms tightly, Eva stifled her shudder. "I hope it doesn't have anything to do with putting your life in danger."

"I can assure you, it does not—at least not any more than the job of a banker or shipbuilder."

"Safer than a policeman?"

His eyebrows arched with intelligence. "I believe I can admit to that."

"Well then." She opened her arms wide taking in a deep breath. "We are standing in the great hall..."

Stepping into her executive roll as if she'd never left, Eva gave him the tour, omitting her private quarters. She wasn't ready to show anyone her hiding place, especially a stranger impersonating William Wallace. Oh no, she wouldn't give her heart to anyone—not for a very long time—even if he did look like William in a modern kilted uniform.

His military, horsehair sporran swung to and fro with his every step.

"Would your men like a private weekday tour?" she asked when they returned to the hall, keeping her distance.

He gave a nod. "That would be verra nice, if it wouldn't be too much of an inconvenience to arrange."

She patted her chest, unable to stop staring at him. "I'm so sorry, but I've been a bit out of sorts. Can you tell me what day it is?"

"Why, it's Monday." A look of concern darkened his features. "Are you unwell?"

"No." Snapping her fingers to her lips, she closed her eyes. "I-I've suffered the death of someone very close and have been wallowing in self-pity."

"I am sorry for your loss. Truly." He rubbed his clean-shaven chin while his crystal blue eyes glanced away. "I was hoping you'd join me for dinner this evening. Perhaps another time?"

Eva shook her head and stepped back while her empty stomach rumbled. Was it time for dinner? "Forgive me, I'm afraid I wouldn't make good company. Besides, I don't think I could hold up in a crowd."

"Unfortunate. You do look like you could use a good meal." The corner of his mouth ticked up just like William's often did. "I ken just the place—a table for two separated from the other diners by an old fashioned screen."

Her gaze drifted aside as she ran her fingers over the medallion. "I don't know..."

"Are you certain? Everyone needs to eat—even when in mourning." He moved his palm over his heart. "Let's share a simple meal. No strings. Just food between two hungry acquaintances."

Her stomach growled so loudly, the noise echoed off the rafters. She glanced down as her face grew hot.

He chuckled. "See? Even your stomach agrees with me."

Biting her bottom lip, she dared meet his crystal blue-eyed stare. "Perhaps a quiet dinner would help these awful tremors."

"Excellent."

Good God, did he have to grin? Eva's knees buckled as she fell into him. Enormous hands encircled her waist and helped her steady. Lordy, he smelled better than a vat of simmering cloves.

"Come," he said. "Let me feed you before you succumb to hunger, then we can discuss that private tour."

CHAPTER THIRTY-FIVE

Eva *never* should have agreed to dinner. She'd picked at her food, sitting across from Bill like a swollen lump of nerves, unable to carry on a conversation. Apologizing profusely, she doubted she'd ever see him again.

But the Special Ops colonel was persistent. He'd asked her out again five times before she gave in and agreed to a night at the symphony. And he'd acted the perfect gentleman—hadn't made a move aside from holding her hand.

But every time Eva looked at him, she wanted to puke. As a matter of fact, she'd thrown up almost every morning since she'd returned to the modern day.

Regardless, simply looking at Colonel Bill Wallace tore her apart.

Tonight, she must end it.

She could not keep seeing the man no matter how much her heart wanted to.

Dammit.

Besides, now she had confirmation from the doctor, he'd drop her for certain—walk away. Eva was almost relieved. Truly, she needed to pick up the pieces of her life and move on. The medallion had used her and she'd played right into the grand plan, telling William about Robert the Bruce. God, what would have happened if she'd kept her mouth shut? If she'd tried not to care?

How on earth could she have thought herself capable of changing the past?

She balled her fists. The only thing she possessed to prove she'd actually been there were William's letter and the pictures she'd managed to snap. Everyone on earth except Walter Tennant would think her a loon if she claimed to have time traveled. Bill would for certain. But Eva needed to give him an honest explanation—she couldn't just dump him. He'd been so damned nice.

At least if he left thinking she was insane, she might not hurt his feelings too badly. He was that kind of guy. Brilliant like William, masculine, considerate, chivalrous, fiercely good looking.

Not for me.

Eva must move on. She couldn't mope around in a quagmire of depression anymore.

Fortunately, as soon as she'd returned from hell, her "modern" life shifted into high gear. The only problem? Things just might be happening *too* fast.

The movie company had e-mailed her tickets to fly to America for the film debut of her book. Jeez, her agent had dropped the phone when Eva finally called. She'd missed all of the promotional appearances and a chance to be on The Tonight Show with the cast, but Eva didn't care about that. However, she was looking forward to attending the debut.

And then she'd spend a couple weeks in Washington DC at the embassy with her parents. Mum was elated. Breaking the news to them would be—well, Eva would just have to do it.

Though her main residence was a townhouse just outside Edinburgh, Eva had invited Bill to Torwood. She could explain things so much better there—kind of keep things in the past as well.

She waited for him in the car park and when the rumble of the Audi's engine approached, her palms grew moist. Every time Eva looked at this man, she shook like a Chihuahua standing in snow. Seeing him was almost akin to an addictive drug—it terrified her, yet she craved his nearness, his scent. He made her think of little else until their next meeting, and by God, that needed to stop.

Driving over the gravel, he waved, smiling the grin she'd fallen in love with. Jeez, looking at him twisted her into a million knots. He cut the engine and stepped out of his shiny black car. "Am I late?"

A deep inhale helped to steady her nerves. "Exactly on time."

She'd told him tonight was casual and he sauntered toward her wearing jeans and a black t-shirt that stretched taut across his biceps and well-muscled chest.

Eva's knees wobbled beneath her sundress and sweater. But she ground her teeth and forced herself to look away.

"It's good to see you." He took her fingers, bowed over them and plied the back of her hand with a kiss—warm breath, lips softer than feathers... "How are you, my lady?" ...a burr that could melt honeycomb.

Forcing a smile, Eva drew away her hand and rubbed the back of it—tried to erase the tingles skittering up her arm. "Coping."

"That doesn't sound good." He bit down on his bottom lip. "Are you certain you wouldn't prefer to go out? I know—"

"I'm positive," she said a bit too insistently. "Besides, I already have everything prepared."

"I'm honored," Bill said with deep sincerity in his voice. He gestured toward the enormous doors. "Shall we?"

Leading the way, a lump of lead sank to the pit of her stomach. This was a bad idea—the worst she'd had yet. Bill's footsteps echoed behind her along the way as they climbed the five fights up the wheeled stairwell.

I cannot back out now.

Exiting into the fifth floor passageway, she regarded him over her shoulder. "I've never brought anyone up here. This wing isn't open to the public."

"No?" His mouth turned up as if he liked the idea but tried to hide a bigger grin. "What other surprises do you have for this evening?"

"You'll soon find out." She unlocked her chamber door and motioned for him to step inside.

He stopped just beyond the doorway. "Wow. This is incredibly *authentic* looking." He turned full circle, his lips slightly parted, then he gave her a pointed look. "Are you sure you didn't show me this chamber on my first tour?"

"Absolutely not."

"Huh." Bill tapped his chin. "I feel like I've been here before."

Eva swallowed against her thundering heart. He'd probably taken a tour at Holyrood Palace and was remembering the King's Bedchamber—though a bit more lavish, it had similar furnishings.

She watched him stroll inside and run his fingers over the round table set for two, a pair of candles burning atop. He then moved to the hearth where a peat fire smoldered. On the mantel, a candelabra cast the most light. Eva had opted not to use electricity this evening.

Turning to the bed, he crossed his arms while a look of surprise arched his brow.

That was her cue. She definitely didn't want him to get the wrong idea about all this. "Clan Forrester has granted me this chamber for my own private use. Did you know the royals once entertained their closest friends and allies in their bedchambers?"

"Ah, no. I didn't." His stance relaxed. "Do you write up here?"

"Sometimes."

He ran his finger down a brass candlestick on the table. "It's perfect—just like the medieval chambers you describe in your book."

"I hoped it would be." Eva pulled out his chair and pointed to it. Having him standing in her chamber—the replica of the one she'd once shared with William, made it nearly impossible for her to focus. "Wine?"

He shook his finger. "*I'm* supposed to pour."

"Very well." She slipped into her seat before he had a chance to hold it for her.

He pulled the cork out of the bottle, then hesitated. "Only one glass?"

She nodded, indicating she wanted him to pour. If she didn't start talking now, she might never address the issues and then this night would be for naught. "Ah…when you saw me for the first time, did you have a spark of recognition?"

He sat and rested the bottle in the pewter holder. "Do you mean did I have déjà vu?"

"Something like that." Eva chewed on the inside of her cheek.

"Come to think of it, I did have a flicker in the back of my mind, but I couldn't put my finger on it." He leaned forward, squinting. "I haven't wanted to sound tactless, but it's been driving me insane. Have we met before?"

"Yes…and no." Lord, she probably had the man entirely confused and she hadn't even touched on the meaty stuff.

"Huh? Ever since we met…every time we're together, there's a sense of-of-of *familiarity* I cannot possibly explain." He pushed the heels of his hands against his temples. "Have I lost my mind?"

Eva managed a smile. "I don't think so, but after I tell you a few things, you might think I've lost mine."

Dropping his hands, he blinked. "Forgive me, but you're not making a bit of sense."

"I know." She cringed. "Sorry—it's just hard to decide where to start."

"You seem nervous."

Licking her lips, she wished she'd allowed herself a half glass of wine. "I am."

He reached across the table and smoothed his fingers down and up her arm. "No need. I'm just happy to be here...with you." He spread his arms wide, taking it all in. "In this amazing chamber."

God, she needed to get this over with before his charm completely seized her heart. "So—you don't remember meeting me, but you felt something...some *familiarity* when we met?" she repeated.

"Yes." He nodded decisively.

She twirled William's ring around her finger. "Well, I remember meeting you."

"You do? Where was it? At university? Because, I have to say I wasn't always on top of my game—"

"No." She reached under the table and grasped the file of photos she'd printed. "I have so much to say, please bear with me."

"Why not take a deep breath and start at the beginning?" One side of his mouth quirked up—as handsome as...

She set the folder down. *Maybe it can wait.* "Would you prefer to eat first?"

He leaned in, his blue eyes sparkling with the candlelight. "I think you're stalling."

"Right. The beginning makes the most sense." Sighing, Eva pulled the medallion from under her blouse. "Um. Over eight years ago, Professor Walter Tennant gave me this medallion..."

"Tennant?" Bill clasped his hands together, satisfaction filling his eyes. "I took a class from him at Glasgow Uni."

"So you know him?"

"Yes—brilliant man."

"Quite," Eva said noncommittally. She showed Bill the medallion's front and back, explained the only rule. Then she sat straight, clenched her bum cheeks, and told him everything from the first occasion she'd time traveled. Showing him the pictures she'd taken along the way, she made her case, trying to convince him to believe the unbelievable, knowing that with each word, she hammered a nail in the coffin of their relationship.

Bill sat very still, listening, not saying a word. Though he studied every picture, running his pointer finger over his— *William's* face.

Did this man have any recollection of the events she unraveled? Was she completely off the mark? God, she didn't even believe in reincarnation.

Or did she?

By the time Eva got to the part about William's trial she was a wreck, shaking like a lunatic. "After the justice finished, I opened my mouth to refute the litany of false accusations against William, and poof, I was gone." She thrust her finger out. "Landed on that bed, and then you were the first person I saw."

Sitting back, Bill picked up his wine glass and swirled the cabernet. Then he took a long drink—a very long drink— drained half of it.

Eva licked her lips and cringed. "Do you still want dinner?"

"Aye," he croaked out hoarsely.

"Are you all right?" She stood.

He took another drink. "Not certain."

Perhaps he needs a little time before he bolts for the door.

She started across to the sideboard. "I have a lamb pottage and fresh bread warming."

"Pottage?"

Picking up the spoon, she regarded him over her shoulder. "Is that all right? Would you prefer something else?"

He poured himself another glass of wine. "I'm sure it'll be fine."

"It's sort of a medieval stew."

"I know…don't ask me how, but I know." His voice sounded strained. What did she expect—she'd just told a decorated colonel that she'd been running around medieval Scotland with his clone.

Eva placed the plates on the table. "I half expected you to have walked out by now."

He took his serviette and unfolded it across his lap. "The thought crossed my mind."

Her heart sank. "Sorry. But at least I can serve you a good meal first. I didn't make the pottage—ordered it from the medieval restaurant at Stirling Castle."

He held up his fork. "Well, thank heavens you have modern cutlery."

She let out a nervous chuckle—ah yes, she'd told him about using an eating knife. "It's time I put all this behind me and move on with my life."

"Good idea." Ignoring his food, he stared across the table as if he were stunned. Did he have any remembrance? Was he about to run? Did he think her a complete lunatic?

She should have just cut things off over the phone before she got on the plane tomorrow. Why in the hell did she think she needed to explain?

Examining her food, Eva shoveled a bite into her mouth. He did the same.

"Mm, this is very good," Bill said, dabbing his lips.

"I'm glad you like it." She swallowed—more like gulped.

He picked up his glass and swirled the ruby liquid. "Have you given it much thought?"

"The pottage?"

"No, what you'll do now that your ordeal is over?"

Eva pushed her food around with her fork. "In the short term, I'm traveling. Hopping a plane for Los Angeles in the morning. Fortunately, I've made it back in time for the film debut of my book. And then I'll stop in Washington to see my parents."

"You're leaving?" His eyebrow's pinched together as he set his glass down. "How long will you be away?"

"A month or so." She shrugged. "I suppose it doesn't matter."

"Pardon?" He picked up one of the pictures—a selfie she'd taken with William in the early days. "Did you think your leaving wouldn't matter to me?"

She sat back with a snort. "Ah…I thought you would have run out of here screaming by now."

"Perhaps I should." He then examined the one she'd taken when William and Andrew were consecrated as Guardians.

"Not before dessert. I made your favorite." Eva again headed for the sideboard. "I had to make it from scratch because they didn't have any at the castle."

Glancing over his shoulder, he pushed his chair back. "So, what *is* my favorite?"

"Plum pudding."

"Wrong. It's plum tart."

Her shoulders dropped. "I knew there had to be some differences. After all, it's been seven hundred years." She tried to laugh, but it came out like a splutter.

Standing, the floorboards creaked as he moved in behind her and placed a hand on her waist. "You seem upset." His whisper sent a shiver across her shoulders.

This time Eva's laugh sounded like a cough. "If only someone besides Walter Tennant would believe me."

Warm breath caressed her neck. "I believe ye, *mon amour.*"

Eva froze, goosebumps coursed down her arms. She hadn't said a word about William's endearment. But then, it was common enough—the two men were similar, too.

"God help me." She closed her eyes and swooned against him. "Do you remember anything from my story?"

"Not a thing…but…"

"Yes?"

"I had a feeling. I can't explain it—but there's something incredibly familiar about your photos—about you—about this room."

"There is?"

"So much so, I cannot walk away—though any reasonable man would have already sprinted to his car and sped down the motorway."

Eva's head spun. It wasn't supposed to turn out this way. He was supposed to be history by now, speeding down that very motorway. She picked up the spoon and scooped some pudding. "Taste."

He opened his mouth and allowed her to feed him. His bold jaw twitched with his chewing, then his eyes grew wide. "Lord, that *is* delicious."

She grinned. "A new favorite?"

He reached for the spoon and scooped some more. "It's a close second for certain."

"I'm glad you like it." She bit her bottom lip. "But there's one more thing I have to tell you before…before…um…"

…you make that mad dash for your Audi.

He stopped mid-chew. "Yes?"

"I'm pregnant," she blurted without hesitation. After all, he needed to know and she had to get this whole thing over with. Jeez, how he'd hung around this long was beyond her.

His Adam's apple bobbed with his gulp. "Oh?" It wasn't a happy "oh". It sounded more like the croak from an adolescent rooster.

Now he'll run for certain. "I just found out yesterday."

Bill's face pinched like he was in complete shock, then he turned and strolled toward the hearth. "And the father?"

Here it comes. Eva clutched her hands against her abdomen. "Ah…as I said, I've been away since February. It's August—and I'm only two months along."

"Good God." Bill buried his face into his palms. Shaking his head with a groan, he then slid his hands over his hair and regarded her. "What other shocking surprises do you have for me tonight?"

Regardless of the fact that she'd prepared for his reaction, the hunk of lead in her stomach dropped to her toes. "I didn't think you'd want me to cut my trip to America short."

"America?"

"The film debut—you know—I mentioned it."

"Er…yeah." Bill paced the floor, his head still shaking. How she'd ever thought there was a thread of hope he'd believe her… Then he stopped. "I…you…I—"

Throwing out her hands, she stepped in. "You don't have to say anything. I know this seems crazy—impossible. I can't even believe you're still here right now."

"Jesus." He looked to the ceiling. "Do you have any idea why I haven't walked out the door?"

"No."

He pointed to her chair. "You'd best sit, 'cause this might take a while."

Holy shit. What on earth? Eva complied and folded her arms. *This ought to be good.*

He stood with his arms crossed, his black t-shirt straining good and tight across well-muscled pecs. "The first time I saw you, your eyes were swollen and red with tears. At that time, my instinct was to leave you to your sorrow, but then a picture flashed through my mind—one that's been with me since the beginning of time—one I've dreamt about as long as I can remember."

Leaning forward, she opened her mouth, but Bill held up his palm.

"Bear with me." His Adam's apple bobbed. "When I looked at your face—really looked at it, you brought all my dreams to life. You made the hairs on my arms stand on end."

He shuddered.

So did she.

Then his crystal blues bore through to her soul. "Every dream is the same—and it's *you*. I'm certain of it. You are always dressed in gold with an aura of light radiating around you." He pulled open her arm, took her hand and turned William's ring around her finger. "Don't tell me how I know this, but I gave you that ring. I know this ring. I know it in my heart and my soul. And God save me, you are the woman I've always known I would be with."

Eva's heart fluttered like a gazillion flashing lights. He *did* know her. "A-and the baby?"

He let out a wee chuckle. "I only wish I'd been dreaming about the time of conception all my life."

Heat burned her cheeks while she tore her gaze away. "I know the responsibility is too much to ask of any man."

"The wee one needs a father." He brought her ringed finger to his lips and kissed the Celtic knot. "Is it safe to travel in your condition?"

Eva nodded. "The doctor said I should be all right this early."

"Well," he said, running his pointer finger around the ring. "I don't think you should walk the red carpet alone."

The fluttering stopped. "But I cannot possibly miss it."

Stroking his chin, his eyebrows shot up. "Look. I have some leave coming." His eyes turned hopeful. "I'd like to go with you."

She drew a hand over her mouth. "You're serious?"

He nodded. "My heart is telling me yes."

"And your head?"

He thumped his temple. "My guess is that it'll catch up—you said Walter Tennant gave you the medallion?"

"Yes."

After he stood, Bill removed the leather thong from around her neck. "I think we should return this to the professor." He pulled her up into his arms. "I don't want you going anywhere that's not in this century, *mon amour.*"

Oh yes. Oh yes, yes, yes. "I like the way you think." Eva let her hands slide around to Bill's back. Her body molded to his, forming that perfect fit—the one she craved. "Sh-should I buy you a ticket to Los Angeles?"

He nuzzled into her neck. "Can you postpone for a day? Give me a chance to apply for leave…then I'll pay for my own ticket."

"Okay." She closed her eyes and swooned into him. "No problem cutting it short. They gave me a couple days to account for jet lag."

"Excellent."

He captured her mouth, his eyelids fluttering closed. With slow swirls of his tongue, he allowed her to savor him, grow to know the modern man—a great warrior she had loved in another time and now would love again.

Taking in a deep inhale, Bill lightly rested his forehead against hers. "Och, I canna believe how much ye feel like home, lass."

Epilogue

One year later

After typing "the end", Eva sat back and regarded those two words with a long sigh. This manuscript was late to her publisher, but having a baby at home took so much time—even with a nanny.

The past year had been one of reflection, filled with new beginnings but not without its share of trepidation. The medallion was safely locked away in Professor Tennant's safe and miraculously Bill had stayed by her side through everything. The best part? He'd picked her up and had taken her to every single Lamaze class. He'd been in London when Eva went into labor, but by the time wee Lachlan decided he was ready to come into the world, Bill had arrived and was holding her hand.

God bless him. God bless them both.

The second miracle of the year, of course, came with Lachlan, a healthy bairn with chestnut hair and blue eyes just like his father. *And just like Bill.* Since the wee lad had been born, whenever Bill hadn't been away on Special Ops business, he'd spent every weekend with Eva and Lachlan. Eva had chosen the bairn's name as a tribute to a young orphan who'd befriended Robbie Boyd, a brave young archer who never had the chance to make his mark on the history books. Eva swore over the lad's grave that she would make sure the world heard his tale. And now she had the honor of naming William Wallace's son for the brave boy.

Things were almost perfect. Too often she longed for the days on Eynhallow when she and William walked along the shore holding hands and talking about important matters like Robert the Bruce and King Edward of England.

But she had a new life now. A rich life. One that she could share with her son and a modern William Wallace—yet another man who could make her heart soar with the eagles.

The doorbell to Eva's townhouse rang.

"I'll get it," called Cora, the nanny.

Eva clicked "save" on her computer as Bill's deep voice cut through the corridor. "Good evening, Cora. Would you mind staying late with Lachlan? I've a dinner planned with Eva."

"Late?" The nanny didn't sound too certain.

"I'll pay you double."

Eva checked her calendar. She didn't have anything marked for the evening. What was Bill up to?

"Very well," Cora agreed. "Who could resist such an offer?"

"You're a lifesaver."

Eva poked her head out her office door. "What's this? You're keeping my nanny late?"

Wearing his dress uniform, Bill stood a bit taller and flashed a wide grin. Dear Lord, every time Eva saw that smile, she melted. He could ask her to fly to the moon and she'd probably agree. "I made reservations…ah…" He looked like a lad trying to hold in a secret he didn't want to keep. Striding forward, he took her hands. "I've some news and the only person I want to share it with is you."

"Sounds intriguing. I just finished the last chapter of my manuscript—so I suppose I have reason to celebrate too. Where are you taking me?"

"Torwood."

She looked sideways. "Just the two of us?"

"Aye."

Arching one eyebrow, she looked him from head to kilt. Oh, how well he wore that kilt. "What are you up to?"

He pulled her key from his sporran and held it up. "You'll see."

She swiped it from his hand. "You took that from my dressing table."

"I borrowed it. Forgive me?" His pleading blue eyes could make any woman turn into a mushy pile of gush, but Eva wasn't about to let him get off too easily.

"Not sure." The key to the castle was hers and no one else's. He should have asked first. She gave him a practiced stern look. "This had better be good."

"We'll be home by ten," Bill said as he ushered Eva out the door.

The trip to Torwood didn't take long and soon they were in Eva's chamber up on the fourth floor.

The table sported two formal settings, a candle and on one plate, a red rose. A waiter stood beside it in a tuxedo with a white towel draped over one arm. He pulled a bottle of champagne from the bucket. "Would you like champagne now, sir?"

Bill held the chair for Eva. "Yes, thank you."

"This looks lovely." Eva picked up the rose and held it to her nose. "But you're killing me here. What's this big news?"

The waiter showed Bill the label, and he motioned for him to pour. "That will be all for now."

"When would you like the first course?" the man asked.

"Give us fifteen minutes."

"What's on the menu?" Eva asked.

The waiter bowed. "Seven courses, compliments of Her Majesty."

Bill leaned forward. "I don't even know what we're eating—but I've no doubt it will be exquisite."

Eva watched in amazement while the waiter took his leave. "The queen? You cannot possibly keep this from me any longer."

Bill held up his glass. "First I'd like to make a toast. To us."

A butterfly flitted in her stomach. "To us."

He set his glass down. "I can't tell you everything about my work, but I can say my squadron and I have made enormous strides toward assuring world peace."

"But you said you weren't doing anything dangerous."

His eyebrows slanted downward. "I think I said I wasn't doing anything that would get me killed."

"But your work is dangerous?" *Oh God, no. Please not again.*

"I mostly gather intelligence—occasional danger, but nothing like riding into battle with a sword strapped to my back."

"Nothing that will get you killed?"

He crossed his heart. "Promise."

Releasing a deep breath, Eva reached for her glass. "So you've made a major breakthrough?"

"We've prevented our enemies from gaining nuclear weapons." He took a sip of champagne while Eva cogitated the news.

"You're serious? Oh heavens, that *is* big."

"And I will be knighted by the Queen in London, two months hence."

Eva gasped. "A knighthood? Congratulations!" She clapped her hands. "Please let me be the first to call you Sir Bill."

Chuckling, he slipped out of his chair and kneeled in front of her. "But I want you to go to London with me."

"Of course, I wouldn't miss it for the world. I am over the moon excited for you." In a blink, Eva recalled the last time she'd been to London—her visit to the dank tower, and worse, the trial. She shuddered. *Seven hundred years have passed. It's time to get over it.*

Bill didn't seem to notice her reaction. Digging his hand in his sporran, his eyes twinkled with the candlelight. "When I am knighted, it is my greatest wish for you to attend not as my girlfriend, but as my *wife*."

She clapped a hand over her mouth as he pulled out a black velvet box and opened it. Inside was a platinum ring in the same design as the one she still wore—the one Bill remembered, but that William had given her. The difference? This one had an enormous diamond in the center.

"I don't expect this to replace that one." He nodded to her hand—to William's ring. "I hope you will always wear it too. But this ring—well, I'd be honored if you would wear it on your left finger. From the first time I set eyes on you, I knew you were the only woman in the world for me. I want to make Lachlan my son. I want to see you pregnant with *our* child and I want to love you until I take my last breath."

Her hands trembling, Eva removed William's ring for the first time and put it on her right finger. After losing William, she never thought she could love anyone again—but this man who kneeled before her *was* William Wallace—Bill was her William as only he could be in this century. "Yes," she said with conviction. This was right. Joining with Bill would make her whole again. "I will marry you. And you'd best promise me you will have a long life. Because my heart cannot endure another loss, *not ever*."

A tear slid from her eye and splashed the back of her hand as Bill slid on the beautiful ring. The perfect ring to pledge his love.

"I promise to care for you for the rest of my life."

Eva held up her hand. "It's beautiful." Tears now streamed from both eyes. "You're beautiful."

Wrapping her in his arms, he stood and together they twirled across the floor. "You've made me happier than any man in Scotland."

"And I'm ever so happy to be with you. I love you."

"I've always loved you, *mon amour*."

When the waiter opened the door, they were joined in an embrace, kissing like teenagers. "Shall I come back, sir?"

"No." Bill grinned, staring into Eva's eyes. "My lady needs her sustenance, for our celebrations this evening will be strenuous, indeed."

"I like the way you think." Eva kissed his cheek then rose to her toes, pressing her lips to his ear. "I want a girl this time."

The End

Autdor's Note

Thank you for joining me for William and Eva's story. When I first plotted this saga, I planned to have Eva figure a way to spirit Wallace from the brink of death. But as the story came together, I felt as though I would be cheating history if I changed it for the sake of a good yarn. I couldn't do that. So, I took a cue from Jude Deveraux's *Knight in Shining Armor*, and conjured up Bill Wallace, a modern day hero.

I laughed and cried while researching and writing both books in this series. Historians dispute many facts about Wallace's life and book two was a bit more difficult to write as there was a wide void in William's history after the Battle of Falkirk in 1298 until his execution in 1305. It is known that he did travel to France in his efforts to raise help for the Scottish army and he was imprisoned by King Philip for about a year. By that time, the king of France had entered into a treaty of peace with England, and thus William's pleas for assistance in Europe fell on unsympathetic ears.

There is no record of his visiting the exiled John Balliol. In 1300, King Philip wrote a letter to the French representative at the court of Pope Boniface in Rome to aid Wallace, but it is unknown exactly what William accomplished in Rome. I should also mention the poet, Blind Harry, wrote that William was forced to fight a lion while in the French court, which may or may not have happened.

After William's return to Scotland, he was pursued by Edward who maintained a driving, psychotic lust to capture him at all costs. The English king pardoned a great many nobles who fought in the Battle of Falkirk, but refused to consider such pardon for William Wallace. Perhaps the big Scot haunted him. Perhaps Edward the Longshanks feared William more than anyone else in Christendom.

As I said, I did take more literary license writing *In the Kingdom's Name*. The connection that arose between Wallace and Bruce developed out of my imagination.

There is no question that William's life was epic. He represented and stood for those common folk who had no voice. He took the weight of a faltering nation upon his shoulders, and with his martyr, became the catalyst for Scotland to regain her freedom under the leadership of Robert the Bruce. Wallace's execution marked a beginning. A new age of hope.

My research for both *Rise of a Legend* and *In the Kingdom's Name* took months and included a trip to Scotland. Aye, Scotland owns a piece of my heart and I hope I can make many more journeys there in the coming years.

Excerpt from Amy's Next Book

The Fearless Highlander
Highland Defender Series, Book One

Chapter One

Fort William, Scotland, March, 1691

The door of the surgery burst open and two sweaty dragoons scooted inside, straining to carry a Highland prisoner sprawled atop a canvas stretcher. Charlotte clasped a cloth between her hands and watched while the soldiers rolled the enormous man onto a cot and chained his leg irons to the metal footboard.

"Another one?" asked Doctor Munro, Fort William's army physician.

"Fevered just like the blighter yesterday and he smells worse than a heap of sh—" The soldier looked at Charlotte and cringed. "Apologies, Miss Hill, but this lump of rancid mutton stinks."

Charlotte's cheeks burned as she looked down at the cloth in her hands and nodded, her fingers twisting the piece of Holland so taught, fibers frayed. Her father's men could be overly insensitive when it came to the Scottish prisoners—and there she stood nodding in agreement. *Blast my shy streak, I cannot allow this heartlessness to pass.* "Truly?" She stepped forward. "And this man is so dangerous he must be chained to the bed? He's unconscious, for heaven's sake."

"I'd not be taking any chances with a blighter the size of Goliath." A gutless dragoon raised his palms. "Who knows what he'll do when he wakes?"

The physician held a kerchief to his nose while he bent over and examined the Highlander. "Why in God's name did you bring him here? He's half dead already."

The two dragoons inched toward the door. One carried the stretcher upright and inclined his head in the direction of the fevered man. "The prisoners made such a ruckus, hauling him to the surgery was the only thing to get them to shut their gobs."

Doctor Munro snorted. "So now we're allowing murderers and thieves to tell us what to do? Colonel Hill received orders to send the lot of them to the gallows—and in short order."

"No!" Charlotte snapped. "Papa is awaiting a pardon from the king."

The physician smirked. "You think the king cares about a handful of bedraggled Jacobites rotting in a remote outpost? Why let these criminals run free? A dead man cannot return and thrust a knife into your back."

A twitch of his eye was the only outward sign the Highlander may have heard Doctor Munro's caustic opinion. By the saints, he was unusually large. The soldiers had propped up his shoulders to prevent the man's legs from overhanging the cot. Oh yes, they were well formed, quite muscular legs at that.

Blinking away the image of the Highlander laying atop the cot like an effigy of Richard the Lionheart, Charlotte picked up the ewer and poured a stream of water into a bowl. "I daresay they were right to demand he be seen," she whispered, hoping no one could hear. So unpopular her point of view, any public expression of it would only invite a terse rebuttal. But her insides roiled with a tempest. How could they all be so unfeeling? Was she the only person at Fort

William who cared an iota about the living conditions of the poor prisoners? It wasn't the Highlander's fault he smelled a tad unpleasant. She'd continually asked her father to provide water and lye for the prisoners to bathe, yet he always responded with the same terse remark. *Dear Charlotte, you are too kindhearted. These men are convicts—animals. And Fort William is no bathhouse of luxury.*

The physician stood, and with brisk flicks of his fingers, folded his kerchief and replaced it in his sleeve. "You men are dismissed." He watched them leave, then turned to Charlotte. By the pinched purse of his lips, he'd overheard her remark. "If I may be so bold Miss Hill, you are too gentle to be tucked away in such a disagreeable outpost. In my opinion, a young woman such as yourself should not be exposed to foul lowlife akin to this man, or any of the other riffraff incarcerated in this prison. 'Tis just not proper."

"Oh please." She dared meet his gaze. She hated looking Doctor Munro in the eye because he always stared at her with the most intense expression—just as he did right now. Curse his gunmetal-grey eyes. But rather than shy away, Charlotte squared her shoulders. "You speak to me as if I'm but a delicate flower."

He stretched his fingers toward her cheek, but when she leaned aside, he quickly snapped his hand to his hip. "Oh, how delicate you are, indeed." He took a step closer. "Your father should have at least sought a post nearer to Edinburgh where *civilized* people reside. This outpost is no place for a lady as well-bred as you."

Charlotte regarded the bowl she'd just filled with water and bit the inside of her cheek. "Indeed?" After taking a hesitant look at the patient, she hastened for the door. The unconscious man could use tending, but presently she wasn't about listen to the physician utter another word about what he thought of her gentility. The man had been growing bolder with such remarks. She took in a sharp breath. "Pardon me, but my father serves the king where he is needed, not where it best suits me." Besides, if Charlotte moved anywhere away from Papa it would be London—where she was born. Placing her hand on the latch, she curtsied. "I shall see you at the evening meal."

"Very well—" he said as she closed the door before he could utter another opinionated word.

At the top of the stairs, Charlotte stopped and drew in deep breaths as she turned full circle. Good, no one was about, as was usual in this part of the fort. Most everyone gave the surgery a wide berth, which she suspected was why her father allowed her to assist Doctor Munro. The physician wasn't too terribly horrible. Though he was teaching her to be his assistant, he watched her with too much intensity beneath his beetle brows. Of course it was only natural for him to scrutinize her closely. He was even somewhat amenable, except when it came to ministering to prisoners. There, his manner was decidedly stiff and insensitive.

She ducked behind the wood stack and waited.

As she expected, it wasn't long before the physician locked the infirmary and headed off. Doubtless, he hadn't taken a second look at his fevered patient. Doctor Munro had the same opinion about the prisoners as everyone else in the Government Army. They were all but wild animals locked in chains where they ought to be.

But Charlotte vehemently disagreed with them. For the most part, she kept her opinions to herself, except when it came to her father. Inordinately shy, she hated the way the soldiers looked at her when she spoke at all, let alone expressed her unpopular beliefs. Of course with Papa she knew what she could and couldn't say. The others? She shuddered. Merely speaking out came with great risk, and a charge of sedition would not only see her hanged, it would ruin her father's prospects for advancement. With civil war an ever-present threat across England, Ireland and Scotland, no one knew what spies lurked at every turn.

Fishing the surgery key from the purse at her waist, she waited until Doctor Munro's footsteps faded. On tiptoes she crept from behind the wood stack and peered in all directions to ensure she hadn't been spotted. Then she lifted her skirts above her ankles, and as fast as a rabbit, pattered down to the surgery and slipped inside.

With the lamp snuffed, the light was dim, and Charlotte stood against the door keeping her hand on the latch while she waited for her eyes to adjust. The Highlander's breathing wheezed. Her heart sped. Tightening her grip on the latch, she nearly fled. But the outline of the man became clearer. Lying on his back, she could see only his profile. A massive warrior, he didn't have a hooked English nose, but his forehead angled to a proud Norse-shaped nose—straight, noble-looking. Like all of the other prisoners, his beard was rather unruly.

The unfortunate soul. By the saints, Papa will send this man to the gallows over my dead body—and I will see to it he survives.

Taking a deep breath to still her jittery nerves, Charlotte lit a candle and placed it on the table nearest the Highlander's cot. She set the bowl she'd filled with water on the table and fetched a small cup of claret. Resting the back of her hand on the Highlander's forehead, she tested his temperature. The patient was afire.

After dousing the cloth, she cleansed his face and neck with swirling strokes. Once she'd cleared the grime, she stood back for a moment. He had a handsome face—rugged as the Highlands. His dark hair was the color of well-oiled leather, and he'd braided his moustache hair into his beard— to keep it clean, she supposed.

How wretched for anyone to be housed in the bowels of Fort William.

At the age of twenty, Charlotte had grown weary of biting her tongue and blindly accepting the brutal treatment of prisoners of war. Goodness, she'd been at Fort William for a month. How much longer must she remain silent? As far as she knew, they had done nothing wrong but fight on the losing side of a battle. The men sharing the dank hold were not common murderers or thieves as Doctor Munro had accused this man of being. They were warriors.

She studied him while curiosity fluttered in her breast. Of course, her concern for his wellbeing is what had her insides flittering about. Unusually captivating, he had lines etched into the corners of his eyes like a man of perhaps thirty. Was he married? Did he have a family? Would she be in danger if he weren't unconscious?

A colossal hand in repose atop his belly sported thin white scars. She'd seen such marks caused by nicks from the sparring ring. His fleshy fingers were long, artistic, but moreover, they looked so powerful, Charlotte had no doubt he could crush her much smaller hands without even a grimace.

Nonetheless, sick with fever and flat on his back, he did not appear too terribly dangerous. *Is he a murderer? No. By the stirring of my blood, I do not believe him to be.*

With an exhale Charlotte's gaze trailed lower. His shirt laces were open, revealing tufts of mahogany curls. Licking her lips, her gaze meandered down the length of the loosened laces. His chest rose and fell with his breathing. She dunked the cloth in the basin and wrung it out. He smelled better already, but she would cleanse that which she could reach.

"I'll run the cloth through your beard and over your chest," she said as if he could hear. Heaven forbid he wake and startle.

Charlotte's hand trembled a little after she moved from his beard to his chest. The Highlander's flesh was nearly as hard as stone—far more muscular than she'd imagined a man would be—especially a prisoner.

Of course, she'd seen her father without his shirt, but at the age of two and sixty, Papa's chest was—well, it wasn't nearly as solid as this man's.

Clearing her throat, she drew her hands away. *That should suffice.*

As she turned to the bowl, the Highlander coughed.

With a backward leap, the cloth flew from her hands, over her head, and landed on the poor man's stomach. "A-are you awake?" Cringing, she tiptoed toward him and snatched the cloth away.

"Mm," the Highlander's deep voice rumbled, but his eyes remained closed.

"You're terribly fevered." Biting her knuckle, she glanced toward the door. She really ought to be dressing for the evening meal. Then she regarded the poor soul chained to the cot. It would be ever so cruel to leave without doing something to ease his suffering.

She picked up the cup of claret and placed one hand under the base of his skull. "You need to drink. I'll lift your head now." Goodness, merely his head weighed a stone. But she held him steady and moved the cup, tipping it up ever so slowly until the red liquid touched his lips. He opened his mouth just wide enough to take a small sip.

His Adam's apple bobbed. "More."

"How long have you been awake?" she asked, testing to see if he was well enough for conversation.

"Please," he grunted.

"Yes, of course." She offered another sip, and this time he took in a mouthful and swallowed it with a gulp. Charlotte eased his head back to the cot.

He sputtered and coughed. "Forgive me."

"You needn't apologize for being ill, sir."

Before she could draw away, his eyes flashed open and those enormous fingers wrapped around her wrist, squeezing so forcibly her fingers went instantly numb. Holy Moses, it hurt but Charlotte clenched her teeth and froze.

"Help me," he growled through his teeth.

"I-I'm trying to." She attempted to pull away, but his grip held fast.

Then as if Satan possessed him, his hand dropped and his eyes rolled back, shuttering his haunting stare with inordinately long lashes. By the saints, the color of his eyes gave her pause—treacle brown like liquid pools of unfathomable depth. How on earth a man as fevered as he could be so expressive with a look, she had no idea. In that moment when their gazes connected, aside from her heart flying to her throat, she'd read so many things. Without a doubt this prisoner had suffered inconceivable pain and hardship. But he wasn't a common crofter. Oh no, there was something special about this Highlander. If only Charlotte could put her finger on it.

***

Hugh's head pounded like someone had taken an iron hammer and bludgeoned him to within an inch of his life. But God's bones, after enduring one year and seven months in the bowels of hell, this woman's voice soothed him as if she spoke with the sweet tenor of an angel. No red-blooded Scotsman could allow such temptation to pass without a mere glimpse even if he was close to death.

He willed his eyes to open. At first the fair-haired beauty posed a blur to him. With all the concentration his fevered head could muster, he forced himself to focus. His heart actually fluttered. Oh, Lord in heaven, such a gift he'd been given in these final moments of life. Her wide-eyed gaze expressed her surprise, almost as if she feared he'd do something ungentlemanly. No, no, no, never in his life would Hugh act out against a woman—especially one with bonny wisteria-blue eyes. He guessed with such an expressive countenance, she'd never be able to keep a secret—not with blues the size of silver coins.

If only he could enjoy such a morsel for himself. If only he could ask her to lie in his arms and succor him until he drew his last breath. Damn the unrelenting hammering against his skull. He smirked at the irony—Hugh may not trick death, but bloody Colonel Hill wouldn't have the satisfaction of putting a noose around his neck. Hugh hadn't heard much the physician had said, but the drivel about the false king not caring about a few miserable souls rotting in Fort William's pit rang true. Christ, he'd known he was doomed all along.

Through his hazy vision, Hugh watched the bonny lass. Wasn't a man entitled to a last request?

How long had it been since he'd held a woman in his arms? At two and thirty, he should be married with sons and daughters at his feet. But war had a way of stalling a man's plans for his life.

"What is your name?" she asked with a gentle coo that sent a shiver along his fevered skin.

"Hugh MacLeod," he replied with the same answer he'd given everyone else since his internment into Fort William's hell. If anyone discovered he was the heir to the lands of Glencoe, the bastard dragoons wouldn't wait to hang him. He'd lost count of all the sordid ways they could ensure he died within these walls. His entire body convulsed. *Death be damned.* He must fight to survive, not for himself but for his clan. Clenching his fists at his sides, he stilled his chattering teeth. "And you?"

"Miss Hill," she whispered, as if ashamed.

Hugh's eyes flew open. *Hill?* Blast his rotten, miserable, bloody luck. "The Colonel's daughter?" he croaked, hanging on to a shred of hope that she was of no relation to the sadistic governor of this ill-fated prison.

"Yes." She turned away and doused her cloth in the bowl.

A lump took up residence in his throat.

Earlier, Hugh had been remotely aware of her gentle ministrations—her lithe fingers upon his chest. He'd come to consciousness enough to consider asking her not to stop—to keep kneading her magical fingers all the way down to… *Boar's ballocks.* Now he knew her father was Colonel Hill, Hugh would immediately cease his errant thoughts. Absolutely nothing positive could come from befriending this lass.

He gasped when she placed the cold cloth on his forehead. She was the bloody daughter of Satan incarnate. Why the hell was she in the surgery? Had the devil put her there to tempt him in his last hours?

Damn, he would be far better off if he had no luck at all.

"Do you think you can take another sip of claret?" she asked. "Doctor Munro gives it to all the soldiers—says it will help them regain their strength."

Jesus Christ, did she have to sound so bloody bonny? With a voice like that, he'd offer to gulp down a draught of nightshade. His mouth dry, Hugh only managed to nod. But this time he watched her while she held his head and offered the cup. The fruity wine slid over his tongue, down his gullet, and instantly swam in his head as if he'd guzzled a healthy tot of whisky. Holy Mary, it had to be the most flavorful ambrosia he'd tasted since his capture at the Battle of Dunkeld.

"Why…" He eyed her well-tailored gown, cinched tightly at the waist. Though petite, she was full-bosomed, yet wore a lace modesty panel to prevent him from stealing a glimpse of the velvety white flesh swelling above her bodice. Just as well. The last thing he needed was to be brought up on contrived charges for ogling the Colonel's daughter's breasts.

"Yes?" She regarded him, the expressive concern painted on her bonny face unwavering. Why on earth did the daughter of the devil have to have creamy porcelain skin and a smile that would melt the snow atop Ben Nevis in winter?

"Hmm?" was all he managed to utter as a wave of nausea clamped his gut.

"You were about to ask something?"

The pain eased. Ah yes, now he remembered. "Why does your father allow you in the surgery alone?" His voice sounded like he'd swallowed a rasp.

She glanced back toward the door. "He doesn't really. Since my arrival, I've been assisting Doctor Munro with simple tasks—rolling bandages and tending ill soldiers whenever necessary." She bit her bottom lip. Indeed, the lass shouldn't be alone with Hugh at all.

"Why doesn't he have a local woman assist him?" With his next shudder, chills fired across his skin.

High color blossomed in her cheeks. "Honestly, I needed something to occupy my time. One can only embroider and practice the violin so much in a day."

"You're a fiddler?" he asked through chattering teeth, willing himself to focus. Why couldn't she have a hooked nose with a wart atop?

"Yes, of sorts."

"I wish…" He shivered. "I could hear you play someday." God, he was daft. *Right. Ask the Sassenach lassie to come down to the pit and play a merry tune for the poor bastards as they wallow in their stench. Och, she could accompany the drummer beating the death knoll as he climbed the steps to her father's gallows.*

A bell rang in the distance. Miss Hill cringed and snapped her gaze toward the door. "I'm afraid I must go." She wrung her hands. "Will you be all right?"

Honestly, this cot was the most comfortable thing Hugh had lain upon since his arrival at Fort William. He regarded the chain securing his leg irons to the footboard and the pounding in his head resumed. But still he eyed her. "How about giving a dying man a last request?"

Standing, she grimaced as she rubbed her wrist. "What would that be?"

Hugh squeezed his eyes shut to block the pain. "The key to these bloody manacles for starters."

~End of excerpt from *The Fearless Highlander*

Other Books by Amy Jarecki:

Rise of a Legend, Guardian of Scotland Book 1

Highland Dynasty Series:

Knight in Highland Armor
A Highland Knight's Desire
A Highland Knight to Remember
Highland Knight of Rapture

Highland Force Series:

Captured by the Pirate Laird
The Highland Henchman
Beauty and the Barbarian
Return of the Highland Laird (A Highland Force Novella)

Pict/Roman Romances:

Rescued by the Celtic Warrior
Celtic Maid

Coming Soon, Highland Defender Series:

The Fearless Highlander
The Valiant Highlander
The Highland Duke

If you enjoyed *In the Kingdom's Name*, we would be
honored if you would consider leaving a review. *~Thank you!*

About the Author

A descendant of an ancient Lowland clan, Amy adores Scotland. Though she now resides in southwest Utah, she received her MBA from Heriot-Watt University in Edinburgh. Winning multiple writing awards, she found her niche in the genre of Scottish historical romance. Amy loves hearing from her readers and can be contacted through her website at www.amyjarecki.com.

Visit Amy's web site & sign up to receive newsletter updates of new releases and giveaways exclusive to newsletter followers.
Facebook: Amy Jarecki Author
Twitter: @Amy Jarecki

Made in United States
Orlando, FL
14 July 2022

19782258R00211